Flaw Less

OCT 2012

CH

Flaw Less

Shana Burton

www.urbanchristianonline.com

Urban Books, LLC
78 East Industry Court
Deer Park, NY 11729

ISBN 13: 978-1-60162-728-5
ISBN 10: 1-60162-728-9

First Printing September 2012
Printed in the United States of America

10 9 8 7 6 5 4 3 2 1

Distributed by Kensington Corp.
Submit Wholesale Orders to:
Kensington Publishing Corp.
C/O Penguin Group (USA) Inc.
Attention: Order Processing
405 Murray Hill Parkway
East Rutherford, NJ 07073-2316
Phone: 1-800-526-0275
Fax: 1-800-227-9604

This book is dedicated to the all of the people who loved *Flaws and All* and encouraged me to go on another journey with these flawfully wedded wives!

It is also dedicated to hopeful romantics like me, who never stop believing in love.

Acknowledgments

I never cease to be amazed by the goodness of God. Not only did He bless me with the gift of writing, but He made it possible for me to share this gift with the world. If I thanked Him every minute of every day, it still wouldn't be enough. "Praise Him for His mighty deeds; praise Him according to His excellent greatness!" I would like to thank my family for always encouraging, supporting, and believing in me. My mother, Myrtice C. Johnson, always has been and continues to be my biggest cheerleader and best friend; my sons, Shannon and Trey, who give me purpose and bring so much joy and happiness to my life every day; my father, James L. Johnson, Sr., who challenges me in ways only he knows how; and my siblings, Myrja, Matthew, and Jay, for continuing to believe in me and be supportive of my endeavors. You are all such a blessing to me.

I would like to thank my friends Deirdre Neeley, Lola Oyenuga, and Theresa Tarver, who not only ride with me when I have book signings, but "ride or die" for me on a daily basis. I couldn't love any more than I do now if I tried. I would also like to thank my writing sisters: Traci Smith Williams, Melissa Jones, Keisa Jones, and Crystal Pennymon. You know I couldn't have finished this book without your help! I'll be the first one in line at your book signings!

Thank you to my play brothers Demetrius Hollis, Scott Harris, Daniel Dukes, Quinterrance Bell, Doug-

Acknowledgments

lass Smith, Adrick Ingram, Damon Wilson, Van Miller, Tony Richards, and Ryan Golphin, who are always there to lend a helping hand, sound advice, or a friendly smile. I love you, guys! A big thanks goes out to Mychal Epps for all the laughs, good advice, and countless text messages. I have no words to express how wonderful you are! Our friendship means the world to me.

To my Virginia College crew: Shameka Powers, Rashada Ross, Lisa Gibson, Tammy Dunlap, Ronda Shirley, Brian Harmon, Marie Grove, Baron Samuels, Melissa Jones, Mel Lotson, and all of my wonderful students and other faculty and staff members, thank you for making it a joy to come to work every day. A special thanks goes out to Andrea Mitchell for giving me such an awesome book title.

To the best publicist in the world, Dee Stewart, thank you for always having my back and being so patient with me. Love ya, chica! I would also like to thank my fabulous editor, Joylynn Jossel-Ross, and the entire Urban Christian family for your continued support.

Thank you to all of my Beulahland Bible Church members and Pastor Maurice Watson for continuing to be supportive of my writing. I promise to make you proud! Also, thank you to Macedonia Baptist Church, Pat Henderson, and all of the women's ministry members who continue to pray for me and choose my books for your reading selections. You have no idea what your support means to me.

I would like to give a special thank you to my radio family at 97.9 WIBB, especially Ronald "Dirty" Jackson, Rod English, and Thomas Bacote, for always coming through for me whenever I ask. You're the best!

Thank you to all of the book clubs, loyal readers, Facebook friends, book reviewers, bloggers, and ev-

Acknowledgments

eryone else who has had a hand in my success. There would be no me without you. I appreciate you giving of your time and talent to support my writing career. Be blessed and continue to be a blessing to other authors.

Last, but certainly not least, thank you, Dwarka Jackson, for just being you. How blessed are we to have found each other twice? I'm so glad you're in my life.

If I left anyone out, please charge it to this book deadline and my head, not my heart. Happy reading!

All scriptures referenced are from the NIV.

Chapter 1

"How did we get here?"
—Lawson Kerry Banks

Lawson Kerry Banks looked around at the four women sprawled across her living-room floor. The idea of starting a new women's outreach ministry had brought them together that cool afternoon in February, but as they pondered the new group's mission and purpose, one question loomed over all five of them. Lawson was the only one bold enough to ask it. She took a deep breath and wondered aloud, "How did we get here?"

The question was met with immediate tension and an uncomfortable silence as the women squirmed nervously where they were sitting. Lawson's best friend, the beautiful and sophisticated first lady of Mount Zion Ministries, Sullivan Webb, simply shrugged her shoulders and passed her hand over the growing belly bump peeking out from underneath her tunic. She had no answer. After all, Sullivan was four months pregnant and didn't know if she was carrying the only begotten child of her esteemed husband, Pastor Charles Webb, or the lovechild of her twenty-five-year-old lover, Vaughn Lovett. If she couldn't even vouch for her child's paternity, how could she account for anything else?

Angel King drew her knees close to her chest and fiddled with her engagement ring. The group's dedicated and kind-hearted nurse didn't have a response either, although she would've loved if someone could explain to her how her pending remarriage to ex-husband Du'Corey King led her to the brink of an Internet affair and a pornography addiction.

Kina Battle tossed her head back and stared at the ceiling. She fared no better than the other ladies. After losing her abusive husband to a bullet fired by her twelve-year-old son and ending a relationship with her lesbian lover, "How did we get here?" was a question Kina simply couldn't answer.

Lawson's younger sister, Reginell Kerry, or "Juicy" as she was known on stage, found it best to stop seeking answers. Working as an exotic dancer had stripped the twenty-three-year-old of not only her clothes, but also her self-worth, faith in God, and the man she loved. At this point, the "how" and "why" of it all didn't matter much anymore. After leaving a music video shoot gone wrong, Reginell decided that making sure other young women didn't fall prey to the lure of the sex industry was more important than trying to figure out why she did.

Not even newlywed Lawson, who posed the question and who usually had all the answers, could properly address the question. She was certainly in no position to advise anyone. She was still reeling from her groom's confession of an extramarital affair less than a year after they'd exchanged vows. She didn't really know how she'd ended up there. Understanding how her husband ended up in another woman's bed was hard enough.

Such were the lives of lifelong friends and Mount Zion Ministries members Lawson, Sullivan, Angel, Kina, and Reginell. Their bond of friendship had expanded over a number of years, transcended socioeconomic status, and forever linked them together in sisterhood.

"Well," continued Lawson, "somebody say something!"

After thinking over Lawson's question, Reginell cleared her throat and revealed her answer in a small voice. "No man has ever told me I was beautiful before. I think that's how I got here."

All eyes darted toward Reginell. "Are you kidding me?" asked Lawson. "You've got men spending their rent and child support money for a few minutes with you. Of course, men think you're beautiful!"

Reginell looked down at the floor. "Yeah, I get told that I'm sexy or fine, but I want to know what it feels like to be *beautiful*, you know? I don't want it to have anything to do with sex or my body. I want someone to look inside and see the real me and match the beauty of what they see on the inside with what they see on the outside. I just want a man to think, despite everything I've done, that I can still be beautiful."

Sullivan touched her hand. "You *are* beautiful, Reggie, whether some guy tells you that or not. You are beautiful, and you are worthy. That's why I give you such a hard time about stripping and some of the questionable men you've dated. I want you to know you're worth so much more than that."

"That's easy for you to say, Sullivan," Kina told her. "You've always been beautiful, you've always had the best of everything, and men have always been naturally drawn to you. Ever since we were kids, you could get any guy you wanted. It's not that easy for the rest of us."

Sullivan huffed. "You think just because I'm pretty or because I've always had a boyfriend that I don't know what it's like to want to be loved? I've craved real authentic love my whole life, but I was never shown how to give or receive it. I was only taught how to use and manipulate people. My mother convinced me that my worth was tied into designer labels, who I was sleeping with, and how much money he had. You talk about when we were kids, and I can't even remember what it felt like to be a child. My innocence was taken before I even knew how to value it. I've told you all a lot of what I've been through, but if I told you all of it, it would blow your mind. Frankly, I'd probably go somewhere and blow out my brains if God allowed me to remember all that mess." Sullivan let out a sigh. "Do you want to know how I got here? By having a selfish, sadistic mother who taught me how to search for love in all the wrong places and the right wallets."

Angel shook her head. "You know you can't blame Vera for everything, Sullivan." She pointed at Sullivan's stomach. "You got into that jam all on your own."

"I'm not blaming Vera for this whole Charles-Vaughn-Baby Daddy disaster, but I do think I'm the way *I* am because of the way *she* is. Do you know what scares me more than anything?"

"What?" asked Reginell.

"Every day when I look in the mirror, I see my mother looking back at me, taunting me, telling me that I'm just like her. She's in my blood."

"The blood of Jesus is stronger than Vera's," Angel assured her.

Sullivan lowered her eyes. "I know, and I remind myself of that when I start hearing those voices. But whenever I do something stupid or have a wrong thought, I feel like I'm becoming her."

Lawson looked around at all of them. "You know what breaks my heart? I look around this room and all of us, with the exception of Angel, have some deep-rooted issues with our parents. I think that's why we have so many issues with the men in our lives."

Angel stopped her. "Even though both of my parents were great, my relationships have been just as screwed up as everyone else's, so I don't know how big of a role mothers and fathers play in it."

"In my case, not having my father played a huge role," admitted Lawson. "Reggie's and my dad was hardly ever around, and I hated him for that. I resented him for all the times he never walked me to school or tucked me in at night. Lord only knows where he was when it was time to take me on my first date.

"I think that's why I am the way I am sometimes. I know I'm too hard on people, and I expect too much. I try way too hard to be perfect. It's all because I want to be far removed from being lazy, undisciplined, and irresponsible as I can. I'm trying to be everything my father wasn't, and I don't want anyone around me who has those same qualities that remind me of him. As a result, I end up driving people away, especially the ones I love. I guess you can say that's how I ended up here."

Reginell squeezed her sister's hand, understanding.

"Looking back on my life, I've always been a victim," admitted Kina. "I think that's how I ended up here. In my house growing up, you didn't talk too loud or make too much noise because you didn't want to set Daddy off. He was such a cold man. He provided for us, sure enough, but nothing beyond the basics. In fact, he would tell us, 'I'm doing what the law requires.' He was cruel to my mom too. He'd hit her; he'd hit us. My brother Kenneth couldn't take it anymore. I think that's why we ended up losing him to the streets. The worst part of it all is that I married someone just like my father and continued that same cycle of abuse.

"When E'Bell died, I finally felt free and in control of my life for the first time. As a result, I made a lot of mistakes and hurt people in the process." She glanced over at Sullivan. "I went from being the victim to victimizing other people. I don't want to be that person anymore."

"You're not," Reginell assured her.

Lawson turned to Angel. "What about you? How'd you end up here?"

Angel exhaled. "I think I ended up here because I've spent my whole life trying to be what everyone else wanted me to be. I don't even think *I* know who the real Angel King is. My parents were great, but they set an impossible standard for me to live up to. I was expected to always get good grades and get into the right schools and be this perfect daughter. I think I carried that mentality over into my relationships. Even with Duke, I bite my tongue when I don't want to, I put up with a lot of things I probably shouldn't—anything to maintain this image I've worked my whole life to create. But now, the cracks are starting to show, and it feels like my life is falling apart."

The ladies huddled around Angel, holding her and holding each other. With their marriages, relationships, and families all hanging in the balance, they were all bonded by the knowledge that God and each other were all they had left.

Chapter 2

"Don't nobody know but the one who's in it."

—Lawson Kerry Banks

Four months earlier . . .

"Don't nobody know but the one who's in it," thirty-one-year-old Lawson solemnly declared upon hearing that one of Mount Zion Ministries' seemingly most stable couples was headed for divorce. "Freddie and Jasmine always seemed like the perfect couple. Then again, we all thought E'Bell and Kina were happy too, but we didn't know the hell she was going through in her own home." Lawson shook her head and shuddered, recalling the years of physical and emotional abuse her cousin and best friend, Kina Battle, endured during the ten-year marriage to her late husband, E'Bell.

Angel agreed. "When I think of what she went through at the hands of the man who was supposed to love her, it breaks my heart. Just knowing the toll it took on Kina's self-esteem and the effect shooting his dad has had on Kenny is enough to make even the most devout Christian speak ill of the dead. Thank God between our prayers and counseling, they seem to be coping."

Reginell began scraping blackend flakes off a burnt-to-a-crisp chicken leg, which was a product of her first attempt at cooking for her sister, Lawson, and their three closest friends. "It just goes to show that you never know what's going on behind closed doors. Remember when the whole church thought Sullivan and Pastor Webb were Savannah's answer to Ruth and Boaz?" She raised her eyes toward Sullivan. "Nothing like a little Internet sex tape to shatter that illusion, ain't that right, Sully?"

Mount Zion Ministries' first lady Sullivan Webb smiled and flung her newly purchased weave over her shoulder with one French-manicured hand to show that Reginell's snide comments about the year-old scandal no longer fazed her. "While my slight indiscretion was a dark cloud over my husband's ministry and my marriage, I can't think of anything as bad as this disaster that you're trying to pass off as dinner. Honestly, I don't know what's worse—the storm brewing outside or your cooking!"

Angel glanced out of Reginell's dining-room window at the ominous clouds gathering across the dense November sky. "It's supposed to get pretty bad out there." She turned and frowned at the foamy lump heaped onto the plate. "But Mother Nature has her work cut out for her if she wants to beat these mashed potatoes. At least, I *think* these are mashed potatoes."

Reginell sprang from her seat and snatched up the bowl of remaining potatoes in a huff, causing her braids to swing wildly across her shoulders as she turned away. "This is the *last* time I try to do anything nice for you heifers!" she spat.

Sullivan raised an eyebrow. "This is your idea of doing something *nice* for us?"

"Hey, lay off my baby sister! She's doing her best," cried Lawson, coming to Reginell's defense as usual. "Besides, we haven't even gotten to the dessert. Reggie,

I just peeked in the oven and saw that beautiful chocolate pie you have cooling off in there. I can't wait to dig into it!"

Reginell looked confused. "Chocolate pie? I don't know how to make no chocolate pie. The only pie I made was a sweet potato pie."

Lawson winced and eased away from her sister. "You might wanna go check on it, boo. It's looking more like *burnt* potato pie at the moment."

Reginell cussed and dashed into the kitchen.

It was a typical Sunday afternoon for lifelong friends Sullivan, Lawson, Angel, and Reginell, who gathered together as often as possible to share the latest gossip, obsess over their most recent man crisis, and thank the Lord for His presence and each other.

Sullivan laughed and raked her fork across the plate. "You'd think with all the money she makes sliding up and down the pole at the club that she would've had the meal catered and spared us this catastrophe. I'm actually embarrassed for her."

"Reggie is trying to show us how mature and domestic she's gotten, Sully," Lawson reminded her.

Sullivan threw down her fork. "Either Reggie wants to be Martha Stewart or Amber Rose. She's got to make a choice."

Lawson inspected her plate, hoping to find something that looked edible. "She says dancing down at that strip club is just temporary. She's still hoping that it'll lead to her meeting some music mogul who'll sign her to a record deal."

"That's the same thing she said a year ago when we found out she was working there," piped in Angel.

"I know," admitted Lawson. "But she's almost twenty-three years old. She's a grown woman. Reggie is going to do exactly what Reggie wants to do."

Sullivan stabbed a foreign congealed substance on her plate. "Judging by this dinner, what she wants to do right now is poison us!"

"Not everybody, Sullivan," snarled Reginell, barging into the room. "Just you."

"Oh, no!" barked Angel. "We are not about to start this again. I swear you two are worse than the girls with all this back-and-forth bickering."

"How are those precious little angels?" asked Lawson in reference to Angel's soon-to-be stepchildren, offsprings from her ex-husband's marriage to his deceased wife.

Angel rolled her eyes. "They may be 'precious' and 'little,' but the jury is still out on the 'angels' part."

Lawson looked up from her plate. "What's happened?"

"Same ol', same ol'. Miley and Morgan miss their mom. They're still adjusting to the idea of Duke and me getting married and having a new stepmother, which is why . . ." Angel's voice trailed off.

"Which is why what?" prodded Sullivan.

Angel lowered her voice, already anticipating her friends' disapproval. "Duke asked me to move in with them, and I said yes."

Lawson frowned and shook her head. "Shacking up—*really*, Angel?"

"It makes the most sense," she rationalized. "Duke needs help with the girls, and I'm over there all the time. I'm practically living there anyway. It's just more convenient this way."

Lawson raised an eyebrow. "Yeah, but you know what the Word says about it: 'Marriage should be honored by all, and the marriage bed kept pure, for God will judge the adulterer and all the sexually immoral.'"

Sullivan sucked her teeth. "Don't be a hypocrite, Lawson. You and Garrett lived together for five years before you got married."

"Yeah, but once we got saved, I kicked his butt out," pointed out Lawson.

"The wedding is in a few months. I don't see the harm in getting started on our family life a little early," Angel reasoned.

"I'm sure you don't. Unfortunately, God does," replied Lawson. "Besides, Angel, you and Duke haven't even been back together that long."

Sullivan leaned in closer to Angel. "Wouldn't you feel weird living there with all of Theresa's stuff still all over the place? It's like she's still living there."

Angel pretended not to be bothered by it. "Duke just keeps it for the kids' sake. He doesn't want them to feel like they have to forget their mother, and neither do I. As for me moving in, it's not like we aren't planning to get married or like we're not already—"

"Sleeping together?" filled in Sullivan.

Angel let out a sigh. "We were married for three years before getting a divorce so—"

"There's no harm in being his wife between the sheets, right?" finished Lawson.

Angel rolled her eyes and forced Reginell's overseasoned green beans down her palate. "Considering all of the commandments broken between everybody at this table, I don't think anyone here is in a position to pass judgment."

"Amen to that," muttered Sullivan.

"Are you sure you and Duke aren't rushing things?" Lawson posed. "I mean, within six months after Theresa's death, you and Duke were already boo'ed up again. Three or four months after that, you were engaged.

Now, you're moving in. His wife hasn't even been dead a whole year. It just seems like things are moving kind of fast."

"Lawson, I've been waiting to be Duke's wife again since our divorce was finalized ten years ago, and you know I've always wanted to be a mother. None of this feels rushed to me. If anything, I've had my life on hold too long. Now, I'm ready to live it." Angel wiped her hands on a napkin. "Enough about that. It's time for a new subject. How is Operation Baby coming, Sully?"

Sullivan's mood spiraled downward. "It's coming along, I guess."

Lawson raised her eyes. "Well, you and Charles, um, making an effort, right? You know you have to do more than just wish for a baby. It requires a bit of work."

"*I'm* making an effort, but getting Charles to the bedroom has been like pulling teeth these days. I've had to all but strap him to the bed and make him take it!"

Angel snickered. "That's a far cry from last year when you were sending him to bed alone with a bottle of lotion and a deflated ego."

Sullivan sighed. "Yeah, I know, but I'm already thirty-one and at forty-eight, Charles is no spring chicken! At this rate, we'll be older than Abraham and Sarah before we have a baby. That's why I may need to take matters out of Charles's hands—*literally*—and into my own."

"Uh-oh," groaned Lawson. "It never ends well when you decide to do that. Why can't you wait on the Lord sometimes, Sully? I believe He's been at this life thing a lot longer than you have."

The doorbell rang. Reginell answered and let Kina in. "You're soaking wet! Can you shake yourself off before coming in? I don't want you messing up this carpet, costing me my deposit."

"Relax, Reggie. No harm done." Kina let down her umbrella and breezed into the dining area. "So what have I missed?"

"It's about time you got here!" Sullivan huffed. "You know we don't like to be kept waiting."

"Says the Princess of CP Time," grunted Angel.

Sullivan sucked her teeth. "Just because I'm usually late doesn't mean I tolerate it in others."

Kina joined them at the table. "The interview ran longer than I thought it would," explained Kina. "On top of that, traffic was slow because of all the rain."

"Well, how did it go?" pressed Angel King, passing Kina a plate. "Did you get the job? Are you going to be the pastor's new administrative assistant or what?"

Kina placed a napkin in her lap. "He said he was going to call me in tomorrow to give me his decision." Angel nodded. Kina reached over and touched Angel's hand. "And I hope you know my quitting isn't about you, Angel. I'm very happy working for you, but now that I'm a single parent, you know I need the money."

"No, you deserve this, girl. There's no way I could pay you what the church is offering."

"Sullivan, you could help the girl out with a little pillow talk with your husband tonight," playfully suggested Reginell. "You know you don't do anything else in bed to get the man excited."

Angel laughed. "You know, Pastor Charles is the only one I'm willing to lose you to! I'm going to miss having you around. You're the best assistant I've ever had at Guardian Angel."

"You'll find someone in no time," Kina assured her. "And you know it's nothing personal. Working at the church just fits into my schedule better now that I'm in school full time. Maybe you should think about hiring Reggie to fill my spot."

Reginell cleared her throat and sat down. "Reginell *has* a job."

"Don't get me started on the kind of job it is," fired Sullivan.

Reginell rolled her eyes. "I know that you all can't see how this is helping my career, but it is. You'll never guess who I met last night. Tron and all of the other guys from that group Intermission. I was *this close* to signing with Down South Records."

"So what stopped you?" posed Lawson.

Reginell shook her head. "It just wasn't the right deal for me, that's all. But I know I can sing. One day very soon, there's going to be a record deal on the table with my name on it, you'll see," she vowed.

"But in the meantime, I assume you'll still be entertaining perverts down there at Paramours," surmised Sullivan.

Reginell stiffened at the snarky remark. "Honestly, I don't know why you all still act like stripping is the worst thing in the world! Personally, I see nothing wrong with celebrating the human body."

"Celebrating the body is one thing. *Selling* the body is another matter altogether," replied Lawson. Reginell flashed a cold glare in her sister's direction.

Kina tried to break the tension. "So what's for dinner?" she asked, looking around at the still-full plates.

"Don't worry, there's plenty left over." Sullivan slid her plate across the table. "You can have mine."

Kina's eyes widened. "Wow, this looks . . ." She gulped and scrambled for something kind to say. "It looks like you put a lot of time and effort into this dinner, Reggie." She passed the plate back to Sullivan. "But I ate a banana on the way over so I'm good." She patted her stomach. "I'm still on my diet, you know. I got to watch what I eat if I want to be able to fit into all these size sixteens I just bought."

"Down to a sixteen from size twenty, huh?" Angel smiled. "Congratulations!"

"Well, a lot of the credit goes to you and all those salads you make me order whenever we go to lunch."

"I'm a nurse, Kina. What else would you expect?"

Lawson poured a glass of tea. "How are your counseling sessions coming, Kina?"

"Everything is fine," she answered quickly and turned her attention to Reginell. "You must've spent all day in the kitchen whipping this up for everyone, Reggie. That was very sweet of you to do."

Reginell began clearing dishes off of the table. "Thanks. You want me to wrap up a plate for Kenny, Kina?"

"God, no!" shrieked Sullivan. "He's only twelve. His stomach can't digest that!"

"Forget you, Sully," grumbled Reginell and plunked down in her seat with a pout.

Angel chuckled at the two of them. "Is everything still going well for you with school, Kina?"

Kina nodded. "It's great. The professors are so kind and helpful. Everybody is really sweet. They all go out of their way to make you feel at home."

Lawson stood up to close the blinds to block out the lightning. "I'm glad you're enjoying it. I know you were a little apprehensive about returning to school to earn your degree after being out of the loop for so long."

"Yeah, well, E'Bell's gone now, and Kenny spends most of his time at school with his friends, or at Lawson's with Garrett and Namon. I needed something to keep me busy. I'm just thankful that Sullivan convinced Charles to give me a shot at this new job."

Sullivan declined taking the credit for it. "It didn't take much convincing. Even I have to admit that you're good at what you do, Kina. Lord knows somebody as holy as you will fit right in over there." Sullivan took a sip of her tea. "Plus, you can be my eyes and ears. It's always good to have an insider."

Kina was concerned. "Why would you need an insider? You think somebody is over there stealing the church's money?"

"I wouldn't be surprised," Sullivan deadpanned. "And it's no secret that more than a few of those lonely witches over there would like to steal my husband!"

"That's a switch," noted Angel. "It wasn't that long ago that you were practically giving him away."

"That was the *old* Sullivan," declared the first lady. "The *new* Sullivan adores her husband and is the paradigm of fidelity, sanctimony, and . . . any of those other words that people should use to describe Mount Zion's first lady."

Lawson rolled her eyes. "Sullivan, you know *exactly* what words people use to describe Mount Zion's first lady. Most of them can't be said in front of children."

Sullivan frowned. "So I had an affair—big whoop."

"You didn't just have an affair. You had a sex tape," clarified Reginell.

"That was blasted all over the Internet," remarked Kina.

"And cost your husband his bid for county commissioner, not to mention made him a laughingstock for months," added Angel, contributing her two cents.

"We've work through all that," retorted Sullivan with conviction. Her confidence faltered after a few seconds. "We're trying to anyway."

"Well, he stood before the entire congregation to publicly forgive you and ask the church to accept you back in," recalled Kina. "He didn't have to do that. I think it shows just how much Charles loves you and wants to make the marriage work."

"I don't know," began Lawson. "I don't think marriage ought to be looked upon as work. It's supposed to be a blessing. I mean, look at Garrett and me. I'm the happiest I've ever been in my life."

"That's because you've only been married six months," replied Sullivan. "Let's have this conversation five years from now when you're studying episodes of *CSI* to see how you can kill him in his sleep and get away with it."

Lawson shook her head. "When you're married to the one God intended you to be with, you don't have those kinds of thoughts; at least I won't."

Sullivan rolled her eyes. "Not to sprinkle any rain on your delusional parade, Sister Banks, but I believe the Bible says, 'Don't boast about tomorrow, for you do not know what a day may bring forth.' No marriage is written in heaven, not even yours."

Lawson was undeterred. "Sullivan, when Garrett and I took those vows, we meant them. Divorce and failure just simply aren't an option."

"*Humph!*" Sullivan laughed a little. "Ignorance is bliss."

"I can't attest to ignorance, but my marriage sure is," boasted Lawson. "I thank God for Garrett every chance I get."

Angel agreed. "Thank Him, girl, because you know there was a time when we weren't so sure we were gonna be able to get the two of you down that aisle!"

"Thanks to your big-mouthed sister over here," mumbled Sullivan.

"It's not Reggie's fault," protested Lawson. "All she did was tell Mark the truth. I should've told Mark we had a teenage son together after we first reconnected, and I definitely shouldn't have let him come between

Garrett and me. All that's in the past now. Mark and Namon are closer than ever, and Garrett and Mark are getting along now that Mark has stopped obsessing over me. All's well that ends well."

"Now that *Mark's* stopped obsessing?" echoed Reginell. "I believe the 'obsessing' was mutual, dear sister."

Lawson bristled at the notion. "My obsession with Mark ended right around the time I was in the delivery room screaming at the top of my lungs while Namon clawed his way out of my sixteen-year-old uterus. Anyway, I married Garrett, didn't I? His proposal is the one I accepted, not Mark's."

"Can you all believe what a crazy year and a half it's been?" asked Kina, thinking back on everything they'd been through. "Between Kenny killing E'Bell, Sullivan getting outed on the Internet, Angel reuniting with Duke, and Lawson's battle with Mark over Namon, it's a wonder we've made it through in one piece!"

"It's no wonder, Kina. The Lord brought us through, pure and simple," attested Lawson. "There's no way we could've survived all that without Him."

"Tell it, girl," affirmed Angel.

"But you know what?" Lawson went on. "I'm grateful for the trials and everything we've gone through. It's made us all stronger in our walk with the Lord, in our friendship, and made us stronger as women. 1 Peter 1:7 says, 'These have come so that the proven genuineness of your faith—of greater worth than gold, which perishes even though refined by fire—may result in praise, glory and honor when Jesus Christ is revealed.' So I praise him, y'all! I have a level of faith and endurance that I've never had before and that I don't think I would have if I wasn't forced to lean on God to get me through. We need to count it all joy, even when we suffer through hard times because it's those experiences that God uses to make us better and more mature Christians. We also have to remember that whatever we go through isn't just for us; it's also so we can help and encourage someone else."

"That's true," said Angel. "Believe it or not, Sullivan, you and Charles are part of the reason I was able to accept Duke's proposal. I didn't think I could trust him again after he cheated on me with Theresa and walked out on our marriage. Seeing how forgiving and loving Charles was toward you helped give me the strength I needed to move past that. It also showed me that a marriage can not only overcome something as devastating as infidelity but can also be stronger as a result.

"And, Lawson, watching the way Garrett is with Namon—the way he treats him like he's his own child—made it a lot easier to love Theresa's daughters like they are my own, unconditionally."

"We can't deny it, ladies. God has been good to all of us," affirmed Lawson. "Even when times are hard, He still works things out for the good of those who love Him. The devil intended all of those trials to break us and to make us give up. God used those same trials for us to build one another up."

Kina swelled with pride. "Well said, cousin."

"At least it's been relatively calm for the past few months," noted Reginell. "Everybody is doing well. Lawson is trying her best to stay off my back about stripping."

"Lawson staying off your back isn't the problem. It's *you* we need to stay off your back," added Sullivan.

"Sully, do you *really* want to go there?" asked Angel.

Remembering her own dirty dalliances, Sullivan retreated into silence.

"It's a little scary, though," admitted Angel.

Reginell began tinkering with her cell phone. "What is?"

"The calm. It makes you wonder when the other shoe is going to drop."

Lawson peered out of the window. "Well, you know what they say . . . Either you're going through a storm, coming out of one, or are about to enter one."

Just then, a loud clap of thunder and blinding flash of lightning shook the room, causing the lights to flicker. The ladies exchanged troubled glances with one another, wondering if it really had been the calm before one heck of a storm.

Chapter 3

"Nobody told me it would be like this."
—Kina Battle

Kina came home to an empty apartment after leaving Reginell's. Kenny was spending the night with Namon at Lawson's house, and she would be spending the night alone with her thoughts, painful memories, and loneliness.

She slipped out of her shoes, unfastened the belt that was restricting her stomach, and felt like herself again. Sometimes it was exhausting to keep up the façade for her friends, like everything was fine in her life, but it was easier than having them worry about her or worse—feel sorry for her. Yes, she was proud to be back in school, and she knew the change of employment would do her good, but those were outward things. Inwardly, not much had changed. She was no longer at the mercy of her husband's fist, and she had the freedom to do what she pleased, but she still struggled with her demons; only now, external demons had been replaced by internal ones.

Kina checked her voice mail messages. There was only one from her therapist reminding her that she'd missed three appointments in a row and that it had been two months since her last session. Kina pressed delete before hearing the rest of the message.

"What good is all that psychobabble doing me if I'm still in the same state I was in a year ago?" she wondered. "I'm still sad, still lonely, still broke. There's no point in wasting the good doc's time or any more of my money on therapy."

Kina picked up her and E'Bell's framed prom picture, still holding its place on her mother's hand-me-down curio. She remembered with misty eyes how happy they were that night. Back then, she couldn't have imagined a future without him. Now, she had no choice in the matter. She sighed and put the picture back in its designated space.

It was times like this that it was tempting to miss E'Bell. Certainly not the abuse or the assaults on her self-esteem, but having someone—anyone—there waiting for her to come home would've been nice.

Kina recalled how, following E'Bell's passing, people told her she would feel a range of emotions from anger and resentment to crushing grief. Even her therapist had warned her about intense feelings of loneliness and mixed emotions about the abuse she suffered at the hands of her husband.

"But nobody told me it would be like this," she said aloud. There was no one else to confide in, so Kina turned to God. "I guess it's just you and me tonight, Lord, *yet again.*"

Without Kenny there, the silence in the house was palpable. She could hear every drip from the leaky faucet, each clank from the old plumbing, even the creaking of the tattered sofa whenever she sat down on it was a constant reminder that she was utterly alone.

"Lord, I know E'Bell wasn't in the running for winning the *Husband of the Year* award. There were times when he made me laugh, and he was a source of companionship."

Kina looked around her empty apartment. Funny, it seemed so small when she, E'Bell, and Kenny were all crammed in there. There were many times that the wood-paneled walls felt like they were closing in on her. Now, it seemed like a huge vacuum of desolate space full of borrowed and broken furniture. It struck her as strange that two years ago, she longed for the peace and quiet she now resented.

She picked up her NIV Bible lying next to the telephone. After flipping through a few passages, her eyes fell on the first six words of Proverbs 6:25: "Do not lust in your heart." She cringed and tossed the Bible aside. She felt convicted, knowing that the Matthew, Mark, Luke, and John she wanted couldn't be found between those sheets.

Kina loved the Lord with her whole heart, but there was a void in her life that not even the most powerful scripture could fill at times like this. As much as she loved her son, Kenny couldn't fill it either. Lord willing, Kenny would only get older, more independent. Within a couple of years, he'd be in high school, and off to college within a few more. Then she'd really be alone. Kina had her friends and her church, but what about the midnight hour when the doors of the church were locked and her friends were snuggled up next to husbands of their own?

Deep down, Kina knew what her real problem was. Even though she'd never admit out loud, Sullivan had voiced it in jest several times before.

"Kina, you just need some *male* in your life, and I don't mean the kind that comes stamped in long envelopes either!" Sullivan had declared.

Of course, Kina rebuked the notion, followed by scriptural quotes about sexual purity and the marriage bed being undefiled. It made her feel like a hypocrite because inside, she was siding with Sullivan. Kina wasn't a nymphomaniac by any stretch of the imagination, but she did long to be kissed, held, touched, and to feel the weight of a man on her own body.

"God, is it wrong to feel this way?" she asked. "Loving you is supposed to be enough, so why doesn't it feel like it? I'm tired of pretending I don't want a man in my life and like I'm not a real flesh-and-blood woman. While my sex life with E'Bell wasn't the best, it did exist, which is more than I can say for my current situation.

"You said you'd send us a comforter," she quietly prayed. "So where is mine? Lord, I've tried to do right by you. I've done everything you've asked us to do in your Word. I've shown love to people, I've stayed away from sin and fornication, I go to church, and I tithe. I even started losing weight and taking better care of my body like you told me to. What more do I have to do before you do your part? You said whatever we ask for in Jesus' name, we shall receive if we're obedient and have faith. Well, I've been asking, Lord. When will it be due season for me? When will my harvest come?"

Kina checked the time. It was only 9:00 P.M., but she figured she might as well turn in early. There was no point in staying up and being tortured by depression and disappointment. She turned off the light in her living room and prepared to take a cold shower and crawl into bed alone.

As she peeled off her clothes, Kina caught a glimpse of herself in the mirror attached to her dresser. "Maybe it's time to add a little 'work' to my faith," she uttered, looking at her body in the mirror. She pinched her plump cheeks to bring needed color to her olive skin. She sucked in her pudgy stomach as best she could for a more flattering profile. "After all, the Lord helps those who help themselves, right?" She tried to rake her pageboy haircut into different positions to give it an edgier look.

Not that she possessed a sense of entitlement, but Kina did feel like, as a child of the King, she should be able to get at least a few of the things she wanted out of life. Considering that God had promised to bless exceedingly, abundantly beyond anything she could imagine, she didn't think a husband for herself and a father for Kenny was asking too much.

Chapter 4

"We've perfected phoniness so much at church and around our friends that you're starting to believe the bull we're putting out to the rest of the world."

—Sullivan Webb

"Charles?" called Sullivan as she entered the ornately decorated foyer of their spacious contemporary Victorian home. "Are you here?"

"Yeah, I'm in the study," he shouted back.

She wasn't surprised to find him there. Charles was spending more and more time in the study. There was a time when he would have been waiting to greet her as soon as she entered the door from one of her many shopping sprees or salon appointments. These days, however, she was more likely to be greeted by the housekeeper, Mavis, than her husband. It wasn't that he was avoiding Sullivan; it just seemed that his life had moved on without her.

Sullivan walked into the study and found Charles staring into his computer's monitor from behind his wire-rimmed glasses. "Hey."

"Hello, sweetheart. How was dinner with the girls?"

"The girls were great, Reggie's dinner, on the other hand, left a lot to be desired."

Charles chuckled a little. "I guess you've got to give Sister Reggie credit for trying."

"She needs to try harder. I'm starving," whined Sullivan, rubbing her hand across her toned stomach, which was a stark contrast to her husband's portly belly. "I think there's still some of that casserole left from yesterday. I can warm some up for you too if you'd like."

Charles still hadn't taken his eyes off of the computer long enough to look at her. "No, don't trouble yourself. I'm not really hungry."

"How about a bottle of water?" she offered.

"I'm fine, Sullivan."

Sullivan stood by idly a little longer, waiting for him to strike up a conversation or otherwise acknowledge her existence. It didn't take long for her to conclude that she was waiting in vain. "I think I'm going to eat, then turn in. Should I wait up for you?"

"No, darling, you go on to bed." He heaved himself out of the chair and kissed her on the forehead. "I'll see you in the morning." Charles seemed anxious for her to leave and slightly annoyed, which *greatly* annoyed her.

Sullivan pressed her lips together and folded her spindly arms across her chest. "Are you sleeping down here again?"

Charles hunkered back down in his seat. "This research paper is due by seven in the morning. It's probably going to be late when I finish up here, and I don't want to wake you."

"So I take that as a *yes*. I hate it when you sleep down here, Charles, and you know it. That bed is too big for me to be in all alone." She curved her lips into a seductive smile and sashayed over to him. "Besides, you still haven't seen me in the oh-so-naughty lingerie I bought last week." She set her glossy pink lips on his neck and ran her hands through his salt-and-pepper hair.

Charles affectionately patted her hand before pulling away. "As tempting as that sounds, I'm going to have to pass. For a few hours, at least."

It was an immediate blow to Sullivan's ego, but she wasn't going to stoop to begging, no matter how much she wanted to be near her husband that night.

Frustrated, she snapped off the computer's monitor. "You said you'd forgiven me, Charles," she blurted out.

He looked up from his computer. "What are you talking about?"

"You said you'd forgiven me for having the affair with Vaughn."

"And I have. We agreed to work on our marriage, and that's what we're doing."

"Then why doesn't it feel like it?" she snapped.

Charles stood up and calmly faced his wife. "What does it feel like, Sullivan?"

"It feels . . . fake and forced, and it has for the past several months. You don't look at me the same way, you barely even touch me anymore."

He sighed. "Sullivan, I love you, and I'm trying, all right? It's just going to take some time for things to get back to the way they used to be."

"And what are we supposed to do in the meantime?" she demanded, temper still flared.

"We keep praying and going to our marriage counselor. We take positive steps toward rebuilding the trust in our marriage, but like I said, it's gonna take some time."

Sullivan rolled her eyes. "How much time?"

"I can't answer that, sweetheart. All I can tell you is that I'm trying."

Sullivan bore holes into him with doubtful eyes. "Really, Charles? Camping out here on the couch, eating in silence—this is your idea of trying?"

Charles exhaled. "I can't get into this with you right now. I have this paper—"

Sullivan cut him off and threw up her hand. "Yeah, you have your paper, you have the church, you have orphans in Africa that need to be fed, souls that need to won for Christ, drowning polar bears that need to be rescued, and whatever else you can think of to avoid our marriage. I get it, Charles."

"Please don't act like this way," he pleaded. "I'm trying, Sullivan, I really am. I honestly think things are getting better between us."

"Why? Because we've said at least two words to each other in the past twelve hours? Or maybe we've perfected phoniness so much at church and around our friends that you're starting to believe the bull we're putting out to the rest of the world."

"Is that what you're doing? Being phony?"

She let out a deep breath. "Sometimes . . . when I'm in public smiling when I really want to scream or when I pretend not to notice that you don't look at me like you used to. It hurts, Charles. I know I screwed up royally, but how long do I have to be punished for my sins?"

"Nobody's trying to punish you, honey, and I love you as much as I always have. It's just a busy season for us right now, but don't read more into it than that."

"How can I not? Truthfully, Charles, I think the only reason you took on all this extra responsibility is to have an excuse to evade me and our issues."

"Maybe at first," he confessed. "But that was when I was still dealing with the affair and the fallout from the election. God has dealt with me on that, and I'm over it now, but I still have obligations and commitments to fulfill."

"Including the ones you have to me!" she interjected. "I love you, Charles. The doctor has already warned you about taking on too much and getting stressed out. I just think the focus right now should be on our marriage and having a baby. Before everything blew up with Vaughn, you had babies on the brain. Since then, you've been quiet about it. You know I want to have all of my children by the time I'm thirty-six. After that, I'm closing up shop, so time is of the essence, especially if we're going to have more than one."

"Honey, we're still five years away from your deadline. Honestly, once you made it clear that you didn't want any kids, I accepted it and put it out of my mind. I've never known you to be a baby person, Sullivan. In fact, you've been very vocal about detesting children, and I know how much you hate directing the children's choir at church."

"I never said I hated children. My issue has always been the fear that I'd be the kind of mother that Vera was to me. Lord knows I wouldn't wish anything that traumatic on any child. I've moved beyond that, though. People can change. Isn't that what you're always preaching to the congregation?"

"Maybe you were right the first time. Perhaps some couples are just meant to be a blessing to other people's children."

Sullivan got riled up again. "What are you saying, Charles? Are you going to deprive me of having children?"

"Have I ever deprived you of anything, Sullivan?"

Sullivan cracked a smile, easing the tension. "There *was* that Louis Vuitton croc I wanted a few years ago."

He chuckled. "You mean the $14,000 purse that you tried to convince me was an *investment*?"

"Charles, I can't help but think that a baby is just what we need to get things back on track between us."

"I'm not saying I don't want to have children, not at all. I think children are a blessing from God, but we don't need a baby to fix our marriage, not to mention that it's not fair to put that kind of responsibility on a child. It's up to us and the Lord to fix whatever is wrong in our marriage."

"Whether it's a baby or you taking on a less strenuous workload, something has to change. Our marriage won't survive if we continue on like this," cautioned Sullivan.

Charles cupped his hands around her arms. "We're fine, Sullivan. If you want, I'll stop what I'm doing and spend an hour or two with you, then come back and finish. If you're hungry, I'll take my beautiful wife out to eat instead of having you warm up day-old casserole. If you're tired, I'll take you upstairs and rub your feet, okay?" He planted a kiss on her lips. *"We are fine, honey."*

Sullivan exhaled and fell into her husband's loving arms, almost convinced that their marriage would be okay.

"There's that pretty smile I wanted to see," said Charles, standing back to look at her. "We're good. Stop looking for trouble."

At that, Sullivan's smile began to fade. The problem wasn't that she looked for trouble. The problem was that it always managed to find her.

Chapter 5

"Baby, I just don't know how comfortable I'd be wearing your dead wife's clothes."
—Angel King

Angel hurried home from dinner with the girls to prepare dinner for *her* girls after picking them up from a play date. She quickly slipped out of her Sunday best, donned one of her mother's old aprons, and forced her natural ringlets of curls into a bun. Had she known they were going to murmur and complain like the children of Israel, she would've served them Reginell's half-baked leftovers.

Miley's pouty lips soured into a frown, and she tossed her fork on the plate after sampling Angel's spaghetti. "I don't like it. It doesn't taste like Mommy's."

Angel sighed. It wasn't the first time "not like Mommy's" was hurled at her and probably wouldn't be the last. Who knew there was an art to making spaghetti?

"Where's the bacon?" asked ten-year-old Morgan, digging through the noodles. "Mommy always put bacon in it."

"I used sausage instead," said an exasperated Angel.

"I don't like sausage," griped Miley.

"You ate three sausage patties this morning," Angel reminded her.

The five-year-old sulked. "I don't like *this* kind. I like the patties."

"Well, you don't have to eat it if you don't want to, but I'm not cooking anything else," threatened Angel.

Miley poked out her mouth in silent protest. Then her hunger got the best of her, and she began taking small bites out of her plate of spaghetti.

"What time is Daddy getting home?" asked Morgan.

Angel poured glasses of juice for them. "He has to work late tonight. He won't be home 'til around ten."

"Can we stay up and wait for him?" asked Miley.

"She's gonna say no," muttered Morgan. "She always does."

"Morgan, that's not true. But you have school tomorrow. If I let you stay up that late, you won't want to get up in the morning, then we'll be late. Remember what happened when I let you stay up waiting for him last week?"

Rather than admit defeat, Morgan found a new way to rile Angel. "Can we go see Mommy this weekend? I want to put some flowers on her grave."

Angel bit her lip. She knew that the girls needed closure and still needed to feel close to their mother, but the weekly cemetery visits were starting to wear on her. "Wouldn't you rather do something fun, like go to the park or go skating?"

Morgan looked down at her plate. "I knew you were going to say no."

"I didn't say no, I just . . ." Angel gave up and gave in. "If you want to put flowers on your mother's grave, that's what we'll do. I know you miss her."

"I miss her all the time, like every day," admitted Morgan.

"Me too," replied her sister in a low voice.

Angel softened toward them. "I understand. She was my friend, and I miss her too. But she wouldn't want us to be sad all the time. She'd want us to be happy."

Morgan pouted while Miley jabbed at her food with the fork as they ate in silence. All three were relieved when they looked up and saw Duke's smiling face. The girls sprang from the table and rushed into their father's arms.

"*Daddy!*" squealed Miley.

"Yea, Daddy's home!" sang Morgan.

Duke kissed them on their cheeks and tousled the afro-puffs sprouting out of the tops of their heads. "Yes, Daddy's home. How are my two favorite girls?"

"Good now," squealed Miley. Angel wondered what they were before Duke got home.

Duke released his daughters and then bent down to kiss Angel on the top of her head. "And how's my *other* favorite girl?"

"Tired and exhausted but good now," she replied with a simper, echoing Miley. "I thought you were working late tonight."

"I was supposed to, but I decided that spending time with you guys was more important than making another dollar." Duke grabbed a plate and sat down across Angel. "This looks good, babe," he commented, reaching for the pasta.

"She didn't put any bacon in it like Mama," grumbled Morgan.

Duke chuckled. "That's okay. There are a thousand different ways to make spaghetti, baby."

"But Mama's way was the *best* way!" argued Miley.

Duke noticed how uncomfortable Angel looked and reached out to give her hand an encouraging squeeze. "Well, let's just see now . . ." He swallowed a forkful. "Honestly, girls, I can't tell whose is better. They're both delicious."

Angel smiled a little. "Thank you."

Morgan shrugged. "I guess it's okay," she conceded, now that her father was on board.

Duke dug in for a second helping. "Um, babe, I noticed that the little end table in the foyer is missing. What happened to it? Did it break or something?"

"It's in the attic," replied Angel. "I got tired of bumping into it when I come in with all my stuff after work. Having it gone makes it more convenient for me. Taking it out opens up the space more, don't you think?"

Duke shifted uneasily in his seat. "It's just that Reese loved that little table. It belonged to her grandmother. She called it her 'what-not' table." He stopped himself from elaborating. "You know what? This is your home too now, and if you think it shouldn't be there . . ."

Angel held up her hand. "No, it's okay. I'll put it back. I didn't know it meant that much to you."

He seemed relieved. "Thank you, sweetheart. Maybe we can just move it to the other side so it'll be out of your way."

Angel couldn't help feeling a little slighted that Duke had sided with his dead wife yet again. First, there was her picture that he insisted on keeping in their bedroom. Then there was his wedding ring that only came off when Angel threatened to break off their engagement a few weeks earlier. She also had to constantly fight the urge to slap Duke every time he slipped up and called her "Reese." Now, she'd have to add Grandma's table to Theresa's growing list of posthumous victories.

"Daddy, can we go upstairs and watch TV?" asked Miley after nearly cleaning her plate.

Duke smiled at his daughters. "Of course, you can."

"After they put their dishes away," stipulated Angel. Seeing as how their favorite television show was about to start, Angel's request was met with downtrodden looks but immediate compliance.

Duke grinned watching them scramble up the staircase after clearing the table. "That Miley looks more and more like her mother every day, doesn't she?"

Angel cleared her throat and steered the conversation in a new direction. "You know we're having that clothes drive at my church next week. Have you thought any more about my suggestion?"

Duke wiped his mouth with a napkin. "You mean donating Reese's clothes?"

Angel nodded. "Yeah, they're just in the closet taking up space. Theresa was such a giving person. I'm sure she'd want her clothes to go to someone who needs them."

"Are you sure you don't want them?" offered Duke.

The thought of wearing Theresa's clothes was more disturbing than Duke siding with Theresa about the table. "Theresa and I aren't really the same size," she answered, not sure exactly how to respond. "Theresa was so tall and lean, and I'm pretty average in size and height. I don't think her clothes would fit me."

"I'm sure there must be one or two pieces that would fit you. I think you wearing her clothes would be a great way to honor Reese's memory."

Angel sighed. "Baby, I just don't know how comfortable I'd be wearing your dead wife's clothes. It would be a little creepy, for lack of a better word."

Duke nodded. "I understand, and I'm sorry. It was stupid for me to even suggest that."

"It wasn't stupid," she assured him. "Just because I can't wear them doesn't mean someone else couldn't get good use out of them. If you want, we can set a few things aside for the girls to grow into." Duke didn't look convinced yet. "Just think about it, okay?"

"I will. Give me a couple of days to think it over."

"Okay, but keep in mind that we're trying to move forward, not stay in the past. Sometimes doing that requires us to make painful choices."

Duke was quiet for a few seconds. He loved his Theresa, but he also adored the woman seated across from him. "You're right, baby. I love you. Reese is gone, and you're the woman in my life now. If you want to donate the clothes, then that's what we'll do."

Angel beamed. The living—one point; the deceased—3,492.

Duke returned her smile, reminding Angel of one of the many things she loved about him. "So how are we coming with the wedding plans? Have you found a dress yet?"

Angel shook her head. "I haven't really started looking."

"What's stopping you?" he asked, surprised.

Her body tensed. "Are you sure this marriage is still what you want?"

"Do you even have to ask?" Duke held up Angel's left hand. Her exquisite white-gold, 1.5-karat diamond engagement ring sparkled under the light. "This is a symbol of my commitment to you, our marriage, and this family. You never have to question whether this marriage is going to happen or my love for you."

"Sometimes, I wonder if I'm going to lose you. I don't think I could survive that again."

"You won't lose me," he promised her, inviting Angel into his arms. "And I can't lose you again either. You know, baby, God allows strange things to happen. Obviously, I don't think my being unfaithful to you when we were married was a part of God's will, but I can't help but think that having Morgan and Miley was. While I regret hurting you, I don't regret having them. I don't think Reese having cancer was God's divine plan either, but I believe you coming here and being a part of our lives was. Reese's illness was the catalyst for us all overcoming years of hurt and unanswered questions. It's also what eventually brought us back together. Now, we have the family we always wanted. I know my girls can't replace the child that the two of us lost, but this seems like the life we were always meant to have."

She nestled in Duke's arms. "I know, but a part of me wonders if you'll ever love me as much as you loved her."

"Yes, I loved my wife," Duke admitted. "But there's only room in my life for one Mrs. King."

That much, she believed. However, the question remained whether he meant his last wife or his future one.

As Angel finished clearing the table, she watched Duke, who sat on the sofa deep in thought. She knew without his having to say so that he was thinking of Reese again. She knew that being threatened by a dead woman was foolish, at best, and borderline psychotic, at worst. Nevertheless, Angel couldn't help but feel like she was still competing with Theresa for Duke's heart. After all, Theresa had come between them before. Who was to say she couldn't do it again?

Chapter 6

"I'm going to come back home and show you why you're so lucky to have me!"
—Lawson Kerry Banks

Lawson's husband, Garrett, crept up behind his diminutive bride and snaked his arms around her waist. "Do you know what you were doing six months ago today, li'l mama?"

"Hmm, let me see . . ." teased Lawson. She dropped a few dishes in the kitchen sink. "Was it the laundry?"

He smirked. "Oh, it's like that, huh?"

"Wait a minute." She pulled Garrett into an embrace. "I think I vaguely remember saying 'I do' to the sexiest, sweetest, kindest, most romantic man on the planet. Does that sound about right?"

He leaned down to kiss her. "So how do you like being Mrs. Garrett Banks so far?"

"It's the best decision I've ever made."

"Yeah, well, you made me work hard enough for it, that's for sure!"

"I had to make sure you were worthy, honey," she replied, playfully taunting him. "You know not just anybody can get this."

"Is that right?" Garrett's mood morphed from frisky to amorous. "What you know about me gettin' some of *that* right now?" he kissed her again.

She giggled. "I may know a little something about that. . . ."

He leaned down and whispered in her ear. "What do you know about going into our bedroom to re-create our wedding night?" Before she could answer, the phone rang. "Don't answer it. If it's important, they'll call back."

Lawson glanced down at her cell phone on the counter. "Baby, it's Mark. I have to answer it." She pulled away from her husband and picked up the phone. "Hi, Mark, what's up?"

Mark's husky voice came piercing through the phone. "Don't panic but—"

Lawson gasped and held her chest. "Oh my God, what happened to Namon?"

"I just told you not to panic," Mark reiterated.

"Mark, what happened to my son?" broke in Lawson. Garrett edged closer, seeing her concern.

"Calm down, he's fine, Lawson," Mark assured her. "Namon had sort of a little accident on my motorcycle."

"*Motorcycle?* Mark, are you crazy? I told you I didn't want him anywhere near that thing! He's a child!"

"Namon is fifteen. He's not a child anymore, he's a young man."

"Ugh!" roared Lawson. "I can't believe that you could be so irresponsible with him. Just tell me what happened."

"All he did was mount the bike. It was a little heavier than he anticipated, and the bike fell over on him. He skinned up his leg pretty bad."

Lawson sighed. "I'll be there in ten minutes."

"For what? I just told you he's okay."

"I want to see it for myself."

"How about I put him on the phone?" proposed Mark.

"How about I just come over there and bring my son home where he's safe?" she shot back.

"Namon is perfectly safe here with me, and he doesn't want to leave. He didn't even want me to tell you about it because he knew you'd react this way."

"So the two of you have been conspiring against me, is that it?" questioned Lawson, becoming more irate by the second. "I'm coming over, Mark, and you can't stop me."

Mark was firm with her. "He's not leaving with you, Lawson. It's my weekend with Namon."

"Whatever! I'll be there in five minutes." Lawson hung up the phone and began searching for her car keys.

"What's going on?" asked Garrett, alarmed.

"Mark let Namon play around with that darn motorcycle of his, and now Namon's hurt. I'm going over there to check on him."

"How bad is it?"

Lawson reached for her purse hanging on the back of one of the high-bar chairs. "Mark says that he only scraped his leg, but I want to see for myself."

"Baby, if Mark says Namon is okay, I believe him. There's no need for you go charging over there, especially not on our anniversary."

Lawson was irked. "Namon is my son, Garrett. If he's hurt, I'm going to be there for him."

Garrett pulled his wife closer to him. "He's not in grave danger. He's a boy, and boys fall down and get hurt. He doesn't need his mother running over there and making a big fuss over him. Let him be a man."

"Is that how we're defining manhood now?" she snapped.

"I'm just saying there's no need for you to go over there making a big deal out of it."

"Garrett, you already know that I'm still not all that comfortable with the idea of Namon spending so much time over there, especially when it's obvious that Mark is letting him run amok and do whatever he wants to."

"Baby, it's supposed to be our night," Garrett reminded her. "Let Mark handle Namon, and let *me* handle *you*."

Lawson shook her head. "Do you honestly think I'm going to be able to focus on anything if I'm worried about my child? I'll be back before you know it. I just want to see how serious it is and if Namon needs to be taken to the hospital."

Garrett groaned. "All right, Mrs. Banks, we'll go. Just let me grab my jacket."

"No, you stay here," advised Lawson. "And I want you waiting for me in bed when I get back, preferably with some soft music and a bowl of whipped cream," she added with a twinkle in her eye.

"Baby, Namon is my son too. Plus I don't like you driving alone at night, even less so when you're this upset."

Lawson slung her purse over her shoulder. "Mark only lives a few miles from here. I'll be fine, and I promise to call you as soon as I assess the situation with Namon. I'm praying that we won't end up having to spend the night in ER."

"Are you sure you don't want me to tag along?" Garrett offered again.

"Yeah, I think if we both show up, guns blazing, Mark will be on the defensive and think we're ganging up on him again. Things have been peaceful between us lately, and I don't want to rock the boat unless I have to."

Garrett yielded to his wife. "Okay, just don't keep me waiting or make me start without you."

Lawson laughed and perched herself up on tiptoes to kiss him on the cheek. "Thank you for being so understanding. I'm just going to run over there for a minute to check on Namon, then I'm going to come back home and show you why you're so lucky to have me!"

Garrett watched his wife duck out of the house. He knew Lawson's primary concern was seeing about her son, but it still irked him that she was also leaving him to see her ex-lover Mark. At that moment, he wondered just how *lucky* he really was.

Chapter 7

**"Ray, my *voice* is the last thing
on his mind, and you know it!"**
—*Reginell Kerry*

Reginell lingered in the bathtub for over an hour. No matter how hard she scrubbed, she could still feel hands all over her. She wasn't one to be prudish when it came to sex, but sleeping with a man she'd just met in exchange for a favor was a new low even for her. She didn't bother praying, fearing that she had gone beyond the perimeters of God's mercy and grace.

Reginell splashed water on her face to wash away the tears and drew her knees up to her body. Dinner with her family had given her a temporary reprieve from the ordeal she'd experienced at the strip club where she worked, but now that everyone had gone home, the images came flooding back.

Lawson's favorite scripture to hammer her with was, "Don't give to dogs what is sacred. Don't throw your pearls to pigs." If by *pigs*, Lawson meant the patrons at the club, Reginell had neither pearls nor anything else sacred left to throw—not after what she'd done.

The twenty-four hours prior initially held such excitement and promise. Reginell's manager and club owner, Ray Stokes, had scored her a singing audition with the up-and-coming R&B group, Intermission, who had performed in Savannah earlier that night and were coming through Paramours to unwind. Ray had promised Reginell that this was the big break she'd been waiting for; the years she'd spent hoping to get "discovered" had finally paid off. By the end of the night, Lawson, Sullivan, and everyone who'd doubted her would have to eat their words once she stepped out with a record deal and a shot at the kind of future she'd only imagined.

Upon Intermission's arrival, Ray escorted Reginell to the VIP section of the club. "Here she is, fellas, Miss Reginell Kerry," announced Ray as he introduced Reginell to the members of the group. "Everybody around here knows her as Juicy."

"I see why," replied a dreadlocked member of the band. "What's up, sexy? I'm Hurricane."

"I can't believe it's really you! I'm a huge fan of your music!" gushed Reginell, shaking his hand profusely.

Intermission's lead vocalist approached her next. "Glad to hear it. My name is—"

"You don't have to tell me," butt in Reginell. "You're Tron, right?"

He smiled, pleased to be recognized. "Yeah, I'm Tron. Ray here tells me that you're a singer."

"More like a hummer," cracked one of the band-mates. The others snickered.

"Man, shut up. I'm trying to conduct some business here," said Tron and put his attention back on Reginell. "So you sing, ma?"

Reginell's face lit up. "Yeah, I can sing something for you right now if you want."

Tron traced her lips with his finger. "Yeah, I bet you can do all sorts of things with that pretty mouth of yours." The group members laughed again.

"Ray said that you're looking for singers for your new record label," stated Reginell, ignoring the inside joke between the guys.

Tron nodded. "I'm looking for talent. You think you've got what it takes?"

"I know I do," guaranteed Reginell. "Just give me a chance to prove it."

"Oh, you'll get your chance," promised Tron. "First, why don't you show me some of those dance moves you were doing on stage up there."

"I thought you wanted to hear me sing," said Reginell, a little deflated. "Ray said that you wanted me to audition."

Tron licked his lips. "So, you wanna audition for me, huh?"

Her smile weakened. "Yes, I thought that was the whole point."

"My office is available if you need her to *audition* in private," offered Ray, obviously in on whatever they were plotting.

Tron nodded. "It looks like I may have to take you up on that, Ray."

"Aye, if you audition for Tron, you've got to audition for me too," spoke up another member of the group.

"Look, we're talking about singing, right?" Reginell asked cautiously. "I'm not down for anything else."

Tron groped her. "We're talking about you doing whatever it takes to impress me. And after you show me how good you are, you've gotta show my brothers too. They get final input on any new artists signed to the label."

"Why can't I just perform for you?" she bargained.

"We're a family around here. What's good for one is good for all," hedged Tron. "Now, why don't you show me where Ray's office is?"

Reginell knew that this so-called audition would include a romp on Ray's couch, which was a common practice for men willing to shell out extra money for the service. Reginell hadn't stooped to having sex with any of the club's patrons but didn't know how she could avoid doing so now. She turned to Ray. "Hey, can I talk to you for a second?"

Ray exhaled sharply and moved off a little distance with her. "What's up?"

"Ray, this feels like a setup," she whispered. "I don't want to go in there with him."

Ray shrugged. "Okay, cool." She heaved a sigh of relief. "Consider this your last day. I'm terminating our agreement. You're fired."

"What?"

"Reggie, I don't have time to play these games with you. I did my part. I got you the audition; I arranged for Tron to come here to see you, and what do you do? You refuse to even go in there and sing for the man."

"Ray, my *voice* is the last thing on his mind, and you know it!" refuted Reginell.

"We've already had this discussion, Reggie. It's no big deal. It's just sex."

"Sex *is* a big deal! I don't even know those guys. You know, just because I work here doesn't automatically make me a ho."

Ray eyed her as if to say it did. "I thought most chicks would kill to kick it with a celebrity."

"This is a little more than just 'kickin' it.'"

"I told you when we first met that my reputation is on the line. When you flake out like this, it makes me look bad. Why would I put up with that when it's easier just to replace you with some other girl?"

"Ray, I'm not trying to make you look bad—"

"Then don't!" he barked. "Just go back there and walk out with your record deal."

"But—"

"Look, Reggie, either you're in or out." He pointed at Tron, who was flirting with another dancer. "You see that? He's already moving on. That's how it works in this business. If you don't take advantage of your opportunities, somebody else will."

Reginell knew that she was losing time and possibly Tron's interest. Her soul couldn't afford to go along with the plan, but her career couldn't afford to let this chance slip away. "All right, I'll do it this once," she stipulated. "I need a drink first."

Ray smiled. "That's my girl. Don't worry, this will just be a footnote on your way to the top. Tron knows a lot of big names. Signing with him can take you places."

Reginell wondered if hell was one of those places.

Tron walked over to Reginell and Ray. "What's up? Are we gonna do this or what?"

"Yeah, you know how it is," said Ray, summoning a bartender. "She just wanted to make sure it was all right with Daddy." Ray pulled out a set of keys and handed them to Tron. "You can go on back to the office while I get her situated."

Tron smacked Reginell on the rear. "Don't keep me waiting."

The bartender brought a whiskey sour to Ray, who handed it to Reginell. "Just show the man a good time," he urged as Reginell woofed it down. "Everybody can walk away from this thing getting exactly what they want."

Reginell thought of what was waiting for her inside of Ray's office. She knew how used and empty she would feel coming out of that room. "Can I have another drink? And some kush too, just to take the edge off."

That night wasn't the first that Reginell depended on the mind-numbing effects of drugs and alcohol to get through her shift at work. Together, they had the phenomenal ability to make her forget that she was in the moment; they made her feel nothing. Feeling nothing was a whole lot better than feeling dirty and used like a whore. Feeling nothing enabled her to withstand Tron, and later his bandmates, desecrating her body with their sweat, their hands, and their bodily fluids, soiling her temple and her spirit. She felt nothing and, to them, she was nothing.

When Reginell returned home early the next morning, she headed straight for the shower. One hundred, fifty, and twenty dollar bills littered the floor. Inside the stall, Reginell sat crying as the water streamed down on her. By now, the high had worn off, leaving her to face the reality of what she'd done in harsh sobriety. She was a whore—worse than that, if possible. She was trash, unworthy of love, of respect, and of anything sacred. She couldn't show her face to God or to the people she loved most. What would they say if they knew what she'd done? She had pawned everything that was special about her in exchange for a record deal that Ray had called to say was now off the table due to "creative differences."

She accepted that she was the slut everyone thought she was. She had done too much to turn back but didn't have the first clue about how to move forward.

Chapter 8

"I think my mother would've preferred that I told her I was gay during my senior year in high school. It definitely would've gone over better than telling her I was pregnant."

—*Kina Battle*

Kina rubbed her hands along her new desk for what must have been the hundredth time that Tuesday morning. After Charles called the day before and offered her the job as his new administrative assistant, she immediately went into praise mode, followed by a phone call to her friends to announce her new position.

Kina set Kenny's picture down on her desk and stood back, beaming with pride. "You did good, girl!" she said to herself before settling into her new leather chair. She swished around a little to adjust the seat to her bottom.

"So are you settling in all right?" asked Charles, approaching her.

She sat upright. "Oh, yes. I've never really had a big space like this to myself," admitted Kina. "Everything is set up so lovely. I can't believe I'm actually getting paid to be here."

One of the associate pastors followed up with a bouquet of flowers to set on her desk.

"And these are for you as well," announced Charles and handed her the vase. "They're from all of us to welcome you to the family."

"Oh, wow!" gushed Kina. "Pastor, you didn't have to do all of that. Just working here is enough for me."

"Well, yours is the first face people see when they walk through the door, so I've got to do everything I can to keep a big smile on it."

Kina blushed. "Thank you."

"Is there anything else you need? I know it's going to take a minute to figure it all out, but I want to make sure you're off to good start."

"Yes, I'm fine. Everyone has been so helpful. I can already tell I'm going to love working here."

"I certainly hope so. It's the Lord's will that every man find satisfaction in his work. Mount Zion Ministries wants to be as big a blessing to you as you are to us."

"You were a blessing to me long before I was on payroll, Pastor."

"You're mighty kind, my sister." Charles returned her smile. "I'll be in my office. Give me a buzz if you need anything at all, and I'll come running. You have a blessed day, you hear?"

Charles was so kind and thoughtful. It made her wonder how Sullivan managed to garner enough favor with God for Him to send her a man like Charles. It also made her wonder if he ever did wrong in a past life to deserve a woman like Sullivan.

A long day at work followed by a longer day at the gym wasn't exactly Kina's prescription for a day of fun, but she was as committed to taking care of herself on the inside as she was on the out, so she dragged herself to Fitness Fanatics with the last bit of energy she had after leaving church for the day.

After expelling 800 calories between the treadmill, free weights, and ten laps around the indoor track, Kina prepared to leave, unaware that someone had been watching her.

"So, how many pounds have you lost?"

Kina turned around. "Excuse me?"

A woman with sister-locked twists offered a kind smile. "I know a success story when I see one. I've been coming to this gym for a while. I've seen you here a few times, enough to know that you've shed some serious LBs, so how much have you lost?"

Kina grinned, ecstatic that someone had noticed. "I've lost thirty-three pounds and counting."

The woman's eyes widened. "Wow, that's impressive. How long did it take to come off?"

"I've been seriously working out and watching what I eat for about six months now."

The woman outstretched her toned arms. Kina caught a glimpse of her strong, sculpted mahogany legs as well. "This is what six days a week for five years in the gym will get you." She put her arms down. "It wasn't that long ago that I couldn't stand to look at myself in the mirror. Now, I can't stay out if it!"

Kina laughed. "I can't wait until I'm at that point, but I definitely like what I see more than I used to. I decided to make some changes after . . ." Kina bit her lip.

"After what?"

Kina shook her head. "It's not important."

The woman encouraged her. "Sure it is. What were you going to say?"

Kina exhaled. "After my husband died a year ago."

"Oh, I'm so sorry to hear that. Was he sick?"

"Not the way you mean."

The woman nodded, understanding. "Well, look, if you ever want to talk about it, I'm a great listener." She laughed a little. "I guess it would help if I told you my name first. I'm Joan." She extended her hand.

Kina received it. "I'm Kina."

Joan smiled. "That's pretty. I like that . . . Kina."

"Joan is nice too," complimented Kina. "It's a name that evokes strength and confidence." She paused. "Plus, I was a huge fan of *Girlfriends*. Joan was always my favorite."

Joan chuckled. "Joan was a little neurotic for me. I always liked Toni. She was just so fiery and sexy."

"And a complete witch—don't forget about that!" added Kina with a laugh. "I actually have a very close friend who's just like that."

"Don't we all?" retorted Joan. They both laughed. Joan's laughter was infectious. "Hey, listen, have you finished up your workout?"

Kina wiped her sweaty brow with a towel. "Yeah, why?"

Joan checked her watch. "It's after six o'clock, and I haven't even had *lunch* yet. You wanna grab a bite to eat? It's my treat. I know we just met, like, five minutes ago, but I'd love the company. Truth be told, I hate eating alone. It's one of the downsides to single life."

"Don't I know it!" Kina patted her stomach. "You know I *could* use a li'l something on the belly, but you don't have to pay for it."

"No, I want to. Don't worry—I'll let you treat next time! Hopefully, this is just the first of many meals together."

Kina was thrown a little by the invitation, but she too hated eating alone and agreed to a bite at a café across the street. Besides, Joan seemed cool. Kina was amazed by how quickly the two of them hit it off.

"So, Kina," began Joan once they'd sat down, "tell me what you like to do for fun."

"*Fun?*" repeated Kina. "I hardly know what that is anymore! Fun is one of those things I'll get to eventually. Right now, everything is all about work, school, my son, and, of course, my church." The corners of Joan's mouth dipped into a frown. Kina picked up on it right away. "Did I say something wrong?"

"No . . . not really."

"So what's the long face about?"

Joan hesitated. "I have issues with some of the doctrines of the church."

"You're not an atheist, are you?"

"Of course not!" scoffed Joan. "I know there's a God, and I believe He loves me just as I am."

"I don't know of any church or pastor who'll disagree with that."

Joan folded her hands together. "Most churches don't accept my lifestyle, Kina. I guess you could say I'm living in sin by some standards."

"How so?"

Joan took a deep breath. "I'm a lesbian, Kina."

Kina froze, stunned. "Oh . . . I didn't know." She gulped. "You seem so . . . heterosexual."

Joan laughed. "That's the first time I've heard that one!"

Kina smiled politely but didn't say anything.

"Does my being gay make you uncomfortable?"

"No, I admit that it caught me off guard, though. I haven't been around many gays."

"I'm sure you've been around more than you think," quipped Joan.

"Don't you think being gay is a sin?"

"I think there are lots of sins. If being gay is one, I don't think it's any worse than others in God's eyes. I definitely don't think I should be ostracized because of it."

Kina nodded slowly and blurted out, "How did you get like that? I mean, have you always been gay?"

"I've always felt like I was different. I have sisters and female friends. I knew I didn't feel the same way about men as they did. I was just always more attracted to women both physically and intellectually."

"So you've never had a boyfriend?"

"Sure. Trust me—it wasn't exactly acceptable to be gay when I was coming up. There was no *Will & Grace* or *L Word* to soften the blow. I had boyfriends, many of whom were gay themselves, but they knew their secret was safe with me and mine was with them."

Kina was intrigued. "So when did you, you know, come *out?*"

Joan thought back. "I was a freshman in college. By then, it was a lot more acceptable in society, and I think my family had their suspicions anyway. No one seemed overly shocked when I brought my girlfriend home for Christmas that year."

Kina chuckled. "I think telling my parents I was gay definitely would've gone over better than telling them I was pregnant when I was a senior in high school. Growing up in the church, I was always taught that homosexuality is an abomination. Then again, it can't be any worse than what E'Bell did to me."

Joan stopped eating. "Who's E'Bell?"

"He was my husband, the one who died. He was . . . um, he was abusive to me and my son Kenny. With Kenny, it was mostly verbal. With me, it was verbal and physical."

Joan put her hand on Kina's. "I'm so sorry to hear that."

"Yeah, he could be a real monster when he wanted to," recalled Kina with tears filling her eyes. "He was always so angry and blamed me for everything. Sometimes, he would even hit me in front of Kenny." Kina closed her eyes. "I was afraid all the time. You never knew what would set him off. It was awful."

"Kina, were you the one who . . ."

Kina shook her head. "I didn't kill him, Joan. One night, we were arguing because I'd decided to take Kenny and leave him for good. He went ballistic. I don't even remember everything that went down. I just know that he beat me unconscious. When I woke up, E'Bell was on the ground bleeding, and my son was there with his father's gun at his side."

"So it was your son?"

Kina nodded. "Kenny shot his father trying to protect me. To tell you the truth, I really think Kenny saved my life. E'Bell was going to kill me—that much I'm sure of."

"What kind of man would terrorize his wife and child that way?" Joan shook her head. "Men can be such beasts, and I'm not just saying that because I swim in the lady pool."

"I'm not trying to defend him, but E'Bell had a lot of issues," explained Kina. "It was a lot deeper than just being abusive. He couldn't read, and his illiteracy and that anger cost him his football career, his future, his family—everything he ever wanted, including his life. A part of me can't help but feel sorry for him."

"I can tell you have a good heart, Kina. Most women I know wouldn't be this understanding. I've dealt with several cases of domestic violence, so I know how ugly it can get and what some women will do when they're pushed to the edge."

"The God that I serve gives me strength and the ability to forgive E'Bell for everything he did to Kenny and me. I'm not the same woman I was a year ago. I'm stronger now, and I've had enough time and distance from it to see everything more clearly."

"You're amazing, you know that?" Joan gazed intently at Kina. "They don't quite make 'em like you anymore."

Kina smiled bashfully. "That's very nice of you to say."

Joan winked and downed her glass of lemonade. "So far, I have nothing but nice things to say about you." Kina blushed. "So, Kina, do you live around here?"

"Unfortunately, I don't. This neighborhood is a wee bit out of my price range, but I'm looking to move soon."

"Oh, really?"

"Yeah, I recently got back in school and got a better-paying job. I can't wait to get my son out that crappy apartment we're in." She stared down at the floor. "We both have a lot of bad memories there."

"What do you do for a living?"

Kina shrugged. "A little bit of everything, I guess, mostly clerical stuff. Actually, I just got a job as the administrative assistant to the pastor at my church. I guess my job isn't all that glamorous, huh? Everybody knows that administrative assistant is just code for secretary."

"Are you kidding me? My sister is the administrative assistant to the president at a college in New York. She's making way more than me!"

A waiter dropped off the bill, which Joan insisted on taking care of despite Kina's protests.

"I guess I better head on back," said Joan once the check issue was resolved. "There's a pile of work waiting on my desk for me."

"I guess I'll see you around the treadmill," teased Kina.

Joan dug into her purse. "Here." She handed Kina
her business card. "All of my contact information is on
there. Give me a call, and we can hang out sometime.
You owe me that lunch, remember?"

Kina nodded. "I remember, and I'll make good on it,
I promise."

Joan waved and sauntered out the door. Kina sat the
table, staring down at Joan's card, actually looking forward to seeing her again. She had been longing to meet
someone new, for someone to ask her out and pay her
some attention. Never in her wildest dreams did she
imagine that the person to do so would be a woman.

Chapter 9

"I think everybody is a little bi-curious."
—*Kina Battle*

Lawson squatted on her bedroom floor that evening, sifting through the last of the clothes she, Garrett, and Namon were donating to their church's clothes drive. She was so engrossed in the task at hand that she didn't notice Garrett emerging from the hallway and into their bedroom.

"Well . . ." prompted Garrett.

Lawson looked at him over her shoulder. "Well, what?"

"Did it come? You know . . . Bloody Mary."

"Wow, you're usually depressed this time of the month," remarked Lawson and tossed aside a worn jacket. "Why the sudden euphoria over the prospect of seeing me in bloomers and flannels all week instead of lingerie?"

Garrett plunked down next to her. "For one, if Mary skipped our house this month like I'm hoping, we could be holding our baby a year from now."

Lawson hated letting him down. "Not this time, honey; maybe next month."

Garrett pressed his lips together and nodded. "I guess this gives us an excuse to keep trying every night, right?"

She rubbed his chest. "I hope you're not too disappointed."

"It's not the news I wanted to hear," he admitted, "but I know it'll happen soon. It probably takes awhile for your body to readjust after coming off birth control. The doctor said this could happen. It must be frustrating for you too. I know you want this baby as much as I do."

Lawson started bagging up the clothes. "God doesn't put more on us than we can bear. At least, this gives me more time to concentrate on grad school."

"Baby, I don't want you throwing yourself into work and school because you're not able to conceive. All that extra stress and pressure you're putting on yourself might be part of the problem."

"I can handle it," she told him. "The minute I do get pregnant, everything else will be put on hold. Until then, I should try to stay active. Speaking of being active, don't you and Namon have plans for tonight?"

"Kicking me out, huh?"

"Never that." Lawson kissed him. "You know the girls are all meeting up here for a clothes-sorting party. We're going through everybody's stuff to get it organized for the clothes drive." The doorbell rang. "That's probably them."

"I hope it's more exciting than it sounds," joked Garrett.

"With that crew, I'm sure it will be!"

The clothes carpeting Lawson's living room looked like fall leaves spread over the ground outside.

"Okay, we need to separate everything by colors and seasons," directed Lawson. "Kina, you take all the summer stuff. Sully, you take spring. Angel, you get fall, and I'll take winter."

Kina began gathering clothes. "You know we complain sometimes, but you can't look at all these clothes and *not* know we've been blessed. These are just the clothes that we don't want. It doesn't include what we still have in the closets."

Angel nodded. "You're right, Kina. God is good."

Lawson shuffled through the pile for winter clothes. "So, what's been going on in the lives of you girls today?" she inquired.

"I got a massage and a facial," replied Sullivan. "I swear . . . that Jennifer can work miracles with my pores."

Angel let out an exasperated sigh. "Of course, this isn't nearly as exciting as Sullivan's shrunken pores, but one of my patients died this morning. As a nurse, I'm glad to see him out of his misery, but it's never easy to see the toll death takes on the family."

"Aw," groaned Lawson. "I'm sorry to hear that, Angel."

Angel smiled in gratitude. "Thank you, but to be absent from the body is to be present with the Lord. At least he's in peace now." Lawson nodded, agreeing.

Kina cleared her throat, anxious to divert the conversation into another direction. "Umm . . . I met a lesbian."

"Well, let's start with that, shall we?" spoke up Lawson with renewed interest.

Angel blinked back. "And just where and how did we meet said lesbian?"

"Power lesbians always have the best shoes," Sullivan noted wistfully.

"Oh, they have powers now?" asked Lawson in a snarky tone.

Sullivan turned to Kina. "I don't know. Do they, Kina?"

Kina laughed. "Don't ask me! I said I *met* one, not that I *am* one! But Joan's cool. I like her."

Sullivan shot her a side-eyed glance and muttered, "Yeah, I bet you do."

"*As a friend!*" finished Kina, glaring at Sullivan. "We met at the gym and before I knew it, we were laughing and crying over our failed relationships and attempts at weight loss."

Angel frowned. "You sure she wasn't just trying to hit on you?"

"Why would she be trying to hit on me?" asked Kina, offended by the assumption. "Do you assume that every *guy* who strikes a conversation is trying to hit on you?"

"Kina, look at me," Sullivan scoffed. "Of course, I do."

"I'm not saying that she's trying to turn you out," clarified Angel. "I just think the whole thing is a little weird."

Kina narrowed her eyes. "Why? Because she likes women? With the men being as crazy as they are, who can blame her?" Kina passed a quilt to Lawson. "Personally, I think everybody is a little bi-curious."

"Not everybody," insisted Sullivan, combing through the pile of spring clothes. "There ain't a woman in this world who can make me turn down a long, stiff—*ahem*—drink."

"Amen!" Lawson concurred, slapping hands with Sullivan. They all joined Lawson and Sullivan in laughter.

Kina sidled up next to her. "You mean to tell me you've never checked another woman out before?" she asked playfully.

"No," insisted Sullivan. "I believe everyone in here knows that I'm a huge fan of the shaft!"

Angel laughed. "If I look at a woman, it's in a *'She's pretty'* or *'Her hair is fabulous!'* kind of way," she revealed. "But not in the *'I kissed a girl, and I liked it'* sense. I don't think you palling around with her is a good idea, Kina. You don't want to give the wrong impression."

"What impression would that be: That I don't judge other people? That I accept people for who they are without trying to change them?" Kina shook her head. "I'm looking at who Joan is as a person, not which box she checks when asked about sexual orientation."

"Just make sure she's not checking for *your box*— that's all I'm saying," replied Sullivan.

Kina huffed. "Sullivan, that was very crass and uncalled for."

Sullivan smacked her lips. "So is all this lesbian talk!"

"Avoid the appearance of evil," quoted Lawson. "Now that's all *I'm* sayin'."

Kina's annoyance flared. "I'm hanging out with an adulterer, a teen parent, a stripper, and a woman who's shacking up with her ex-husband. Someone could make that same argument about all of you!"

"Don't get all sensitive, Kina," piped in Sullivan. "You know what we mean."

"I do, and that's the problem! I'm not going to shun this woman because we don't play for the same team. I couldn't care less who she sleeps with. I think it's sad you're not more open-minded, especially in this day and time."

"The times don't have anything to do with what the Bible says is right and wrong," asserted Lawson. "Now, I know that everyone here has made her fair share of mistakes and has broken more commandments than a few, but homosexuality is on a whole other level."

"Don't tell me you're homophobic, Lawson," countered Kina.

"No, Kina, I'm *Lord-a-phobic*."

Kina shook her head. "Homosexuality isn't more or less of a sin than anything else. If you want to hate something, hate the sin, not the person."

"I'm not saying I hate gays or anything like that. You know how crazy I am about Uncle James."

"You mean *Miss Penelope*," Kina corrected her. "He stopped going by James years ago."

Lawson rose. "Whether he's Penelope or James, I'm still going to love him, but wrong is wrong. If the Bible calls it perversion, I do too. Do I have to remind you what 1 Corinthians says? 'Do not be deceived: Neither the sexually immoral nor idolaters nor adulterers nor men who have sex with men nor thieves nor the greedy nor drunkards nor slanderers nor swindlers will inherit the kingdom of God.'"

Kina cocked her head to the side. "What if you're born that way?"

"We're all born into sin," disputed Lawson. "You can get born-again."

Angel nodded in confirmation. "You better say it!"

Kina rolled her eyes. "Well, lesbian or not, Joan seems like a genuinely kind person who I would like to get to know better. There's nothing wrong with the two of us being friends."

Angel raised an eyebrow. "The same way there's nothing wrong with a little bump and grind?"

"There will be no bumping *or* grinding," maintained Kina. "Just a little coffee and conversation every now and then."

Angel reached for more clothes to fold. "Just be careful about what you get yourself into. . . ."

"Or what gets into you!" added Sullivan.

Lawson held up a charcoal double-breasted wool coat and pressed it against her five foot two inch frame. "I'm surprised you're giving this away, Angel. It's beautiful."

"Yeah, I don't think I've ever seen you wear this before." Sullivan checked for the designer's label. "And I *know* I've never known you to invest in Burberry."

"You would see me in it if Duke had his way," murmured Angel. "This label says Burberry, but this is actually from the Theresa King collection."

Lawson was surprised. "Wow, Duke finally decided to get rid of Theresa's old things. I think that a positive step in the right direction, don't you?"

"I would if he'd thought of it! You have no idea what an uphill battle it was to get him to agree to do it," lamented Angel. "Did I tell you that he asked if I wanted to keep Theresa's clothes for myself?" She shook her head and continued to sort through the clothes. "The whole thing just weirds me out sometimes."

"Maybe he's just sentimental," suggested Kina.

"Maybe he's still in love with his dead wife!" spat Sullivan. Lawson and Kina glared at her with stone faces. "What? Was I not supposed to say that out loud? All of you were thinking it."

"Duke's not in love with Theresa; he's in love with *me*," contended Angel. "It's just taking all of them awhile to grieve. You have to give people the time and space to mourn in their own way."

"You had to know this was going to be an issue, Angel," voiced Sullivan. "He was married to you for two years, but he was married to her for nearly ten. They have children together, and if Theresa hadn't gotten sick, they'd probably still be married."

"He wouldn't have asked me to marry him and move into his home if he didn't love me."

Lawson stepped in. "We've never doubted Duke's love for you, Angel, but don't underestimate his love for Theresa either."

"Dang, is this what it's come down to?" asked Kina. "I used to think women had to look out for anything in a skirt. Apparently, now we've got to be worried about anyone in the *dirt* too!"

Angel remembered her mother's warning given to her as a teenager. "Mama always said there are two people you can't compete with for a man's attention because you can never be either one of them: a white woman or another man. I'm starting to wonder if 'dead wife' needs to be added to the list."

"Angel, you know you don't have to put up with that, don't you?" rendered Sullivan. "You don't have to come second to any woman, especially not to a dead one who stole your husband! Duke's got a lot of nerve thinking he can treat you this way."

Angel released a breath to calm down. "This is just the devil trying to plant doubt seeds and play with my mind. Duke and I will be okay. We're coming up on the anniversary of Theresa's death. Once we get through that and the holidays and really start planning this wedding, everything will go back to normal."

Lawson flapped her lips. "Normal? What's that for any of us?"

Angel snickered. "Yeah, I know, right?"

Sullivan held up one of Miley's frilly baby dresses. "You mind if I keep this, Angel? It's adorable!"

"It's not really your size, Sully, or your style—the designer being OshKosh and all."

"It's not for me, silly. I think it would look absolutely fabulous on Christian."

"Christian?" repeated Lawson.

Sullivan nodded. "That's what I'm thinking of naming her . . . or him."

Kina dumped a load of clothes out of a box and onto the floor. "Who's *her?*"

Sullivan put the dress to the side. "Our baby, of course."

Lawson looked around the room, puzzled. "Did you and Charles procreate while I was in the kitchen?"

"No, but I have every confidence I'll be barefoot and pregnant by Christmas."

"I think Christian is a beautiful name," said Kina dreamily. "What better way to honor Christ?"

Sullivan looked down at her red-bottomed stilettos. "Well, the Christian I had in mind is usually followed by the words Dior or Louboutin, but the Christ thing works too."

Lawson rolled her eyes. "I'm sure our Lord and Savior is flattered."

"Speaking of babies," began Angel, "what's up with baby number two, Lawson? Are you as anxious to be a new mom as Sullivan?"

Lawson stopped folding and sighed. "Can I be honest with you?"

"Yes, you know that," answered Angel.

She peeked out of the window to make sure Garrett's car was out of the driveway and that he'd taken off with Namon. "I know it sounds selfish, but I don't really want any more kids right now. My career is finally taking off, Namon is independent, and I really just want to enjoy this time with my husband. We're still newlyweds, for God's sake!"

Kina shook her head. "I don't think it's selfish, but I think you need to tell Garrett how you feel."

"I know, but it'll crush him. He really wants to be a dad. I feel like such a bad wife for not giving him the child he wants, especially since he's been so good to Namon."

"It only makes you a bad wife if you don't tell him," replied Angel. "Garrett loves you, Lawson. He'll understand if you want to wait."

"Just don't keep any more secrets from him," warned Kina. "You know what happened when you didn't tell him about Mark proposing to you and the disaster *that* was!"

"Yeah, I know," said Lawson, remembering how devastated he was after discovering secrets she and Mark were keeping from him. She dropped her head. "I know."

". . . there is nothing concealed that will not be disclosed, or hidden that will not be made known. What I tell you in the dark, speak in the daylight; what is whispered in your ear, proclaim from the roofs," quoted Angel from Matthew 10:26–27. "Honesty is always the best policy—"

"Until it's not!" asserted Sullivan. "The Bible also says, 'He who holds his tongue is wise.'" Sullivan shook her head. "I've seen it backfire too many times when people go blabbing their mouths when they shouldn't. Some men simply can't handle the truth. Then the new best policy becomes, 'We're all entitled to have our secrets.'"

Chapter 10

"I didn't realize how much we don't have in common anymore."
—Angel King

"You'll never believe what I just got us!" proclaimed Duke, coming home from work.

"I can't imagine what it is." Angel smiled up at her fiancé from behind the stems of roses she was arranging into a vase. "You've already given me the world, not to mention these gorgeous roses you had delivered to me at work today." She planted a kiss on his lips. "You know how to make your woman feel like a queen, don't you? Your efforts are greatly appreciated and shall be richly rewarded."

"The rewards don't stop there, babe." He handed her two tickets.

"What's this?"

"Two tickets to see comedian Kevin Hart!" announced Duke. "He's in town for a show the day after Thanksgiving, and we'll be in the front row laughing our butts off all night long!"

Angel's face fell. "Oh . . ."

"What's the matter? I thought you'd be thrilled. You used to love stand-up."

"Yeah, ten years ago, but I gave all that raunchy stuff up when I started to get serious about my walk with the Lord. I'd love to go see a Christian comedian, though," she proposed.

"I admit, he cusses a li'l bit, but it's not exactly what I'd call 'raunchy.'"

"All it takes is allowing a little spark of that stuff to get into your system. Before you know it, there's a whole fire burning."

Duke apologized. "I'm sorry. I thought you'd get a kick out of going. I'll see if I can sell the tickets or give them away."

"No, just because I don't want to go doesn't mean you shouldn't. You can call up some friends and make it a night out with the boys."

"Are you sure?"

"Yes, baby, I want you to go and have a good time," she assured him. "The girls and I will stay home and find G-rated ways to entertain ourselves."

Duke draped his arms around her. "How did I get blessed with such a good woman, huh?"

Angel smirked. "God must really love you."

"He must—He sent you. I love you, Angel. I do."

"You're going to love me even more when I tell you what I'm cooking for dinner," she hedged, rising from the sofa.

"What's that?"

"Shrimp Newburg. I haven't made it in years, but I do remember that it's one of your favorites."

This time, *his* face changed. "Um, about that . . ."

"What?"

"I don't really eat that anymore. Reese was allergic to shrimp, so I pretty much stopped eating it too."

"Wow . . ." She sighed. "I didn't realize how much we don't have in common anymore. It's scary how fast things can change."

He pulled her into his arms. "We may have changed our tastes in food and entertainment, but we still have a lot in common, including *this*." He kissed her. "It doesn't feel so scary now, does it?"

She shook her head and smiled. "No, it doesn't. I guess we don't have to be afraid of change when we serve a God who is the same yesterday and today and forever."

At that moment, Duke's phone rang. "I'm going to go in the kitchen to take this."

"Okay."

Duke disappeared into the kitchen while Angel set her new flower arrangement in the foyer.

When he returned a few minutes later, the color was gone from his face. "That was my aunt Jackie," he began slowly, still in shock. "My cousin Channing was shot in Afghanistan last night. Apparently, the Humvee he was driving was shot up by some Afghan locals. He was trying to get his comrades out of Dodge when a bullet went through the door."

"Oh my God!" Angel held her chest. "Is he dead?"

"No—thank God—but his knee was damaged pretty badly. It's shattered. There's no way he can complete his physical training now. My aunt believes he'll probably be medically discharged from the military."

She was relieved. "That seems pretty minor compared to what could've happened."

Duke shook his head. "You don't know Channing, babe. He's a soldier from the heart. If he can't serve, that bullet might as well have killed him."

"Maybe God has a different calling on his life. Did anyone consider that?"

"Angel, the army is the only thing he's known since he was eighteen. He's been in the service for fifteen years. God's call or not, this is going to crush him."

Angel slid her arms around his him. "Well, let's send him a care packet or something. Where's he going to be staying?"

"He'll be in a hospital overseas for a couple of weeks. I don't know his plans after that. You know, Chan's single, no kids, and no real family outside of my aunt and a few cousins. Aunt Jackie isn't in the best health herself. I was thinking about inviting him to stay with us for a little while, just until he can get back on his feet."

Angel backed away. "I'm sure a house full of kids is the last thing he needs right now. He's going to want a quiet place to rest and recover. He can't do that here."

"Babe, my cousin sacrificed his body and risked his life for this country and for us. There's no way I'm going to turn my back on him or ship him a box of cookies and send him on his way."

"I didn't say you shouldn't support him. I just said that our home may not be an ideal place to recuperate."

"Why not? I think it's perfect. We have all this room, and you're a nurse."

"I'm *a* nurse, not *his* nurse. Duke, I work. I can't provide round-the-clock care for him."

"Nobody's asking you to, but, Angel, he's family. I wish you wouldn't fight me on this."

Angel sighed, knowing that she would give in to Duke yet again. "All right, fine. I guess taking him in is the Christian thing to do. What's one more mouth to feed?"

"Thank you, sweetheart. This means so much to me." He pulled his cell phone back out. "I'm gonna call my aunt and let her know that Chan can stay with us."

Duke returned to the kitchen, and Angel sunk into the sofa, defeated. She knew in her heart that taking in Duke's cousin was the right thing to do, but the last thing she needed was another King to serve.

Chapter 11

**"Can you imagine having Vaughn's
bastard seed trapped inside of me?"**
—*Sullivan Webb*

Sullivan spent the morning in her pajamas and sipping on coffee. Nostalgia and an old Christmas CD had inspired her to look through old photos. Her eyes began to water as she flipped through her wedding album. Charles looked so dapper in his tuxedo and, of course, she was effortlessly beautiful. That day was filled with so much joy and promise. Now, she feared that her marriage was one wrong decision away from divorce.

Sullivan was startled out of her thoughts by a knock at the door. She opened it to find Kina on the other side.

Sullivan stood in the doorway with her arms crossed. "Shouldn't you be tending to the business of the Lord?"

Kina let herself in. "The pastor left his laptop at home. I offered to swing by and get it."

Sullivan closed the door behind her. "That was nice of you."

"Truth be told, I needed a little break. Plus, I wanted to see you. How've you been? You look sad."

Sullivan invited Kina into the living room. "I was traipsing down memory lane." She showed Kina one of the pictures. "Remember this?"

Kina reached for the album. "Yeah, you were such a beautiful bride. And, Pastor . . . when we saw the way he looked at you and when he started crying saying his vows . . ." Kina sighed. "I don't think there was a dry eye in the church at that moment. Well, you know, except for yours."

"Kina, I was not about to ruin a two-hundred-dollar air-brushed makeover for the sake of sentiment. But you're right, it was a beautiful ceremony," recalled Sullivan. "It's funny how quickly things change."

Kina and Sullivan both sat down on the sofa. "Things aren't any better, huh?"

"Charles isn't mean or anything like that, but there's definitely been a shift in the tide. He doesn't look at me the way he did on our wedding day anymore."

"Sullivan, a lot has happened, and a lot of it isn't pretty. Even before the Vaughn thing, you and the pastor had problems."

"Charles was always the one fighting for our marriage and trying to keep it together while I self-destructed. Now . . ."

"It's not so much fun when the shoe is on the other foot, is it?" gibed Kina.

Sullivan shook her head. "No, it's not."

"I can relate to what you're going through. When E'Bell was alive, I was always the one trying to hold the marriage together. He acted like he couldn't care less. I felt so alone. You don't marry someone expecting to be lonely in that relationship." Kina hung her head slightly. "Loneliness probably isn't a feeling you can really relate to. You always seem to love your own company so much."

"Well, you know I *do* love me some Sullivan Webb," she joked, then turned serious again. "But, as humans, we still need to connect. I never had a lot of that growing up. You remember how my mom and I were always moving. You and Lawson were my only sources of stability until I met Charles. Even with him, it's often felt like I was in competition with the church and God. I think that was the impetus for my affair with Vaughn. I thought I was just bored and needed some fun interjected in my life, but when it came down to it, Vaughn was someone I connected with."

"Do you miss him?"

Sullivan flinched. "God, no! What I miss is having that connection to someone."

"Well, I still think you got off kind of easy," grunted Kina.

"How, Kina? Thanks to the Internet, the whole world knows about my little indiscretion with Vaughn. I was humiliated, Charles lost his bid for county commissioner, and my marriage is still trying to recover. What part of that is *easy*?"

"It could've been worse, Sully. Pastor could've walked out on you or you could've gotten an STD. Heck, you could've gotten pregnant! Then what would you have done?"

"Good point." Sullivan shuddered at the thought. "Can you imagine having Vaughn's bastard seed trapped inside of me?"

Kina laughed. "No, especially not when you put it that way! You were lucky, the young ones are always fertile! I'm glad you made him don a raincoat before jumping in the pool, if you know what I mean."

"Thank you for that very poetic way of putting things, Kina," Sullivan replied dryly.

"We can dress up the pig as much as we want, Sully, but a pig is still a pig." Kina stood to leave. "I guess I better grab that laptop and get out of here."

"It's in the study, down the hall. You can't miss it."

As Kina made her way to the study, Sullivan's mind wandered back to Vaughn, more specifically to his virile, strapping, young twenty-five-year-old sperm. If only the situation had been in reverse and Charles had been the one who had the libido of a frat boy and the reproduction capability of a jackrabbit.

"Too bad I didn't freeze some of that good sperm when I had the chance," she muttered. She halted, struck by a new thought.

She laughed to herself. It was an idea crazy even by Sullivan's standards. She had every confidence that, with prayer and plenty of practice, Charles's half-a-century-old sperm would produce a little Webb of their own in no time.

Then again, she thought, there was nothing wrong with having a little insurance on the side.

Chapter 12

"I'm sure my husband would rather spend time working on a baby than me working on another degree."
—*Lawson Kerry Banks*

"You went on them today, didn't you?" teased Mark as he and Lawson filed out of the media center following the faculty meeting at North Central High School, where they both worked. "You've got a lot balls for a second-year teacher."

"I'm taking that as a compliment regardless of how you meant it," Lawson responded with a wry smile. "I take my job very seriously. You, of all people, should know that. I can't sit around and watch these students fail and not say something about it. Half the teachers in that meeting were more concerned about planning the holiday party than they were making sure our students can pass the standardized tests."

"After that speech you gave, I don't think you'll have to worry about that anymore. And after the way you called out most of the staff, I don't think you have to worry about getting an invitation to the faculty Christmas party either."

Lawson laughed. "I don't know how I'm going to sleep tonight with that hanging over my head."

Mark looked at her intently. "Seriously, Lawson, I admire your passion. We need more people like you on the frontlines making a difference."

"Thanks, Mark, but I've come to realize that if I really want to make a difference, I've got to get out of the classroom. There's only so much I can do from there."

"You're not thinking of leaving the profession, are you?"

She unlocked the door to her classroom. Mark followed her inside.

"No, nothing like that. I've started working on my master's in administration. I think if I was a principal, I could implement the changes I'd like to see happen."

"Got your eye on the big chair, I see. I'm impressed."

Lawson sat behind her desk. "So do you think I've got it in me?"

"Lawson, I believe you can do whatever you set your mind to. Isn't it tough, though, balancing work, school, Namon, and a new husband?"

"No tougher than it was being a single parent trying to go to school and look after Namon and Reggie between my shifts at Pic-'n-Pay."

Mark became solemn. "I still feel guilty that I wasn't around to help you with our son."

"You shouldn't, Mark. You didn't even know Namon existed. Besides, now I have the kind of support system most people dream about." She looked away. "Although I'm sure my husband would rather spend time working on a baby than me working on another degree."

"Garrett isn't giving you a hard time about grad school, is he?" asked Mark, concerned.

"Oh no, Garrett's not like that. He's very proud of me. I think it's more about him getting older and not having any biological children of his own. We've talked about having kids, but the timing's never been quite right."

"You can't always wait for the perfect time. If we did, do you think Namon would be here? Ambition is cool and wanting to make a difference is even better, but nothing compares to family and being able to watch your kids grow up."

"I hate you didn't have that time with Namon. I know now how wrong I was to try to keep you from him."

"Namon and I are making up for lost time. I'm just saying, at the end of the day, work isn't what matters. Family is."

She nodded slowly. "You're right. When did you go and get so wise?"

"After two kids and thirty-three years, I ought to know a little something, right?"

She laughed. "Mark, I'm really glad we've gotten back to a place in our relationship where when we can talk like this. Things had gotten pretty bad between us for a while."

"I know, and I apologize for my part in it. I shouldn't have threatened to take our son away from you and Garrett. I actually have a lot of respect for your husband. He's been a good father to Namon. I hope he's been as good a husband to you."

"He has. He's everything I prayed for in a mate."

"You did the right thing choosing him over me," acknowledged Mark. "It makes me feel good to see you so happy."

"I think it's important that we support and can be happy for each other for Namon's sake. So will we be getting you down the aisle any time soon?"

Mark laughed. "I don't know if marriage is in the cards for me. I've popped the question twice and have gotten two rejections. Twice might be my limit."

"Third time's the charm, remember? You just haven't met the right one, but you will. I'm sure of it."

"Yeah, we'll see."

"Don't give up. She's out there, maybe even closer than you think."

"Your lips to God's ears." Mark kissed her on the cheek. "I'll catch you later."

He disappeared, and Lawson busied herself with paperwork. "Oh my! Look what the cat dragged in!" exclaimed Lawson, seeing Sullivan in her classroom doorway. "Is this where you're stashing the bodies these days?"

"Ha-ha." Sullivan set her purse down on one of the empty desks. "Can't I come by and see one of my oldest and dearest friends without having some kind of ulterior motive?"

"You can, but you usually don't, so what gives?"

"Nothing," she replied in a sing-song voice. "I just wanted to see you."

"Uh-huh. What's up, Sullivan?"

Sullivan slid into one of the student's desks. "Same crap, different day. Is Mark around?"

Lawson erased her board. "He's here somewhere, probably down in the gym."

"Isn't it awkward having him work here? I'm sure by now everyone knows he's dipped his hands, not to mention his other parts, in your cookie jar."

"It's not like we've broadcasted it over the morning announcements, Sully. A few people around here know, but we keep things very professional. Nobody's bold or crazy enough to ask us about it."

"I think it's amazing that the two of you have managed to still be friends, all things considered."

"It's better for Namon this way. It's not hard, though. Mark is a good dude. Now that we've firmly established the boundaries in our relationship, we're free to just enjoy each other as co-parents and friends."

Sullivan sat upright. "What about Garrett? Where does he fit into all of this?"

"He's my husband, Sully. Everything begins and ends with him. Mark is cool, but if my relationship with him ever jeopardized my marriage to Garrett in any way, I would end it, no hesitation or questions asked."

Sullivan nodded. "What about Namon? Now that Mark's in the picture, how does that affect Namon and Garrett's relationship?"

"It doesn't. Namon knows who his biological father is, and I think he's really grown to care about Mark and his little sister Mariah. But Garrett is the one who raised him. Garrett will always be Dad in Namon's heart."

"Does Garrett feel the same way?"

"Of course. The two of them couldn't be any closer if they were biologically father and son. Heck, they even kind of look alike. God knows they act alike! Most people think Namon is Garrett's son. For all intents and purposes, he is."

Sullivan drummed her fingers on the desk, thinking—or more to the point—scheming. "So you think it's possible for a man to unconditionally love a child who's not his own?"

"Yes, my family is living proof." Lawson grew skeptical. "What's up with this line of questioning? Is there something going on with you I should know about?"

"I'm just weighing my options with this baby situation. You never know how these things are going to turn out. Something might happen that forces Charles and me to resort to adoption or artificial insemination. I just want to be sure that Charles would love the baby as much as he would if the child came from his own body."

"Of course, he would! Don't even waste time wondering about that, but don't start driving yourself crazy with worst-case scenarios either. You and Charles will have your baby when it's time and not a moment sooner or later than that. Just be patient. I know asking you to be patient is like asking the sun not to be hot, but you have no other choice."

"I always have a choice, Lawson," stated Sullivan.

"Yes, you do, but it's always best to wait on the Lord, my wayward friend. The Bible says God knows His plans for us, and He's not going to move at our beck and call."

"Waiting and patience aren't really my strong points," huffed Sullivan.

"That's a tidbit we know all too well! But when we try to force things to happen, we go from God's divine will to His permissive will. He'll allow certain things to happen, but then you're subject to the laws of nature and society as well as the consequences. Nature and society aren't always as forgiving as our Lord and Savior."

"How can you say it's not God's will for Charles and me to have a child when the Word clearly tells us 'be fruitful and multiply'?" asked Sullivan, contradicting her.

Lawson gave up. "Just promise that you won't do anything stupid. I take that back—promise that you won't do anything stupid without running it by someone first, namely the Lord."

Sullivan exhaled. "I promise that I'm not going to do anything I haven't thought out and planned very carefully."

"For some reason, that's not very reassuring coming from you."

"Lawson, you know me. One way or another, I always get what I want, and right now, what I want is a baby."

"Those are the key words—*right now!* What about six months or a year from now? Better yet, twelve years from now, will you still want this kid? It's not like buying a pair of shoes, Sully. You can't take the kid back or donate him to charity when you get bored and want to try something else."

"Don't you think I know that?" she snapped. "I actually want to have this baby. Why does everyone find that so hard to believe?"

"I guess because we can't figure out why you want it. You're not exactly the poster child for motherhood. If this is about trying to please Charles, your husband adores you and is committed to you with or without a baby. If it's to keep your marriage together, a newborn will only add stress to an already bad situation. If Charles wants to leave, he's going to leave—baby or no baby."

"Maybe it started out being about Charles, but now having a child is something I want for me. I want to be a mother. I need to have at least one thing in this world I've done right. Being a good mother can be that one thing."

"Sully, you've done a lot right in your life. You survived your sociopathic mother for one; you graduated at the top of your class in college. You're a brilliant artist and an even better friend. Even when you mess up, you pick yourself right back up, hold your head high, and keep movin'. You don't need to have a baby to prove anything to anybody."

"I have something to prove to myself, Lawson, and to God. I want to prove to Him that I can be trusted with something as precious as one of His children. I want to prove to me that I'm capable of loving another human being more than I love myself."

"I get that," Lawson assured her. "I just don't know if that's a good enough reason to bring a child into this world."

"That's not fair!" shot back Sullivan. "Look at you and Mark. What profound reason did you have for bringing a child into the world aside from the fact both of you were too ravenous to insist on throwing on a condom? Are you saying that, at sixteen, you were more equipped and prepared to be a mother than I am now?"

"I'm not saying that at all. At the time, I had no idea what I was getting myself into. If I could do it over again, I would've waited. That's why I'm not rushing into having more children. True, Garrett wants more kids, but deep in my heart, I know I'm not ready."

"That's the difference between us, Lawson. I *am* ready, and it's *going* to happen, one way or another."

"Yeah, and it's that 'other' way that usually gets you in trouble."

Sullivan shook her head. "Not this time."

Lawson yielded. "Okay, just don't do anything you're going to live to regret, Sully. Let the Lord do His work without any interference from you. Remember Rachel, Jacob's wife in the Bible? She desperately wanted a baby too, and the child she thought she wanted so badly was the very thing that killed her."

Chapter 13

"I've got grown woman bills, so I've got to do what grown women do."
—Reginell Kerry

"Hey, I'm here to pick up li'l man," announced Reginell when Mark opened his front door the next evening and found her there instead of Lawson.

Mark let her into the house. "Where's Lawson?"

"She's finishing a paper for class, and Garrett's working late, so here I am."

"You know I'm always happy to see you. Come in, sit down." He made room for her on the sofa. "Namon is doing his homework. He'll be out in a minute."

"Homework on the weekend?" Reginell frowned. "I used to hate teachers who did that! Just because they didn't have a life Friday through Sunday didn't mean I didn't."

Mark chuckled. "Imagine how hard it was for me trying to cram in James Baldwin novels after playing football on Friday nights!"

"I bet you had some cute little cheerleaders doing that work for you. I know—I used to be one of those cheerleaders doing the football players' homework!" They both laughed. "How is everything going between you and Namon? He talks about you much more than he used to."

"Good things, I hope," ventured Mark.

"Of course."

The relief showed on Mark's face. "We have our moments here and there when it gets a little tense, but most of the time, it's like we were never separated. I can't tell you how good it feels having him around. He and Mariah have gotten pretty close too."

"Yeah, Namon is crazy about his little sister. If Garrett has his way, Namon will have another little brother or sister to dote on real soon."

"You said *Garrett*. I guess you know Lawson isn't exactly gung-ho about popping out another kid."

"Lawson wants to climb the corporate ladder. You know how she is, Mark. She's not satisfied with just being a teacher. Lawson wants to run the whole doggone school!"

"So I've noticed," he replied with a laugh. "But I know she loves Garrett. I'm sure she'll slow down long enough to give him that baby he wants."

"What about you? Do you want more kids?"

Mark shrugged. "I don't know. My hands are pretty full with Namon and Mariah. If I met the right woman, I might consider it."

"You're not dating anyone?" she asked, surprised.

"Here and there, but nothing serious. What about you? No doubt you get more than your fair share of men vying for your attention."

"That's business. They don't want me, they want Juicy, and even that's just for one night. I want more than that."

"I thought you were pretty hot and heavy with some guy awhile back. I remember seeing the two of you at Lawson's wedding. It looked like you were going to be next in the bridal line."

"Yeah, things seemed like they were getting serious for a minute, but he couldn't handle my job and seeing other guys around me that way. We broke up a couple of months ago."

"So you chose stripping over the man of your dreams?"

"The man of my dreams will love and accept me whether I'm stripping or not."

"True, but it's gonna take a strong brother to be willing to overlook all that. Wouldn't it just be easier to stop dancing?"

"For some, maybe, but I'm not stripping just to be doing it. I know none of you believe it, but it really is a career move for me. I've met a lot of people in the music industry at Paramours, people who can help me get my singing career off the ground. I know it's going to pay off eventually. Plus, it ain't like I'm out there shaking for pennies. I bet I make more in a week than you and Lawson, with all them degrees, make in a month."

"You're probably right, but it makes a difference when you can look at yourself in the mirror, knowing that you're doing some good out here in the world."

"I'm good at what I do too," she crowed.

He licked his lips. "I bet you are, but I'm talking about making a positive difference in someone's life. You can't put a cash value on that."

"But you *can* put a cash value on my rent, my car, my clothes, and everything else I got to pay for. No five-and-dime job is gon' cut it for me. I've got grown woman bills, so I've got to do what grown women do."

"You don't have to do *that*, Reggie. Don't short-change yourself."

Namon emerged from his bedroom, slinging his duffle bag over his shoulders.

Mark took his eyes off Reginell and looked up at Namon. "You got everything finished?"

"Yes, sir." Namon waved at Reginell. "Hey, Auntie Reggie."

"Hey, Big Nay! Your mom sent me to come get you. You ready?"

Namon grinned. "Cool. You gon' let the top down on the car?"

"Boy, you know Lawson hates it when I have you in car with the top down." She broke into a smile. "That's *exactly* why I'm going to do it!" They all laughed. She tossed him the keys to her Mustang. "Go load up your stuff. I'll be out there in a minute."

"All right." Namon embraced his father. "Are you coming to my game next week?"

"Do you even have to ask? I'll be there, embarrassing you as usual," guaranteed Mark. "Call me when you get home so I'll know you got there safely, all right?"

"Okay." They hugged again and then Namon walked out.

"You're real good with him, you know that?" complimented Reginell once Namon was out of earshot.

"Well, I love him. He makes it easy." Mark paused. "Listen, I know you got a lot of slack from your sister and her friends for forcing Lawson's hand about introducing me to Namon and telling him who I was, but I'm so thankful for that, Reggie. Who knows how long it would've taken if you hadn't. I'll always be grateful to you."

"No thanks necessary. Lawson was wrong for ever keeping the two of you apart. I think it's wrong to keep any two people apart who ought to be together."

He nodded. "I couldn't agree more."

Reginell smiled. "Well, let me go on and get this boy home before his mama starts blowing up my phone.

You know what a worrywart she is. I'll see you later, Mark."

Reginell headed for the door. Mark grabbed her hand. "Wait a minute, Reggie."

She turned around. Her eyes met his. "Yeah?"

"You know, maybe you and I should get together for coffee or lunch one day this week. What do you think about that?"

Reginell thought it over. "I guess that would be okay," she replied, questioning if Mark was being nice or if he was asking her on a date.

"I guess it's a date then," he said, answering the question for her. "I'll give you a call tomorrow, and we can set everything up."

"Okay," she confirmed, blushing. "I'll talk to you tomorrow."

Reginell walked to her car, still asking herself what had just happened. She giggled. Truth be told, she'd always thought that Mark was cute and that Lawson was a fool for not going after him.

"Looks like Lawson's loss is my gain," Reginell said to herself. The moment was quickly followed by two other thoughts. The first was that an attractive, successful, single man had just asked her out. The second was that she'd just accepted a date from her sister's baby's daddy.

Chapter 14

**"I'm having dinner with someone
I enjoy spending time with, who enjoys
spending time with me, and who just so
happens to be a woman."**
—Kina Battle

Kina entered Angel's great room and playfully twirled around to make her strappy yellow sundress flutter and fall at her knees. "You like?"

"Wow, don't you look pretty!" raved Angel, as she and the other ladies decorated for Miley's birthday party. "What's the occasion—a hot date?"

Kina blushed. "I don't know if I'd call it all that, but I do have dinner plans."

"Ohhh, so you've been holding out on us!" teased Lawson. "Who's the mystery date, Kina? Do we know him?"

Kina's mood shifted. She pressed her lips together and dropped her eyes. "It's no one special."

"Does 'no one special' have a name?" asked Angel.

Kina pouted. "I don't want to talk about it."

"Why not?" snapped Sullivan.

"You'll just ruin it for me," whined Kina.

Sullivan tied string around one the balloons. "We're not going to give you a hard time about him. Trust me, I'm just glad you're getting out of the house and away from that les-ho you've been running around with. I've gotta tell you, Ki, we were worried about you for a minute there."

Kina was offended. "Why? Joan's great."

"Yes, but *Joan* lacks a *shlong!*" Sullivan pointed out. "You don't need to get caught up in her girl-on-girl drama."

Kina frowned. "Sullivan, just shut up! You have no idea what you're talking about."

Lawson was taken aback. "Dang, why are you so sensitive today, cuz?"

"And secretive," added Angel. "Why don't you want to tell us who this guy is?"

Kina stomped her foot. "Because it's not a *guy*," she confessed. "I'm having dinner with Joan."

They were all stunned into silence, followed by judgmental grumbling.

Lawson was the first one to recover from the shock. "So, is this dinner as in a *date?*"

"What's so wrong with that?" argued Kina. "I go out to eat with you ladies all the time."

"The difference between the two is that we're only interested in eating what's on the menu," replied Sullivan. "We can't say the same for your little lezzy friend."

Kina rolled her eyes. "Sully, don't be gross."

"Honey, you can't replace your problems with men by turning to women," spoke up Angel. "This isn't a good idea, Kina."

Kina set her hands on hips. "Why not?"

Angel draped her arm around her. "You're still really vulnerable. I mean, E'Bell's only been dead a year—"

Kina broke away from her. "So has Theresa, but that hasn't stopped you from moving in on Duke, literally *and* figuratively!"

"Sometimes I think I shouldn't have," admitted Angel. "Besides, my situation with Duke is nothing like yours."

Kina snorted. "I don't know why you think that. From where I stand, it's exactly the same."

"For starters, it's legal for Duke and Angel to marry in this state," tossed in Sullivan.

"And I've known Duke my whole adult life, Kina. I was his wife long before Theresa was."

"Look, I know that this whole thing with Joan has caught you all off guard, but I think you're all blowing this way out of proportion," explained Kina, attempting to allay their concerns. "It's not like I'm coming out of the closet or am about to go lead the Gay Pride Parade. I'm having dinner with someone I enjoy spending time with, who enjoys spending time with me, and who just so happens to be a woman."

Joan greeted Kina at the door with a smile. "You look nice. Come on in."

Kina returned the smile at the compliment. "Thank you. So do you."

Joan welcomed Kina into her home. Her apartment was as eclectic as Kina imagined it would be with anomalous furnishings accentuated with bright lights and large candles. A few pictures of Africa's lush landscapes punctuated the walls.

"Sit down, make yourself comfortable." Kina sat next to her on the sofa, being careful to keep a respectable distance between them. "The food is ready, but I thought we should talk first."

***

"All right," replied Kina, swallowing hard. She could feel the sweat beading on her palms. Being so far out of her comfort zone was daunting.

Joan picked up on the tension. "You're nervous, aren't you?"

"Is it that obvious?" Kina laughed nervously.

"A little, but there's no need to be. I want you to feel comfortable in my home, Kina. In fact, I hope to have you here more often. Would you like some wine?" Joan didn't wait for Kina to respond. She pulled two glasses and a bottle of wine from her buffet. "I have to say, I was a little shocked when you accepted my dinner invitation."

"Why?"

"It wasn't exactly a platonic invitation."

Kina wrung her hands together. "I know, but I'm trying to keep an open mind about things these days. I guess you could say that I'm sort of experimenting."

Joan shook her head and poured Kina a glass of wine. "You know, women like you can be dangerous. A girl could get her heart broken once the novelty wears off and you realize you like men after all. A lot of women start dating the same sex because they're frustrated and have had it with men. They don't realize that it's not enough to be through with guys. You've got to *want* to be with a woman."

"I think I could do that. I mean, I can appreciate a beautiful woman as much as any guy can."

Joan smiled. "Do I qualify as a beautiful woman?"

Kina bashfully averted eye contact. "Yes, you do."

"Goodness, you're so tense, Kina. Let me loosen you up." Joan stood to massage Kina's back. Kina involuntarily jerked away. Joan looked a little hurt. "You don't want me to touch you?"

"It's not that. I just wasn't expecting it, that's all. You know, this is the first time I've been on a date with any-one, male or female, since my husband died. The fact that I'm here with a woman is . . ."

"It's a little overwhelming." Kina nodded in agree-ment. "I understand. It's a little overwhelming for me too."

"Why?"

Joan cupped Kina's face. "Because you drive me crazy, you know that? I think about you all the time. It's like I crave you."

Joan admission's shocked and fascinated Kina. No one had said anything to her like that in years, and she'd ceased to think that anyone ever would. "What kind of thoughts have you had about me?"

"I think about holding you, touching you . . . kiss-ing you." Joan moved in closer to her. "Have you ever kissed a woman, Kina?"

"No, I mean, I've kissed my mother on the cheek and forehead, but not kissed another woman, no," she stammered.

"I want to kiss you."

The revelation made Kina dizzy, but she knew it was time to pee or get off the pot. She resigned herself to at least being open to the idea of kissing another woman. "Okay," she whispered.

Joan planted a kiss on Kina's cheek. Then she looked into Kina's eyes and tenderly kissed her lips. Kina flinched. Undeterred, Joan leaned in and kissed her again. Kina forced herself to sit still while Joan kissed her. She relaxed a bit and began to feel a sensation that she hadn't expected. Joan's lips were warm and soft on hers, and she found herself returning the kiss.

Joan broke away from her and smiled. "See, that wasn't so bad, was it?"

"No, it was kind of nice," admitted Kina.

Joan initiated another kiss. Wrapping her arms around Kina's waist, she moved her mouth from Kina's lips to her neck. The transition snapped Kina out of her trance.

"I've got to go," she announced abruptly, bolting from the sofa.

Joan was dumbfounded. "What's wrong?"

"Nothing. Kenny has an appointment with his counselor today, and I totally forgot about it." She grabbed her purse and inched toward the door. "I should get going . . . right now!"

"He has an appointment this late at night?"

"It was a last-minute thing."

"Well, you're already late. What difference would a few more minutes make?"

"A lot! I've got to go, Joan. Bye." Kina raced out of the apartment and into the hallway to catch her breath.

She could still feel Joan's lips on hers. She closed her eyes and leaned against the wall. She was thinking of the kiss when she felt Joan's presence again, only this time it wasn't in her head. Joan was standing in front of her.

"Your son doesn't have an appointment today, does he?" Kina shook her head. "I know why you ran out like that," said Joan. "You were scared by what you felt back there. There's nothing to be afraid of. Come back inside."

"I can't," whispered Kina.

"Yes, you can. I know you want to." She grabbed Kina's hand, gently pulling her back toward the door.

Kina closed her eyes, trying to decide whether go with Joan or bolt in the opposite direction. She couldn't deny the influx of emotions she felt whenever

Joan looked at or touched her, but was that enough to classify her as gay?

Kina had been attracted to men all her life, yet not only had she let another woman kiss her, she didn't stop her. She wondered if she was bisexual or just desperate. Did it really matter that Joan was a woman? After all, what man had treated her like anything other than a piece of meat? She asked herself if Joan, with one kiss, had shaken everything she believed about herself and what she wanted.

Chapter 15

"I'm officially one of the good girls now."
—Sullivan Webb

Sullivan had spent most of the night tossing and turning, so much so that she was tempted to break nearly two years of sobriety for a quick shot of Patrón to calm her nerves. She decided against it, realizing that she needed all of her wits about her if she was going to go through with what would be the scam of a lifetime.

It had taken several days, some serious self-talk, and a positive ovulation test for her to finally settle on a decision. She considered adoption and artificial insemination, but she wanted to experience being pregnant, and she wanted to know who her child's father was. She knew God would never give His approval, so she didn't bother seeking it. Besides, hadn't she given Him ample time to act? Charles was making a modest contribution in the bedroom, but Sullivan feared that his lethargy the last two times they'd made love could have a negative impact on his sperm. She could've very well waited for another month to pass to try again, but waiting was never her style. She didn't wait for sales, she didn't wait in lines, and she definitely wasn't going to wait another thirty days before trying to get pregnant.

As Sullivan slipped into a red dress that left all of her dangerous curves exposed, she thought, of all things, about *The Scarlet Letter*, the Nathaniel Hawthorne novel she'd been forced to endure for American literature in high school. She likened herself to heroine Hester Prynne. Like Hester, she was also destined to bear a child conceived under less-than-ideal circumstances, shrouded in a veil of secrecy and shadowed by adultery. Sullivan was adamant that her story wouldn't end like Hester's, however. After all, this wasn't Colonial America, and she was far craftier than the simple-minded, scarlet letter-bearing Hester.

Vaughn was a creature of habit, and weeks of a sordid affair with him made her quite familiar with his routine and favorite haunts. One thing she knew for sure was that he never failed to start his day without a cup of coffee from the McDonald's around the corner from his apartment. She decided to accidently bump into him on purpose that fateful morning.

Before condemnation had a chance to set in, she spotted Vaughn's car outside of the restaurant as soon as she wheeled into the parking lot. She gave her makeup a quick inspection before hopping out of the car and heading for the glass entrance.

Sullivan spied him right off, sitting at his usual booth—newspaper in one hand, coffee in another. Not much had changed about him. Although he'd traded his trademark cornrows for a more conservative Caesar cut, he still had that velvety dark skin and athletic build, as well as that boyish swagger and those ruggedly handsome features that attracted her to him in the first place. Much to Sullivan's chagrin, he still looked good.

As she stared at him, Sullivan recalled their last liaison, which was also their traumatic breakup. After announcing that he was tired of sleeping with her, Vaughn tossed Sullivan out on her posterior and locked the door behind her. Not only had he embarrassed

Charles, but Vaughn had humiliated Sullivan, and *no man* humiliated Sullivan Webb and lived to tell about it!

She wanted to move, but her feet felt cemented to that spot in front of the entrance. She'd sworn to her husband and herself to never see Vaughn again. She had promised to be faithful from now on. How could she do this to Charles? How could she spit in the face of God, who had shown her so much mercy?

"This isn't a good idea," Sullivan murmured to herself and turned in the opposite direction toward the door. Just at that moment, Vaughn stood up to grab some sugar from the condiments stand. Sullivan ducked out of his line of vision.

Meeting Vaughn had profited her nothing except a few mind-blowing sin sessions. The way she saw it, he still owed her something. The perfect atonement for his nearly destroying her marriage could be his providing the one thing that could possibly save it.

Why not use him the way he used me? she thought. *An eye for an eye, right?* She compromised with herself and the Lord by promising not to enjoy it. . . . Well, maybe just a little bit.

Sullivan took a deep breath. The decision was made.

She strolled up to him. "Vaughn, is that you?" she asked with all the shock she could assemble.

Vaughn almost knocked over his coffee, surprised to see her. He sprang to his feet, "Sullivan . . . hey."

"Long time no see." The tension between them was stifling. "You're looking well. I hope life is treating you as such."

"I can't complain. You're looking good, but you always do." He stuffed his hands into his jean pockets. "What are you doing over here? I thought you hated this part of town."

"Well, I'm here for my mission work," she lied. "I, um, I'm feeding the homeless this week."

Vaughn cracked up. "You—Sullivan? Feeding the homeless?"

"You don't have to sound so surprised," she barked.

His eyes drifted over her body. "Well, you don't really look dressed for the occasion."

She glanced down at her dress, scrambling for a logical explanation for feeding the homeless in heels and a curve-fitting frock. "Red triggers the appetite."

"Yes, it does." He dragged his tongue across his lips, practically salivating over her. "This is a switch. The Sullivan I knew couldn't give a rat's behind about the homeless."

"Maybe I'm not the Sullivan you remember," she drawled, holding his gaze in a fearless stare.

He sucked his teeth and looked her over. "Nah, she's still in there somewhere."

"I've turned over a new leaf, Vaughn. After all of that campaign drama and nearly losing my marriage, I decided to straighten up and fly right. I'm officially one of the good girls now."

He smirked a little. "I hear you, but you know what they say, once a good girl goes bad, she's gone forever."

"There's an exception to every rule, Vaughn, and I fully intend to be the exception. I love my husband, and we are very happy together. I love the life we share, and I don't intend to jeopardize that ever again," vowed Sullivan, almost meaning it.

"That's good if that's what you want. I kinda miss the old Sullivan, though. She was my kind of woman."

"Yes, I'm sure she was. She was a heathen and an adulterer who lived for pleasure." She piously folded her hands together. "Thankfully, all of that riotous living is a thing of the past. Now I live for the Lord."

"Is that right?" he asked, making no attempts to hide his skepticism.

"Perhaps one day we can sit down together, and I can tell you about my transformation from the girl you used to know to the woman I am now."

"Yeah, we'll have to do that. Are you still painting?"

"Yes, when I can."

"I'm sure feeding the homeless and building temples keeps you pretty busy. Hopefully when you get some free time, you'll let me see some of your artwork."

She paused before responding. "I guess there's no harm in that."

"All right, well, you know where I live. Stop by anytime."

"Do you mind if I bring my husband with me?"

Vaughn laughed a little. "You can bring whoever you want, Mrs. Webb. I'm sure your husband is just *dying* to get reacquainted the man who was breaking his wife's back while he was on the campaign trail."

A quick flashback made her tingle. "I don't like it when you talk like that."

His lips plunged into a seductive smile. "Don't worry. I still remember *everything* you like, Sister Sullivan." He brushed a finger across her cheek before scooping up his coffee and newspaper. "It was good seeing you again. You're still as beautiful and sexy as ever. Take care."

Vaughn disappeared from view. He'd played right into her hands. This would be as easy as taking candy from a baby. She could only hope that *making* a baby would be just as effortless.

"I thought you were bringing your ol' man," teased Vaughn when Sullivan turned up at his door one hour and one strategically placed phone call later.

"He's busy, and he's not that old." Sullivan pushed her way inside and looked around. With the exception of a few portraits, nothing had changed inside the modest studio apartment since the last time she was there.

"I see you've added some paintings," she remarked, taking off her jacket and laying it across a chair.

"Yeah, I've had a lot of free time on my hands since getting canned for messing around with you."

This was news to Sullivan. "Mike fired you from the garage?"

"Yeah, he gets a lot of business from your church. He said keeping me on would be disrespectful to the pastor. It didn't help that my name and face were plastered across the Internet."

"Things must've worked out for you. I don't see you living on the streets."

"I know how to land on my feet. Being infamous actually helped me sell a few paintings."

"Really?"

"Yeah, I've got a couple people interested in commissioning me to do some work. I'm thinking about moving up North for a while to check out the art scene up there."

The prospect of Vaughn moving to parts unknown was almost too good to be true. Sullivan had been contemplating a tactful way to shake him once the deed was done. Now, it was apparent that the work was being done for her. Somebody was definitely on her side. She just couldn't figure out if it was God or the devil.

Vaughn offered Sullivan a seat on the bed and sat down next to her.

"Are you moving for real?" she asked.

He balled up a piece of paper and tossed it into his wastebasket. "Yep, time to move on. There ain't really nothing keeping me here no way."

Sullivan's lips began to quiver, and her eyes watered. She was a pro at making herself cry. It was a skill that had come in handy ever since she started dating.

"Hold up . . . Are you crying?" Vaughn asked incredulously.

"No." She sniffed. "It's just my allergies."

Vaughn wiped a tear from her cheek. "Sullivan, are these real tears, baby?"

Sullivan covered her face with her hands and sobbed into her lap. "I'm sorry. It's just that the thought of not seeing you again . . ." She began wailing.

Vaughn stroked her back. "Dang, baby, I never expected you to react like this. I mean, if you don't want me to go—"

Sullivan's head popped up and her wailing came to a halt. Perhaps she was actually *too* good of an actress. "No, you have to follow your destiny, Vaughn. I'd never ask you to give that up, especially when the two of us could never be," she added with affectation.

"I'm sure our paths will cross again someday."

Sullivan reached for him. "Yes, but *someday* could be years from now. I just wish . . ." Her voice trailed off.

"You wish what?"

"I wish that we could have one last memory, something that I could treasure and carry with me always."

Vaughn scooted closer to her until their bodies were touching. "What about your husband and all that jazz about being a good girl now?"

"That hasn't changed, but this isn't about Charles. It's about here and now and possibly seeing you for the last time."

He fiddled with a strand of her weave. Sullivan silently prayed that it wouldn't come off in his hand and kill the mood. "So what you wanna do?" he asked breathlessly.

"This . . ." Sullivan closed her eyes, then kissed him lightly on the lips.

Vaughn was pleasantly surprised. "Is that all you want to do?"

"No." She stood up. "But I should go before we do something we might regret."

Vaughn pulled her into his lap. "Don't you think you'll regret it more if we walk away now? I mean, like you said, this could be the last time we're ever together like this."

She kissed him again. "Yeah, you're right."

Their kissing turned passionate. Vaughn picked her up, with her legs still straddled around him, and lay her down on the bed. Sullivan pushed back thoughts of Charles, fidelity, and marriage and indulged in the moment.

He abruptly stopped. "Shoot!" hissed Vaughn.

"What?"

He pulled his shirt back over his head. "I ain't got no condoms. I gotta run to the store and get some."

"Don't worry about that!" cooed Sullivan, drawing him into another kiss. "I've got it covered."

"Oh, you brought some with you?"

"No, I'm on the pill."

He groaned. "Now, how many dudes have fallen for that line?"

Sullivan sucked her teeth. "Do you honestly think I'd lie about something like that? Besides, I'm very happy in my marriage. The last thing I want to have to tell my husband is that I'm carrying your love child. Now, come on. Kiss me."

Vaughn set his lips down on hers, allowing raging hormones to take the place of better judgment. Sullivan peeled off his shirt, and Vaughn snatched off her scarlet dress. The discarded dress landed on a heap of clothes in the middle of the floor along with Sullivan's vows, pledge to God, and her promise to only enjoy it a little bit.

Chapter 16

**"I just want a good man who cares about
me and can see who I really am outside of
being Juicy up there on stage."**
—Reginell Kerry

Mark invited Reginell to a restaurant that she'd never heard of or been to before. She was far more at home in a place where the menu was on the wall behind the cash register. The white linen tablecloths and waiters in suits were intimidating to her. She knew she had no business in a place like that and got the feeling that everyone else there knew it too.

Mark was waiting for her near the entrance.

She greeted him with a simple, "Hey."

"Hello, yourself." He kissed her on the cheek and took off her coat. "Our table is ready." A hostess escorted them to their table. Mark pulled out Reginell's chair for her. "You look nice, Reggie."

"Thank you." Reginell looked around anxiously. "I feel like I'm underdressed," she admitted, wishing she hadn't chosen the hip-hugging black mini and knee-high stiletto boots.

"Are you kidding? You look great . . . very sexy." Mark took his seat. "What's wrong? You look nervous."

"I've never been in here before. It's kind of fancy for lunch."

"I like to spurge a little, especially if I have a good reason to," he added with a wink.

By the time they'd placed their orders, Reginell had started to relax. "I bet you've taken a lot of women here, huh? I know the drill, you spend a lot of money to make 'em feel like they owe you something."

Mark grinned. "Now, I'm not one to brag, but I've never had to spend money to get a lady to give up the goods."

"Yeah, I bet!" Reginell agreed with a laugh.

"What about you?"

"What *about* me?"

"Do you make them drop a truckload of dough before you drop them drawers?"

She laughed again. "I make them drop some dough to even *look* at the drawers! But that's just work, you know. My man doesn't have to spend a lot of money on me or anything like that. I just want a good man who cares about me and can see who I really am outside of being Juicy up there on stage."

Mark stared into her eyes. "So who are you?"

"What do you mean?"

"I mean who are you outside of the club and your sister's shadow and behind all those masks that we wear out in public every day?"

Reginell thought about it. "I think I'm someone who is kind and loyal, who goes hard for what I want—even if my sister doesn't understand what I'm doing or why I'm doing it. I'm a beast if you get in my way," she warned. "But I'd lay down my life for the people I love. I like to make people happy. I love singing, I love performing, period. Even though it's stripping, I still get a chance to get up and entertain people and make a wad of money while I'm doing it."

"You forgot one. You're strong, Reggie. You'd have to be to make it in that business. You're a survivor, and you're not afraid to go for yours. I admire that about you." Reginell giggled. "What's so funny?"

"Nothing." She blushed. "It's just that I've never heard anyone say they admire me before, especially not lately."

"Well, I do. I can't believe none of the guys you've dated never told you that before."

"I don't go on that many dates anymore," she replied. "Besides, if you date one man, you've dated them all."

"Oh, Lord," grumbled Mark, "another angry black woman."

She rolled her eyes and frowned. "You haven't seen angry yet."

"Put your claws back—I'm just kidding! I can think of a lot of words to describe you, and *angry* isn't one of them." He tilted his head a little. "Reggie, can I ask you a personal question?"

She laughed. "You *been* asking 'em! I don't know why you're trying to get my permission to do it now."

Mark smiled. "Well, this might be kind of a sensitive subject, but it's something I've been wondering about. How is it that a smart, vibrant girl like you got into stripping?"

Reginell groaned and rolled her eyes.

Mark reached for her hand. "I don't mean it like that. I mean, like, *how*. What happened to make you walk into the strip club that day and apply for a job?"

Reginell exhaled and leaned back in her chair. "I didn't walk into the club looking for a job, not one stripping anyway."

"So how did you walk out with one?"

She shrugged. "Just kind of happened."

Mark shook his head. "Taking off your clothes doesn't just 'kind of happen.' I know there's more to it than that."

"Ray said it was what I needed to do if I was serious about breaking into the music business," she recalled.

"Ray's the guy who owns the club, right? Lawson says he's kind of shady. Is that true?"

Reginell laughed a little. "Well, I guess he's as honorable as the next pimp, if that answers your question."

"How did you get mixed up with a dude like that?"

"My homeboy Black gave me Ray's card. Black thought Ray might be able to help me find a record label. I figured it wouldn't hurt to call and see what was up. Say what you will about Ray, but he has a lot of connections in the music industry."

"And you have a lot of talent! You don't need his connections."

Reginell sucked her teeth. "Mark, we're in Savannah, Georgia—not exactly the music capitol of the world. It's going to take more than a good voice to get discovered out here."

"So what exactly did this Ray character promise you?"

"The world," she replied with a bitter chuckle. "You should've seen me strolling into his office wearing my borrowed suit, trying to look all professional." She shook her head. "It didn't take long to find out my voice wasn't the only thing Ray was interested in."

Mark took a sip from his water. "What did he do?"

"What he does best. He let me talk about my dreams and how bad I wanted to sing. I told him about leaving college to go to New York to sign with this independent label and how it all blew up in my face. He said that I had guts and that he liked that I was 'hungry' and down to do whatever it took to get a deal."

"Dropping everything to follow your dreams *did* take guts, Reggie. I know Lawson gives you a hard time about dropping out of school, but sometimes you've got to be willing to take risks."

"Well, Ray asked me to sing for him, and I did. He said he loved my voice and was going to hook me up with some people to produce my demo. He even offered to be my manager."

"Your *manager*?" he asked warily.

"At the time, I believed he really wanted to help me."

"When did you change your mind?"

"Around the time I understood what being willing to do *anything* meant."

Mark caught her drift. "I take it that he wanted you to do a little more than run errands and get coffee."

"Yeah, he wanted me to do *way* more than that. He started talking about his manager's fee and how he was taking a chance on me and needed something for him in order to prove that I was a worthy investment."

"Is that when stripping came up?"

"Not really. He wanted something else first. He started saying things like, 'We need to get to know each other better,' and that he wasn't going to waste his time on some scared li'l girl and whatever I wasn't willing to do for a chance at stardom, the next girl would be willing to do. Then he said I could go out that door and keep singing for pennies or I could turn off the light and show him how much I appreciated him making me a star."

Reginell closed her eyes. "I remember just praying and asking God to give me a way out. Immediately, I felt the strength to run, to flee and resist the devil. I told Ray I wanted a record deal but not like that."

"So you walked out?" concluded Mark.

She looked away. "Not exactly."

"What happened?"

"Mark, I don't know if I should get into all this with you. You're my nephew's father. If you knew some of the stuff I've done, you probably wouldn't let Namon anywhere near me."

"I'm not here to judge you, Reggie. We've gotten to know each other pretty well over the past year or so. There's nothing you can say that would change my opinion of you. You can trust me. Tell me what happened with Ray."

Reginell took a deep breath. "Ray started talking about how other chicks were givin' it up for up for beats, tracks, contracts, and everything else in between and that sex was just another bargaining chip.

"I told Ray that some people do make it without having to compromise themselves or their principles, and that I planned to be one of them. Then he said, 'Sweetheart, you ain't Beyoncé. You ain't Alicia Keys or Mariah Carey or none of those other chicks who can make it just off talent. This is the only way you're going to get ahead in this game.'"

"And you believed him?"

"I think at that point, I figured I could give it up for free or I could put a price tag on it and make it work for me. I just told myself to do it and get it over with. I could repent afterward. Then I just turned off the lights and pretended it wasn't happening."

Mark empathized. "That had to have been hard for you. I imagine something like that changes a person."

"It did for me. I haven't quite looked at men, or myself, the same way since. I know I strip and everything, but I believe in God and I know He's not happy with the way I'm living my life. I always think about my mother watching me from above and remember all those sermons where the pastor talked about the body being bought and paid for by Christ."

Mark's heart went out to her. "It's never too late to change direction. You've got a story to tell, Reggie, but the best part is that it isn't over. You can write the ending however you choose. Dancing at the club doesn't have to be it for you."

"I know it's not!" she boasted. "I'm going to be a star, Mark. Just watch."

After having their fill of lunch, dessert, and conversation, Mark accompanied Reginell to her car. "I had a really nice time with you," said Mark. "I hope we can spend some time with each other again."

"I don't know. . . ." She grinned. "We'll see."

"I guess it's not a real date unless it ends with a kiss, so . . ." Mark leaned into her, and she closed her eyes. He planted a soft kiss her on the forehead. Then he lightly brushed a finger across her lips. "Was that okay?" he asked.

"Yes, that was nice." She'd never known a guy to not go straight for the jugular. "Good-bye, Mark." she said flustered. She climbed into the car, and he shut the door behind her.

Reginell floated all the way home. She knew Mark to be a good father and coach; now he'd given her something else about him to like. He seemed like such a nice guy.

Then reality set in: Nice guys didn't go for women like her. And even if they did, they either never stayed put or rarely stayed "nice" for very long.

"Mark is probably no different from any other joker you meet in the club any given night," she told herself. "You'd be stupid to put your heart into this. You'll just end up hurt and disappointed again."

In her heart, she knew he was just like the rest, but there wasn't anything she wouldn't have given to believe that he wasn't.

Chapter 17

"Ladies, I'm in crisis! This is not the time to abandon me."

—*Kina Battle*

Thanksgiving was two days away. Sullivan, Reginell, and Angel crowded into Lawson's small kitchen to help her prepare Thanksgiving dinner, expecting to feed no less than twenty people over the next couple of days.

"Can you believe in a month it'll be Christmas?" posed Lawson, mixing batter for her famous six-tier coconut cake.

"Oh, I can believe it!" exclaimed Angel, chopping onions. "I'm in the house with two kids who've been counting down to Christmas since Labor Day."

"I hope this year will be easier on them. It was hard for any of us to be in the Christmas spirit so soon after Theresa's and E'Bell's deaths last year," noted Lawson.

"Speaking of E'Bell, where's Kina?" asked Reginell, who had been assigned to "corn bread duty" for her sake and everyone else's.

Lawson peered out into the driveway. "She's pulling up now."

"Look . . . if it isn't the lesbian du jour," joked Sullivan as Kina joined them in the kitchen.

"I never said I was a lesbian, Sully."

Sullivan tapped the side of her face. "Yet your girlfriend is, so you'll understand if I jump to conclusions."

"Joan is not my girlfriend," upheld Kina.

"Right, I believe the politically correct term is *life partner*," teased Lawson.

Kina rolled her eyes and turned around. "I'm leaving."

"No, you're not," insisted Angel, dragging Kina back into the fold. "Ladies, give her a break. Kina, I know I speak for everyone when I say that we love you even if we don't agree with some of the choices you're making."

"Forget all that," spat Reginell, wiggling in her seat with excitement. "I wanna know what happened with Joan the other night!"

"Yeah, I kinda wanna know that too," admitted Angel.

Kina sighed and sat down at Lawson's kitchen table. "It was nice. We had a good time."

"A good time or a *gooood* time?" fished Sullivan, sitting down next to her.

Kina hesitated. "She kissed me."

Sullivan slapped her hand across her forehead. "Oh my God! Kina's officially crossed over!"

Lawson shushed Sullivan. "Let her finish, Sully. It's not as serious as all that . . . is it, Kina?"

Kina looked around at all of them. "I don't know."

Angel narrowed her eyes as if trying to process this new information. "What does that mean? Exactly what is it that you *don't* know?"

"We're probably going to go to hell just for listening to this foolishness!" ribbed Sullivan.

"If you're going to hell, it won't be for this. You started paving that road a long time ago!" fired Kina.

Angel wiped her hands and joined them at the table. "So, are the two of you, like, a couple now? Are you dating?"

Kina shrugged her shoulders. "It's like I said, I don't know."

Reginell leaned in. "You admitted kissing her, but did you . . . *you know* . . ." She raised her eyebrows up and down.

Kina's eyes bulged. "No, nothing like that, but . . ."

"But what?" pumped Reginell.

Kina swallowed. "I thought about it. She got to second base. I really think I'm attracted to her. I can't promise that she won't get all the way home next time."

The ladies let out a collective *"Eww!"*

"Ladies, I'm in crisis!" cried Kina. She stood up to wash her hands and pitch in. "Maybe I should let you guys meet her. We can all meet up for dinner or something. That way, you can feel her out and tell me what you think."

"Feeling her up and out is *your* job, Kina," said Sullivan. "Honey, I love you, but there's nothing in the best friends' handbook about this. The last thing I need is for the church to catch Pastor Webb's wife walking in or out of one of Joan's gay establishments. I can see the headlines now: PASTOR'S WIFE NOW SEEKS LESBIAN LOVER! I don't think so."

Kina frowned. "Why do you always make everything about you, Sullivan?"

"Because everything always is!"

"Well, this isn't!" declared Kina and faced her friends. "This is not the time to abandon me. What do you think I should do?"

Sullivan gave her a hard look. "Seek therapy!"

Kina stomped her foot. "I'm serious!"

"So am I!" replied Sullivan. Lawson and Angel laughed.

"No, really, I mean . . ." stammered Kina.

"What?" asked Lawson, still laughing.

Kina turned somber. "I mean, it's been over a year."

"Since E'Bell died?" Angel inferred.

Kina wrung her hands together nervously. "Since . . . the last time."

"The last time what?" asked Reginell.

"You know . . ." Kina seemed embarrassed. "Since the last time I've been with a man."

"*What*?" squawked Sullivan. "You haven't had sex in over a year?"

"Don't say it like that, Sully," jeered Lawson. "You make it sound so depressing."

"That's because it is!" blabbed Sullivan. "My goodness, no wonder you've turned to women. At this point, you'll turn to anything with a pulse!"

"It almost feels like it," admitted Kina. "How am I supposed to handle these urges? I've been *active* for the past fourteen years. I'm used to being intimate on a regular basis. I'm ashamed to say it, but my hormones have been out of control."

"It sounds like you're dealing with a lustful spirit," concluded Lawson.

"No, it sounds like she's horny!" exclaimed Reginell.

"I agree. It definitely sounds like a job for good ol' Bob," resolved Sullivan.

Angel looked up. "Who's Bob?"

Sullivan reeled back. "Are you serious? Considering how long you were celibate, I thought you and Bob would've been joined at the hip."

Kina was confused. "I'm with Angel on this one. Who's Bob?"

"B-O-B . . . Battery-operated boyfriend," supplied Reginell.

Angel giggled. "Really, Sullivan? Toys?"

Sullivan narrowed her eyes. "Don't act like you've never—"

"I didn't say that, okay?" inserted Angel. "I just don't advocate it."

"Why not?" asked Reginell. "It's safe sex in its highest form."

Kina filled a pot with water for boiling. "Don't you guys think it's a sin?"

"The Bible says anything you know is wrong is a sin," Lawson reminded them.

"It's not sin, it's sex with someone I love," challenged Sullivan.

Angel laughed. "Maybe it's a necessary evil, like carbs and calories."

Kina set the pot on the stove. "Yeah, but why is it wrong, especially if you're thinking about your husband in the process?"

Lawson poured her batter into a floured pan. "At the very least, I think it's an impossible standard for any man to live up to. I mean, all those multiple speeds and settings. No human being can compete with that."

"Sounds like we're speaking from experience," muttered Sullivan.

Lawson grinned. "Well, I *was* celibate for those three years before getting married!"

"So it is wrong?" Kina asked again.

Angel cleared her throat. "Right or wrong, no battery-operated device can replace having your own husband in your own bed. Bob, as you so eloquently call it, can't hold or kiss you—"

"You haven't seen the new stuff they're coming out with," threw in Sullivan.

Angel went on. "No toy or vibrator can take the place of a real man. It's not a part of God's plan for sex and marriage, so I don't think it should be a part of ours. You can dress it up however you want; it's still lust and thinking about sex. Biblically speaking, the sinful act

starts in the mind. The physical act is just a manifesta-
tion of that." Angel took a breath and continued. "That
said, sometimes a girl's gotta do what a girl's gotta do!"

They all hooted.

"Maybe I should bring this up in Bible Study," suggested Kina.

"Um, maybe you *shouldn't!*" cautioned Lawson. "I
don't know how to work your vibrator questions into
the pastor's series on grace and mercy."

"Grace and mercy aside, if a sex-toy box is going to
keep Joan out of *your* box, I'm all for it, Kina," said
Sullivan.

Reginell laughed. "While we're on the subject of odd
couples, guess who I had lunch with the other day."

"Whose husband or boyfriend was it this time?"
asked Sullivan. Reginell gestured a finger from her free
hand in Sullivan's direction.

Lawson checked on the food she had in the oven.
"Who, honey?"

"Mark."

Sullivan looked up with a confused expression on
her face. *"Mark who?"*

"Mark Vinson—who else?"

Angel shuddered and shook her head. Kina looked
away.

Reginell noticed the looks on everyone's face.
"What?"

"Reggie, I know you're not the brightest bulb on the
chandelier, but even you should know not to go after
your nephew's father. Are the pickings getting that slim
at the strip club?"

"Sullivan, chill out. They only went to lunch," reiterated Lawson. "No need for you to get your panties in a
bunch."

"As if she doesn't go commando," threw in Reginell.

Angel's eyes widened. "Lawson, you're okay with this?"

Lawson shrugged. "Why wouldn't I be?"

A scowl registered on Sullivan's face. "Well, it's icky to say the least! I mean, I've heard of hand-me-down-clothes, but hand-me-down—"

"Don't even say it!" butt in Angel, sensing where Sullivan was about to go.

Lawson calmed the fray. "Ladies, you're acting like Reggie and Mark are ready to jump the broom. Besides, Mark and I were never in a real relationship. He can date whoever he wants."

"Thank you!" said Reginell. "If I said you all couldn't date anyone I ever slept with—"

"There would be no one left to date," piped Sullivan.

Reginell ignored her and addressed her sister. "So you're really okay with me hanging out with Mark?"

"Girl, don't listen to Sullivan. I said yes, didn't I? It was only lunch. Don't make such a big deal out of it."

"What if it was more than lunch?" pressed Reginell.

Lawson was a little unnerved. "Did something happen between the two of you afterward?"

"No, nothing like that. I just meant, like, if we were to go out again."

"Reggie, you're a grown woman. You can do whatever you want." Lawson paused a moment. "I just hope Mark is different now."

Reginell went on alert. "What do you mean?"

"Honey, Mark wasn't as interested in getting to know me *personally* as he was getting to know me *biblically*, if you catch my drift."

Angel brushed it off. "That was fifteen years ago, Lawson, he was just a kid. What teenage boy isn't interested in sex?"

"I agree, and we all know that sex is a man's first need. It just so happens that you work in an establishment where sexing it up is a part of your job description, Reggie. For some guys, hooking up with a stripper is a fantasy. Mark might be one of those guys."

"So you think all he wants from me is sex?"

"I'm not saying that definitively. I have no idea what Mark wants from you, but Mark and I talk a lot. I can't say that I've ever heard him express having an interest in you."

Reginell was crushed. "Oh . . ."

Lawson put her hand on her sister's shoulder. "Sweetie, I'm not saying that a man wouldn't be genuinely interested in you. I'm saying you shouldn't take anything Mark does or says too seriously. He's a natural flirt, and I'd hate for you to misread his signals and think there's something there that doesn't exist. You're my baby sister, and I don't want to see you get hurt again."

"You're probably right," resolved Reginell, shattered by the revelation. "I don't know what I was thinking."

"Don't worry, sis." Lawson hugged her. "The right man will come along. Just don't expect him to be Mark Vinson."

"Lawson, can you come open this?" Sullivan held up a jar of relish for the potato salad. "You know you're all manly and strong."

Lawson strolled over to her. "Insults are not the quickest way to get me to do you any favors."

Sullivan pulled Lawson off to the side. "The relish was just an excuse to get you away from Reggie. What was that about?"

"What was what about?"

"All that blocking you were doing," charged Sullivan. "Don't you think that was a little harsh?"

"Excuse me for trying to protect my sister from getting hurt."

Sullivan stood akimbo. "Maybe you really were trying to protect Reggie . . . Maybe you were really trying to protect *you*."

Lawson drew back. "*Protect me?* From what?"

"From being jealous of the fact that your ex-boyfriend might actually be falling for your baby sister."

"Mark doesn't want Reggie, not for anything outside of the bedroom, at least."

"How can you be so sure?"

"Because I know Mark," insisted Lawson.

"Did you know he was going to ask her out?" Lawson shook her head. "Then maybe you don't know Mark as well as you *think* you do."

Chapter 18

"You don't have to apologize for me! I haven't said anything I didn't mean."
—*Angel King*

Angel came home exhausted from Lawson's. Duke greeted her with opened arms when she walked into their home. "There's my beautiful fiancée."

"Hey, baby." She kissed him. "Where are the girls?"

"Upstairs, washing up before dinner."

Angel couldn't fathom the prospect of preparing yet another meal. "It's been such a crazy day, Duke. Why don't we just order a pizza for the girls and make it an early night?"

Duke caressed her back. "I was sort of hoping for a home-cooked meal."

"Well, you're home. Why don't you cook it?" she snapped.

"The occasion warrants something a little more special than pizza, and you know my home-cooked specialty is cereal."

Angel slid out of her jacket. "What's the occasion?"

"Channing is flying in today for Thanksgiving. I'm picking him up from the airport in about an hour."

Angel felt a rush of anger. "Thanks for the warning, Duke! This house is a wreck. We're not prepared for company."

"Chan is not coming here to inspect our house. He's coming home to see his family."

"Wouldn't you rather take him out?"

"Angel, he's been flying all day. I'm sure he wants to sit back and relax, not deal with waiters screwing up his order and obnoxious patrons." He kissed her hands. "Please, baby, for me. . . ."

Angel rolled her eyes. "You're going to owe me big time, Du'Corey King!" she warned him.

He winked at her. "You know I'm good for it."

"Yeah, I know *exactly* what you're good for," grumbled Angel.

Duke pulled her into his arms. "And you love every minute of it."

"This is so frustrating," screeched Angel into the phone with Lawson as she hunted for a boiler in Theresa's seemingly never-ending collection of pots and pans. "I don't understand this woman's organizational system at all. Who even buys this much cookware? It's like Pots 'R' Us in here!"

"You're just stressed out, Angel. Calm down; it's just dinner. Don't make such a big deal out of it."

"It's not 'just dinner,' Lawson. It's the way he just expects me to drop everything to—"

"You need some help in the kitchen?"

Angel didn't recognize the low tenor voice speaking to her. "No, I got it. I just . . ." She turned around. It felt as if the world had stopped spinning the moment she laid eyes on him. He was far more handsome in person than he was on any of the pictures of him she'd seen. Angel told herself to blink and to breathe.

"I have to admit, I love seeing a woman in an apron. Something about it is wholesome yet sexy." He smiled.

Even on crutches, he had a swagger about him that rivaled any movie star on the red carpet. "Hi, I'm Channing. You must be Angel."

"Hi." She managed to climb down without killing herself or taking her eyes off of his luscious butterscotch skin. "Lawson, I'll call you back." She dropped the phone.

"Oh, you didn't have to get off the phone. I just wanted to come formally introduce myself. Obviously, I've heard a lot about you, but with me spending most of my life on foreign soil, we've never had a chance to meet face-to-face."

She shook his hand. "It's a pleasure to finally meet you. How's the leg?"

He looked down at the cast. "They didn't amputate it, so anything short of that is good."

She laughed a little too hard—a telltale sign for Angel that she was giddy and far more attracted to him than she should've been.

"I hear congratulations are in order . . . *again*. When is the big day?" asked Channing.

"What day?"

"Your wedding," he answered.

"Oh, right! Um, late spring. June fifth."

Channing nodded. "Okay. I hope I'm able to fly back for it, and I apologize for just showing up out the blue. I was supposed to fly out Saturday, but I couldn't resist the chance to be home with family for Thanksgiving."

"It's okay," she said quickly. "I'm glad you could make it for dinner."

"Really? Duke kind of hinted that you were less than thrilled about having an extra mouth to feed."

"I don't know where he got that idea from," she lied.

"That's good. I'd hate to put you out."

"Oh, I don't mind putting out." She winced when she caught the Freudian slip. "I mean, it's no big deal, honestly." Angel swallowed and wiped her sweaty palms. "I bet Duke and the girls are wondering where dinner is. They're not a bunch who like to be kept waiting."

"I think all of us Kings have that in common." He smiled flirtatiously. "We've got to have what we want when we want it."

Angel finished the dinner and brought it out to her starving family. Knowing she was cooking for such a handsome guest made the task a little less arduous. Duke blessed the food, and they all began digging in.

Angel passed the salad bowl to Channing. "I bet it feels good to be home, huh?"

"I'm happy to see my family, obviously, but my heart is out there on the ground with my combat unit."

Angel fixed Miley's plate. "The troops have my utmost respect and my prayers, but I'd be lying if I said I agreed with everything you all are doing out there."

Channing blinked back. "Exactly which part don't you agree with, Angel? Liberating people? Taking down oppressive dictators? Feeding starving children on the street?"

"No, occupying another country without sensitivity to their culture, their beliefs, and their way of life. I don't think imposing our will on them is right. Neither is bombing villages and killing innocent civilians."

Duke attempted to diffuse the exchange. "Angel, chill out now. We're trying to enjoy a nice dinner."

"Well, Duke, I'm sure there are families all over the country who would love to be having a nice dinner with a loved one who's life was sacrificed for a senseless war."

Channing countered her argument. "Since when is fighting for freedom senseless? This country was built on the backs of soldiers. It's 'senseless wars,' as you put it, that provide the freedom that you're able to enjoy."

"So the torture and killing of innocent people and the increased risk to our own national security are just causalities of war too?" challenged Angel. Channing was starting to become less attractive.

Channing gulped down his glass of tea. "It's war, Angel. Sometimes it gets bloody and gruesome. All of it's not pretty and, yes, sometimes innocent blood is shed. But as they say, sometimes the needs of many outweigh the needs of a few."

"Fine . . ." Angel heaped food onto her plate. "You tell that to the parents having to bury their son today or to the child whose mother isn't around to kiss him good night because she's on her third or fourth tour of duty."

"Every soldier knows the risk involved when he or she enlists. To most, dying for their country is honorable."

"I don't know what's so honorable about dying on foreign soil, maimed and gasping for life, never even being able to tell your family good-bye."

"You watch too much sensationalized television," charged Channing. "You have no idea what's on going out there."

"You're right. It's probably much worse than the politicized version we get on television."

Duke rubbed Angel's shoulders. "Baby, go easy on him. The man has been fighting in a war zone. He put his life on the line for us and almost lost his leg in the process. That's a heck of a sacrifice."

Angel turned to Duke. "I know all about sacrificing for this country."

"Chan, I hope you're not offended. My fiancée can be a little passionate and high-strung." He kissed her on the cheek. "But we love her anyway!"

Angel pushed Duke away. "You don't have to apologize for me! I haven't said anything I didn't mean."

"I know, baby, but don't you think you're being a little hard on him considering what he's been through?"

Angel faced Channing. "I'm sorry if you think I'm being insensitive, but this is a very touchy subject for me."

"Angel lost her father in combat," explained Duke. "He was killed in the first Iraq war."

"My father was everything to me," Angel told him. "He was a soldier, but he detested senseless killing, and he had great respect for other people's differences." She took a breath. "His death devastated my family. I would never want to see anyone else's spouse, sibling, child, or friend go through what we went through. My mother has never completely gotten over it."

Channing now understood her combativeness. "I'm sorry for your loss, Angel. For the record, no one looks forward to being deployed, separated from loved ones, and not knowing how or if you're going to return. However, it's what we signed up to do."

She nodded. "I respect your commitment and loyalty to this country."

Channing smiled. "So are we cool again?"

Angel blushed. "Yeah, we're cool. Nothing wrong with a little difference in ideology, right?"

"You're right," replied Channing.

"Well, you know what Aunt Jackie used to make us do after a big fight," Duke said. He gave his cousin a slight shove. "Go on over there and hug it out!"

Angel laughed nervously and shook her head. "Oh, that's not necessary, Duke."

"No, it's cool," disputed Channing, rising from his seat. "I mean, we're practically family now."

Channing held out opened arms and invited her in. Angel accepted, inhaling his cologne as he held her.

She released him before the hug could be considered anything but amicable. Angel knew they'd soon be family, but what she felt in that embrace was anything but familial.

Chapter 19

"You all won't admit it,
but I think you like it when I sit
around being contrite and obedient, doing
whatever *you* think is best, living my life
according to *your* standards."

—*Kina Battle*

"Sullivan, that husband of yours knows he can preach!" declared Kina after they all returned to Sullivan's house following the church's Thanksgiving Day service for dinner. "It felt like he preached that sermon just for me."

Lawson removed a pan of dressing from the oven. "It never hurts to be reminded that this battle we're waging is a spiritual warfare, not a physical one. When we find ourselves at odds with one another, it's good to remember that." She glanced over at Sullivan, who sat quietly while everyone else scurried about preparing dinner. "By the looks of it, Sully, you're fighting your own spiritual warfare over there with yourself. What's going on with you? You've been quiet since we got here."

"I'm just a little preoccupied today. The holidays have that affect on me," she explained. *The holidays and Vaughn*, she thought, racked with guilt following their baby-making liaison. She discovered that sinning wasn't as easy or painless as it used to be.

Lawson slipped off her oven mitts. "You and Charles okay?"

Sullivan grimaced. "He keeps saying that everything will work out. I suppose at some point I ought to believe him."

Angel whisked ingredients for the gravy. "If you think your marriage is so shaky, why are you trying to have a baby?"

Sullivan pitched off a little of the dressing. "I think having a baby will bring us closer and remind us of all the love there is still left between us. Giving him a child is my way of proving to him how committed I am to our marriage; my way of atoning for having an affair."

Lawson swatted her away from the dressing. "Sully, you don't atone for cheating by having a baby. If you want to atone for your affair with Vaughn, just don't have any more affairs with Vaughn."

Sullivan cringed, struck with the memory of the romp at his apartment. "Could you not say his name please?"

"Are you the only one who gets to holler out his name?" ribbed Reginell, relegated to tea making now.

"At least I know his name, which is probably more than you can say for majority of the men you wake up next to," hurled Sullivan.

"Come on now, it's Thanksgiving. Let this be the one day out the year that the two of you don't argue," pleaded Kina.

"Kina, did you invite your little friend to join us?" asked Angel.

Kina was annoyed. "If you mean Joan, no. She's spending Thanksgiving with her family in Florida."

Lawson wiped her hands on a dishtowel. "So what's the status on that whole thing?"

"We're friends," Kina replied.

Reginell smirked. "Are you friends of a beneficial nature?"

"No! Why are you making this about sex? Joan and I enjoy each other's company. Sex hasn't even really come up."

"And when it does?" prodded Lawson.

"I'll deal with it then. Joan understands that I need to take things slowly."

"Just remember that the Bible calls same-sex relations detestable."

"The Bible also says you shouldn't date relatives. Did you remind Reggie and Mark of that?"

"Hold up! When did *I* get into this?" protested Reginell.

"When Mark got into *you*," replied Sullivan and scratched her head. "So what's your therapist saying about all this, Kina?"

Kina avoided eye contact with anyone. "She's fine with it."

"She actually considers this to be a healthy development?" Sullivan shook her head. "What kind of quack-job therapist is she?"

"Dr. Shaw is not a quack." Kina exhaled. "She's . . . She's no longer my therapist."

Lawson grew concerned. "Why did you change therapists?"

"I didn't change. I just decided I don't need therapy anymore," stated Kina. "I have the Lord, and I have all of you. You all know me better than anyone."

"Yes, we're your friends and all, Kina, but you've been through some stuff we aren't equipped to handle," cautioned Lawson.

Angel faced Kina. "Do you have any idea what you and Kenny have gone through and the psychological impact it can have for years to come? Kina, your husband used to beat you, and your son witnessed that. He made you feel responsible for his failed football career; you carried around the guilt from that for over ten years, only to find out it was a lie and that you'd endured all that pain for nothing. On top of that, Kenny shot and killed his father. You both watched him die. That's a lot for anyone to process. While we have the Lord, who the Bible calls a wonderful counselor, we also have people on earth ordained and appointed by God to help us. I believe that God can give you a miraculous healing, but until then, you and Kenny need to get back in counseling immediately."

"Kenny still goes," revealed Kina.

"When's the last time you went?" asked Sullivan.

Kina didn't answer.

"When is the last time you went, Kina?" asked Lawson in a stern voice.

Kina replied in a voice barely above a whisper. "Around August or September."

"That's why you've been so confused and making questionable decisions," Angel concluded.

"Spending time with Joan isn't a questionable decision. She's a good person. She's kind, she listens to me, she—"

"She's a lesbian!" blurted out Lawson. "And you're not!"

"I may be," asserted Kina.

Lawson rolled her eyes. "You're not a lesbian, Kina. You're lonely and confused. Leading her on isn't fair to you or to Joan."

"Is your problem that I'm seeing a woman or is the problem that I'm finally standing up for myself and not doing what you want me to do?"

Lawson squinted her eyes and responded with a terse, "What?"

Kina spoke with a newfound confidence. "You all won't admit it, but I think you like it when I sit around being contrite and obedient, doing whatever *you* think is best, living my life according to *your* standards. You're just as controlling as E'Bell was. If I want to be with Joan, I'll be with Joan. I don't need permission from my cousin, my therapist, or my friends to do so."

"What about God? Do you need His permission?" inquired Angel.

Kina retreated quietly to the stove without answering.

"I'm glad to see you're less pissy than you were when I called you last night," Lawson said to Angel, who was polishing the silverware. "How was the dinner?"

Angel opened her mouth to speak, but a girlish giggle came from her lips instead.

"Umph, I know that look," said Sullivan. "I guess we all know how Duke snatched that frown off your face last night."

"Last night, I met the most gorgeous, most charming, most provocative man ever!" announced Angel.

Sullivan gave her a side-glance. "I thought those kinds of adjectives were usually reserved for Duke."

"They still are. His cousin Channing was the guest of honor for dinner last night. What a man! Obviously, the apples don't fall far from that family tree."

"You're not going to make a play for Duke's cousin, are you?"

"Of course not!" she balked. "I just said he was fine."

"You said a lot more than that," teased Sullivan.

"Well, that's all I meant!"

Lawson laughed at the two of them. "Will this Adonis be joining us for dinner?"

"No, Channing, Duke, and the girls are eating with Reese's family."

Sullivan frowned. "Why didn't you go with them?"

Angel examined her work. "Apparently, Thanksgiving was one of Theresa's favorite holidays. They're all spending the day doing and eating all of her favorite things. I didn't think I should be a part of that."

"Why not?" quizzed Reginell. "You're family now, and she was your friend too."

"I know. I just wasn't up to spending the day in her shadow."

Reginell was distracted by a text message coming through on her phone. "Um, I'll be right back. I've got to handle some business." She took off before anyone had a chance to question her.

"What's up with that?" wondered Kina. "Do you think she went to go see Mark?"

Lawson shrugged. "Who knows? With that child, 'handling some business' could mean anything."

Kina smiled. "Call me crazy, but I think they make a cute couple."

Sullivan cleared her throat. "I believe we've already established that you're a little cray-cray, and, no, there's nothing 'cute' about Mark mating with Reggie. It's borderline incestuous."

Kina disagreed. "I don't think a good man should go to waste just because Lawson slept with him once more than a decade ago. I could see if Lawson wanted him, but she doesn't. She's in love with Garrett. You're fine with Mark and Reggie dating, aren't you, Lawson?"

Lawson pressed her lips together and grabbed a covered dish. "It's getting late. We should go ahead and start setting the food out on the table." She scampered out without responding to Kina's question.

"I guess that's a no," surmised Angel after Lawson left.

Charles clanked a butter knife against his glass to gain everyone's attention once the table was set and the food brought out. He rose from his position at the head of the table, passing his eyes over the nine faces seated around the dinner table.

"It certainly is a blessing to be able to share this wonderful occasion with all of you. You know, the Word tells us to 'give thanks to the Lord, for He is good. His faithful love endures forever.' Thanksgiving shouldn't just be the third Thursday out of November. For the Christian, there shouldn't go one day where we don't give thanks to the Lord for His many blessings."

Lawson looked lovingly at her husband and son, seated to her left and right. "Amen."

Charles continued. "Each year at this time, however, I like to take time to publicly thank God for everything He's done for me. If y'all don't mind, I'd like for each of us to go around and tell the Lord and each other what we're thankful for." He turned to Sullivan, who was seated to his right. "Honey, you want to start?"

"Sure." Sullivan smiled politely and stood up. "As most of you here know, this past year was a challenging year for my family and me. Through God's grace and mercy, we've started to reclaim everything the devil tried to steal from us, and I'm thankful for that. I'm thankful to be blessed to live in this beautiful home, but that would mean nothing if I didn't have all of you to share it with. I'm so thankful for you, Lawson, Kina, Angel, and even you, Reginell, for being the sisters I never had.

"I'm eternally thankful to have a husband who loves me unconditionally." She turned to Charles. "Charles, I know I'm far from perfect, and I know I probably keep you on your knees in prayer more often than you'd like to admit, but I love you. You may not be God's gift to women, but you're God's gift to me. I just thank you so much for loving me. No matter how many times I break your heart, you still love me. I believe our Heavenly Father is the same way. He keeps right on loving us no matter what. I'm thankful for that."

Charles hugged his wife. "I love you too. Thank you for loving me."

Angel rose. "Um, like Sullivan, this has been a trying year for me too. Twelve years ago, I met the man I was destined to love for the rest of my life. It was a fairy-tale wedding, but it ended in a bitter, painful divorce. Not only did I lose my husband, but I lost my child too. If it wasn't for the ladies seated around this table, I probably would've lost my life as well."

Angel took a few seconds to swallow the lump in her throat. "But God had another plan. He saw me through that painful time in my life, and like Job, He called me out of the storm. He blessed me to finish college, start my own business, which allows me to use my gift as a nurse to minister to other people, and He brought all of you into my life. The biggest miracle of all, though, is that He brought me back to the only man I've ever loved. Just to show the goodness of God's mercy, He allowed us to be reunited by the very person who drove us apart. It was through Theresa's love for Duke and, eventually, her love for me, that Duke and I are together again. We have the family that I thought we'd lost forever, and I'm just so thankful that God used Theresa to help me open my heart to receive forgiveness and be forgiven and to love without limits." She raised her eyes toward heaven. "Thank you."

Namon staggered to his feet. "I just want to say that I'm thankful for my mom. I know she's sacrificed a lot for me, and it hasn't always been easy for her, but she did it because she loves me. She works hard to provide for our family; she teaches me about God and the Bible; and she's never too tired to go to one of my games or help me with my homework or to yell at me when I mess up."

They all laughed. Lawson wiped a tear from her eye as Namon went on. "I'm also thankful that I have, not one, but two dads now. For a long time, I didn't have any. It was just me, my mom, and my Aunt Reggie. Now, I have all of you here and my little sister Mariah, and that's what I'm thankful for." He sat down.

Charles nodded. "Well said, son."

Lawson dotted her eyes. "Wow, I don't know what to say after that. Thank you for such kind words, Namon. When I became a mom at sixteen, I had no idea that I'd end up needing my son as much as he needed me."

Lawson exhaled. "If I tried to tell you all everything I'm grateful for, we'd be here all night, so I'll keep it as brief as possible. I'm thankful that God allows me to wake up surrounded by love, family, and His peace every day. I'm thankful that I have a church where I'm ministered to and a pastor who is not only my spiritual leader, but he's also my friend. I'm thankful to have a job where I can make a difference in the lives of children. I'm thankful for my health, my intelligence, being clothed in my right mind, and that I know from whom my help and strength comes from.

"I'm thankful for my baby sister." Lawson turned to Reginell. "I don't approve of everything you do, but I'd give my life for you, Reggie; no hesitation, no questions

asked." She reached for Garrett's hand. "I'm thankful
for my wonderful husband, who God created purposely
to love me and for me to love. Garrett, you're the best
man I know. I love you, now and forever. I'm thankful for this crazy, unrestricted, unpredictable group of
ladies I call friends. You all are my sisters just as much
as Reggie is. And, Namon, I'm so thankful that God
choose me to be your mother. I love you, bud."

Namon kissed his mother on the cheek. "I love you
too."

Lawson turned to Garrett. "Baby, you're up next."

Garrett cleared his throat. "Everyone who knows me
knows that I'm a man of few words, so I just want to
say I'm thankful to God for blessing me with the life I
have. I thank Him for letting me see almost thirty-eight
years on this side of heaven. I thank Him for my beautiful wife, who I would do anything for, and for my son,
Namon. I thank Him for giving me a thriving business
and surrounding me with good hardworking people,
and I'm thankful for all of you. Lord willing, Lawson
and I will have a new son or daughter at this table and
have even more to be thankful for."

Kina stood up. "I've been sitting here, listening to
all of you, trying to stop myself from crying. There's so
much love at this table, and God is love, so what I'm
really saying is that there's so much God at this table."

Angel concurred. "Amen."

"This time last year, I'd just lost my husband. But I
didn't just lose E'Bell. I lost my sense of who I was. I've
been defined by that relationship since I was seventeen
years old, so I didn't know how to be anything other
than Kenny's mother or E'Bell's wife. I'm thankful that
God is showing me how to be Kina. I'm grateful to be
in school again and to be blessed to be working at the
church that's like a second home to me. I'm thankful

that I have the coolest son in the world, who I'll love until I take my last breath, and I'm thankful for all of you and for the new people that have been introduced into my life."

Sullivan grunted at the reference to Joan. Angel elbowed her.

"You want me to go, Mama?" asked Kenny. Kina nodded. He stood. "Well, I guess I'm thankful for God, my Xbox, my friends, my mom, my cousin Namon, my therapist, and my grandma Hattie." He paused. "I'm also thankful that my dad can't hurt my mom anymore and that he told me he wasn't mad at me for shooting him before he died." Kina held her son.

"I guess it's my turn." Reginell stood on her feet. "I know I'm the black sheep of the family. I'm the one who everybody expects to mess up, but y'all love me anyway. I'm very thankful for that. I know I don't know as much about the Bible as everyone else at this table, but I know that it says to treat everyone the way you want to be treated, and you all try real hard to do that. I can't act like God is pleased with what I do for a living and some of the people I hang out with, but I'm trying. I just hope He doesn't give up on me."

"God's love and compassion never fail, my young sister," replied Charles.

"Thank you, Pastor Charles. I guess I just want to say I'm thankful I have all of you watching my back, praying for me, and for accepting me as I am, with all my flaws. I'll just try to flaw a little less as time goes by."

Charles addressed the group again. "My heart is so full right now. Sister Battle, I think you said it best. This table is full of love, so this table is full of our Lord. I love all of you so much, from the youngest to the oldest. Well, I guess I'm the oldest, huh?"

They all chuckled.

"We can't ever forget everything the Lord has done for us, and what He's doing for us even at this moment. No matter how bad you think it is, it could always be worse. And for someone else, it is worse. I thank God I have a friend in Jesus; I'm thankful that I'm made righteous through His blood, and that I have a blood-bought right to everything God has promised me. So do all of you. I'm thankful that He's blessed me to be a blessing to others. I'm thankful that God has blessed me with this gorgeous woman I get to call wife. I'm thankful for everyone seated here who I get to call friend. I'm just thankful. If God never does another thing for me, He's already done enough."

His speech was met with a round of "Amens."

"Well, let's ask the Lord to bless this bountiful harvest, then let's dig in!"

As they feasted and fellowshipped, they knew the good times and euphoric feelings wouldn't last forever, but, at least for now, all was right with the world.

Chapter 20

*"I'm a stripper, so the first
thought that comes to mind is,
'Oh, she's easy. She's a ho.'"*
—*Reginell Kerry*

"I've got to say, I was surprised when you called me over," said Mark, entering Reginell's apartment the next day. He looked around. "I like how you've got everything set up in here. It's nice." Mark stood back and took another look at her. Her thick twists were pulled back into a bun. "Speaking of nice, look at you! I like your hair like that. It shows off your face more."

Reginell pointed to the sofa with a stern look on her face. "Sit."

"Ohh-kay," he slowly enunciated. "What's up with the military routine that you've got going on here?" he asked after sitting down on the couch. Reginell sat down next to him and pulled back her robe. She wasn't wearing anything underneath.

Mark was floored. "Reggie, what are you doing?"

"You don't like it? Don't you think I'm sexy?"

"Of course! Not that I'm complaining, but what's going on here?"

"Nothing," she answered curtly. "I called you here to give you what you want. This is what you want, isn't it?"

"I'm a thirty-three-year-old heterosexual male. I'd be lying if I said no," confessed Mark, looking down at her seemingly flawless body.

"Good," she replied. She lay back on the sofa and gapped her legs open.

His mouth flew open. "Reggie, *what* are you doing?" he asked again.

"I'm giving you what you want. Do you have condoms? If not, I have some in the back."

Mark was taken aback. "Are you serious?"

Reginell crossed her arms in front of her. "I'm very serious, Mark."

"So, are we supposed to be having sex today?" he asked for confirmation.

"Yes, Mark, we are having sex today, but we do need to go ahead and get started. I'm getting my braids taken out at three, and I don't want to be late." She huffed and stiffened her body. "Okay, do your thing."

"If this is some kind of test, I'm telling you now that I'm in great danger of failing." He glanced over at Reginell, who looked stoic and bored. Then he leaned down to kiss her.

She stopped him when he was about an inch shy of her lips. "You know we really don't have to do all that. Just in and out, no extras. You can skip all that foreplay."

"Okay." Mark shrugged his shoulders and stood up to take off his shoes and pants. He started pulling his shirt over his head.

"You don't have to that either," cut in Reginell.

"Do what? Get naked?"

"Yes. I mean I know that you have to take off your boxers, but you can leave your shirt on. I only took my clothes off because I'm more comfortable this way."

Bewildered, Mark pulled his shirt down. "Well, do I at least get to touch you?"

"You can," she said and frowned, "but I told you it's really not necessary."

Mark caressed Reginell's face. She only stared uncomfortably at the ceiling and blinked rapidly like she was trying to figure out what he was doing. He thought he felt her wince. Mark tried massaging her shoulders. The only response he received this time was Reginell clearing her throat and swallowing. "Okay, what in heaven's name is wrong with you?" he asked, frustrated.

"What? I'm just lying here."

"That's my point!"

"Look, Mark, are we going to do this or what? I told you that I have other things to do today." She saw the confused look on his face. "Honestly, I thought we'd be done by now or at least made more progress than this. What are you waiting for?"

Mark sighed. He knew that he would live to regret passing up this opportune moment, but he couldn't go through with it. This was a cold, mechanical act, and he didn't want it to be that way with her.

"What's going on, Reggie? You've got me over here feeling like a rapist or something, and I want to know why." He looked down at her again, her crotch staring him in the face. "Please, just close your legs for my sake." She sat upright. He handed her the robe. "Here, cover your breasts too."

Reginell covered her body. "I wasn't playing games with you, not like you've been playing with me."

"What are you talking about?" he asked, pulling up his pants.

"You men are all so transparent. You don't think I know why you're so interested in getting to know me?

I'm a stripper, so the first thought that comes to mind is, 'Oh, she's easy. She's a ho.' That's why I called you here today. Since this whole thing is just about sex to you, I'd rather get that over with and send you on your way than get caught up in your games and lies under the pretense of us trying to form some kind of relationship."

"I never thought that."

"Yeah, right, so I'm supposed to believe that you asked me out because you actually like me?"

"That *is* the real reason."

"Yet you couldn't pull your pants down fast enough when you thought I was going to give you some."

Mark shook his head. "Reggie, it's not even like that."

"It's *exactly* like that, Mark! You're no different from any of those fools sweating all over me at work. You just came wrapped in a nicer package, that's all."

"Not all men are like the dudes you deal with down at the strip club."

"Yes, they are! Despite all this talk about wanting to get to know me, what you really want to know is how many lies you've got to tell me before I'll sleep with you."

"I've never had to lie to a woman to get her to sleep with me, nor would I. I respect women, and I have a mama who won't hesitate to go upside my head if I don't."

"But your mom ain't here," countered Reginell.

"She's not, but the values she gave me are."

Reginell sucked her teeth. "Whatever."

"I'm not out here looking for a good time. I can't deny being attracted to you, but there are a thousand other reasons that I like you too."

"Name one."

"For starters, you're the most upfront woman I've ever met and, for reasons I can't explain, I actually like that. But I can tell that there's a big heart underneath that tough exterior. You make me laugh, and you keep me on my toes. You're sassy, but you're fun too. I'm feeling you—I can't lie."

"Mark, you don't have to say that."

"I know I don't. Stop acting like you don't deserve to have nice things said about you."

"I don't know that I do. I mean, I know what I do for a living, and I know what people think of me, especially my sister and her friends."

"Your sister loves you, Reggie, that's why she goes overboard. She doesn't want to see you get hurt or live beneath your potential. Quite honestly, neither do I."

"Dancing is just a stepping-stone," she explained. "Why can't anyone see that?"

"I'm sure that's how you see it, but you're so much more than some sex object. You're pretty and smart and funny. You shouldn't sell yourself short."

"Now, you're starting to sound like Lawson," groaned Reginell.

"That's because I care."

"That's what I don't get. Why do you care?"

"There's something about you, I guess. You were the only one on my side when I was trying to get my son, and that means a lot to me. You've got a good heart. Plus, I just like being around you."

"Somebody certainly has taught you how to lay it on thick," responded Reginell, not swayed by his flattering words.

"I'm speaking from the heart. I don't know what more I can get you than that."

"Mark, I deal with lying, sleazy, triflin' men every day. It's hard to believe you'd be any different."

"You have a point," he conceded. "But I *am* different. You'll see."

"Every man claims he's different, which makes all of you pretty much the same."

Mark gripped Reginell's shoulders and looked her in the eyes. "I like you, Reggie, and I can't promise you that I'm going to always act like a Boy Scout around you, especially when you come to the door dressed like that. Even if I had been thinking with the other head when I first saw you, it's different now."

"How is it different, Mark? How are *you* different?" She gently removed his hands and walked a few feet away from him. "You barely even know me."

"But I want to get to know you. I feel something when I'm around you that I haven't felt with anyone else, and it's not just a sexual attraction. I actually sit around thinking about you like a lovesick teenager. You've got me open. I don't know how or why, but you do. If I was to be honest, you have ever since the first time I saw you in Lawson's living room. If it means taking our time and being just friends until you feel comfortable with being something more, then we'll do that. No strings attached."

"You can't say that you just want to be friends, but every time we're together, you're trying to get in my pants. I get enough of that at work. I don't need it from you too."

"And you won't get it from me. Not all of us are over-sexed swine, you know?" Mark slipped his shoes over his feet.

"That's remains to be seen."

"Now, I want you to answer a question for me. Would you really have gone through with it a few minutes ago?"

She smiled coyly. "I guess we'll never know."

"Well, know this, Miss Kerry, you've got me for as long as you'll have me. Now, why don't you go slip into something a little *less* comfortable so we can talk?"

Reginell couldn't help laughing. "Are you always this silly?"

"Maybe. Why don't you spend some time with me and find out."

Reginell went into her room and returned wearing jeans and a T-shirt. "Is this better?"

Mark made a face. "Not really, but definitely more appropriate."

Reginell sat down next to him. "Can I ask you something?"

"You can ask me anything."

"Are you still in love with Lawson?"

Mark dropped his head a little. "I don't recall ever saying that I was in love with her."

"You asked her to marry you, and I know that you weren't too happy about her marrying Garrett."

"That was more about Namon than it was my feelings for her. I didn't want to be cut out of his life. I admit, there was a time when I thought there might be some potential for something to happen between Lawson and me, but it was more of an attraction than love."

"How do you feel about her now?"

"I care about her. I want to see her happy, and I think Garrett does that for her. I want her to have a great life because whatever she does affects my son. I value our friendship and the relationship we've managed to establish, but that's pretty much it."

Reginell nodded. "I just thought that maybe . . ."

"What?"

"I thought you had me here because you couldn't be with her, you know, kind of like a substitute."

Mark shook his head. "Lawson was the furthest thing from my mind when I invited you to lunch or came here today. In fact, lately, all women have been the furthest thing from my mind, except you."

"Really?" He nodded. "I've been thinking about you lately too. I think you're pretty cool, Mark."

"What—for an old guy?" he inferred.

"You're not that old . . . are you?"

Mark laughed. "I've got about a decade on you."

"I've dated guys a lot older than you. Believe me, they weren't nearly as nice either."

"So that's what we're doing? We're dating?"

"Um, well . . ." stammered Reginell. "I didn't mean, like, you're my boyfriend or anything."

"Not yet," replied Mark. "But I definitely like the thought of dating and seeing you more often."

"For real?"

"Yeah . . . I mean, if you're okay with that."

She paused for a second, still in shock. "That's cool. I would—" she took a deep breath, gaining confidence— "I would like that very much."

"I'm glad to hear it."

"What about Lawson? Are you going to tell her?"

"Is what we do really any of her business?"

"In this case, it is. She's your baby's mama."

"Reggie, you can tell her if you want. I don't feel obligated to fill her in on who I'm dating whether it's you or anyone else. Lawson's only concern should be how the woman I'm with is treating our son. That's a nonissue with you. You love Namon as much as we do, so it shouldn't be a problem."

"It shouldn't, but you know how people are. You know somebody is going to have something negative to say about it."

"I thought you didn't care what people think about you."

"I don't, but I'm kind of worried about what they might think about you. My last boyfriend broke up with me because he couldn't handle his friends and family giving him a hard time about me being a stripper. Not only are you dating a stripper, but she's also your son's aunt.

"I care about what other people have to say about as much as I care about the latest episode of *Keeping Up with the Kardashians*, which is very little."

"You seem like a really nice guy, Mark," she paused, "then again, you all do until you get what you want."

"Well, I *am* a nice guy, and all I want is to get to know you."

"And you wanna date me?" she asked skeptically.

"Very much so," he admitted. "It's all I can do to stop myself from kissing you right now." Reginell exhaled loudly. "I'm not going to, I'm just thinking about it."

They talked for hours, and she loved every minute of it. Reginell couldn't remember the last time she laughed so much or felt so much like her old self. With her history and her job, she knew she wasn't worthy of a man like Mark, and it was only a matter of time before he knew it too. But she was bound and determined to enjoy it while it lasted.

Chapter 21

"When it's meant to be, you just know."
—Angel King

"Did you buy out the stores?" asked Channing when Angel came in carrying her weight in shopping bags following her Black Friday shopping.

She set the bags down. "I rationalize by only purchasing items that are more than 50 percent off." She looked around the house. It was unusually quiet. "Where's everybody?"

"The girls are spending the night with Reese's parents, and Duke went to the comedy show with some of his frat brothers," reported Channing.

"I forgot about that. Why didn't you go with him?"

Channing rapped on his leg. "I'm still in recovery, remember?"

"You're able to get around so effortlessly that it's easy to forget." She put her hands together. "Well, I'm about to go into the kitchen and whip up something to eat. You hungry?"

Channing put his hand over his stomach. "Famished!"

"What are you in the mood for?"

"Anything other than turkey!"

Angel remembered the frozen shrimp she didn't make for Duke. "How do grits smothered in shrimp gravy grab you?"

He smiled. "Sounds perfect."

***

"So where did you learn to cook like this?" asked Channing, helping himself to a third serving.

"Big Mama, of course! I was her official helper in the kitchen."

"Are you close with your family?"

"I try to be," she replied. "It's sort of hard with everyone else living farther north, but Duke and the girls are my family now. Having them here definitely makes it easier."

"Did you ever think you and Duke would get back together?"

Angel shook her head. "I prayed for it for a long time, but once he moved back to D.C. and married Theresa, I gave up hope."

"For the record, I never agreed with his decision to leave you and walk away from his marriage. None of us did, but once my cousin gets an idea in his head . . ."

"Nothing can talk him out of it!" finished Angel. "I know that better than anybody."

"But despite all that, you two found your way back to each other. I think that was nothing short of a miracle."

"Even though I didn't know if Duke and I would ever be together again, I've never had any doubt about him being the love of my life."

"Duke must've felt the same way too," gathered Channing.

"When it's meant to be, you just know. We know," boasted Angel with a smile.

Channing nodded. "It's good to be so confident about something in a world full of so much uncertainty."

"Isn't that how you feel about being a soldier?"

"Yeah, it's what I was born to do. Serving my country is what I want to die doing."

Her eyes widened. "Wow, that's powerful. I'm really in awe of your commitment and integrity."

"Believe me, I'm no saint," he hinted. "I guess that's the wrong thing to say to an angel."

"None of us are saints, but you're an honorable man. That's a rare find these days."

"That's a trait we Kings have in common."

Angel averted his gaze. "Not all of you . . ."

"Are you talking about my cousin, your fiancé?"

Angel recalled their first failed attempt at marriage. "There was a time when Duke was anything but honorable."

"You're talking about when he left you for Reese, right?" She nodded. "I tried to tell him it was a bad move. We all did. You didn't deserve to be treated that way."

"Thank you for saying that. Duke and I are fine now, but it took us a long time to get here."

"If you can get through that, maybe the two of you *are* meant to be."

"We are. It's destined." She began eating again. "Speaking of couples who are meant to be, why are you still single?"

He chuckled. "Trust me, it's by choice! Honestly, I move around so much that it's hard to settle down long enough to establish a real connection with anyone."

"Don't you get lonely?"

"Sure, who doesn't? I didn't say I don't date or spend time with women, Angel. I just said I haven't found the one I want to marry."

"Have you ever come close?"

"To let a couple of ex-girlfriends tell it, I have," he answered with a sly grin. "But truth be told, I haven't found the woman who makes my heart go pitter-patter."

"You can't if you never put yourself out there."

Channing paused. "Isn't this the pot calling the kettle black?"

"How so?" she balked.

"You haven't been serious about anyone either, have you? Aside from Duke, I mean."

"That's different," stammered Angel. "I've been busy with work and my other obligations."

"So have I."

"And I didn't want to start a relationship I knew I couldn't finish. Deep down, I've always known that I was still in love with Duke. It wouldn't have been fair to the next man."

"I think the one you've been unfair to is you. You've never opened yourself up to the possibility of loving someone else."

Angel was quiet. "I guess I didn't."

"All's well that ends well, right? You and Duke are together now, you have the family you've always wanted, and you've never been happier." He stopped and looked up at her. "You *are* happy, aren't you?"

"Yes . . . very."

"Then that's all that matters."

Angel wondered how true that was. "So when do you take off for the VA hospital in North Carolina?"

"In a week. Leaving will be harder than I thought. I've loved spending time with the girls and hanging out with Duke. I've also thoroughly enjoyed getting to know you better."

"Same here," she admitted. "It's too bad you don't come around more often."

"I'll be back for the wedding. Hopefully, by then, I'll be all stitched up and ready to go back out into the world."

"Duke said once you're medically discharged, you can't reenlist. What are you going to do with the rest of your life?"

"Get a job, I guess, maybe go back to school. The military is the only thing I've done since I graduated high school. It's kind of scary to imagine doing anything else."

"Just pray and ask God to place you where He can use you the most," Angel suggested.

"Is prayer your answer to everything?"

"Pretty much."

"Is that what you did before accepting Duke's proposal?"

She wriggled in her seat. "Of course."

"What about before moving in with him? Doesn't the Bible tell you not to do that?"

Angel sighed. "That part is complicated."

"No, it's not. Either the Bible says you can or you can't. Or are you one of those Christians who twist the Word to make it fit whatever you want it to?"

"Channing, I'm not like that," decried Angel.

"You don't have to convince me. Personally, I think you're far more interesting when you're not hiding behind that cloak of religion."

"I don't want you to get the wrong idea, though. I'm very sincere about my walk with the Lord."

"I'm sure you are, but clearly you're not above indulging in a few sinful acts here and there either."

"Duke and I were married. In the eyes of God, we were never really divorced."

He laughed. "Whatever gets you through the night, Angel."

"The Lord does."

"Yes, the Lord does, and, apparently, a few other things too."

"I know it's wrong for me to be living with Duke, and we aren't married, but it's just for six months. Primarily, it's to help him out with the kids."

Channing agreed. "It's clear how much they rely on you. I just hope they appreciate you."

"They do. Duke lets me know how much he loves and appreciates me every day too."

Channing grunted with disapproval. "You weren't there last night."

"So?"

"So you didn't hear him going on about Reese with her parents and the kids. I don't think he's completely gotten over her."

"I know he hasn't," acknowledged Angel. "I still grieve over her too, but we're all ready to go to the next phase in our lives."

"I don't know if you're incredibly strong or . . ." He dropped his head.

"Or what?" demanded Angel.

"Incredibly stupid."

Fuming, Angel sprung from her chair. Channing caught her by the arm before she bolted off. "Why do you put up with that?"

She rolled her eyes and snatched her arm out of his grip. "Put up with what—you?"

"No, put up with the way they treat you around here."

"I love them, Channing. I've loved Duke my whole adult life, and I've loved those girls from the second I met them. They're my family."

"I get that. I love my cousin and his kids too, but if it were me, I don't think I could do it."

"It's a good thing you're not me, isn't it?"

"Look, I'm not trying to stir up trouble. I know my cousin loves you, and, obviously, you love him too. I'd just hate to see you get hurt again or taken for granted."

"Duke is committed to me. He loves me," she reiterated.

"Nobody's saying he doesn't, but does he treasure you? Does he make you feel like the most beautiful woman in the world? Like you're the only thing that matters to him?"

Angel fought back the word no. "We'll get there. It'll just take some time."

"The question is *how much time*." Channing reached out for her hand. "You're an incredible woman, Angel. You need a man who appreciates you."

"Like who? You?"

Channing eased away. "No, but someone who can. I'm not sure if my cousin is ready. I know he's a king and all, but at some point, he's got to recognize you for the queen you are."

Chapter 22

**"A few lunches and maybe a lap dance
here and there is not exactly dating."**
—*Lawson Kerry Banks*

"Thank you so much for taking Namon to the doctor for me at the last minute. I really appreciate it," said Lawson after meeting up with Mark following Namon's appointment.

Mark offered her a seat on his couch. "Lawson, he's my son. You don't have to thank me for doing my job."

"I'm just used to having to do everything on my own where Namon is concerned. Old habits die hard."

"You're not alone anymore, and I don't want you apologizing for leaning on me. I love him, and I'm happy to do it. I'm just as much vested in this parenting thing as you are."

Lawson smiled. "You've really surprised me, Mark. You've turned out to be an excellent father to our son. I know that you don't want me to say I'm grateful, but I am. You could've very easily looked the other way when I told you about Namon, but you didn't. You stepped up and forged a relationship with your son despite all my interference and resistance. You did the right thing. I shouldn't have tried to keep you apart."

"Water under the bridge now," he said. "Besides, I know where you were coming from. You didn't know me or what my intentions were. You were just trying to protect your son. Any good mother would do the same."

Lawson nodded. "I want to thank you for what you're doing for Reggie too."

Mark squinted his eyes. "What did I do for Reggie?"

"You know . . . spending time with her and trying to be sort of the big brother she never had. The breakup with Jody was really hard on her. I think it's great that you reached out to her. Lord knows I can't get through that thick skull of hers! You're a good influence and a nice contrast to those losers at the club."

"Thanks, but I don't mind at all. Yeah, she's a little misguided at times, but I think Reggie is a great person."

Lawson nodded slowly. "I would just be cautious if I were you. I mean, Reggie's young, and she may start to read more into the situation than there is."

Mark rose slowly. "I don't think that's what's happening, Lawson."

"Of course, *you* don't, but I see the way she looks whenever your name comes up. I believe my sister may have a little crush on you," cautioned Lawson with a wink.

"You talk about her like she's Namon's age. Reggie's a grown woman."

"A grown woman with stars in her eyes," she pointed out. "It doesn't take her long to form attachments, including unhealthy ones. I just don't want her to get hurt again. She's had enough disappointment when it comes to men."

"I understand your concern. It's sweet, really, but no need to worry. Your sister and I have it all under control."

"Mark, come on. You have to admit that it's not a good idea to lead her on. Sure, it may be flattering to have a beautiful young girl hanging on to your every word, but that's my baby sister. You can't play her like you do these other women."

"I have no intentions of hurting Reggie. Heck, I hope she has none of hurting me."

Lawson was thrown. "Why would you be the one to get hurt in all of this?"

"Lawson . . . I'm not playing games with your sister. I honestly dig her. She's smart, talented, beautiful, and the fact that she can do a Chinese split doesn't hurt at all!" he added with a chuckle.

Lawson stood up with her hands on her hips. "Will you stop playing around? This is serious."

"So am I. Reggie and I are . . ."

"Are what? Sleeping together?" she assumed.

"No, we're dating."

Lawson crossed her arms. "A few lunches and maybe a lap dance here and there is not exactly dating, Mark."

"It's more than that. When I say we're dating, I mean we're *dating*."

She wrinkled her nose. "So is she your girlfriend or something?"

"We haven't put labels on it yet, but she's the only woman I'm seeing right now."

"Mark, you can't date my baby sister!" spewed Lawson.

"Why not?"

"You just can't!" replied Lawson, arms flailing. "She's Namon's aunt, and she's almost ten years younger than you. Not to mention—"

"Not to mention what?"

"Not to mention that you and I slept together! We have a child, Mark. Look, I know she's pretty and flirtatious and all that, but there are just some things you don't do."

Mark tried to calm her down. "I appreciate the concern, Lawson, but Reggie and I are two consenting adults. We can date or do whatever we want. I don't care if she is your sister, it's not your call. As far as you and I are concerned, it was just a one-night stand, as you have pointed out to me several times. Yeah, we got a son out of it, but it's not like we were in love or anything. We didn't even date."

Lawson's ego took a direct hit. "If it was all so casual, why did you propose to me last year?"

"I thought it was the only way Namon could be a part of my life, but we both know that wasn't about love. I was trying to do right by my kid."

"Mark, don't act like it was *all* platonic *all* the time."

"It was platonic enough. We didn't do anything I'm ashamed to tell Reggie or Garrett or even Namon, for that matter."

"I just don't know why out of all the women in the world you had to pick the one who's my sister."

"Lawson, you said yourself that the woman I've been looking for could be just around the corner. As fate would have it, she was."

"How do you intend to explain this to our son?"

"Like I would any other woman I was serious about," he remarked. "Why is this bothering you so much?"

Lawson was flustered. "I don't know," she admitted. "It just does."

Lawson knew the reason, but she'd never admit it to anyone; she barely admitted it to herself. The truth was that she had gotten used to having Mark to herself and couldn't stand the thought of having to share him, *especially* with her sister.

Chapter 23

"You're my husband and my best friend. I thought I could tell you anything."
—*Lawson Kerry Banks*

Garrett came into the kitchen to grab something to drink. He found Lawson hunched over a mountain of books and paperwork.

"I guess I don't have to ask how you'll be spending the rest of the night," he grumbled.

She didn't look up. "No, you don't. All this stuff is due first thing in the morning."

"Can I do anything to help?"

"That depends." Lawson put down her pen. "What do you know about the War of 1812?"

"That it was fought in 1812," he quipped.

The joke irritated her, and Lawson continued to work.

"It's okay to smile, you know." Garrett rubbed her shoulders. "You're so uptight. I think you need me to put my special touch on you."

Lawson shirked away from him. "Could you *not* do that right now?"

"Do what—touch my wife?"

"No, *irritate* your wife," she snapped.

Garrett was taken aback. "So I irritate you now?"

Lawson exhaled and kissed his hand. "I'm sorry, baby. It's not you, it's work and grad school and Namon and Mark and Reggie. . . ."

"Mark and Reggie?" Garrett stepped away from her. "What do they have to do with it?"

"Nothing," huffed Lawson. "Let's talk about something else, *anything* else."

"I think we need to talk about *this*. You've been on edge all week, and from the way you're acting, I'm guessing it has something to do with your sister and new boyfriend."

"It has nothing to do with them as a couple," she lied and swept her hair behind her ears. "I'm just under a lot of pressure right now."

"No more than usual. In fact, you were handling things fine before Mark started seeing your sister."

"Can you blame me?" Lawson exclaimed. "It's not *exactly* an ideal situation."

Garrett leaned against the refrigerator. "That depends on how you look at it. I mean, for the longest, you've wanted Reggie to find a good man. While I'm not Mark's biggest fan, I do know that he's a stand-up guy. I realize your sister dating your baby's daddy may be a little taboo, but, hey, who are we to stand in the way of true love?"

"I'm sure it's more like *true lust* between those two," grumbled Lawson.

"Then there's even less for you to worry about. Let them do their thing." He wrapped his arms around Lawson. "And speaking of lust . . ."

"The Bible is very clear," argued Lawson, thwarting his advances. "No one is to approach any close relative to have sexual relations."

"What about approaching my sexy wife for sexual relations?" Lawson crossed her arms and pouted. "Look, babe, all you can do is tell 'em. They're both adults, and they're going to do exactly what they want to do. Hopefully, you'll let me do exactly what *I* want to do as well."

Lawson broke away from him. "Will you get off me? I'm trying to have a conversation with you, and all you can think about is getting in my pants!"

Garrett threw up his hands and backed away. Lawson tried to reach for him, but he moved out of her grasp.

"Honey, I'm sorry. I didn't mean it like that."

"No, I think you said exactly what you meant. What I don't understand is why this is bothering you so much. You have a man. Why does it matter to you who your ex is sleeping with?"

"It doesn't, not in the way you're suggesting. This isn't even about Mark. It's about my sister and her incessant need to make bad choices."

"Maybe you should worry less about Reggie's choices and more about your own," Garrett replied.

"What's that supposed to mean?"

"Lawson, I love you, but I'm not going to stand here and listen to you whine about your old boyfriend and his new girlfriend. Do you know how disrespectful and insulting that is to me?"

"I'm not trying to disrespect you, Garrett. I'm telling you because you're my husband and my best friend. I thought I could tell you anything."

"Then tell me this—do you want to be with Mark?"

"If I wanted to be with Mark, I'd be with Mark," she fired back. "But I love *you*. I married *you*."

"Yeah, that's what your lips say, your actions say something totally different, though."

"You're missing the point, Garrett." She gave up and slammed shut the textbook. "You know what?—I don't even know how the conversation even got here. Let's just go to bed and call it a night."

Garrett shook his head. "Nah, you go. I think I'm going to go out back to shoot some hoops to clear my head."

"You were itching to go to bed five minutes ago."
Garrett looked her squarely in the eyes. "You'd be
surprised how much can change in five minutes."

Chapter 24

"So you're going to let a man come between us?"
—Lawson Kerry Banks

"Wow . . . Now *that's* what I call a tree!" declared Angel, admiring their handiwork after helping Kina decorate the church's Christmas tree in the vestibule.

Kina stood back and looked. "Yes, it's beautiful. I hope the pastor likes it."

"I can't imagine why he wouldn't. He likes everything else you've done around here," revealed Sullivan.

Kina was pleased. "Your husband is a great boss, and this is such a wonderful place to work."

"Oh my God!" shrieked Reginell, staring down at her phone.

Lawson looked up. "What?"

"Someone just sent me a text," she answered with hesitation, as if she was trying to get her thoughts together.

"It's called text messaging. Welcome to the nineties," Sullivan replied sarcastically.

Kina looked over Reginell's shoulder. "What does it say? Who's it from?"

"It's from Mark." Reginell held up her phone. "He said he loves me. That's the first time he's ever said it."

"Aww, Reggie, that's so sweet!" gushed Kina.

"Is it?" Sullivan frowned. "He didn't even have the guts to tell her in person."

Reginell slowly broke into a smile. "You, guys, *Mark loves me!*" she squealed.

Lawson grabbed the phone out of Reginell's hand and read it for herself. "Apparently so." She handed the phone back. "Maybe he meant agape love, you know, that whole Christian brother-sister love."

"I don't think so," said Angel. "Just look at that Kool-Aid smile on her face!"

"Are you going to say it back?" asked Kina.

Reginell exhaled, still beaming. "I don't know."

Angel set a box of unused ornaments down next to Reginell. "Well, do you love him?"

"I don't know." Reginell lifted her eyes. "I think so."

Lawson eased in between them. "Wait a minute! Reggie, you are *not* in love with Mark. The two of you have only been out a few times."

Reginell cut her eyes at Lawson. "That doesn't have anything to do with how we feel about each other." She turned to Sullivan, Angel, and Kina for support. "Should I text him back? No, I think I should call him, don't you?"

"I think you and Mark need to stop this nonsense!" advised Lawson. "The two of you are no more in love than Kina and Joan."

Reginell stepped to her sister. "What is your problem with Mark and me? Why are you hatin'? You don't think I'm good enough for him or something?"

"That's ridiculous, Reggie. You're my flesh and blood. If anything, I don't think anybody is good enough for *you!*"

"So what's going on, Lawson?" asked Angel. "Are there some lingering feelings between you and Mark?"

Lawson exhaled. "No, it's just . . ."

"What?" pumped Reginell.

"I get it," piped in Sullivan. "You don't want your sister sloppin' up your leftovers like some beggar."

Lawson shook her head. "It's not even that. It's . . ."

"Just say it, sweetie," coaxed Angel.

"It's not that I want Mark because I don't," explained Lawson. "I love my husband. He's the only man that I want."

Reginell put her hands on her hips. "Then what is it?"

"I hate that Mark . . ." She took a deep breath. "I hate that he wants *you*, all right?" she said at last. "Where was this kind, sensitive, caring guy when *I* needed him? When I was drowning, trying to raise our son by myself, where was he then?"

"Lawson, he didn't know," Kina reminded her.

"I know that. All those years I was raising my son alone, I convinced myself that Mark was this jerk that Namon and I were better off without, but he's not. Mark has turned out to be a really good guy and—"

"Do you know how selfish and crazy you sound right now?" charged Reginell.

Lawson was convicted. "Yes. I want you to be happy, Reggie. I do. I want you to find a good man and get married and have babies . . . just not with him."

Kina wrapped her arm around Lawson. "It's okay, honey."

"No, it's not!" screeched Reginell. "Why are you even worried about Mark and me? You have a husband, and you have a good life. All I want is a little piece of happiness for myself, and it sucks that my sister—my best friend—can't support me!"

"Reggie, I would be supportive if it was anybody else, you know that!"

"But it *is* him. Mark is the one I want."

Lawson appealed to her sister's sensitive side. "Even if it hurts me?"

"This ain't about you, Lawson! Mark doesn't want you. He wants me. You have Garrett, who loves you. He loves you so much that he's practically begging you to give him a baby, but you're here trying to break up my relationship. What you need to do is focus on your own man before you lose him too."

Kina moved in between Lawson and Reginell. "Okay, let's just settle down and fall back for a minute."

"No," insisted Reginell. "I'm not backing down because Lawson is too stouthearted and jealous to be happy for me. I'm not giving up Mark either."

"Well, I, for one, can see where Lawson is coming from," spoke up Sullivan. "This is some Jerry Springer, trailer-park mess! How are you going to date your sister's baby's daddy, Reggie? What's Namon supposed to call you now—Aunt Stepmother? It's confusing to me as an adult. What's a kid to think?"

"I could see if Mark and Lawson had some long, beautiful romance, and I came in and stole her man, but it's not like that," said Reginell. "They had a one-night stand, and she got knocked up. It's no different from—"

"What you do every day?" supplied Sullivan.

"It's no different from what *people* do every day! Lawson, you just need to live your life and let me live mine. How many times do I have to remind you that you're not my mama?"

"I'm not trying to be. Look, you asked me to be honest and tell the truth. I did that. Don't get mad with me if you don't like the answer. Some people just can't handle the truth."

"No, Lawson, *you're* the one who can't handle the truth, which is that Mark chose me. You can either deal with it or get dealt with."

"There's no need to make threats, Reggie," cautioned Kina.

"Believe me, y'all ain't seen nothing yet, but you will, Lawson, if you don't back off."

Lawson stood aghast. "So you're going to let a man come between us? Your very own sister?"

"No, *you* are!" Reginell stormed off, slamming the door behind her.

Angel rubbed Lawson's back. "Do you want me to go after her?"

Lawson sighed. "If you think you can talk some sense into her."

"Or *knock* some into her," added Sullivan as Angel raced to catch up with Reginell. Sullivan turned to Lawson. "Are you all right?"

Lawson rubbed her forehead. "I don't want to lie. We're in church."

Sullivan laughed a little. "I want you to know I understand."

"You do?" Lawson was grateful for the empathy.

"Yeah, I know this sounds a little selfish and shallow . . ."

"Selfish and shallow is what you do best, Sully," teased Lawson.

Sullivan playfully elbowed her. "Like I was saying, it sounds selfish, but once mine, always mine! Even if I don't want a guy, that doesn't mean anyone else can have him either, especially not someone I'm close to."

"I don't know if I should be relieved or ashamed. You just made me sound very egotistical and self-absorbed."

"Not egotistical . . . just a little territorial and with good reason! Mark isn't just someone you once dated. He's your son's father. The two of you will always be connected. If he and Reggie seriously hook up, it could get messy. What if they have kids? How would you explain that Namon is both their brother and their cousin? It's just too weird."

"But she's my sister, and he makes her happy," Lawson conceded. "Who am I to mess with that?"

"No one, if it was that simple, but it's not, and you both know it."

Lawson sighed. "I don't know, Sully. I hate feeling this way, not to mention what it's doing to my relationship with Reggie."

Sullivan bit her lip. "What is it doing to your relationship with Garrett?"

"Garrett and I are fine," she insisted.

"Honestly?"

"Yes, he knows Mark is no threat to him."

"Are you serious? Lawson, you slept with Mark, and you have a child together. Mark will always be a threat to Garrett."

"My husband isn't insecure like other men. We're solid, Sully. Trust me."

"If you say so . . . Just don't let Garrett see you get so worked up about Mark. I don't care how solid you think you are, no marriage is written in heaven, and even the most solid foundation can be destroyed by a single crack."

Chapter 25

"Did you say the doctor said you were sterile?"
—Sullivan Webb

Sullivan studied the calendar. It had been almost six weeks since her encounter with Vaughn, and her period was officially five days late. She didn't want to get her hopes up too high. It had been late before. Unlike the previous times, however, this time was a welcome surprise. The only dilemma would be pinpointing the exact date she conceived. Not that it mattered, though. For all intents and purposes, any child that came out of her body would only know Charles Webb as its father.

Charles dragged into house looking downtrodden and defeated. "Hey, honey." He gave Sullivan a peck on the lips.

"You look sad, but I think I have news that will cheer you up."

Charles sighed and sank down onto the sofa. "My spirits certainly could use a lift."

Sullivan rushed to his side, laying a hand on his shoulder. "What's wrong, honey? What's going on?"

He reached for her hand. "My doctor called with my test results from my physical a couple of weeks ago."

Sullivan covered her mouth with her free hand and braced for the worst. "Charles, please don't tell me it's cancer."

Charles patted her hand and chuckled a little. "No, nothing like that, sweetheart."

She exhaled, relieved. "So what did he say? Does he want you to lose some weight, start working out more?"

"Yes. My cholesterol and blood pressure are a little higher than he'd like it to be, and he's worried about atherosclerosis."

"My God!" gasped Sullivan. "What's that?"

"It's buildup of plaque in the artery walls. Sometimes it can lead to a heart attack or a stroke, but that's not what concerns me."

"Well, that's what concerns *me!*" exclaimed Sullivan. "I keep telling you those hens at the church aren't doing you any favors by cooking all that fried, lard-infested soul food." Charles didn't say anything. "What's the matter, honey? What aren't you telling me?"

He took a deep breath and looked Sullivan in the eyes. "The doctor says I might not be able to have children, Sullivan. He says most of my sperm aren't active and haven't been for a long time."

Sullivan froze, the air and life seemingly sucked out of her. She began trembling. "Did you say the doctor said you were sterile?" She had to make sure she'd heard him correctly.

"Well, not completely sterile, but it's definitely what the doctors consider to be a low sperm count. Without some intervention, there's a very slim chance of you getting pregnant the old-fashioned way."

"Wa-wa-wait, Charles," she stuttered, clutching her chest. "Doctors can be wrong. Those tests can be wrong!"

Charles shook his head. "He ran the test twice, honey."

"It's a mistake!" denounced Sullivan. "There's got to be some kind of mix-up or something!"

She began panting. Thoughts began racing through her mind. She'd slept with Vaughn. She didn't use any birth control, and now her period was late. She was prepared for the letdown of not being pregnant. She was even prepared for a possible miscarriage or a stillbirth. Being pregnant with no possible way to pass Charles off as the child's father was the one scenario she hadn't considered.

Charles folded Sullivan into his arms. "I know you're disappointed, sweetheart, but there's still hope. I'm already taking steps to remedy the problem."

"How?" she wailed.

"Well, the doctor's got me started on these fertility pills to increase my sperm count. That alone will increase our chances by about 25 percent. But, Sullivan, there are so many children out there who need homes and two parents to love them. Maybe God wants us to take in and love one of those children instead of trying to make some of our own."

Tears sprang to her eyes. "How could this happen?" Sullivan wondered aloud. "Is this some kind of sick joke?"

"I'm just as disappointed as you are," said Charles and released her. "But the Lord knows His plans for us. He's always right. Don't ever question that. We have to trust Him."

"Charles, I want you to get that doctor on the phone. No—we need a different doctor. We need a second opinion." She began rummaging through the room looking for a telephone directory. She found one inside the ottoman. "That test can't be right. It just can't be!"

Charles took the phone book out of her hands. "Another test is not the answer, sweetheart." He felt her hands. "You're trembling, Sullivan. What's wrong?"

Sullivan swooned, falling back a little. "All of sudden, I don't feel so good." Charles caught her, and she leaned on her husband for support.

"Come over here and sit down." He walked her back to the sofa. "Take it easy."

Sullivan tried to breathe normally. Then she felt bile rising in her throat. She muttered, "I think I'm going to be sick . . ." before vomiting all over their sofa and coffee table.

Charles held her hair back while she hacked up everything she'd eaten that day. "Did that make you feel a little better?"

Sullivan sat up and nodded. "A little bit."

"I'm sorry, Sullivan. I didn't mean to upset you this much."

"It's fine," she croaked. "I just need to clean all this up, brush my teeth, and jump in the shower."

"Baby, you go on upstairs and take care of yourself. You need to go lie down. I'll clean this up and come check on you in a few minutes."

"Okay, thank you." Sullivan stepped over the mess and made her way upstairs to her bathroom.

"It's just stress," she told herself to calm down. "That's all it is." Stress, virus, terminal illness—anything would've been preferable to the reality that she might actually be pregnant with a baby no one would ever believe was her husband's.

Chapter 26

"Friends support each other; they're there for each other. And when necessary, they lie and cover up the truth about paternity for each other!"
—Sullivan Webb

"See, it's like I told you on the phone," Charles explained to Lawson as they watched Sullivan swaddled in their bed, crying softly. "She won't talk; she barely eats; and she won't get out of bed."

Lawson touched Sullivan's shoulder. "Sullivan, are you all right?" Sullivan didn't respond.

Charles sighed. "She's been like this for the past two days, ever since we got that doctor's report."

Lawson swung around, alarmed. "What doctor's report?"

"Oh, I thought she told you." Charles seemed a little embarrassed. "I'll spare you all the details. Suffice it to say that it's not going to be as easy to conceive as we'd hoped."

Lawson's heart went out to him. "I'm so sorry, Charles."

"I'm still praying for a miracle, nothing is too hard for God. It was a major setback to Sullivan, though. She had her heart set on being pregnant by Christmas."

"Is it okay for me to have a few minutes alone with her?"

"Of course. I actually have to get over to the church, but I didn't want to leave her alone. If you could sit with her for a little while, I would certainly appreciate it."

"Okay, you go do what you need to do. I'll keep an eye on Sully."

"Thank you, sister." Charles leaned down and kissed Sullivan on the forehead. "I'll be back in a couple of hours, sweetheart."

Lawson listened for the door to close behind Charles before saying anything. "Okay, Charles is gone, so you can stop the drama queen act. What's going on, Sully? What's this all about, other than a pathetic attempt to get some attention?"

"It's over," sobbed Sullivan. "It's all over."

"What is—this charade?"

"My life, my marriage," she groaned.

"Is this about the baby? Sully, Charles isn't going to leave you if you don't have a child. If he was going to leave you, it would've been because you slept with Vaughn."

This made Sullivan bawl harder.

Lawson sat down next to her. "What in the world is wrong with you? Do I need to call in the troops?"

Sullivan sat up and wiped her eyes. "No, don't call them, especially not your stupid sister."

"If you want any sympathy from me, you'll need to refrain from calling my sister stupid."

"Well, she is, Lawson!"

Lawson rose from the bed. "Okay, I'm going to leave now that I see what this little stunt of yours was all about. I strongly suggest you find more productive uses for your time, Sully. You might want to consider getting a job."

Sullivan shooed her away. "Go on, leave! Walk out like everybody else!" she cried.

Lawson rolled her eyes. "You know these hysterics only work on Charles, right?"

"You would be knocking on hysteria's door too, if you knew . . ." Sullivan buried her face in the pillow.

"Knew what? That you and Charles may have to adopt? Look at it this way—at least you wouldn't ruin your stick figure with pregnancy pounds. If you don't like that option, you could exercise your faith and wait for God to bless you and Charles with a child of your own."

Sullivan propped her head up. "When have you ever known me to wait on God or anyone else to make things happen?"

"That's the part that frightens me." Lawson reached for her phone after hearing it vibrate. "It's Angel." She answered the phone. "Hello?"

"Did you and Sully forget that you're supposed to be meeting Kina and me for lunch? We've been waiting thirty minutes!" barked Angel through the other end of the phone.

Lawson slapped her hand over her forehead. "I'm sorry. I totally forgot; I'm sure Sullivan did too. I'm at her place right now. You two may want to come over. She's in the middle of another meltdown. I haven't quite gotten to the bottom of it, other than knowing it has to do with Charles and the baby."

"Is she pregnant?"

"Why don't you two just swing by, and we'll let the first lady explain it for herself."

Minutes later, with Kina in tow, Angel pulled her car up to Sullivan's gated entrance. Lawson let them both in and led them to Sullivan's bedroom.

Angel squeezed Sullivan's hand. "Sully, Lawson told us the doctor's report about Charles. I'm so sad to hear that."

"There's still a chance you could get pregnant," Kina reminded her. "Plus, there are so many children just waiting for a couple like you and Charles to adopt them."

"It may already be too late for that," disclosed Sullivan.

"Why, because of the application and waiting process?" asked Angel. "I know that sometimes adoptions take years, but if you go ahead and get on some lists now or start looking into foster care—"

Sullivan stopped her. "It may be too late for me to worry about getting pregnant because . . . I may already be pregnant."

"Oh my God, really?" exclaimed Angel. "Sullivan, you should be praising the Lord! That's wonderful news."

Lawson was bewildered. "Sully, if that's the case, then what have the long face and the tear faucets been about? Are you afraid something could be wrong with the baby and don't want to get your hopes up?"

"No, I'm praying to God that I'm not pregnant at all!"

Angel squinted her eyes, confused. "What? Five minutes ago, you wanted a baby with Charles and now you don't?"

"Yes, I want a baby *with Charles*, and no one else," stated Sullivan.

Lawson shook her head. "Sweetie, you're talking in circles. One minute, you want a baby, the next you don't. Now you want a baby with Charles, but you're praying that you're not pregnant. Just come out and say whatever it is you're trying to tell us."

Sullivan moaned. "You know that scripture that says, 'Confess your sins to each other and pray for each other so that you may be healed?'" asked Sullivan.

"Yes, that's somewhere in James, I think," answered Angel.

Sullivan threw up her hands in capitulation. "Well, I'm confessin', and you heifers better get to prayin'!"

Lawson dropped her head. "How did I know another one of your deathbed confessions was coming next? To be honest, I don't even want to know all the dirty details. Just tell me which side it falls on, illegal or immoral?"

"Lawson, don't be mean," admonished Kina. "Let Sullivan get whatever this is off her chest. Remember, the Bible says we are called to bear one another's burdens. It shouldn't matter that Sullivan makes us bear more burdens in a week than most people do in a lifetime."

Sullivan smacked her teeth. "Kina, I'm really too stressed out right now to try to figure out whether you're trying to insult me. All I know is what I'm about to say may be a little bit shocking and my methods slightly unorthodox, but remember that everything was done with the best intentions."

Angel closed her eyes. "Sullivan, just so we can be prepared, on a scale of one to ten, how bad is it?"

Sullivan thought for a moment. "Possibly an eleven." They all groaned and grimaced. "Hear me out before you make those judgmental faces, all right?"

"I probably need to sit down for this," said Angel, scooting in next to Sullivan.

"What exactly did you do?" grilled Kina.

"Well, I was ovulating. As you know from being a nurse, Angel, there was a very small window for me to conceive if I wanted to get pregnant within that month."

Angel nodded. "Okay, so what's your point?"

"With Charles being knee-deep in paperwork, he hasn't exactly been in an amorous mood when I need him to be, so I helped the situation out," Sullivan took in a deep breath, "by going to my local sperm bank."

"Jesus Christ!" sputtered Lawson. "Please don't tell us that you had yourself artificially inseminated!"

Sullivan chewed on her nails. "Well, it wasn't exactly artificial . . . and it wasn't actually a sperm bank."

"This just keeps getting worse by the second," uttered Angel.

Lawson shook her head. "Sullivan, please explain what you mean by, 'wasn't actually a sperm bank' and 'wasn't exactly artificial' because it almost sounds like . . . I can't even say it. The thought is just too crazy, and I know you would never do anything that reckless and stupid."

Angel gestured her hands toward Sullivan. "Lawson, look who we're talking about here! Reckless is a way of life for her."

"Angel, don't talk like I'm not in the room," snapped Sullivan. "I'm upset enough as it is."

Angel exhaled. "Okay, Sully, you're right. We just really need to hear you say that you had yourself inseminated with Charles's sperm. As sick as that it, it's a lot better than the alternative."

"Which is what?" demanded Sullivan.

"*You being inseminated with someone else's sperm!*" answered Lawson.

Sullivan silently looked away, fiddling with the tassels on one of her decorative pillows.

Angel studied Sullivan's body language. "Oh no! Whenever she's quiet and fidgety, that means she's either plotting or she's guilty."

"Stop being ridiculous!" retorted Kina. "Sullivan would never do anything like that, would you, Sully? She loves Charles too much, and she would never hurt him that way. Go on, Sullivan, tell them."

"If you'd stop and look at this thing from my point of view, you'd see that I did it *for* Charles," rationalized Sullivan.

"So, it's true," concluded Lawson. "You could possibly be carrying another man's baby."

"Sullivan, no . . ." The disappointment registered on Kina's face. "How could you do that to Charles?"

"I didn't do anything *to* Charles. I did it *for* him!" she insisted.

"No, you did this for *you*, Sullivan!" argued Lawson, pointing her finger at Sullivan. "I don't even know what to say to you right now."

"It would absolutely crush Charles to find out," said Kina. "It would more than crush him, it would kill him."

"Don't you think I know that, Kina? I wasn't thinking about the magnitude of what I'd done. That's why I've spent the last two days praying I'm not pregnant and hoping at least one of Charles's convalescent sperm was able to beat all odds and make it to my eggs before Vaughn's did."

"*Vaughn!*" spewed Lawson. "*You slept with Vaughn of all people?*"

"How long having you been sleeping with him again or did you never end the affair in the first place?" questioned Angel.

"It was one time, I swear." Sullivan raised her hand as if taking an oath. "Yes, I admit I didn't think the whole plan through."

Lawson clasped her hands together. "What in God's name was the plan, Sullivan?"

"It was just some insurance," detailed Sullivan. "I was desperate, and I knew that Vaughn was moving away and taking all of that untapped sperm with him. It was a shot in the dark, just an added measure to ensure I got pregnant."

"As ridiculous as this plan of yours sounds, you knew there would always be a chance that it would be Vaughn's baby," said Angel.

"Biologically, yes, but he was simply a surrogate. It would be Charles and my baby in every way that mattered." She sighed. "Of course, now that we know he's practically sterile . . ."

"It'll be a lot harder to pass off this bundle of joy as Charles's," summed up Lawson. Sullivan nodded her head in agreement.

Kina broke her silence. "Sullivan, I don't think I've ever been this disappointed in you—in anybody! I mean it. This is as low as it gets."

"Hopefully, this whole debacle never has to be brought to light," implied Lawson. "She might not even be pregnant."

"Have you been feeling any different? Any nausea or tiredness? Have you missed a period?" interrogated Angel.

"I threw up when Charles told me what the doctor said, but that was brought on by the shock of it all. I'm a few days late, but that happens from time to time."

"There's only one way to be sure," said Lawson. "You've got to take a pregnancy test."

Angel shook her head. "This is too big to chance like that. Sullivan, you need to go see your doctor. If he does an ultrasound, he may be able to pinpoint the conception date by the size of the baby."

"I can't go to my doctor," Sullivan objected. "He's a member of the church."

Lawson massaged her temples. "This is such a nightmare."

Angel hopped off the bed. "Let me make some phone calls. I may be able to get you in somewhere." She walked out into the hallway as she scrolled through the contacts on her cell phone.

"Kina, you're being awfully quiet," noted Lawson.

"I just . . . I don't know what to say. I mean, Sully, you're my friend, but Charles is my pastor and my boss. How am I supposed to keep something like this from him?"

"You'll find a way," commanded Sullivan. "Charles can't know anything about this, Kina. My marriage would be over, and you know it."

"How can you knowingly let him raise another man's baby?" questioned Kina.

Sullivan flung back her comforter. "First off, we don't know that I'm pregnant. Second, if I am, we don't know for sure it's Vaughn's child. Furthermore, this is between my husband and me. It's not up to you to say anything."

Kina crossed her arms in front of her. "What about my duty as a Christian?"

"What about your duty as one of my best friends?" shot back Sullivan.

Lawson interceded. "Kina, we can sort all of that out later. The first thing we need to do is find out if Sullivan is really pregnant."

Angel reentered the bedroom. "Okay, I called an OB friend of mine. Sullivan, she can see you if you come within the next thirty minutes."

"She's not anyone from the church, is she?" inquired Sullivan.

Angel helped Sullivan out of bed. "No, your secret will be safe, at least for now."

Lawson tossed Sullivan some clothes. "Why does it feel like we're aiding and abetting?"

"Are you going to have a moral crisis right now?" hissed Sullivan. "If so, we can leave you and your conscience here."

Lawson shook her head. "I'm already an accessory to the crime. I might as well see it through. It amazes me that I continue to let you talk me into getting involved with shenanigans only the Lord can get you out of!"

"Because that's what friends do!" insisted Sullivan. "Friends support each other, they're there for each other. And when necessary, they lie and cover up the truth about paternity for each other!"

"Congratulations, Mrs. Webb. You're pregnant!" announced the gynecologist after reviewing Sullivan's sonogram. "Based on the size and position of the baby, I'd say you're about six weeks along."

"Did you hear that, Sullivan?" asked Angel, grinning. "You're going to be a mommy!"

Sullivan sat on the doctor's examination table and tried to catch her breath. "Really? I'm, like, really pregnant for real?"

"Yes, you are. The first thing you're going to want to do is make an appointment with your regular OB-GYN. Your top priority right now needs to be making sure you and this baby stay healthy. Your doctor is going to run a series of tests to make sure everything is functioning the way it's supposed to. In the meantime, I can get you started on some prenatal vitamins, and you can start the countdown to your due date."

Sullivan smiled politely. "Um, Dr. Oyenugal, is it possible to tell exactly when the baby was conceived? Like pinpoint the exact date?"

"Seeing as how I wasn't there when it happened, it's kind of tough to give you specifics like that." Dr. Oyenugal looked down at her chart. "My best estimate is that you got pregnant around the twentieth."

Sullivan nodded. "Thank you, doctor."

"I'm going to let you get dressed while I check on those vitamins for you. Congratulations!" The doctor left Sullivan alone with Angel.

Angel moved to comfort her friend. "Are you okay?"

"Hand me my purse, will you?"

Angel passed it to her.

Sullivan scrolled through the calendar on her phone. "Okay, I had sex with Vaughn on the nineteenth, and with Charles the day before and two days afterward."

"You've been a busy girl!"

"I was on a mission." She blew out a breath and shook her head. "It doesn't matter. Either way, it's going to be Charles's baby." She rubbed her hand across her stomach. "You hear that, little one? You're going to make your daddy very happy, you know that?"

Angel chortled. "Which one?"

"The only one that matters!" snarled Sullivan.

"It's official," proclaimed Sullivan when she and Angel reunited with Kina and Lawson in the lobby of the doctor's office. "I'm pregnant!"

Lawson didn't make a move. "I'm not sure how we're supposed to react. Are we sad, are we happy . . ."

Sullivan gave her a reassuring smile. "We're happy, Lawson."

"So you're going to keep it, right?" double-checked Lawson before joining in Sullivan's enthusiasm.

"Of course, I am. I've seen the inside of an abortion clinic enough to last a lifetime," said Sullivan, lowering her voice. "I'm definitely keeping this baby."

"What if the baby is Vaughn's?" raised Kina.

"We will never speak that name again, all right?" issued Sullivan. "We'll never even *think* it! This baby is Charles's . . . It has to be."

"But what if it's not?" repeated Kina.

Sullivan huffed. "Did you hear what I just said? This is *Charles's* baby!"

"There's nothing wrong with speaking things that be not as if though they were," recited Lawson.

"I'm all for speaking things into existence," affirmed Kina, "but, Sullivan, you can't pretend like the chances of this baby being Vaughn's don't outweigh the chances of it being your husband's."

Sullivan rolled her eyes. "Miracles happen every day, or did you holy rollers forget that? God has the power—"

"Please don't put God in the middle of this foolishness," argued Kina. "God did not tell you to go out and sleep with Vaughn, and He certainly didn't tell you to try to pass the baby off as Charles's."

"Just shut up for a minute!" squawked Sullivan. "I can't think with you yammering in my ear like this!"

"Well, you better think fast, sister," Lawson warned her. "Timing is everything in this situation."

Sullivan copped an attitude. "You think I don't know that, Lawson? But I just found out that I was pregnant. Can I have a minute to think about that and be happy and thankful for this new life before you all desecrate it with your doom-and-gloom predictions?"

"You're right," granted Angel. "Regardless of how it happened, this is a very special moment for you, and I'm glad we're here to share it. Obviously, we're not thrilled about the child's conception, but if you're happy about this pregnancy, so are we."

"Thank you," said Sullivan. "That's all I wanted to hear."

Angel and Kina offered a lukewarm congratulation.

"Maybe we ought to pray for her," suggested Kina.

"Pray for what, that her sins not find her out?" posed Lawson.

Kina shrugged. "I don't know. We should pray for the baby if nothing else. This kid is going to need all the prayers she can get."

"Why, Kina? Because I'm its mother?"

"No, because you're pregnant, Sullivan! We've got to start thinking about and praying for this baby. Now is as good a time to start as any." Kina grabbed Sullivan's hand with Lawson and Angel reluctantly joining in. "Lord, we come to you full of praise and thanksgiving. We thank you that our sins are forgiven through the blood of Jesus. We come now thanking you for this child that Sullivan is carrying. While we don't know what the future holds, we know that you know the plans you have for us and the plans you have for this baby. You knew this child when she was stitched in her mother's womb. This baby may not have been conceived under the best circumstances, but, Lord, we know that you can take a mess and turn it into a masterpiece.

"Be with Sullivan as she goes through this pregnancy. Give her the wisdom to handle every situation, Lord. Supply all her needs and her child's needs, as you promised in your Word. Let her know that you hate the sin, but you love the sinner. Keep your hedge of protection around them. Lord, right now, we also come asking you to watch over her husband and our pastor. Give him the strength he needs. Give him a loving heart toward his wife and new family. Surround him with godly counselors. Bind and destroy all tricks of the devil designated to harm him. Help them to raise this child in love and in the knowledge of you. We declare the baby will be anointed and a soldier in your army. Let him or her be strong, healthy, and a blessing in the lives of everyone he or she touches. We believe that it's done. We claim it and thank you in advance. In Jesus' name I pray. Amen."

"Amen," echoed Lawson and Angel.

Sullivan was touched. "That was beautiful, Kina. Thank you. I appreciate you putting your personal feelings aside for this child and me."

"I won't hold the child accountable for the sins of the mother," resolved Kina.

Lawson exhaled. "I guess the real fun starts now. Are you going to tell your husband?"

Sullivan nodded. She seemed detached. "I am . . . but not tonight."

"Why not?"

"Because the baby . . ." Sullivan was unable to finish her thought. The severity of her situation came crashing down on her all at once. Her heart began to race, and she started to frantically search for her car keys. "I need to get out of here. I've got to think."

Angel instinctively reached out for her. "Sully, are you okay?"

Sullivan's eyes glassed over. "It feels like my heart is about to jump out of my chest. Oh my God, I can't breathe!" she panted and doubled over to keep from hyperventilating. "I can't breathe! What's happening to me?"

"You can breathe, Sullivan, you need to calm down," ordered Angel, rubbing her back. "Take deep breaths in and out very slowly."

"What's wrong with her, Angel?" Kina asked, concerned.

"She just panicked a little."

Lawson stooped down to be eye-level to Sullivan. "Are you okay?"

Sullivan inhaled and exhaled a few more times before pulling herself up. "I'm all right. I just had a moment there."

"I know you're feeling overwhelmed, but try to stay calm for your baby's sake," lectured Angel. "Everything you do affects that baby."

Sullivan shook her head and began crying again. "You were right, Kina. This is a mess. I don't know what I was so happy about."

"Don't listen to me, Sully," refuted Kina. "You have every right to love and be excited about your baby."

"Girl, you know you can count on us," Lawson assured her. "You've got three friends who'll stick closer to you than a brother."

"We've got your back," chimed in Angel.

"No matter how many times you lie on it," joked Lawson, forcing a laugh out of Sullivan.

"I appreciate it. Your support means the world to me." Sullivan recovered from crying. "I especially thank you for keeping this a secret, at least for now. I know I'm asking a lot, but I need time to figure out how I want to handle this."

Lawson hugged her. "It's not our secret to tell, honey. Be prayerful and trust God's direction."

"You ready to go home?" asked Angel, jingling the car keys.

"I can't go home," said Sullivan. "I'm not ready to face Charles yet."

"Where are you going?" inquired Kina.

Despite the prayers and support from her friends, Sullivan knew how dire the situation was. She needed help now, and there was only one person vile enough, manipulative enough, and heartless enough to understand what she did and why and how to get her out of this predicament.

Sullivan looked up. "I think it's time I paid a visit to my mother."

Chapter 27

"I hope this isn't good-bye forever."
—*Angel King*

Angel made her way down to Channing's room and lightly tapped the opened door. He was standing over his bed supported by his crutches, zipping a duffle bag.

When he looked up and saw her, his face lit up. "You tryin' sneak up on me? Did Duke send you to make sure I didn't steal any of the silver?" he joked.

She managed a faint smile. "I wasn't checking up on you, I promise. How's the leg this morning?"

He playfully nudged Angel in the arm. "It's fine. I'm a survivor, you know that."

"You're really leaving today, aren't you?" she asked, already knowing but dreading the answer.

He nodded. "My plane takes off in a couple of hours. A part of me was sort of relieved when you got called into work. I already knew I'd have a hard time saying good-bye. Seeing you makes it harder."

The look in her eyes let Channing know she felt the same way. "Are you ready to be a civilian again?" she asked him.

"Yeah, I'm kind of looking forward to it. I've even decided to go ahead and take advantage of the GI Bill and finish college."

"That's great, Channing. I'm really happy for you."

"If you're so happy, why do you look so grim? You look like you've lost your best friend."

"It almost feels that way," she admitted.

"Angel, I'm going to North Carolina, not to Mars," he said lightly.

"There's no chance of you moving back here after you recuperate?"

"I don't know. We'll just see how it goes."

Angel thought it over. "It's probably best that you don't. I really need to focus on planning this wedding and getting the girls acclimated to all of the changes. We'll be very busy for the next few months."

"That's good, and I'm sure that things will work out for you all. Please let the girls know that I'll be thinking about them, and I'll be sure to send them lots of presents if I'm not able to come back for birthdays and Christmas."

She nodded. "I just wish that you didn't have to go. I could really use some of your sound advice."

He touched her face. "You're stronger than you give yourself credit for, Angel."

Angel opened her mouth to speak but was interrupted by Duke knocking and opening the door. "Hey, you ready?" he asked cheerfully.

"In a minute," answered Channing.

Duke grabbed Channing's suitcases. "I'll take these down for you. I'll be outside when you're ready." He turned to Angel. "Babe, you coming with us to the airport?"

Angel shook her head. "I don't think so. I've got to get back to work."

Duke kissed her. "I'll see you after work then." He trotted out the door.

"I guess this is it." Angel exhaled and clasped her hands together.

"Guess so," he replied.

"I'm going to miss you," she whispered.

Channing swept her in his arms and held her tightly. "I'll miss you too. You take care, all right?"

"I will, and you call to let us know how you're doing and when you get there." She let go of him. "I hope this isn't good-bye forever."

"It's not." He looked at her, tempted to hold her again. "You be good, Angel."

"Always—I'm an angel, remember?"

They stared at each other, wanting to say more but not knowing what to say.

"I'll call you all when I land," he promised.

"Okay."

He hesitated before walking out. "Hey, Angel?"

"Yeah?"

He wrapped his arms around her, with her offering no resistance. Then he set his lips down on hers in a tender kiss. "Sorry . . . I've been wanting to do that since the second I laid eyes on you." He winked at her and walked out to meet Duke. Angel watched as he walked away until he was out of sight.

She sank onto his bed. Channing's scent still lingered there; his touch still lingered on her lips. It was as if she felt knotted to him somehow. She pushed the thought away from her head. Channing was gone. Now, she could put her focus back on where it should be: becoming Duke's wife.

"Aren't you coming to bed?"

"Not yet," answered Angel, staring into the computer screen. "I've got to finish this tonight if we're going to make payroll next week."

"Do what you have to do, babe." Duke turned over on his side, away from her. "I'm tired. I'm gonna go on to sleep."

Angel scrolled through her e-mails looking for a missing invoice. The last thing she expected to see was a message from Channing King. Seeing it made her heart stand still.

She glanced over at Duke to make sure he hadn't seen it. "You know what, honey? I think I'm going to take the laptop downstairs and finish this up. I don't want to disturb you." She closed the laptop and tucked it under her arm. Then she leaned down and kissed him.

"Don't be too long," grumbled Duke, already half-asleep.

"I won't."

Angel crept down the stairs and made her way to the living room. She plunked down on the sofa and popped open the laptop. With trembling hands, she opened the e-mail from Channing:

> Dear Angel,
> I tried not to write you. I tried not to miss your touch, your scent, your laugh, and your smile, but that's like trying not to take my next breath. Thinking about you has become the new constant in my life. I keep reminding myself that you don't belong to or with me. I know you love my cousin, but that doesn't stop me from wishing I was in his place.
> Yours truly,
> Channing

Angel must have read his e-mail twenty times before deciding to respond. Nothing she wrote quite sounded right, so she settled on a simple, "I miss you too."

After working her expense reports for a few more minutes, Angel checked her account and found another e-mail from Channing.

Angel,

So you miss me too, huh? I know it's wrong, but I couldn't be happier to hear it. I have to admit that I'm kind of nervous and confused because I never expected to feel this way, especially about my cousin's ex- and soon-to-be wife. I don't think it's really a good idea to e-mail and text each other. I wouldn't want Duke to see anything and get the wrong idea. I don't want to hurt him because I know hurting him would hurt you. There's a site I know of that we can go to and chat in real time. I'm sending you the link. Sign up and join as a member (don't worry—it's free!). I just want to be able to talk and be ourselves. Please join me there at 1:00 A.M. I'll be waiting. . . .

Angel agreed with Channing. Communicating this way was definitely wrong and would most certainly hurt Duke. She could've decided not to reply, but that would've been rude. She followed the link to the site.

She gasped. Immediately, she was met with explicit pictures of couples plastered all over the monitor. It was clearly a pornographic Web site.

"This can't be the right Web site," she said to herself. Nevertheless, Angel proceeded with the site's registration. As she created a profile, she reminded herself that there is always a moment when a person steps over the line between flirting with danger and moving into dangerous territory. This was definitely crossing over into the latter.

After creating a profile, she was able to join Channing for a live chat.

"Isn't this better?" he asked once they were both logged on. "We can talk in real time."

"Channing, exactly what kind of site is this?"

"It's a private, secure site where we can get to know each other better."

Angel shook her head. "I don't know about this. This feels wrong. I . . . I should go."

"Don't log off, baby. Do you have any idea how bad it's killing me that I can't there with you for real?"

"Don't say things like that, Channing. It only makes it worse."

"There are so many things I want to do to with you. Do you know what we'd be doing if you were here right now? You've got me hot just thinking about it."

Angel felt uncomfortable. "Channing . . ."

"I want you to touch yourself everywhere you'd want me to touch you."

"What?"

"It would make it feel like we're together. Please, Angel."

"I can't do that. I can't do *this*. This is wrong!"

"All right, I don't want to pressure you." He tried a different approach. "Can you send me a picture?"

"Of me in my pajamas?"

"Of you in nothing," he answered.

"Channing, I'm not even supposed to let Duke see me naked, let alone his cousin," she argued.

"Why are you always worried about what you're 'supposed' to do? Do what feels good to you for once."

"This doesn't feel good to me," she told him. "It doesn't feel right."

"I'm not trying to make you feel right," said Channing. "I'm trying to make you feel good."

Chapter 28

"I didn't want to lie to you. I just didn't know how to tell you the truth."
—*Lawson Kerry Banks*

Garrett put down his cell phone when he heard Lawson's keys jingling as she unlocked the kitchen door. "There you are. I was just about to call you."

"Before you ask, I didn't forget about dinner with your parents tonight. I had to make a quick run to the drugstore." She pulled out a box of tampons. "I was out of these."

Garrett's face dropped. "I guess that means we won't be making any announcements this month."

"No," she replied sadly. "But, you know, we can try again in a week or so. Maybe this time next year we'll be buying diapers instead."

"That's what I'm praying for."

"It'll happen, baby. We've just got to be patient. Besides, it's not like we won't be having fun trying, right?" she joked to lighten the mood.

"It's just frustrating sometimes, that's all."

Lawson hugged him. "I know, honey. We've just got to trust God and have faith that it'll happen in due season. The Bible says there's a time and season for everything under heaven."

Garrett gently pulled away from her. "Maybe it's time we thought about getting a second opinion. You know, make sure all of our parts are in working, baby-making order."

Lawson grew uneasy. "Baby, I just had a checkup with my gynecologist a couple of months ago. She assured me that everything is fine. It takes some women longer to conceive than others."

"It wouldn't hurt to talk to a specialist."

"I'm sure nothing is wrong with either of us. This is probably a side effect from the birth control pills."

"Yeah, but you've been off the pill for about two months now."

Lawson gulped. "I just think we need to give it a little longer before we start wasting time and money going to see a specialist who's going to confirm what we already know. I'm fine, baby. Plus, we haven't even been trying that long."

"The specialist wasn't just for you." Garrett sighed, a little uncomfortable. "You might not even be the problem. Maybe it's me."

"Garrett, don't say that. We're not even going to speak that into existence. There's absolutely nothing wrong with me or my brilliant, sexy husband or his brilliant, sexy sperm." They both laughed.

"You're probably right, but I want to make an appointment with my doctor to be sure."

"Look, it's almost six!" interjected Lawson, eager to change the subject. "We've got to hurry up and dress if we're going to meet your parents by seven. Where's Namon?"

"Back there in his room glued to the computer."

"Ugh! I bet that boy didn't iron that blue button-down like I told him either. Let me go back there and straighten him out."

Lawson marched down the hall to Namon's room. Garrett began unloading the shopping bags Lawson brought into the house. After putting up the paper towels, his eyes landed on a small white sack with a prescription attached.

Lawson reentered the kitchen. "All right, Namon is in the shower, and I'm about to—" She struggled to catch her breath when she saw Garrett holding the pharmacy bag.

"Lawson, what's this?" he asked, more accusing than curious.

She walked over and plucked the bag out of his hands. "It's a prescription; it's nothing."

"A prescription for what?"

She shrugged, brushing off the question. "My doctor said that my iron is a little low. It's some kind of iron supplement."

"So, this makes, what, the second lie you've told me in the last five minutes?"

Lawson narrowed her eyes. "What are you talking about?"

"Are you seriously going to stand there and play innocent while you lie to my face?" charged Garrett. "Then again, you've been doing it for months. Why would today be any different?"

She feigned ignorance, hoping against hope that he'd drop the issue. "Baby, I honestly don't know what you're talking about."

He snatched the bag from her. "Do you think I'm that stupid, Lawson? I can read. I know what this is!"

"Garrett, it's not . . ."

"It's not what? It's not your prescription for birth control pills?" he fired. He hurled the bag across the room, startling Lawson.

She couldn't say anything. She definitely couldn't carry out the lie anymore, so Lawson lowered her head and said nothing.

"So you're mute now?" asked Garrett. "You had plenty to tell me when you were going on about our having a baby being the Lord's will and timing. Obviously, by *Lord*, you meant *Lawson*."

"I don't know what you want me to say," she replied meekly.

"I want you to do the one thing you obviously haven't done in God knows how long. I want you to tell me the truth. Do you think you're capable of doing that?"

"Of course I'm capable of telling you the truth, Garrett. The truth is that I love you very much, and I'd never, ever want to do anything to hurt you. You and Namon mean everything to me. *That's* the truth!"

"Yeah, that sounds real nice, Lawson, but you're leaving out one very important part of this *truth* of yours, aren't you? Come on, just say it."

"Say what? That I renewed my prescription?"

"No, that you never canceled it!" he answered. "You never had any intention of getting pregnant, did you?"

"Baby, that's not true," she sobbed. "I love you, and I want to have your child. I just needed a little more time."

"Lawson, you stood there and let me go on and on about getting my sperm checked and going to specialists when you knew all along."

Lawson smeared tears from her face. "I didn't want to lie to you. I just didn't know how to tell you the truth."

"Did you know how to tell the girls? Do they know?"

She shook her head.

"What about Mark? Does he know?"

"Of course not!"

Garrett raised his voice. "I'm shocked. You talk to him about everything else."

"Don't make this about Mark."

"Why not when everything else is about him? Your job, Namon, Reggie . . . It all goes back to Mark. We can't even have a conversation without Mark being in the middle of it."

She sniffed. "Garrett, you're not being fair."

He laughed bitterly. "I'm not being fair? You've been lying to me for weeks, but *I'm* not the one who's fair? You know, I should've . . ." He bit his lip to keep from saying anything he might regret.

"Should've what?" pushed Lawson.

"I should've thought longer and harder before asking you to become my wife."

Lawson's heart sank to the floor. "Why would you say that to me? How could you even think that?"

"I mean it, Lawson. Look at the way I let you string me along for ten years, then how you and Mark carried on behind my back, now this!"

"I wasn't carrying on with Mark, and you know it."

"You were practically engaged to the guy. You have no respect for me, Lawson, none at all."

"I have the utmost respect for you." She tried to hold him. "I love you."

Garrett rebuffed her. "Love and respect are not the same things. You can't say that you respect me and turn around and pull stunts like this—you just can't!"

"Okay, I admit that what I did was wrong and selfish and stupid. I know that hearing this right now doesn't mean anything to you, but I really am sorry, Garrett. I was afraid to tell you the truth."

"Why? I'm your husband!"

"You haven't exactly made it a secret that you resent the fact that I have a child with Mark."

"Don't go there, Lawson. You know I love that boy like he was my own son."

"I know that, but he's not yours, not biologically. Whether you admit it or not, a part of the reason you want this baby is because I have a child with Mark, and you can't stand the fact that he and I share something that you and I don't."

"Whatever. . . ."

"No, you said you wanted to be truthful, so let's be truthful. You're jealous of my connection to Mark and his bond with Namon."

"Are you sure you don't have my jealousy confused with yours over his relationship with Reggie?"

"So what are we fighting about, Garrett—the pills or Mark?"

"Take your pick."

Lawson was flustered. "This isn't getting us anywhere. Let's just go to dinner with your parents. We're going to be late." She turned to walk toward their bedroom.

Garrett stopped her. "Are you kidding me? I'm not about to go front for my parents like everything is cool between you and me."

"Garrett, we can't stand them up."

"Namon and I are going. You and your pills can stay here. I'll just tell them you got sick. What's one more lie, right?"

She didn't bother protesting. "Can we finish talking about this when you and Namon come home?"

He shook his head. "No, I'm done talking about this. I'm through talking about babies. I'm through talking about Mark . . . I'm through talking about us."

"What are you saying?"

He sighed. "I'm tired. I love you, but I'm tired."

"Of me?"

"Of this."

***

Lawson waited for Garrett in bed, a part of her wondering if he was going to come back. She thought back to how many times she'd chided Sullivan for lying to Charles and being secretive. Now, she was forced to eat her words.

She turned over and began speaking to the Lord. "God, I know you are a loving and forgiving Spirit. Thank you for forgiving us over and over again when we mess up. You already know exactly what I've done, but I need to ask for your forgiveness. Lord, forgive me for lying to my husband and for going behind his back. Forgive me for letting my feelings toward Reggie and Mark interfere with my marriage. I ask that you speak to Garrett on my behalf. Touch his heart, and let him forgive and love me the way you do. Lord, I know I can live without him as long as I have you, but I don't want to. Please let him love me enough to get past this."

Relief flooded Lawson's body when she heard his footsteps coming down the hall. He came into the room without speaking to her.

She sat up in bed. "How was dinner?"

"It was good. I needed that time to get away and think."

"Where's Namon?"

Garrett hung up his sports coat. "He's tired. He said he was going to bed."

Lawson pulled back the blankets to invite him in. "That sounds like a good idea for all of us. Come on, let's get some sleep."

Garrett unbuttoned his shirt. "I think I'm going to sleep on the couch tonight."

She looked down. "You're still mad at me, I see."

"I wish it was that simple. I really do."

"It can be."

Garrett shook his head. "Lawson, I know you had your reasons for what you did. Maybe they're valid—I don't know. I just know what it did to me as your husband."

"Baby, I know I hurt you, but we can get past it. We've gotten past things before."

"This feels different. You don't love me enough to have a child with me. I'm good enough to play step-daddy for Namon, but not good enough for the real thing."

She brought her hand to her chest. "Don't say that. That's not how I feel at all."

"That may not be how you *want* to feel, but that's the reality. I've finally come to accept it."

Lawson reached for his hand. "I don't like to hear you talk like this. It scares me."

"You don't think I'm scared too? I feel like I'm losing the only woman I've ever really loved. I'm losing my family."

"I'm not going anywhere, honey. I'm here," she assured him.

"Whether you realize it or not, you left this marriage the minute you started lying to me." Garrett let go of her hand and grabbed a pillow from the bed. "As far as I'm concerned, you left a long time ago."

Chapter 29

**"In thirty-one years, the only
thing you ever really taught me was
how to be a whore."**
—*Sullivan Webb*

Vera Jackson answered the door in her customary satin robe, glass of vodka and cranberry juice, and a lit cigarette and growled, "What are you doing here?"

Sullivan rolled her eyes and sidestepped her mother to force her way into the St. Simon's beach house. "It's good to see you too. Of course, I don't mean that literally. You have enough bags under your eyes to put Kroger out of business. And your hair . . ." She tugged on a lock of Vera's disheveled bob wig. "This wig is as old as I am."

Vera slapped Sullivan's hand away. "Can you please get on with the reason for this visit? I have a facial at four."

Sullivan looked around for Vera's live-in boyfriend. "Where's Cliff?"

Vera pulled on her cigarette and flung her hand. "He's out scouting locations or something. He'll be back on Sunday."

Sullivan laughed. "*Scouting locations?* He directs porn! How hard is to find a bed and bad lighting?"

"He directs *movies*, not porn!" countered Vera, sprawling across the sofa.

"Funny . . . I don't recall his cinematic masterpiece, *Heels and Thongs, Volume One*, making its rounds to my local theater."

"Say what you will, but Cliff's job has afforded me to live the lifestyle I've grown accustomed to. Now back to my original question—why are you here? You in trouble or something?"

"What makes you think that?"

"Because you're here!"

"It's the holidays. Is it so hard to believe that I wanted to see the woman who gave me life?"

Vera rolled her eyes. "Sullivan, please don't insult my intelligence. I haven't spoken to you since your obligatory birthday call back in June, and you haven't set foot in this house since Christmas '08. It doesn't take a genius to figure out you're in trouble."

Sullivan sat down across from her. "I'm glad to see that you haven't totally lost your mothering instincts and intuition. You're right. I am in trouble," she admitted. "The old-fashioned kind, to be exact."

Vera shot up, spilling a little of her drink in the process. "Good Lord, Sullivan, are you pregnant?"

"Yep." Sullivan rubbed her hand across her stomach. "This time next year, you'll be a grandma."

"*Humph!*" Vera shook her head and sat back down. "Ain't that a blip? You know, I thought you looked a little fat around the jaws, but I didn't want to say anything just yet. I figured you had enough on your mind without worrying about fattening up like some farmhand's prized pig."

"A simple congratulations would have sufficed, you know."

"I haven't decided if the occasion is worth celebrating yet. Judging by the look on your face, I'd say it's not. The question is *why*."

"You know me. Do you think I'm the maternal type?"

"I *do* know you, Sullivan, and I know how I raised you. Any fool worth her weight knows that having a rich man's baby is better than winning the lottery, so what gives? Did Charles lose his money?"

"Charles's financial state, which is none of your business, is fine."

"Is he seeing another woman?"

"Of course not!"

"Then what's the problem? And don't give me some crap about not being ready for kids. We both know that you're just going to pawn the poor thing off on Charles or some nanny to raise."

Sullivan's voice went up an octave, as it often did whenever she was lying. "Nothing's wrong. How many times do I have to tell you that?"

"Listen, honey, you can lie to Charles all you want, but me?" She bumped the ashes off her cigarette into the ashtray. "I can see bull coming from a mile away."

"The baby might not be Charles's," confessed Sullivan.

"What difference does it make as long as he doesn't know that?"

"He will once I tell him I'm pregnant."

"How would he know? Are you over here crazy enough to think that God is going to reveal it to him?"

"Not God, Charles's doctor. He just found out that he has low sperm."

Vera dropped her head. "Then who's the father?"

Sullivan swallowed hard. "Vaughn."

"That grease monkey you were all over the Internet with?" Vera closed her eyes. "I need another drink. You want one?"

"Did you forget that I'm pregnant?" she asked, appalled that her mother would offer a pregnant woman a drink.

Vera smacked her teeth. "I drank all the time when I was pregnant with you. Then again, that might explain how in the world you could do something so stupid."

"I know it was wrong to cheat on Charles again—"

Vera interrupted her. "It was wrong to not know how to avoid getting caught! I honestly don't know where I went wrong with you. I thought I raised you better than this."

"Why? Because you raised me to be a gold digger and to use what I got to get what I want? What did that get me?"

"It got us a full bank account, a house I never made the first payment on, and a brand-new car in the driveway when you turned sixteen, that's what!"

"That's because Samuel Sullivan was married! He had to do *something* to keep you quiet."

"He gave you his name. He didn't have to do that."

Sullivan contradicted her. "He didn't give me his last name, the one that actually mattered."

"What actually matters is that you didn't have to want for anything a day in your life. We always had the finest, and we didn't get that because your mama made careless mistakes. We got that because your mama knew how to bring a man to his knees and how to play the game. You had it for a while too, but now . . ."

Sullivan shook her head and rose. "This isn't helping. It was a mistake to come here."

"You're free to go, Sullivan. Or you can stay and let me tell you how to get out of this mess."

Sullivan turned around and sat back down.

"I would suggest the obvious, which is to have an abortion and pretend like this whole thing never happened, but if you were going to do that, you would've done it already. I suppose you had your fill of the surgeon's table in high school and college."

"Thanks for reminding me," Sullivan hissed.

"Sullivan, you know I'm not one to mince words. I'm here to give it to you straight." Vera took a final puff from her cigarette before crushing it. "It definitely complicates things with Charles's soldiers being just as dried up as he is, but you need to thank your lucky stars that he told you before you told him you were pregnant."

Sullivan became irritated. "Can you just tell me what the plan is?"

Vera began thinking. "Charles is a praying, God-fearing man, right?"

"Well, he *is* a pastor, Vera, so I would think so."

"You're going to have to pass the baby off as Charles's, pure and simple."

"I don't know if I can do that," Sullivan disclosed.

Vera shook her head. "That's always been your problem. You never made a good hustler because you always ended up thinking with your heart instead of your head."

"Forgive me for actually loving the man I'm married to," Sullivan replied sarcastically.

"You don't love that man, Sullivan. You don't love nobody but yourself." Vera stood up to retrieve more cigarettes. "That's the way it should be. When you start worrying about other people, you forget to look out for number one."

"So what are you saying? Are you finally admitting that you never loved me?"

"I took care of you, didn't I?" countered Vera.

"It's not the same thing."

"It is in my world. Look, Sullivan, all this love crap that you're so interested in is completely overrated. Get all that fantasy stuff out of your head, you're too old to be thinking like that. Life is all about gettin' the jump on the next man before he can get the jump on you. What is it that guy called in *Raisin in the Sun?*" She lit a new cigarette and inhaled. "Oh, yeah, 'the takers and the tooken,' that's it! You don't ever want to be one of the tooken, honey. You save that for men like Charles."

"I refuse to live that kind of selfish existence or bring this child up in it."

"We're selfish people, Sullivan. That's what we do."

Sullivan fanned the smoke away from her face. "Don't throw around words like *we*. I'm nothing like you, Vera."

"No, you're not because I don't get caught. You want to be like me, but you never figured out how." She puffed on her cigarette. "It wasn't for my lack of teaching, I'll tell you that!"

Sullivan reeled back. "What exactly do you think you taught me, Vera?"

"I taught you everything you know. You were never much in the brains department, but you did have your looks going for you. Thanks to me, you learned how to use your looks and that pot of gold between your legs to get what you want."

"In thirty-one years, the only thing you ever really taught me was how to be a whore."

Vera didn't deny it. "Considering the situation that you've gotten yourself into, it looks like I didn't even do that right. A real whore wouldn't be in this mess. You're an ungrateful wench, Sullivan—always have been, always will be."

"You know, I used to sit and fantasize about what it would be like to have the kind of mother I could go to for sound advice, one who would take me shopping as opposed to shoplifting. The kind of mother who would talk to me about boys, not teach me how to seduce men."

Vera was undeterred and resolute as she continued. "I raised you the way I was raised. And my mama raised me how she was raised, and her mama raised her how she was raised, and we all turned out just fine."

"I intend to raise this baby better," asserted Sullivan.

Vera took offense. "Better than what?"

Sullivan threw her hand up at the blatant ostentation that filled Vera's living room, relics from a lifetime of money-grabbing and bed-hopping. "Better than *this!*"

"What, because you go to church now and you're the first lady, that makes you better? Huh?" Sullivan didn't answer. "Maybe I need to remind of you where you came from!"

"I don't need you to remind me of anything. Trust me—the memories are here to stay."

"No, I think I better refresh your memory because you seem to have forgotten a few things. You remember the eight months you spent locked up in juvie for shoplifting?"

"I was thirteen years old!" cried Sullivan. "You dropped me off in front of the mall with no money and said I better have my school clothes by the time you came back. What did you expect me to do?"

"Hmm . . . Maybe I need to remind you of the time I caught you messing around with my boyfriend when you were fifteen."

"I wasn't 'messing around' with him. He was molesting me, Vera. There is a difference between the two!" Sullivan shook her head. "You didn't even do anything about it. The counselors at school had to intervene for me to get any kind of help."

Vera went on. "Oh, and we can't forget about your sophomore year in college when you got knocked up by your professor—your *married* professor, I might add.

I believe that resulted in abortion number two, or was it three?"

Having her past flash before her all at once was almost more than Sullivan could bear. "I was young and stupid. He said he loved me and was going to leave his wife, and I believed him."

"I can go back even further, Sullivan. I can dredge up the football player you blackmailed when you were sixteen. You remember—the one you threatened with statutory rape charges. Though I must say, that garnered us a nice li'l payday. Well played, my angel."

"And I did it all under my mother's guidance and coaching," surmised Sullivan, on the brink of tears. "What kind of mother does that to her own child?"

"It paid for your degree, didn't it?"

"Yeah, and it was worth every penny to get me away from you."

"Don't put this all on me, Sullivan. You wanted that lifestyle—the cars, the clothes, the money. I didn't have to force you to do anything."

"No, but you could've shown me a different way. You've could've instilled values in me and some sense of the Lord. You didn't have to make me like you." Sullivan paused to compose herself. "You have no idea what this kind of upbringing did to me, do you?"

"Sullivan, you had everything a child could want. Who else was going to school with Chanel purses and Jimmy Choos on their feet? To this day, you ain't worked a single day in your life. I may not have been 'Mother, May I,' but I taught you how to survive and get what you want out of this world."

"You think you taught me how to survive?" repeated Sullivan in horror. "You taught me how to hate myself and how to feel like all I was good for was sex. You broke my spirit, Vera. You robbed me of the chance at having any kind of normal childhood. I had no values, no morals." She hesitated. "No love."

Vera lit another cigarette. "Don't give me this Lifetime movie sob-story mess, Sullivan! You turned out just fine."

"Because I have the Lord in my life and Charles. It has absolutely nothing to do with you." Sullivan whirled around and marched out of the room.

Vera came barreling down the hall after Sullivan, waving her cigarette. "You think you better than me? Huh? Well, look in the mirror, sweetheart." She snatched Sullivan by the arm and forced her to the mirror. "You're just like me!"

Sullivan stiffened her lip, refusing to give in to her tears. "I'm *nothing* like you."

"Oh, yeah? You romance for finance, so do I. You messed around and got knocked up by the wrong joker, and I did too. You don't give a flying flip about nobody in this world but yourself, and you know what?" Vera took a pull from her cigarette. "Neither do I."

"I care about this baby, and I care about my husband," affirmed Sullivan.

"Yeah, I see. That's why you're sleeping around, carrying another man's baby, ain't it? Because you *care* so much?"

"It wasn't like that," she tried to explain.

"Sure, Sullivan . . . Say whatever lets you sleep at night," Vera replied flippantly.

Sullivan scolded herself. "I can't believe I actually came here looking for advice and encouragement."

"Me either. You already knew what I was gonna tell you."

"I guess I was crazy enough to think that you might've changed."

"I ain't never gonna change!" declared Vera. "Neither are you."

"I have changed," swore Sullivan. Vera shook her head in disbelief and puffed on her cigarette. Sullivan was tempted to tell Vera to go hell and walk away, but she couldn't. Charles didn't give up on her; how could she give up on her own mother without at least trying?

"Do you believe in God, Vera?"

Vera frowned. "What?"

"Do you believe in God and salvation and Jesus being crucified for your sins?"

"Sullivan, don't come at me with that foolishness. Save that for Charles and them folks up at the church."

"It's not too late for you to change, to be redeemed," Sullivan told her.

"To be redeemed from what? This house? My cars out in the garage? The money we got in the bank? The broke and the weak rely on all that religion crap to justify being in that situation. I don't need God or religion. I got everything I want right here."

Sullivan reached out to her mother. "Your life could be so much more than this, Vera. I know it's hard to believe, but God loves you, and He's waiting for you to reach out and acknowledge that you need Him. All you have to do is accept Him into your life. It doesn't have to be this way."

Vera seemed to be listening and actually softening for a moment. "Sometimes I want to believe that . . ." Her words trailed off, and Sullivan could see the ice come over her again. Vera brought the cigarette back to her lips and inhaled. "You can stay the night, but you need to be gone by the time Cliff gets back," she ordered before waltzing off to her bedroom.

"You were wrong about one thing," Sullivan called after her. "You said I don't love anybody, but I do. I love this baby, and I'm going to make sure he or she gets everything you deprived me of."

Vera turned around. Her cigarette ashes fluttered to the ground. "You can try, but you know what we are, Sullivan, and there ain't nothing you can do about it."

Chapter 30

"I guess I'm just tired of doing things God's way and ending up with nothing."
—*Kina Battle*

"Pastor, if you don't need anything else, I'm going to go on and leave for the day," said Kina, poking her head into Charles's office.

"Come in for a minute before you go. I want to talk to you."

"Sure." Kina eased into his office and closed the door behind her. "Did I do something wrong?"

Charles offered her a seat. "Sister, what's all this business I'm hearing about you dating a woman? Is this true?"

"Did Sullivan tell you that?" Kina fumed. "That girl can't keep a secret if her life depended on it, unless it's one of hers, of course!"

"No, Sullivan didn't tell me that; I'm hearing things from other members. Sullivan is not out spreading rumors about you, but she didn't deny it when I asked her about it. She's concerned about you. She told me I needed to talk to you, so that's what I'm doing."

Kina nodded. "It's true. I have been spending a lot of time with a woman. I guess you could say we're dating."

Charles frowned. "Why would do something like that?"

Kina shrugged her shoulders. "I don't know. Maybe I was curious." She sighed. "Or lonely."

"The Lord will be your comforter, sister. Lean on Him."

"I do. But sometimes, it helps to have an actual person to lean on as well."

"Sister Battle, you're in a position of leadership now. This doesn't mean I or anyone else expects you to be perfect, but I am looking for you to uphold a certain moral standard when it comes to your decisions and lifestyle choices."

"Pastor, this thing with Joan isn't that serious. We're just hanging out."

"I'm sure I don't have to remind you of what the Word says about homosexuality either. Do you think the Lord is pleased with what you're doing?"

"I think me and the Lord are on the outs these days," divulged Kina.

"Why do you say that?"

"Pastor, you know me. I've tried to be the best Christian I know how to be. I pray, but it doesn't seem like my prayers get answered. I tithe, but I'm still broke. I tried to be a good, faithful wife to E'Bell; all I got was broken and beaten in return. It just doesn't seem fair. I look around at people who ain't even *trying* to live right, and they have it all! I'm tired of doing things God's way and ending up with nothing."

"It sounds like you're in offense, Kina."

"I'm not offended. I know I can't sit here and work for you and the church and be in what's considered a sinful relationship. If this is your way of asking for my resignation—"

"I'm not talking about being offended by me. I'm talking about you being offended at God."

Kina sat quietly, convicted.

"Sister, I know you're hurt and frustrated, and it seems like nothing is happening the way you want it to, but don't get mad at God. Who else is going to help you?"

"Pastor, I know you're a man of the cloth, but every time the doors of the church open, I'm here. I help people, I'm in four different ministries, and I try to live right. This may not be politically correct to say, but it seems like the Lord owes me something!"

Charles leaned back. "I don't know that He owes you anything, Sister Battle."

"You know what I mean," mumbled Kina.

"I do. Like you said, you come to church, you pray, and you do all of the things a good Christian is supposed to do, right?"

"That's right."

"Then perhaps you need to examine your reasons for doing it. Are you doing it because you want to have a relationship with God or because you want God to be obligated to do something for you?"

Kina was quiet. This was a possibility she hadn't considered.

Charles continued. "Sister Battle, you're familiar with John the Baptist and his death, right?"

"Yes."

"Do you know what killed him? The very thing you're dealing with now, offense."

Kina shook her head. "John was killed after Herodias's daughter asked for his head on a platter."

"Obviously, that happened too, but let's delve a little deeper in Luke." Charles opened the NIV Bible on his desk. "You remember when John was locked up and he sent for Jesus asking, 'Are you the one who was to come or should we expect somebody else?'"

Kina wrinkled her nose. "What's wrong with that?"

"*What's wrong* isn't so much that he asked as much as it is the implication behind the question. John was in offense because Jesus hadn't come to get him out of jail. In his sarcastic way, what he was really asking was, 'Are you coming, Jesus, or do I need to find someone else to come do your job?' And do you know what the Lord's response was?"

"No, not really."

"He said, 'Go back and report to John what you have seen and heard: The blind receive sight, the lame walk, those who have leprosy have been cured, the deaf hear, the dead are raised, and the good news is preached to the poor. Blessed is the man who doesn't fall away on account of me,'" read Charles. "Translated, he tells John, 'You know I'm *the one*. The proof is in the pudding! But blessed is the man who does not get offended at God.'"

Kina felt small. "I didn't realize that I was acting that way."

"Now that you know better, I have faith that you'll do better." Charles squeezed her hand. "You've got to watch how you question God too. It's one thing to ask Him how He wants you to handle a situation. It's something else to question His authority and sovereignty. You don't want to do that."

"I know." Kina lowered her head. "You're right."

"Trust in the Lord to know what's best for you. I know that waiting is hard, and it can be very tempting to circumvent the Lord's system and way of doing things for the world's way, but there are lessons He wants you to learn and pitfalls God wants you to avoid because He loves you. He knows how it's all going to end, and He tries to shield us from unnecessary hurt. Now, if you're bound and determined to do things your way, He's gonna let you, but it'll take you a lot longer to reach the destiny He has planned for you."

"What about all these feelings, Pastor?"

"That'll pass, sister. Emotions are designed to lead you to or away from the Lord. One path is life, the other one is death. The danger is that emotions can often be fickle, and their impact is too far-reaching for you to make decisions based off of how you feel. Your decisions need to be based on what the Word says, not emotions."

"I think a lot of my problem is that I'd gotten so used to being married. I hate being alone. I think if I had a husband or someone truly special in my life, I'd be okay."

"You can't look for another person to take God's place in your life, sister."

"I know you're right, but I have all this love inside and all these feelings. I feel like I need to put them somewhere or on someone."

"Put them on the Lord, your son, your neighbors, your church members, and yourself."

"You left out husband," Kina exhaled. "You must think I'll never get married again."

"Of course you will, if that's what you're believing God for, but treasure this time you have right now. Enjoy being single. Use this time to concentrate on improving your relationship with God and your relationship with yourself. Finish school and take care of your son. Continue your ministry work and try to be a blessing to others. When those elements are well-established, you'll be ready to receive your husband."

Kina felt the weight taken off of her. "You're so wise, Pastor. As a church, we're all very blessed to have you."

"Thank you, but I can't take the credit. Any wisdom I have comes from the Lord."

"So you think there's still hope for me?"

"There's always hope. Trust me, sister, you're going to be just fine."

Charles hugged her. As he held Kina in his arms, she felt a sense of peace and belonging she'd never felt before. It was almost as if she were being embraced by God Himself.

Charles let her go. "Are you feeling better now?"

She nodded. "You make everything so clear, Pastor. How do you do that?"

He chuckled. "Sister, things aren't nearly as complicated as we try to make them. The Bible reminds us that there's nothing new under the sun. The issues we face today are the same ones they faced during biblical times. As long as you let the Word be your final authority on all decisions, you'll be all right."

"I just wish I could hear the Lord's voice as clearly as you can."

"That comes from spending time with the Lord and spending time in His Word. God will start to reveal all kinds of things to you if you ask Him and if your spirit is receptive to it. Keep Him first and all the other things will be added onto you. He promised to give you the desires of your heart. Have faith that He'll do what He said He'd do." Charles checked his watch. "Well, I better get on out of here and do some shopping. Sullivan has been a little down lately. I want to surprise her with a few new pretty things when she gets back. Presents always make her feel better."

"I hope she appreciates it and knows what a blessing she has in you."

"We're a blessing to each other." Charles tilted his head toward her. "You have a pleasant evening, Sister Battle, and think about what I said."

"I will, Pastor."

As Charles retreated down the hallway, a revelation hit Kina like a freight train. Charles had told her to have faith and that God would send her the kind of mate that she needed. Intuitively, Charles knew that she needed a man who was grounded and rooted in the Word of God, who knew her secrets and would accept her anyway, who could love her unconditionally, and who could help her grow in her relationship with Christ.

Charles also needed something. He needed the kind of wife who'd respect and honor him, who relished working along beside him in his ministry, who didn't mind catering to his needs, and someone who was equally yoked to him in every way.

The weight of her newfound revelation was almost too much to comprehend. "Lord, are you telling me what I think you're telling me?" Kina asked aloud.

She eased down into her seat, trying to make sense of it all. It didn't make sense, yet it made perfect sense at the same time. She heaved, amazed as all of the pieces started to crystallize and form right before her eyes.

"Reflect on what I am saying, for the Lord will give you insight into all this," recited Kina, recalling 2 Timothy 2:7.

Nothing happened by accident. E'Bell's death, her working there as Charles's assistant, Sullivan's affair with Vaughn and subsequent pregnancy—it was all a part of God's plan. It was all to bring her to this moment.

Kina burst into laughter. How could she not have seen this all along? The answer had been so obvious that it was invisible. That is, until the moment Charles took her in his arms—the place where she was meant to be.

Kina knew that it would be controversial and that there would definitely be some explaining to do, but eventually everyone would see for themselves what was now blatantly obvious to her: It was she, not Sullivan, who God had called to be Charles's wife.

Chapter 31

"I think my marriage is over."
—*Lawson Kerry Banks*

Lawson accidentally brushed up against Mark while passing him in the hallway at work. She mumbled a brusque "Excuse me" before pressing on to her room.

"Hold up, Lawson," called Mark.

She stopped and turned around, clearly agitated. "What?"

"Lawson, are you okay?" he asked, genuinely concerned.

"Like you care," she snapped.

Mark followed her into the classroom. "Of course I care. Why would you say something like that?"

Lawson sighed. "I'm sorry, Mark. The problem isn't you, not entirely anyway."

"So what is it?"

"It's Garrett." She paused. "I think . . . I think my marriage is over."

"Come on, don't be so dramatic," scoffed Mark. "You guys haven't even been married a year. I seriously doubt that it's over."

"You weren't there. You don't know what happened."

"You had your first real fight, that's all," reasoned Mark. "Just kiss and make up."

Lawson shook her head. "We had our first fight two days after we got back from the honeymoon. This was more than just some newlywed spat."

"How much more?"

"He's furious with me. We haven't talked in four days, and he didn't come home last night. He called to say he won't probably won't be home tonight either. He's thinking about moving out."

The news took the wind out of Mark. "I'm sorry to hear that, Lawson. Don't assume the worst, though. Sometimes a little time apart can be a good thing. He probably just needs a minute to clear his head."

"That's sweet of you to say, but you have no idea what I did to him, Mark."

"No, I don't, but I know he loves you, and I know that you love him. You'll work it out."

"What if we don't?"

"You will. Have faith, Lawson."

She smiled for the first time since Garrett discovered her stash of birth control pills. "You're a good friend. I'm glad we can talk like this."

"Are you sure that's not part of the problem?"

"Huh?"

"You said whatever you and Garrett are going through wasn't *entirely* me, which means it at least has *something* to do with me. It can't be easy on him knowing that we talk and confide in each other."

"My husband knows there's nothing going on between us, Mark."

"But he also knows that we were intimate in the past. We have a kid together, and, if I'd had my way a couple of years ago, we'd be married by now. Having to deal with all that can't be easy for him."

"I married him, not you. Shouldn't that count for something?"

"I can't speak for Garrett, but it's probably best for everyone involved if I fall back a little. Maybe we should keep our relationship strictly about Namon for now."

Lawson crossed her arms in front of her. "So by 'everyone involved,' you really mean Reggie, right?"

"I mean all of us. But the reality is that I'm trying to make this relationship with Reggie work and you want to make your marriage work. I think both of those relationships have a better shot if we limit the amount of contact we have with other."

Lawson threw up her hands. "That's just great. It's not enough that I've lost my husband. I also have to lose my friend and my baby sister in the process."

"You haven't lost anything yet, but God has a way of giving us the things we ask for. Only say what you really want to happen."

Chapter 32

"What if I screw up again?
Screwing up is in my DNA, you know."
—Sullivan Webb

Sullivan sat in her BMW outside of her house. She knew Charles was inside waiting for her. She also knew she couldn't keep her pregnancy a secret much longer.

"I screwed up, didn't I?" she muttered, more to God than to herself. "How come I always do this? Am I like Paul—the things I don't want to do are the things I end up doing and the things I do want to do are the things that I don't do?" She unbuckled her seat belt.

Sullivan closed her eyes and spoke to the Lord from her heart. "Heavenly Father, how precious is your name! No matter how big of a mess I make of my life, you said you'll never leave or forsake me. Your grace and your mercy sustain me; your goodness and love know no boundaries.

"Lord, you made me. You know even the numbers of hairs I have on my head. You know what I'm going to do, how I'm going to do it, and who I'm going to do it with before I do. You tried to warn me, but as usual, I had to do things my way. And, as usual, my way sucks, except it's not just me or Charles who stands to get hurt. This child I'm carrying will be the one hurt most of all, and she's completely innocent in all this, Lord. I don't want my child to suffer for my mistakes. Lord,

I know what I did was awful. Even though I tried to rationalize it, I knew that sleeping with Vaughn was wrong. I sinned against you and my husband, even Vaughn. But, Lord, I know if we confess our sins, you will forgive us.

"I don't just want to confess my sins this time. I want to *repent*. I want to change, Lord. I don't want to be this lying, manipulative person anymore. I don't want to end up like my mother. She's not only in my DNA, she's in my mind, in my blood. The only way I'm going to free myself from her and the bad thinking, the wrong values, and all the other generational curses that have plagued our family for years is to surrender myself completely to you.

"I want to be the kind of wife my husband can be proud of and the kind of mother my baby deserves to have. I want to change, but I know I can't do it without you. I'm too weak, too flawed, and too selfish to do it on my own, so I'm turning my life over to you. Do with it as you see fit. Make me over. Save me from myself.

"Lord, I'm not going to ask you to get me out of this mess. I created this situation, and I know I have to deal with the consequences, but I do ask that you protect my child in the midst of it all. God, I'm already in love with this baby, regardless of who the father is. At this point, I don't even care what happens to me as long as she can grow up safe and loved. I don't want her to be afraid and exploited like I was. If she's okay, I know I'll be okay."

Sullivan sat alone in the car for another half hour, alternating between crying and praying. She knew she couldn't sit in there forever, but she also knew things may never be the same once she crossed the threshold into her home.

She took a deep breath before putting the key into the lock of their front door. She'd resolved to tell her husband about her pregnancy; whether or not it would be perceived as good or bad news was still to be determined.

"Oh, you're back!" exclaimed Charles, rising from the sofa to greet Sullivan at the door. He met her with a kiss. "Let me help you with your bags."

"Thanks, honey." Sullivan passed her suitcase to him. "Did you miss me?"

"Every second you were gone," he replied, still smiling. "How's Vera?"

Sullivan set her purse and keys down. "Vera is very much still Vera. She's as self-centered and evil as ever, but she does send her love."

Charles shook his head. "Bless her heart. Just keep praying for her, sweetheart."

"I will, but seeing her this weekend brought back a lot of old memories, most of which weren't too pleasant."

Charles wrapped his arm around her and walked her into the great room. "Sullivan, those days are long behind you. The girl you were back then doesn't even exist anymore."

"I know. Seeing my mother just reminded me of how messed up I used to be." She braided her fingers into his. "It really made grateful for you, Charles. You saved my life."

"Now, don't go giving me the credit for the Lord's work."

"Accepting the Lord into my life was definitely the turning point, but you gave me something I never had. You gave me unconditional love and a home. Our marriage gave me purpose, and you helped me see that I was a lot more than a pretty face or a hot body. Yes, it's the Lord who made me whole, but you had everything to do with getting me to the point of even *finding* the Lord."

"Sullivan, you're not giving yourself enough credit. I couldn't have led you to Christ if you weren't ready to receive Him and make some changes in your life."

"All I know is that I was lost and dead inside until the day Angel dragged me to church with her. It was the best thing that ever happened to me."

Charles was taken aback. "Wow, your visit with Vera must've been really intense. I haven't heard you talk like this in a long time."

"I was hoping in vain that Vera would change, at the very least be apologetic. I was basically prostituted out from the time I was fourteen until I went off to college. She doesn't even see what she did wrong. She had the nerve to tell me that I'm ungrateful."

"Vera is sick, sweetheart, and lost. You can't really blame her. She's in darkness. We just have to keep praying that one day the Lord is going to touch her heart, and she'll see the error in her ways."

"I'm not holding my breath for that miracle. Vera is so far gone that the devil himself will probably convert before she will."

"I've seen souls worse than Vera's be turned around by the Holy Spirit."

"I hope you're right." Sullivan settled into Charles's arms. "I love you, honey. More every day. When I think of how close we came to losing everything . . ."

"Shh," Charles quieted her. "We're going to be just fine. You believe that, don't you? The Lord has His hand on this marriage. If we keep Him first and each other second, everything else will fall into place."

"How can you be so sure?"

"We've been put through the test, Sullivan, and we came out stronger and a little closer to God and each other in the process. I don't think there's anything we can't get through."

"What if—" Sullivan pursed her lips together.

"What if what?"

"What if I screw up again? Screwing up is in my DNA, you know."

"I don't receive that, and neither should you. Nobody expects you to be perfect; I certainly am not! But the more we learn about the Word and God's will for our lives, it stands to reason that we won't fall prey to the same temptations."

"What if I did? Could you forgive me?"

Charles's expression changed. "Obviously, as a Christian and a pastor, it's what the Lord has commissioned me to do."

"What about as a husband and as a man?"

"I would forgive you. . . ."

"But you couldn't stay married to me, right?" inferred Sullivan.

"I didn't say that."

"You didn't have to."

"It would be difficult," he confessed. "But I'm in this with you for the long haul."

"You know I'd never do anything to intentionally hurt you, don't you?"

"I know that, sweetheart. I'm just thankful that we've gotten past all that adultery stuff. I think we both see how important marriage is, and we're both equally committed to making this work."

Sullivan became uneasy. "Charles, I have something I want to tell you."

"Good news, I hope."

"I think it is. I'm hoping you do too."

"What is it?"

She shook her head. "I don't want to tell you about it right now. It's a surprise, but I'll tell you tomorrow over dinner. I want to do a little shopping first."

"Uh-oh," groaned Charles.

Sullivan laughed. "I'm not buying for me, but I am shopping for someone I love very much."

"Are you're sure this is going to be a surprise that I'll like?"

"It'll be a surprise that you love."

"No hints?"

"Nope!"

"I guess I'll have to trust you then." He lifted her chin and looked her in the eyes. "And I do, Sullivan. I trust you. I know you don't always believe that, but I trust you. You have my heart and all my love."

Sullivan decided to tell him and let the chips fall where they may. Either news of the baby would solidify her marriage or destroy it.

Chapter 33

"I don't think being with you is a part of God's plan for my life."
—*Kina Battle*

"What's wrong?" asked Joan when Kina shied away from her touch for the third time that evening. "Why won't you let me touch you? Are you mad at me? Did I do something wrong?"

"No, but Kenny will be home soon. I wouldn't want him to walk in on something I'm not ready to explain."

"You've had me dipping and dodging your son for weeks now. I don't like feeling like we're sneaking around any more than you do. Maybe it's time I meet him."

Kina stood up and vigorously shook her head. "I'm not ready for anything like that!"

Joan rubbed Kina's forearm. "It's okay; it was only a suggestion. Come on, sit back down."

Kina moved out of her reach. "Joan, there's something we need to talk about."

"What's up? Don't tell me it's no big deal because I can see it all over your face."

Kina took a deep breath. "Joan, I like you; I really do. You're smart, beautiful, and protective—just so many wonderful things." Joan smiled bashfully. *"But . . ."*

"There's a 'but'?" Joan's smile vacated the premises. "Hold up—is this *the speech?*"

"What speech are you talking about?"

"The kiss-off speech! I've heard this speech before. Heck, I've even given it a few times."

"Joan, it's just that I've been catching a lot of flak about us . . ."

"From who?"

"My friends, my boss, people at the church."

"You can't listen to all that negative stuff, Kina."

"My friends are very loud, and my conscience is kind of hard to ignore."

"So are your feelings for me! Anyway, who cares what anyone else thinks? You can't be in a relationship for other people's convenience and comfort. You have to be in it for you and what makes you happy."

Kina shook her head. "I wish it were that simple."

"It can be."

"This isn't just about people giving me a hard time about us being together. It's also about my walk with God."

"Kina, God wants you to be happy. You said yourself that I make you happy."

"I know. . . . But I just don't think being with you is a part of God's plan for my life." She looked up at Joan. "I had to come to some harsh realities, Joan. When I imagine my life ten or fifteen years from now, I don't see myself with a woman. I see myself married, possibly having another child or two."

"And you can't see this life with me because, what, I have a uterus?"

"No, because we want different things."

"Like what?"

"Well, we want different body parts, for one."

Joan was taken aback. "Are you kidding me?"

"Joan, you should be with someone who wants to be with you and can accept you just as you are. I can't stand here and honestly say I can see coming to church with you on my arm or introducing you to Kenny as my girlfriend. I'm sorry."

"I deserve to be with someone who is proud to be with me. Obviously, that's not you."

"I'm sorry. I'm not trying to be hurtful."

"I guess that part is just a by-product, right? I knew this would happen," muttered Joan to herself. "Why did you even start this relationship, Kina? I asked you if you were sure and you said you were."

"That was before . . ."

"Before what?"

"Before I realized who God wants me to be with."

"Let me guess—it's a man!"

"Yes, it is. He's a very good, spiritually grounded man who loves God and lives by the Word."

"Well, Kina, I wish you luck with your new *man*. Maybe he can figure you out. Lord knows I couldn't!"

Kina hummed to herself as she bounced around Kenny's room collecting dirty laundry.

"Why are you so happy today?" he asked, looking up from his book.

"God is blessing us, baby, can't you feel it? I just know that good things are about to start happening again."

"I got an A on my math test. Does that count?"

"It sure does! I'm so proud of you." She kissed him on the forehead. "Other wonderful things are happening too."

"Like what?"

"Well . . ." She set the laundry basket down on the floor and sat on the bed next to Kenny. "I think that God is sending someone into our lives who's going to be everything you ever wanted in a dad and all I've ever wanted in a husband, a real God-fearing, spirit-filled man."

Kenny was surprised. "You got a new boyfriend, Mama?"

She giggled. "Not exactly, but I'm hoping I will soon."

"Who is he?"

Her smile faded a little. There was no easy way to say that her perspective new husband was her best friend's current one as well as their pastor. "I don't want to jinx it by talking about it too much. Just know that he's a wonderful man who makes your mother very happy."

"Do I know him?"

Kina playfully pinched him. "What did I say about jinxing it?"

"I know. I was just wondering . . ." Kenny exhaled. "Does he know what I did?"

Kina gave him a reassuring smile. "Yes, he knows."

"Does he think I'm a killer or something?"

"No, sweetie. Nobody thinks that. You saved my life, Kenny. No one blames you for what happened."

"That's what my therapist always says, but I still feel bad about it."

"Well, don't," commanded Kina. "You're a wonderful son, and you deserve nothing but the best." She kissed on him the cheek. "And for once, that's exactly what we're both gonna get."

Chapter 34

**"I won't discuss your marriage to Sullivan.
I'll discuss the kind of life you could have
if you were married to me."**
—*Kina Battle*

"What's smelling so good?" asked Charles, getting a whiff of Kina's candied yams, fried chicken, and collard greens.

Kina strolled into his office and proudly presented Charles's meal to him in a covered plate. "I made you some dinner. I knew you'd be hungry after putting in so much extra time, and I know Sullivan doesn't like to cook."

"She hasn't lately," Charles admitted. "She's been so tired for the past few days. I haven't had any luck getting her to go see her doctor."

"Don't you want to see what I cooked for you?" asked Kina. The sooner they stopped talking about Sullivan, the better.

Charles lifted the foil covering the food. "You made enough for Pharaoh and his whole army, didn't you, Sister Battle?" He smiled. Kina loved that she was the one who put that smile on his face. "That was mighty kind of you. Maybe some of this good home cookin' will help my wife get her strength back and start feeling better."

Kina was miffed. Sullivan wasn't supposed to be part of the package. "You don't really have to share it if you don't want to," Kina told him. "I made it especially for you."

"That was thoughtful, but if it's just the same to you, I don't want to deprive my wife of such a fine meal. It wouldn't be right."

"Suit yourself," muttered Kina in a huff.

Charles picked up on the attitude. "Is everything all right between you and Sullivan?"

"I'm sure it will be . . . eventually."

"Well, I won't pry, it's none of my business. I hope you both remember that the Word says we are to 'live in harmony with one another, be sympathetic, love as brothers, be compassionate and humble. Do not repay evil with evil or insult with insult, but with blessings, because to this you were called so that you may inherit a blessing.'"

"I also know what the Word says about a wife honoring and respecting her husband," hinted Kina. "I just don't like the way she treats you, Pastor."

"I hope that's not what you two are in strife about!" revealed Charles. "My wife treats me just fine, Sister Battle. I don't know what it looks like to you from the outside, but Sullivan and I understand each other. I give her what she needs, and she gives me what I need. That's all anyone can ask for."

"Don't you ever think there could be another woman out there who's perfect for you?"

"No," he answered without leaving room for doubt. "I'm married to the one the Lord sent to me."

Kina pouted. "What do you even see in her? I mean, I know she's beautiful and all that, but that's just surface. What can she offer you other than that?"

Charles squinted his eyes, confounded by Kina's bitter words against his wife and her friend. "She's my wife. I love her."

"But why?" Kina whined. "I mean, she doesn't . . . She doesn't deserve someone like you. You're kind and decent. You're everything she's not!"

"That's enough," Charles said sternly. "Now, sister, I know that we've known each other a long time. Because you and my wife are friends, you're privy to more information than most people. That said, my wife is not up for discussion, and neither is my marriage. Is that clear?"

"Fine, I won't discuss your marriage to Sullivan." Kina inched closer to him. "I'll discuss the kind of life you could have if you were married to me."

"What?" spewed Charles. It was the only thing he could muster, not believing what he was hearing.

"Pastor, you and I have so much in common. We're more equally yoked than you and Sullivan will ever be. I would appreciate you, she doesn't. I don't mind cooking for you and helping out at the church. You'd never have to worry about me lusting after every young preacher you invite to the church or bringing shame to your ministry. I can be the kind of wife that you prayed about if you give me a chance."

Charles held up his hands. "Don't say anything else. I've heard enough." He distanced himself from her. "Now, Sister Battle, I like you. You do excellent work around here, and I believe you have a good heart, but I absolutely cannot tolerate this kind of behavior from you or anyone else on my staff. I'm in love with my wife, I'm committed to Sullivan Webb and only Sullivan Webb, do you understand that?"

"I don't know why," griped Kina.

"You don't have to know why!" he roared. "She's my wife, and that's all you need to know. Sister Battle, I realize that you're a single parent, and this has been a difficult time for you. I'd really hate to release you from our staff, but perhaps it's time we consider moving you somewhere else. I don't think this arrangement is working out quite the way we'd hoped. I really think you should leave before one of us gets into the flesh and say something that doesn't need to be said."

"Are you firing me?"

"I don't want to act in haste, and I don't want you to do or say anything out of emotion. Why don't you just go home for a few days to give me a chance to pray about this and give you a chance to put things in perspective, all right?"

"If my working here is the reason we can't be together, I'll quit."

Charles stood firm. "The reason we can't be together is that I'm married, and I have absolutely no interest in being with you!"

Kina was heartbroken. After laying it all on the line and pouring her heart out to Charles, he still wanted Sullivan. "You're married to a woman who doesn't respect you. She doesn't love you. Sullivan wants a sponsor, not a husband! You can do better than that. I'm offering you better than that." She moved in to kiss him.

Charles quickly rebuffed her advances. "I thought we were going to be able to work this out amicably, but you're not listening to me. I need you to leave this office right now. Don't return until and unless I call you."

Kina snorted. "She's really got you fooled, doesn't she?"

"Sister Battle, I asked you to leave. Please don't force me to call security."

Without thinking, Kina fired the best weapon in her arsenal. "Did she tell you she's pregnant?"

Charles picked up the phone. "I'm calling security."

"I'm not lying to you, Pastor. Sullivan's pregnant. That's why she's been so freaked out lately. That's why she went to go see her mother," blurted out Kina.

Charles slowly hung up the phone. "My wife is pregnant?"

Kina nodded. "Yes."

Charles appeared disorientated. "If that was true, Sullivan would've told me that. She's been trying to get pregnant for months."

"She didn't want to tell you because she knows the baby isn't yours. It's Vaughn's child, but she was planning to pass it off as yours."

Charles seized the back of the chair for support. "No . . . Sullivan wouldn't do anything like that. You don't know Sullivan if you think she'd do that."

"*You* don't know Sullivan if you think she *wouldn't!* This shouldn't even come as much of a surprise. She has no morals, Pastor. She's a whore just like her mother, and not even you can change that."

Charles struggled to catch his breath. "I want you to leave."

Kina saw that the color in his face had changed. He looked to be in pain. "Pastor, are you all right?"

"Go!" he barked. "Just go!"

The tone he'd spoken to her put fear into Kina. She quickly snatched up her purse and scurried out.

Kina stood outside of the church offices, dizzy with emotion. What had she done? She replayed the last ten minutes over in her head again. Had she really just confessed her unrequited love to the pastor, lost her job, and destroyed her best friend's marriage, all in one fell swoop?

Kina leaned against the wall and slid to the ground. "Oh my God!" she cried. "What did I just do? What have I done?"

She quickly composed herself. Perhaps if she acted quickly, something could still be salvaged. She had to make a move before Charles could call Sullivan, before Charles could call anyone.

She raced back inside. "Pastor!" she called frantically. "Pastor!"

Kina barged into his office, but she didn't find him standing at the desk where she left him. "Where could he be that quick?" she asked aloud.

Kina looked down and gasped at the sight before her. Charles's seemingly lifeless body lay facedown motionless on the floor. She shook him to rouse him. "Pastor Webb?"

She tried in vain to roll him over, but he was too heavy and too limp. Then she tried to check for a heartbeat, pulse—any sign of life. She didn't feel anything.

"Oh my God!" she screamed. *"Help! Somebody help me!"*

Chapter 35

"Oh, God, tell me we didn't lose him!"
—Sullivan Webb

Despite all the prayers and positive affirmations being sent her way, there were no words that could comfort Sullivan since receiving Kina's frantic phone call telling her that Charles had collapsed and was being rushed to the hospital. When Sullivan arrived, she was met by Kina, Angel, and Lawson as well as key leaders and prayer warriors from the church.

"How did this happen?" Sullivan wailed. "He was fine when he left home this morning. He seemed okay when I talked to him a few hours ago."

Angel tried to console her. "We don't really know what happened, but he's alive, and he wasn't out that long before Kina found him and called the paramedics."

Sullivan turned to Kina. "Do you have any idea what he was doing right before he passed out?"

Kina shook her head. What was she supposed to say—that she'd tried to seduce the pastor away from his wife, then revealed that Sullivan was pregnant by another man right before he collapsed?

"No, I was out of the office," said Kina. "I'm not really sure what happened."

"Had he been complaining about not feeling well?" asked Sullivan.

"Not really. I mean, I think he may have a headache or something."

"How did he look, Kina?" fished Sullivan. "Was he breathing?"

"I think so. Everything happened so fast. I just remember him looking very pale," recalled Kina, visualizing the pained expression on his face.

"It sounds like it could have been a stroke, maybe even a heart attack," concluded Angel. "It's a blessing that you were still there and able to get help."

"Yes," Sullivan agreed. "You probably saved him."

Charles's doctor emerged from the operating room. The look in Dr. Golphin's eyes told everyone the news wasn't good before he could even say a word. They all circled around him. Lawson reached for Sullivan's hand.

"Dr. Golphin, how bad is it?" asked Sullivan, trembling. "Oh, God, tell me we didn't lose him!" she cried.

"He's alive," the doctor confirmed. "He had a stroke, Mrs. Webb." Sullivan knees buckled.

One of the associate pastors caught her before she fell. "Are you all right, Sister Webb?" he asked.

Sullivan regained her equilibrium and took a few deep breaths. "I'm fine. I need to find out about my husband." Sullivan's eyes began to water. "Just tell me he's going to be okay. Please tell me he's going to live."

"It's too soon to definitively say anything," Dr. Golphin expounded. "Right now, he's stabilized and sleeping."

Sullivan thanked God before asking the doctor more questions.

"How did this happen, Doctor?" asked Angel. "What kind of stroke did he have?"

"It was a thrombotic stroke. That's a blood-clot stroke," explained Dr. Golphin. "It can occur due to blockage to one or more of the arteries supplying blood to the brain. It impairs blood flow, resulting in blood clots. These kinds of strokes can happen as the result of unhealthy blood vessels clogged with a buildup of fatty deposits and cholesterol. They can also be linked to stress and other health factors."

Kina gulped and clutched her chest. Angel began praying quietly.

Sullivan was still shaking. "What does all this mean? Do you think he'll have any long-term damage?"

"Every stroke is different. When the brain is deprived of blood like that, it can cause paralysis, muscle loss. A lot of people have difficulty talking afterward. There can also be some memory loss," he explained. Dr. Golphin reviewed Charles's patient chart. "He's experiencing some numbness right now. He's very weak. Thankfully, you were able to summon help very quickly, so the lack of blood flow to his brain wasn't as severe as it could've been."

"Praise the Lord," uttered Kina.

"Wait, you said something about numbness," recalled Sullivan. "What does that mean? Is he paralyzed?"

"We've noted some paralysis on the right side of his body. I'm going to recommend in-patient rehab. With time and physical therapy, he could make a full recovery."

"How long before he goes home?" asked Lawson.

"I can't give you a firm date right now. At this point, things are still very much wait-and-see. We're going to hold him here at least three days to monitor his blood pressure and to check his progress, but I can guarantee that he's going to need around-the-clock care when he is released. You may want to consider bringing in a nurse."

"Will he ever be the same again?" Kina asked meekly.
Sullivan reached over and held her hand.

"I can't answer that," admitted the doctor. "But we
can pray and hope for the best. I want to assure all of
you that we're giving him the best care possible."

Sullivan nodded. "When can we see him?"

"I want to hold off on that for a little while. He's not
able to communicate with you at this point, and you
can't really talk to him." Sullivan hung her head. "Now,
if you'll excuse me, I want to look in on my patient, and
I'll alert you as soon as you can go in and see him or if
anything changes."

Lawson wrapped her arms around Sullivan's shoulders. "Honey, I know that the report wasn't that encouraging, but the important thing is that Charles is
alive, and he's got the best doctors looking after him.
More than that, he's got all of us praying for him to
pull through this. Remember Jeremiah 33:6: 'Nevertheless, I will bring health and healing to it; I will heal
my people and let them enjoy abundant of peace and
security.'"

Angel stepped forward. "If you need a nurse, Sully,
you know I'd be more than happy to pitch in, or I can
give you some names of other nurses if you want."

Sullivan declined. "No, he's my husband. I want to
be the one who takes care of him."

Angel was touched. "Sully, that's mighty noble of
you, but no one expects you to take on this responsibility by yourself. A lot of people in your situation opt to
hire caretakers or check into temporary living facili-
ties."

Sullivan shook her head. "No . . . I owe him that
much. If it gets to be too much, I'll get some help, but
I've got to at least try to do this on my own."

"You won't be alone, sister," the associate pastor promised her. "All of the ministers and ministry leaders and the congregation are here to support you and give you whatever you need."

"Thank you, Pastor Straws. It means a lot to know I can lean on all of you if I need to." Sullivan turned to Kina. "Thank God you were there, Kina. I can't imagine what would've happened if you weren't. I don't even want to think about it. You may have saved my husband's life."

Kina was paralyzed with guilt. There was no way she could accept Sullivan's praise. "I'm no hero. The Lord just put me in the right place at the right time."

"You're a hero to me and to Charles. I'm planning to see to it that you get a raise," Sullivan half-heartedly joked before succumbing to tears again. "Thank you so much. I love you." She pulled Kina into a hug and whispered, "My baby thanks you. You saved her daddy."

Kina held her friend, overcome with a range of emotions. "I just did what anyone else would've done."

Sullivan pulled away and wiped her eyes. "Not necessarily. You were there, you got help, you stayed with him, and you were praying for him the whole time. Not everyone would've done that."

"The Lord is the Savior in this situation, not me."

"He worked through you, Kina, and I'm glad He did," said Sullivan.

Once things calmed down, Kina slipped away to the hospital's chapel. She clasped her hands together and fell to her knees at the altar. "Lord, I come humbling myself, seeking your face and turning from my wicked ways. I need to hear from heaven right now. I need your forgiveness." Tears began streaming from her eyes.

"Oh, God, what have I done? What have I done? Please let Charles be all right, Lord. All I wanted was for my pastor to be happy and have the kind of woman you'd want him to have. I didn't mean to do or say anything to hurt him, it just sort of came out. Don't let him and his family suffer because of my mistakes. I admit that I was jealous of Sullivan. I coveted the life and the husband that she had. God, sometimes, it just seems like she has *everything*! I believe Charles would give her the moon if she asked for it, but I was wrong for trying to come between them, and I know that now. Punish me, Lord, but don't do it to Charles. Your Word says that whatever has happened to us is the result of our own evil deeds and out of great guilt, and yet, you have punished us less than we deserve. I know I deserve your wrath, but he hasn't done anything wrong.

"Lord, I know you can heal him. I know you can bring him back to his family and congregation. If you bring him out of this, I swear I won't do anything else to interfere in their lives. Help, Lord, please!" Kina succumbed to her emotions.

"It's okay, Kina. The Lord hears your prayers."

Kina looked up and gasped. She saw Lawson standing over her. Kina's heart began pounding so hard that she could feel the reverberation through her whole body. "How long have you been here?" she asked, swallowing hard and hoping Lawson hadn't heard her confession.

"Not long. I figured I'd find you here." Lawson stooped to Kina's level. "You're taking this pretty hard, aren't you?"

Kina nodded. "I feel like it's all my fault."

"Don't be silly, Kina. There was nothing you did to cause this, and there's probably nothing you could've done to prevent it."

"Then why do I feel so guilty?"

"I'm sure seeing him lying there and being in this hospital brings back a lot of emotions for you. It wasn't that long ago that we were here praying for E'Bell, not knowing whether he was going to pull through."

"He didn't. What if that happens to the pastor?"

"It won't," insisted Lawson. "But even if it does, God is still in control. Right now, the most important thing we can do is try to be there for Sullivan. She's going through a tough time right now. She needs us more than ever." Lawson tilted her head to meet Kina's eyes. She still felt as if her cousin was more emotional than expected. "Are you sure you're all right?"

"I will be as soon as I know the pastor will be fine."

"Are you sure *you're* okay?" Lawson still wasn't convinced. "Did something happen in the pastor's office that you wanna tell me about?"

A part of Kina wanted to confess, and there was no better time or better person to pour her heart out to. "Do you think I'm a bad person, Lawson?"

Lawson was caught off guard by the question. "I think we're all capable of doing bad things, but, no, I don't think you're a bad person. Why?"

"Sometimes I get frightened by the things I think I'm capable of doing," she confessed.

Lawson couldn't follow. "Are we talking about what happened tonight at the church or something else?"

Kina lost her nerve. "Neither. I was just thinking aloud. Come on, let's go check on Charles and Sullivan."

As they made their way back to the lobby, Kina recalled Sullivan telling them that honesty wasn't always the best policy. For once, she agreed with her.

Chapter 36

"I know a lonely man and a desperate woman when I see one. If you're not sleeping with her now, you will be soon."
—Reginell Kerry

Following a long day and visit to Charles at the hospital, Reginell sought solace in the form of one of The Lady and Son's flourless chocolate tortes, deciding that the decadent delight was worth the extra time she'd have to put in on the pole to burn off the calories.

She put in her to-go order and sat down at the bar to scope the scene. The usual crowd of Paula Deen fans and Southern cuisine lovers were there; however, there was one familiar but unexpected face in the bunch. She spotted Garrett and, to her surprise, he was not alone.

Reginell stealthily strolled up to them. "Well, well, what do we have here?"

"Reggie?" Garrett's tone was a mixture of surprise and shame.

"Better me than your wife, right?" she asked wickedly. Reginell smiled in the direction of his companion. "Hi, I'm Reginell, Garrett's sister-in-law. His *wife's* sister, to be exact."

"Reggie, this is Simone. Simon, Reggie," introduced Garrett.

"It's a pleasure," said Simone, extending her hand.

"Yes, I'm sure it has been," snapped Reginell, disregarding the outstretch hand. She turned her attention back to Garrett. "Can I talk to you for a minute . . . in private?"

"Actually, they're about to bring our food out now," said Garrett, nodding toward the waiter approaching the table with their orders.

"Great, it'll give Simone here something to do while we talk." She yanked Garrett up by the arm. "Excuse us, Simone." She dragged Garrett a few feet away. "Wow, moving on so soon?"

"It's not what you think. I'm not cheating on your sister."

"Hmm . . . We have a dark, romantic setting and a woman sitting across from you in her brand-new freak'um dress. You're right—how could I *possibly* think you're cheating on my sister?"

"Simone is just an interior designer I'm working with."

Reginell rolled her eyes. "Spare me, okay? Did you forget what I do for a living? I know a lonely man and a desperate woman when I see one. If you're not sleeping with her now, you will be soon."

"Does it even matter if I do?" he asked curtly. "My marriage has one foot in the grave anyway."

"Garrett, don't say that! Things could still work out for you and Lawson."

Garrett shook his head. "Your sister has made her choices."

"Yes, she has, and she chose you."

"Yeah, right," he remarked with a bitter laugh.

Reginell exhaled and crossed her arms in front of her. "G, I know that you and Lawson have been together a long time and you think you know her pretty well, but there are a few things about my sister you may not understand."

"Like what?"

"I don't remember my dad coming around more than two or three times when I was growing up, and I lost my mom when I just turned fourteen years old. At the time, Lawson was barely out of her teens and was raising Namon by herself. Despite that, she stepped up and did whatever she had to in order to take care of us, whether it was working two or three jobs or going without so we could have. She's always sacrificed her life and her dreams for other people, and never once have I ever heard her complain about it. She just asks God for strength and keeps moving."

"I never said she wasn't a strong woman."

"She's more than strong, Garrett. She's phenomenal, and she's my hero. You'd be a fool to walk away from her and your marriage."

"Some people might say I'd be a fool to stay."

"Those people don't know her like you and I do."

"If Lawson wanted to be with me and truly wanted to be in this marriage, she wouldn't have betrayed me the way she did."

"Cut the girl some slack! Lawson has been raising children and taking care of other people since she was twelve years old. All that time when my mom was battling cancer, it was Lawson who was right there taking care of her, making sure she got back and forth to the doctor and had her medication. After Mama died, all of Lawson's time went to looking after me and raising Namon. Now that I'm grown and she has Mark to help with Namon, she wants something for herself. I can't blame her if she's not in a hurry to give up work and school to have more babies."

"It hurts like crazy that she doesn't want to have my child, but I can handle that. What I can't handle is the way she went about it, with all the lies and deception."

"Look, I know this is going to sound ridiculous, but she did it that way because she loves you."

Garrett stared at her in disbelief. "You're right, Reggie. It sounds ridiculous."

"Just hear me out, all right? Lawson loves you so much that she'd rather lie than disappoint you. My sister has lost so much already. It's killing her to think she's lost you too."

"She hasn't exactly been fair to you either. Why are you going to bat for her?"

"I know my sister, Garrett. She gets very possessive about things, even people, because she's so used to having it all taken away. That's why she got so crazy when Mark was trying to establish a relationship with Namon, and that's why she lost it when Mark started dating me. It wasn't that she wanted him back. She just felt like she was losing her sister to him and the friend she'd found in Mark to me."

"I hear you. It just seems like it's always something, you know? We'll be happy one minute, then it's all shot to hell the next. She's so independent and will shut me out when things aren't going the way she wants them to."

"She's not used to having someone she can lean on. It's going to take her awhile to get used to that. Of course, you don't do anything to help the situation when you keep running out whenever she needs you the most. You've got to be patient with her."

"I've been patient with her, Reggie! I waited ten years for her to marry me. If that's not patient, I don't know what is. The problem is that Lawson takes me and this marriage for granted. I understand Namon taking top priority, but everything else? If it isn't school, it's work, or church. If it's not church, it's her friends. If it's not her friends, it's Mark. There's always something that has more of her attention than I do. On top of that, now we're dealing with this birth control issue. I'm an afterthought to her, and I refuse to be in a marriage like that."

"Oh, cry me a river, Garrett! You think Lawson takes you for granted? What does that even mean? Shouldn't she take for granted that her husband loves her, and he'll be there no matter what? Why shouldn't she believe that you ain't going nowhere regardless of how real it gets? Isn't that what marriage is supposed to be about?"

"It's not that simple."

"You do still love her, don't you?"

"I'll always love her."

"Then fight for her, G. Fight for your marriage and your family."

"I feel like I've been doing that my whole life. At some point, you get tired of fighting, and you just have to accept that things will never change. I can stay in it and be miserable." He glanced back at Simone. "Or I can move forward and see what else is out there."

"Lawson likes the scripture that says, 'The Lord will fight for you; you need only be still.' Maybe you should try being still before you rush to move on."

"Reggie, you just don't understand . . ."

"Maybe I don't, but I don't understand how a man can walk out on his wife and child either."

"I'm not *that* guy, and you know it."

"Really? Then prove it, Garrett. Forgive your wife and go back home. Lawson needs you, so does Namon. Believe me, I know what it feels like to be judged and not accepted for who you are and not be loved in spite of all the flaws, the mistakes, and the screwups. Lawson thought she had that in you. We all did."

"I just don't know if I can keep putting myself through this, Reggie. I love your sister, but sometimes love isn't enough."

"Are you kidding me? Love is *always* enough! When it comes down to it, love is all we have, the only thing that matters anyway. Lawson makes me mad enough to strangle her sometimes, but that's my sister. I love her, and I'd die for her, and I know she'd do the same for me. I'd never totally abandon her. Surely you, the man who claims to be so in love with his wife, loves her as much as I do."

"Look, Reggie, I've got to get back to my table. Simone's waiting."

"Yeah, well, so is your wife!" fired Reginell before stomping out with her torte.

Garrett returned to his table and sat down. "I'm sorry about that. Reginell can be a little intense, to say the least."

"Is everything okay?"

"It will be," replied Garrett, eager to put the conversation with Reginell and his marriage to Lawson behind him.

Chapter 37

"I was tricked into it."

—Angel King

As she had started to do every night after Duke had drifted off to sleep, Angel crept downstairs for a virtual liaison with Channing. The guilt that plagued her the first few nights had subsided. Not only did she indulge in these erotic fantasies with Channing, but she was starting to look forward to them. She had the best of both worlds. Her open, loving family and church life with Duke and her exciting, unpredictable, virtual life with Channing.

Channing's grinning face appeared on her monitor. "Do you miss me?"

She smiled. "Don't I always?"

Channing blushed into the camera. "Stand up, let me see you. What are you wearing?"

"My scrubs, what else?"

"Go put on something sexy and let me see it."

"You're crazy!" replied Angel with a laugh. "I'm not doing that!"

"Why not?"

"Because . . . It's inappropriate."

"Having phone sex the other night was inappropriate as well, but you still did it."

"I was tricked into it," she insisted.

"Maybe at first, but you became a willing participant shortly thereafter."

"I shouldn't have, though."

"Why not? Why do you keep second-guessing everything like that?"

"I'm getting married, Channing, to your cousin, I might add."

"I'm well aware of that, ma'am. You and Duke will get married and live happily ever after just like you'd planned. We're just playing around—no harm done to that sexy li'l body of yours."

"Maybe not to my physical body, but the spiritual one is another story."

"Speaking of bodies," he went on, "did you get the picture I sent to you?"

"Yes."

"What did you think?"

She blushed, a little embarrassed. "I think you're crazy. That picture was the definition of inappropriate."

"Well, what did you think aside from that?"

"I thought it was kind of sexy," she admitted.

"How did it make you feel when you saw it?"

She smiled seductively. "Don't make me answer that."

"Come on . . . How did it make you feel?"

Angel cleared her throat. "Like I wanted to do some things to you."

"What kind of things?"

"I'm not going to tell you!" she shrieked.

"You don't have to tell because I already know," boasted Channing. "You want to do all of the things to me that I want to do to you. You've got me excited just thinking about it. You don't want to know what I'm doing underneath this desk."

"I can just about imagine . . ."

"You don't have to imagine because I'm going to tell you." He proceeded to go into graphic detail describing it all to her.

"How long do you think we can keep this up before someone finds out?" she posed to him.

"Nobody is going to find out unless one of us tells, and my lips are sealed, baby,"

"God sees all," she reminded him.

"Then let Him worry about it. We're not hurting anybody. I'm a war hero. I think I'm entitled to share a few fantasies with an incredibly beautiful, sexy woman, don't you?"

"So what's my excuse?"

"You're a hardworking nurse, stepmother, and fiancée. You need a break from the monotony sometimes."

Angel agreed but could feel the battle being waged in her spirit. She knew by giving in to Channing, she was allowing sin and lust to take a stronghold in her life. She knew that her secret lusts grieved the Holy Spirit.

At first, she'd told herself that after the first night, she'd only go to the site to talk to Channing. A few days later, he'd talked her into looking at pornographic pictures. Now, it had progressed to cybersex and lewd acts.

Angel brushed off the condemnation. After all, there were far greater sins than the ones she was committing. This was just fooling around on the computer, and who didn't do that these days?

Chapter 38

"No one wins if the truth comes out."
—*Sullivan Webb*

Charles had been home for a week, with Sullivan tending to his every need around the clock just as she said she would. It didn't matter to her that he'd lost his ability to speak and the movement in his arms. She was just so happy that her husband was alive. The only time she left his side was during his occupational therapy sessions. Even then, she was never more than a stone's throw away.

"You're looking mighty handsome today," remarked Sullivan, brushing his hair as Charles sat virtually motionless in his wheelchair. Though he couldn't speak, his eyes followed her everywhere. She often caught him staring at her.

"Why are you always looking at me like that?" she asked playfully. "Are you as shocked as everyone else to see me playing Nurse Nightingale?" She stooped down in front of him. "You know you're the only person in the world I'd do this for, right?" She touched his hand. "But it's an act of loving service. You've been taking care of me from the moment I met you. It's my pleasure and honor to be able to return the favor."

Charles was still staring, boring holes into her with his eyes. Sullivan became concerned. "Are you trying to tell me something, sweetie? Are you in pain?"

His expression didn't change.

"Knock, knock," ventured Angel, peeking into Sullivan and Charles's downstairs guest room. "Everything is set up to start Charles's therapy session."

"Okay, thank you." Sullivan kissed Charles on the cheek. "I'll be right here when you're done."

The occupational therapist nodded and wheeled Charles out of the room and down the hall.

"Stop looking so worried, Sully. Ann's a pro. She knows what she's doing."

"I just want him to get better, you know? It has to be frustrating to him to be in this state. I can tell he wants to tell me something but can't get the words out."

"He probably wants to tell you how much he loves you," surmised Angel. "What about you? How are you coping with all of this?"

"But by the grace of God go I," she quoted. "I'm fine as long as Charles and the baby are okay."

"I must admit, I didn't think you had it in you, Sully," Angel confided, helping Sullivan make up the bed.

"Didn't have what in me—a heart?"

"Yeah, that too but mostly this nurturing, caring side to you. I've been very moved by the way you've been taking such good care of Charles."

"Trust me, I'm just as shocked as you are!" They both laughed. "Being pregnant seems to have brought out the maternal side of me. You know what else it's brought out? My boobs!" She pulled her shirt tightly against her chest. "Aren't they fabulous? And to think I was considering breast implants at one point. I just hope it lasts. Charles has always been a bit of a breast man."

"There's the self-absorbed, shallow Sullivan I know!" joked Angel. "You'll stay in the double Ds for a while if you decide to breast-feed. Do you plan to do that?"

"I'm thinking about it. It'll definitely save her daddy and me from having to get up every five minutes to hunt down a bottle." Sullivan referencing Charles as the baby's father made them both a little uncomfortable.

Angel held her tongue and fluffed one of the pillows before setting it down on the bed. "So are we going to talk about it?"

Sullivan smoothed out the comforter. "Talk about what?"

"The proverbial elephant in the room, rather in this case, the proverbial mountain."

"You mean Vaughn?"

"Sullivan, you know that truth is going to come out eventually, as in seven months when this baby comes out looking like Vaughn!"

"Can you say that a little louder, Angel?" hissed Sullivan and rushed to close the door. "Discretion, please!"

"Sorry, but I'm serious. You can't keep this secret of yours forever."

"First off, Angel, there's still a chance that Charles could be the father of this child." Angel shot her a sideglance. "Well, there is!"

"Whatever," mumbled Angel. "Okay, so assuming he's not . . ."

"This will be my husband's baby in every way that matters. Charles will be the only father my child ever knows."

Angel shook her head. "Sully, didn't you learn anything from Lawson trying to keep this same kind of secret from Mark?"

"This situation is totally different."

"You're right. This is so much worse!"

"Can you refrain from being Debbie Downer right now?" Sullivan cradled her stomach. "Stress isn't good for the baby."

"Oh, now you're worried about what's best for the baby?" Angel asked with sarcasm.

"This child always has been and always will be my top priority, Angel! My baby will grow up loved, safe, and secure. I refuse to put this child through the kind of childhood I had. That's why Charles has to be the one raising this baby, not Vaughn. DNA doesn't have anything to do with it."

Angel squeezed her friend's hand. "I'm so worried for you. I just know that it's all going to blow up in your face. *Be sure your sins will find you out.*"

"I know that's what the Bible says, and I know one day the truth may reveal itself, but Charles will be so in love with me and our child by then that it won't matter," predicted Sullivan.

"What about Vaughn?"

"What about him? The last thing Vaughn wants or needs right now is another mouth to feed. He can barely feed his own! I'm doing him a huge favor."

"I know you have to tell yourself that to go through with this but—"

"But what," cut in Sullivan. "The truth shall set me free? What does it benefit anyone to tell the truth— this child? Charles? Vaughn? No one wins if the truth comes out. Plus, there's still a chance that it could be Charles's kid. I'm not going to risk my baby's future for the sake of the truth setting me free."

"Have you ever considered that you may be underestimating Charles? He forgave you before. Who's to say he wouldn't do it again and gladly raise this child as his own?"

"Angel, my husband is a good, patient man, but I don't even know if I could forgive me under the circumstances. If Charles ever found out that I slept with Vaughn again and that this baby could be his, it's over.

He'll leave me for real this time. I can't even say I would blame him. I can't do that to him, Angel, especially not after all he's been through with the stroke and having to relearn how to live his life. He saved my life. I'm not about to destroy his. He's been too good to me to do that. You remember how messed up I was when you met me. I was so selfish and self-centered."

"And you're not now?" asked Angel, baffled.

"Even you have to admit it used to be much worse. When I look back over my life, it makes me eternally grateful for my husband. I thank God for him. I literally don't know where I'd be if it hadn't been for Charles and the Lord."

"I remember when we were in college how you never wanted to go home, not even during the holidays. When you finally broke down and told about everything you'd gone through with your mother and how bad things were at home, my heart went out to you."

"I was pretty much a train wreck back then. All that changed after I met Charles. God sent him into my life at just the right time. He was the first one to believe in me and actually saw something in me that was good. He gave me a home. I never had that growing up. Vera wasn't exactly the paradigm of stability and motherhood. Going away to school was the best thing I ever could've done." She cracked a smile. "Besides, it brought me to you, didn't it?"

Angel smiled. "And, ultimately, to the Lord."

Sullivan nodded. "And to Charles. I really do love him, Angel. I don't know where I'd be without him."

Angel rested her hand on Sullivan's shoulder. "I know you love Charles, Sully. Charles loves you too. He'll make sure this child knows nothing but love."

"That's why it's so important to me that Charles raise this baby. I know I can be self-sabotaging," she admitted. "In my defense, my schemes always seem like a good idea at the time . . ."

"That's because the ways of a man seem right to him," quoted Angel from Proverbs. She hugged Sullivan. "Aw, baby girl, you'll be all right. I believe there's hope for you yet. No doubt about it, you definitely keep things interesting around here! I have no idea how you're going to pull off this Charles's-baby-Vaughn's-maybe situation, but you're a tough cookie. If anybody can make it work and look fabulous while doing so, it's you."

Sullivan squeezed Angel's hand. "I've got to do this right, Angel. This baby can't be one of the millions of other things I've screw up. She has to be my legacy, the one thing people remember me doing right."

"I didn't realize being a good mother was so important to you."

"Being a good mother means everything to me, especially after this last visit with Mommy Verest. I hate that she's even my kid's grandmother."

"Maybe having a grandchild will encourage her to make some changes."

"Girl, *please!* I doubt that Vera changes this child's diaper, much less her life for the better." Sullivan thought for a moment. "Do you know what fear keeps me up at night?"

"What?"

"Being afraid that I'm going to end up just like her."

"God won't let that happen," vowed Angel. "Neither will Charles or any of us. Even if you did, love is strong enough to conquer all."

"You mean like you and Duke?"

The comparison made Angel uneasy. "Don't compare yourself to Duke and me, Sully."

Sullivan sighed. "You're right. You'd never cheat on him or do any of the things I've done to Charles. Why can't I be more like you, Angel? You know, boring and wholesome and faithful."

Angel smiled a little, wondering why she couldn't be *less* like Sullivan.

Chapter 39

"I dance, I flirt, and I take my
clothes off. I do whatever I have to
do to get the money."
—Reginell Kerry

Mark stopped sautéing the spring vegetables in the skillet and glanced over at Reginell. "What's your purpose?"

Reginell, sprawled across his sofa, looked up from the music industry magazine she was skimming through. "Huh?"

"What's your purpose? What's your reason for being here?"

Reginell turned the page. "You asked me to come over for dinner, remember?"

"No, not for being *here* at my house, for being here on earth."

She paused. "I don't know. I guess to bless people through my music. You know, make them happy and feel things through my songs. Why?"

"I've been thinking about it a lot lately. Have you ever thought God might want you to do that through gospel music and singing for Him instead of the world? I think that's the call on your life."

Reginell stared at him for a second before bursting into laughter. "Me, Mark, a choir girl?"

"What so funny about singing for the Lord? Stranger things have happened."

"They don't come much stranger than that." She began laughing again. "You can't be that stupid."

"Okay, now I'm insulted." He removed the pan from the stove. "Maybe you ought to go back home."

"All right, I'm sorry," she replied, stifling her laughter. "I shouldn't make fun. Go ahead, tell me about this, um, *calling* you think I have. Did you wake up and hear a voice booming out of the sky or spot a bush burning out front?"

"Don't be cute," he snarled.

"I can't help it," she bragged and joined him at the stove. "Am I supposed to drop everything and follow the Lord?"

"I didn't say that. I just think you should change your focus with the whole music thing. I don't think you're going to be blessed with the way you're going about it."

"I already told that I'm not going to give dancing up for anybody. It's a part of my career plan."

"You're not dancing, you're stripping. Call it what it is."

"Call it whatever you want, but I'm not giving it up. I'm not changing who I am for you or anybody else."

"I'm not asking you to change. Right now, the only thing I'm asking you to do is listen."

They were interrupted by Reginell's phone vibrating. She checked her messages. "Shoot, I've got to go. Ray needs me to fill in for one of the dancers at some bachelor party tonight." Mark blew out breath and slung the pan away from the stove. "Don't get mad. I'll come back afterward, and we can eat then."

Mark was incensed. "You're going to leave me to go dance for a bunch of oversexed, drunk men?"

She exhaled. "It's not personal, Mark. This is business."

He turned away from her. "Yeah, *business*, okay."

"That's my job, Mark. I'm going there to work. Like it or not, this is what I do. I dance, I flirt, and I take my clothes off. I do whatever I have to do to get the money."

"Reginell, you're better than this."

"No, right now I *am* this. You're just going to have to accept it."

"Do you have any idea what these guys are saying about you? To them, you're just a piece of meat, a way to get off."

"Don't you think I know that? I don't have any delusions about why I'm supposed to be here, and neither do they. The only one who's confused here is you. You're the only one trying to be Captain Save 'em."

"How can you go out there and get treated like a prostitute? Don't you have any self-respect?"

"Yes, I do," Reginell snapped, "which is why I'm not going to let you stand here and judge me."

"Do you expect me to say nothing and watch you get taken advantage of?"

"I'm not asking you to do that. Nobody's forcing you to be with me. Honestly, Mark, I had given you more credit than this. I thought that you understood what it is that I do and had accepted it, had accepted me."

"But this is *not* you, Reginell. You don't have to stoop to this." They were both silent as they pondered what to say next.

Reginell grabbed her purse. "Mark, I've got to go. I'm going out there, and I'm going to shake my behind and smile and do what they are paying me to do. If you can't handle it, maybe you shouldn't be with me."

"I'm just trying to look out for you. Do you think anybody else there gives a flip about you?"

"I'll be fine. I don't need you to protect me. You're my man, not my manager."

Mark relented. "You're right, I'm not your manager. I'm just someone who cares a lot about you, who can't stand to see you living your life this way. You're my girl, all right? I don't like seeing you treated like a hooker."

"If this is the beginning of some lecture, you can stop before you start. I get an earful from my sister on a daily basis, and I don't need more of it from you."

"She's just concerned about you, and so am I. The strong, confident woman standing in front of me right now is not the trick about to go make a display of herself at the bachelor party. You're acting like some two-bit slut who would sell her soul if the price was right."

"*Two-bit slut?*" repeated Reginell, now hurt. "Is that all you think of me? What about all that talk about accepting me for who I am and respecting me?"

"Try respecting yourself, Reggie. How can you just stand there and let those men . . ." He ran his hands over his face. "How can you expect me, as your man, to stand back while other men touch you, knowing what they think about you and what they want to do to you?"

"I'm not asking you to accept what I do. I'm asking you to love me enough to see past it."

"I don't know if I can do that, Reggie. I don't. Why can't you just give it up, get a regular job, and—"

"And what—go back to waiting tables? Move back in with my sister? I'm trying to move forward, Mark, not backward. Like it or not, this is a real career move for me. I'm gaining exposure and getting my name out there. Do you know what Ray told me the other night?"

"Do I want to know?"

"He said that someone called asking about putting me in a music video. Not some low-budget local act either, Mark. That video is going to be seen by millions of people. I wouldn't just be some extra. I'd be the lead, a principal role. Do you know what that could do for my singing career?"

"They're just gonna typecast you as some video vixen, Reggie."

"Or this could be the big break that I've been waiting for. I'll be on the set with directors, producers, and record label execs. Who knows what'll happen for me after that."

Mark sighed. "Reggie, I care about you. I've fallen completely, heads-over-heels in love with you, but I can't . . . I just can't support you in this."

Reginell shook her head. "You call yourself a man of God? Whatever happened to accepting people as they are and not passing judgment?"

"Is it passing judgment when you're trying to stop someone from making a mess of her life?"

Reginell snatched up her jacket. "I knew that getting mixed up with you was going to be a mistake. It's funny—you weren't this concerned about my soul when you were trying to sleep with me."

Mark grabbed her arm. "Reggie, I don't want you to leave like this."

"I never should have come. From now on, you just stay in your world, and I'll stay in mine."

"Reggie—"

"Just stop it, okay? All you people make me sick! You want to sit around and pass judgment on people when you have skeletons in your own closets. I can say one thing for Ray and everybody else at the club: They don't judge. They accept me for who and what I am. They don't try to put me down or hurt my feelings.

They've got my back." She went to the door. "The so-called sinners have more God in them than any of you fake Christians."

"Where are you going, Reggie?"

"Back to where I belong," she said, looking around at his house, "I can see that it's not here, probably never was."

Chapter 40

**"I'm not doing anything worse than any-
one in this room has ever done!"**
—*Angel King*

"How's your husband doing today?" asked Lawson
while the girls were over to help Sullivan clean and
cook for Charles.

"He's getting stronger every day," reported Sullivan.
"They've been performing miracles with his therapy.
He's getting some movement back in his limbs. I can
tell he wants to speak. The only thing that still kind of
bothers me is the staring."

"Staring?" repeated Kina.

"Yeah, he just kind of looks at me all the time. I think
he wants to tell me something but can't."

"Maybe he's starting to notice the changes in his
wife's figure," hedged Lawson. "You can hide it with
these baggy clothes now, but sooner or later, the world
is going to know you're pregnant, including your husband."

"I'm going to tell him," claimed Sullivan. "I just
haven't figured out when."

"Just do it before your water breaks!" warned Lawson. "Angel, why are you so quiet over there?"

Angel shrugged her shoulders, still looking down at
the floor. "No reason."

"Okay, first tell us why you're lying, then answer the question," said Sullivan.

"I'm thinking. I'm trying to decipher whether it's cheating if there's no actual physical contact involved. I'm talking no touching, no kissing, no penetration— none of that."

Lawson eyed her. "You mean fantasizing?"

Sullivan flung her hand. "Child, please! I fantasize while I'm actually having sex with Charles. I think it spices things up a bit."

Angel sighed. "Sullivan, nothing you do surprises me anymore."

Lawson spoke up. "Personally, I don't see how it's *not* a sin unless you're fantasizing about your husband. I guess since Duke is practically your husband now anyway—"

"The fantasies aren't about Duke," Angel informed them.

The ladies were briefly silenced.

"Well, now," crackled Sullivan, "this just got a little more interesting! Who's starring in these erotic fantasies of yours? Is it Channing?"

"Yes, and it's a little more than fantasizing."

Kina frowned, confused. "How? He's in Carolina, and you're in Georgia."

"She means phone sex," Sullivan explained.

"No, it's not phone sex," Angel corrected her. "It's kind of like a Web site . . ."

Lawson's mouth flew open. "Oh my God, have you been visiting porn sites?"

Kina blinked back. "Angel, that's so . . . *ick!*"

"I'm not looking at any of the porn," she maintained. "We're just chatting."

"Why do you have to go to a porn site to chat?" Sullivan wanted to know. "You can just set up a camera and Skype to chat."

"The Web site is sort of his thing, I guess," replied Angel, not knowing quite what to say.

"So, it's just talking, right?" Kina asked for clarity.

Angel bit her lip.

"Well?" grilled Lawson.

Angel covered her face with her hands. "I can't talk about it. It's too embarrassing."

"This whole conversation is embarrassing," concurred Lawson. "I don't think you could shock us much more than you already have."

"Well . . ." Angel exhaled. "He asked me to do some things . . . and he did some things . . ."

"Okay, by some *things*, you mean . . ." urged Sullivan.

"You know," supplied Angel, hoping they'd figure it out before she had to go into explicit details. "Touching and stuff like that."

Sullivan was taken aback. "Dang, I guess all that celibacy you'd been stockpiling has finally manifested itself. I didn't know you had it in you, Angel!"

"The only thing keeping me from feeling like a total whore is the fact that I *didn't* have it in me up until now," confessed Angel.

Lawson looked Angel in the eyes. "Honey, I know that this is hard for you to talk about. But if it's making you feel this bad about yourself, obviously you shouldn't be doing it. Outside of it being a gateway to allowing all kinds of sin into your life, you're also cheating on Duke. The fact that it's with Duke's cousin makes it that much worse."

"I guess my question is *why*," pondered Kina. "You and Duke are engaged. You're planning a life together, so why would you even go there? Are you falling in love with Channing?"

"It's not about love or being unfaithful to Duke," Angel explained. "It's sort of like a release or an escape, you know? It gets me out of my reality for a few minutes."

"But the reality is that you're about to make a lifelong commitment to this man and his children. Why do you want to escape that?" Lawson asked.

"There's a lot pressure, Lawson. I have this wedding to plan, I'm working, and I'm trying to raise these girls, trying to be there for Duke, volunteering with the church, not to mention dealing with all the baggage left behind from Theresa. Do you have any idea how hard it is to constantly live in her shadow? Do you know what it's like for me trying to fit into that family?"

"Angel, if you're feeling this way, talk to Duke, don't start talking dirty with his cousin," said Lawson.

Angel blew her off. "I do enough good in the world that I ought to be entitled to relax and unwind sometimes."

"No one is saying you aren't. The problem is the way you're choosing to unwind. I can only imagine how much time you're spending a day on porn."

"You're making me sound like some creepy old guy stalking young boys on the Internet. I'm an adult watching another adult take pleasure in life. You know, a lot of people who go to these sites are married, God-fearing people. They just choose this an outlet to express themselves," argued Angel.

Lawson narrowed her eyes at Angel. "Do you hear yourself right now? You're practically equating porn to a religious experience!"

"That's not what I said," Angel fired back. "It's not what I meant, anyway."

"Sweetie, denial is a powerful thing," Sullivan reminded her. "Remember how long I denied having a problem with alcohol? I couldn't see it despite the fact I was hitting up the liquor store at least twice a week.

As long as I could rationalize it, I felt like it was under control. It wasn't until I sought help that I realized how far gone I was."

Angel exhaled and turned to Sullivan. "Sully, I'm very proud of you for seeking treatment and maintaining your sobriety, I really am. It took a lot for you to acknowledge that you had a problem, but you'd been drinking since you were a teenager. This is different."

"Why? Because you're the saintly one, and I'm the big ol' cheatin', alcoholic heathen?" asked Sullivan.

Angel's defenses flared up. "Look, I'm not endangering anyone. I'm not wasting money or doing anything illegal. I'm not doing anything worse than anyone in this room has ever done!"

Lawson shook her head. "You know you sound like one of those 'I-can-quit-whenever-I-want drug addicts, right?"

"I'm not addicted," insisted Angel. "It's not considered a full-on addiction until it interferes with your daily life. It's not interfering with anything. I still work, I still go to church, and I still look after Duke and the children. Yes, I admit that it's an unholy pastime, but it's not an addiction."

"We make our habits, and our habits turn around and make us, Angel," warned Lawson. "That goes for Bible reading as much as it does for visiting porn sites."

Angel sulked. "It's just a way to release stress and get lost in the fantasy, that's all."

"That's all *you* think it is, but you must always remember that God is the final judge."

"Who was the judge when you were lying to your husband for weeks?" threw in Angel.

Lawson shook her head. "Trying to deflect blame isn't going to resolve it, Angel. Learn from my mistakes. Do you have any idea how much I regret lying to Garrett? I've apologized 'til I was blue in the face, but the damage was already done. Deal with this porn thing and nip it in the bud! If you don't, it's going to deal with you."

Chapter 41

"Oh, God! Father, give me strength."
—Lawson Kerry Banks

Lawson had always considered herself a strong woman, but nothing weakened and humbled her more than watching her marriage fall apart. Garrett was spending more time away from the house and hadn't slept there in two weeks. He basically came only to see Namon and pack up more belongings.

Lawson met Garrett at the door after he'd called to say that he was coming over. "Did you come to get more stuff?" she exhaled and shook her head in frustration. "Do you have any idea how much it kills me to see you carting more stuff out of here every day? Each time, it's like losing you all over again. Either get all of it and be through or do it when I'm not here."

He set his keys down on the counter. "I came to get one last thing."

"What's that?"

Garrett held his breath and came humbly before her. "Your forgiveness."

It was the last thing Lawson expected to hear. "What?"

"I never should've left, Lawson. I vowed for better or worse, and I vowed to be with you until I took my last breath. I don't take my promises lightly."

Lawson moved away from him. "I don't want you here out of a sense of obligation."

"It's not just that. I'm here because I love you, and I don't think I can go another day without waking up and not seeing you lying next to me."

She melted inside. "Really?"

"Yes, babe. I miss you and Namon and our life together. I finally wised up and came to the conclusion that I'd rather have my wife than my pride."

"I'll never lie to you again, I promise, Garrett," she vowed.

Garrett shook his head. "Don't do that."

"Do what?"

"I don't want us to make promises we can't keep. You're probably going to lie to me again. You may even hurt me more than you did this time. I may do the same to you. But, baby, I promise I'll never walk out that door again, not unless I have you and Namon with me."

"Thank you, God." She kissed him. "I love so much. If it means I have to quit school for a while—"

Garrett stopped her. "I'm not going to let you do that, Lawson. I want you to be everything God created you to be. What kind of husband would I be to ask you to live beneath your potential? I refuse to be threatened by your ambition and success. I want you to get that degree and go as far as the Lord will take you. Just make sure you bring us along for the ride."

"I'll take you wherever you want to go, just as long as we're together."

He folded her into his arms. "I love you, baby. I missed you so much."

"I missed you too. Please don't ever leave me again."

Garrett kissed her forehead. "I won't. You and Namon mean everything to me, you hear me?"

She smiled. "I hear you."

Garrett slowly released her. "But, sweetheart, there's something I need to tell you. We can't start over with secrets still between us."

"There aren't any more secrets, Garrett. I told you everything—I swear!"

"I'm not talking about you. I meant me."

Lawson felt the air go out of her body. Something in the way he looked at her told her to brace for the worst. "What about you?" she asked in a low voice.

Garrett seized her hands. "First off, I want to say that I take full responsibility for what I'm about to tell you. Yes, after I found out about the pills, I was hurt and felt betrayed. I also admit that I was insecure about your relationship with Mark."

Lawson swallowed. "Okay . . . Garrett, you're scaring me. Just say what it is you have to say."

His eyes welled with tears as he squeezed her hands. "I made a mistake. I was reckless and stupid. I fouled up big time." He paused. "I cheated on you, Lawson."

"Cheated? I mean, what is that? Did you go out with another woman? Did you kiss another woman?"

"I slept with someone else," he admitted. Lawson crumpled into the chair. "Baby, I'm so sorry. If I could take it back—"

"You can't!" she screeched. "You can't take this back!" She doubled over, holding herself. "Oh, God! Father, give me strength."

Garrett kneeled down in front of her. "Lawson, I know this is a lot to take in. Baby, I'm begging you to please forgive me. I love you, and you're the only woman I want. I was hurt and made the worst decision of my life by being unfaithful to you. But, baby, if I could forgive you, I pray that you could find it in your heart to—"

She pushed away from him. "Don't do that! Don't you dare try to act like it's the same!"

"I know it's not. I'm just asking that you take it into consideration."

Lawson crossed her arms in front of her. "Who is she? Is she someone I know?"

"No, she's a designer I was working with on a project."

Lawson rolled her eyes. "Is it still going on?"

"No, baby, I swear! I told her I could never see her again. It was one time. We both know it was wrong. She had the project reassigned to someone else. It's over. It was only once."

"Just so you know, telling me that you only made love to another woman *one time* really doesn't help."

"Baby, I'm so sorry. Please tell me what I need to do to fix this," pleaded Garrett.

"Fix it?" Lawson was livid. "How do you propose to do that? My God, Garrett, how could you do this to me? To us?"

"I wasn't thinking. I believed our marriage was over." He tried to touch her.

Lawson shirked away. "Is that the hand you used to touch her, Garrett? Is that how you did it, the same way you're touching me?" She closed her eyes as the tears streamed from her eyelids. "I've been with you my whole adult life. We've never been unfaithful to each, Garrett, *never*. That's what kept us connected despite everything else that was going on. I had a level of trust with you that I've never had with any man. Now, it's gone."

"We can get that back," maintained Garrett.

Lawson thought for moment. "You know, Garrett, between this, the birth controls pills, and all the fighting, I'm not so sure I want to anymore." She looked up at him. "Maybe this time it really needs to be over."

Chapter 42

**"How could you not tell me this?
You're my sister!"**
—*Lawson Kerry Banks*

"I can't believe Garrett would do something like this," sobbed Lawson, cradled in her sister's arms. Kina, Reginell, Sullivan, and Angel were all gathered in Lawson's bedroom, having made a beeline to Lawson's house after receiving her tearful summon. "I mean, I know I screwed up by not telling him about the birth control pills, but for him to have sex with another woman? Was he trying to get her pregnant? Does he not find me desirable anymore?" She shook her head. "I don't understand this."

Reginell sighed. "Maybe it's like what he said. Garrett was hurt and confused and wanted to lash out at you for everything that happened."

"So this is what I can expect whenever my husband is hurt or confused?"

Angel brought Lawson a steaming cup of tea. "Sweetie, you know Garrett is not like a serial cheater. He made a mistake."

Lawson accepted the tea. "A *mistake* is leaving the toilet seat up or forgetting to pay the cable bill. This was more than a mistake. This was an absolute betrayal."

"Dang, I bet it was that chick from the restaurant," surmised Reginell.

Lawson's head sprang up. "Wait—what chick? Who are you talking about, Reggie?"

"I saw him having dinner with someone right after he moved out."

"And you didn't tell me?"

"Nooo . . . I confronted Garrett about it, and he swore nothing was going on between them."

"You believed him, Reggie? Really?" Sullivan shook her head in pity.

"Not really, but I thought I'd gotten through to him about trying to make his marriage work."

"How could you not tell me this? You're my sister!" Lawson cried.

"I figured telling you Garrett might be hooking up with his interior designer would only make things worse between you two. Plus, it really was none of my business. I'm not trying to get in the middle of what's happening between y'all. I fulfilled my sisterly obligation by trying to talk him out of it."

"She has a point," said Angel. "If a man is going to cheat, there's really nothing anyone else can do to talk him out of it once that's what he's decided in his heart to do."

"I don't care. You're my sister, and you should've come to me," fired Lawson. "Or is your head so far up Mark's behind that you can't think about anyone else?"

Reginell reeled back and threw up her hand. "Hold up—why are you putting Mark in this? He isn't the one cheating, *Garrett* is."

Lawson drew up her lips and narrowed her eyes. "And how much longer do you think that'll be? Do you really think Mark is going to put up with you taking it off for every man and his daddy much longer? Do you honestly think he wants a stripper around his daughter? Only God knows who or what else you're doing for money."

Angel quickly intervened. "Lawson, please don't say anything else. You're hurt and you're angry, and you're taking it out on the wrong one."

"That's all right, Angel." Hot tears burned Reginell's eyes. "Forget you, Lawson. You walk around here acting like you're so perfect, like you don't make mistakes, but you don't have the right to look down on nobody else. That's why you can't keep a man, and that's why you'll always be alone!"

Lawson pointed to herself. "I've got my dignity."

"Yes, and somebody else has your man!" With that, Reginell grabbed her purse and stood up to leave.

Angel tried to stop her. "You can't walk out on your sister like this, Reggie, especially not now."

"Oh, yeah? Watch me!" Reginell stormed out.

"Let her go!" hissed Sullivan. "Good riddance."

Kina turned to Lawson. "How are you going to handle this situation with Garrett?"

"What can I do? He broke our vows without so much as a second thought. I can't be with a man who thinks so little of our commitment to each other. Even the Bible has an out clause for cheating." Lawson sighed. "I don't think I can stay married to him. I told he had to move out. It may be for good this time."

"Believe me, I know how you're feeling right now, but don't make any rash decisions," cautioned Angel. "You're too emotional. Give it some time and prayer."

Lawson shook her head. "No amount of time or prayer is going to change the fact that he slept with another woman. He kissed her. He touched her. He consciously planned to have sex with her. He gave her the same part of himself that he gives to me like it was nothing when it's everything sacred to me."

Sullivan sat down next to Lawson. "I know it hurts, but it's possible to forgive him and move on. Look at me and Charles."

"Yeah, look at you and Charles," retorted Lawson. "He forgave you, and what happened? You went out and cheated on him again, only this time, you're knocked up to boot!"

Sullivan huffed. "Obviously, I wasn't talking about *that* part."

"Garrett said that the affair is over," cited Kina. "Don't give your husband over to this other woman, especially when they're not even seeing each other anymore. He made a bad decision. He's remorseful and repentant. Don't lose your family over this."

"Why is the burden on me?" questioned Lawson. "He's the one who cheated. He broke our vows, not me."

Angel agreed. "True, Garrett is the one who cheated. He took the coward's way out of dealing with your problems, but you're not blameless, Lawson. Between you obsessing over Reggie and Mark and the whole fiasco with the pills, you practically drove him to it."

"You can't hold Garrett to one standard and yourself to another," said Sullivan. "You both screwed up, but you're newlyweds. Stuff happens. You've got to find a way to fight through it."

Lawson released a breath. "Y'all don't get it." She looked up through watery eyes. "Garrett broke my heart."

Kina came to Lawson's side. "I'd never tell anyone to stay in a marriage where they're being disrespected, abused, or mistreated, but that's not the case with you and Garrett. He wants to come home."

Sullivan squeezed Lawson's hand. "Lawson, you're principled, and that's one of the things we love about you. We can always depend on you to bring us back when we start to stray. You call us on our mess, and you don't allow us to sin and feel like it's okay. I actually appreciate having someone like you around to give me that kick in the butt when I need it, but you need to learn how to let stuff go sometimes, like this grudge against Garrett."

"I'm not holding a grudge against him. I'm just having a hard time accepting that he could do something like that. What does it say about the kind of man he is and his principles?"

"It says he's human," said Kina, still bearing the guilt from her confession to Charles. "He made a horrible decision, but at least he was honest with you about it. He ended the affair; he repented and took full responsibility for what happened. I don't know what more the man can do. He can't change it." Kina looked at Sullivan, speaking for herself as well as Garrett.

"Lawson, I know what you're going through," conceded Angel. "When I found out that Duke cheated on me, I felt utterly betrayed. It made me feel like less of a woman, like I couldn't satisfy him like she could. I was humiliated and confused. I couldn't understand how this could happen after I did everything I could to be a good wife to him. But believe me when I tell you that there's nothing like the pain of going through a divorce. I see why God hates it and calls it violence. That was a kind of pain I don't wish on anybody. I don't have to tell any of you how bad it got for me. You already know I tried to kill myself. I had to be in an excruciating amount of pain to think death was better than divorce."

Lawson began crying again. Angel tried to comfort her. "I know you're hurting right now, and you feel like you don't even know the man you married. God knows that. That's why He gives us an out where infidelity is concerned. If there's any way you can find it in your heart to forgive him and make your marriage work, you need to try. You don't want to walk in my shoes, and you don't want to spend the rest of your life regretting that you didn't give your marriage a fair shot."

Sullivan stepped in. "Lawson, I know you don't want to hear this, but you've got to take some responsibility in this too. You're not the only one who felt hurt and betrayed. I don't by any means excuse him for cheating on you, but you made it real easy between your fixation on Mark, school, work, and Namon, and that was all *before* he found out you lied about taking birth control. You can't put your marriage on the back burner and expect everything to be okay. Believe me, I know."

"I'm going to be honest with you," revealed Angel. "Even though Duke was the one who stepped out and broke our vows, if he'd been willing to change and work things out, I would've stayed with him and kept my marriage together. I'm just so thankful that we've been given a second chance to get it right this time."

"I just feel like it makes me weak to stay," admitted Lawson. "What kind of woman stays with a man who would betray her this way?"

Kina spoke sincerely. "He deserves another chance, Lawson. I know you don't think so, but God gives us grace and mercy all the time, whether we deserve it or not."

"So you expect me to just welcome him back with opened arms and no consequences for what he did? As much as I love my husband, I would've understood if he didn't take me back."

"He *is* suffering the consequences," explained Sullivan. "There's no worse feeling in the world than losing your family and the person you love. I promise you Garrett's feeling like crap right now. How much more suffering do you want him to have?"

"Enough that he doesn't cheat again," argued Lawson.

"It's not your place to punish him," Angel reminded her. "It's the Lord's. The way I see it, if God can forgive Garrett, surely you can too, especially considering that you've hurt him just as much as he hurt you."

"I hear what you're saying, but what kind of example does that set for Namon?" inquired Lawson. "Do I want him to be the kind of husband and father who'd go out and cheat on his wife or marry the kind of woman who'd accept being disrespected that way?"

"It could also be an example of being like Christ and showing mercy and forgiveness. It'll mean more to Namon to know that he can be redeemed than to feel like he's doomed forever if he misses the mark sometimes," said Kina, reflecting on her own situation and hoping to be extended that same kind of forgiveness.

Lawson sighed. "I just don't know, y'all. I love Garrett, but I just don't know how I'll be able to trust him after this."

"Through faith and prayer," answered Angel. "The same way he was able to trust you and give you another chance after you hurt him."

"That's the thing—we keep hurting each other time and time again. At what point do you say enough is enough and walk away? At what point do you finally admit that it's over?"

Chapter 43

"God has never asked us to help Him do His job. It's when we decide to help Him out that we get into trouble."
                                        —*Angel King*

Kina unlocked the door to her apartment expecting to find everything the way she left it. Instead, she opened the door to new furniture she didn't recognize and her friends' smiling faces.

"Surprise!" they exclaimed as soon as Kina opened the door.

Kina grabbed her chest, caught completely off guard. "What's all this?"

"What does it look like, silly?" teased Sullivan. "Happy birthday!"

"No, I mean *all this!*" Kina gestured toward the new living-room suite. She was beyond stunned to see her worn, borrowed, and hand-me-down furniture replaced by a brand-new sectional, entertainment unit, a flat-screen television, and coffee table. "Is this for me?"

"Yes, Kina," replied Sullivan. "Don't you like it?"

"Of course, but I can't accept this." She shook her head. "It's too much. I appreciate the effort, but it's got to go back. You know I can't afford all this."

"Kina, relax and enjoy it," said Lawson. "It's all paid for. The only thing it'll cost you is a great big smile."

"This is so nice," said Kina, looking around at her newly furnished apartment. "Y'all didn't have to do this for me."

"Obviously, *we* didn't," replied Lawson. "Miss Moneybags over here did most of it." She picked up a crystal bowl, which was the centerpiece of Kina's new coffee table. "Reggie bought this, though, and sends her love. Happy birthday, cuz!"

Kina hugged her. "I love it! Please tell Reggie thanks for me." She released Lawson and turned to Sullivan. "I can't believe you did all this for me. Why?"

"Aside from the fact that your old furniture bordered on hideous, you saved my husband's life, Kina. This is the least I could do to thank you."

Kina shook her head, overcome with guilt. "I wish you would stop saying that, Sullivan. I didn't save him, God did. Believe me . . . I don't deserve any of the credit."

Sullivan put her arm around Kina. "If nothing else, you deserve credit for being such a good friend to me. Kina, I know I probably don't say it enough, but I love you. You're my family. I know keeping this secret about the baby and Vaughn has been hard on all of you, but I know it's been the hardest on you, Kina, since you work with Charles and have to see him every day. I know how much you respect and admire him, so I especially appreciate that you've let all that take a backseat to your loyalty to me."

Kina couldn't receive the adulation. "This is just too much . . ."

"Kina, you have earned all of this," insisted Lawson. "You've been through so much, but you never let it break your spirit and change who you are. No matter how much we all fight with each other, you're always the one who brings us back together and who keeps the peace and reminds us of how much we all love one another. You've been so selfless. You're constantly putting other people's needs ahead of your own, whether it's Kenny's or the church's or your friends' needs. It's time someone did something for you for a change."

"Sullivan, this is all very generous, and I thank all you for your kind words and faith in me, but I can't accept this."

"Kina, stop being magnanimous and let us bless you, okay?" teased Sullivan.

Kina was adamant. "Sullivan, I can't keep this."

"I'm not taking it back!"

"Fine . . . I'll just donate it to the church or something."

"You will do no such thing!" objected Angel. "Kina, learn how to let other people help you. You're not in this by yourself. We didn't do this because we had to or because we felt sorry for you. We did this because we love you and wanted to show you how we appreciate you, especially Sullivan.

"And I'm going to keep on spoiling you whether you like it or not, so get used to it!" demanded Sullivan with a smile. "As soon as Charles gets back on his feet, expect him to be just as kind."

Kina dissolved into tears.

Angel rubbed her back. "Why are you crying, honey? Charles is going to be fine. Your prayers, love, and support are part of what's getting him through this."

"He's never going to forgive me," sobbed Kina.

"Forgive you for what?" asked Sullivan, confused.

"The stroke—all of it! It's my fault," sobbed Kina.

"Are you talking about the food you made for him? One helping of soul food didn't do this to Charles. This was the result of years of anniversary dinners, fish fries, and church picnics where fried chicken was as much a part of the scenery as checkered blankets. The doctors and I have been trying to get Charles to take better care of himself for years. Please don't blame yourself."

"I know all that, but the doctor also said this could've been brought on by stress."

"Yeah, but that doesn't have anything to do with you. If anybody is the cause of stress in Charles's life, it's me."

Kina shook her head. "Not that day. He was eager to get home. He couldn't wait to see you."

Sullivan smiled. "That's sweet of you to say, Kina."

"I'm not just saying it, Sullivan. He wanted to go home to you. He loves you."

"I know. I love him too."

Lawson sensed that something was off. "Kina, where are you going with all this?"

Kina covered her face and cried into her hands. "I can't keep this secret anymore."

Angel draped her arm around Kina. "What are you talking about? What secret?"

"Kina, did something happen that day you didn't tell us about?" asked Lawson.

Kina nodded. "It's my fault! It's all my fault!"

Lawson peeled back Kina's hands, revealing a face that was beet red and wet with tears. "Sweetie, what's going on? This is obviously eating you up inside."

"It is. It has been ever since Pastor's stroke," Kina admitted.

Lawson held her cousin's hand. "Talk to us. What's going on?"

Kina closed her eyes to gather her thoughts. "I don't even know how to tell you this."

"Just say it," persisted Sullivan, now both curious and worried.

Kina inhaled, her eyes fell downcast. "I didn't tell you or the doctors everything that happened that day."

Angel wrinkled her brow. "What did you leave out?"

"The part I said about coming to Charles's office to bring him dinner was true. I did do that, but I didn't just drop the plate off and leave like I said."

The tone in Sullivan's voice changed. "What did you do?"

"Something I'll regret for the rest of my life . . ." She looked up at Sullivan. "I told Charles I love him."

Sullivan shrugged her shoulders. "Charles knows you love him. Why would that cause a stroke?"

"I wasn't talking about agape love. I meant that I was *in love* with him." Kina dropped her head. "Then I kissed him."

Sullivan sprang up. *"What?"*

Kina continued. "I told him I was the woman he was supposed to marry, the one God wanted him to be with."

Lawson grimaced. "Kina, why would you do something like that? How could you even think that?"

"I was so confused about Joan and dealing with E'Bell's death and being alone. I convinced myself that Charles could be the one to rescue me from all that."

Angel groaned. "Kina, this is—"

Sullivan broke in. "She's not telling us everything. I know Charles. Kina isn't the first lonely, pathetic, underhanded woman to come on to him. He's used to dealing with that, so that wouldn't have been stressful enough to trigger a stroke." Sullivan's eyes morphed into icy slits. "Kina, *what else* did you do?"

Kina paused before going on. "He told me that he loved Sullivan and that he'd never leave her. I couldn't handle it, I just couldn't take another rejection. I felt like you didn't deserve him, Sullivan, and that he would've been better off with me. He was just too blinded by love to see it."

"So what did you do?" repeated Sullivan.

"I told him," squeaked Kina, barely audible.

Sullivan placed her hands on her hips. *"Told him what?"*

Kina took a deep breath. "I told him about Vaughn and the baby. I told him that you were pregnant and that you'd been making a fool out of him all this time. I told him you didn't love him, that you only wanted his money. I said that you were going to pass the baby off as his—"

Without warning, Sullivan swooped down and slapped Kina across the face with full force. "How could you do that? What kind of monster are you?" screamed Sullivan.

Lawson rushed to Kina's side. Angel winced. "Sully, calm down. This isn't the right way to handle this."

"Oh, I'm sorry," Sullivan replied sarcastically. "What's the right way to deal with this, Angel?"

"Not by hitting on my cousin," spoke up Lawson. "She's had to deal with that enough as it is."

Kina stood up, hold her stinging cheek. "Sullivan, I know you hate me right now, but I couldn't keep the truth from you anymore."

Sullivan glared at her. "You need to get out of my face before I do more than just slap you," threatened Sullivan in an even, acidic tone.

Kina tried again. "Sullivan, we can get past this if you just try to understand where I was coming from and forgive me."

Sullivan stood akimbo. *"Forgive you?* You want me to *understand* you? Are you freakin' kidding me, Kina? Do you have any idea what you've done?"

"I wasn't thinking clearly," Kina tried to explain. "I'm sorry."

"You're about to be *real* sorry," threatened Sullivan and lunged toward Kina, locking her hands around Kina's throat. She wrestled Kina to the ground.

"Sullivan, you're hurting her!" cried Angel. Kina was practically powerless against Sullivan's rage and years of street fighting.

Lawson tried to wedge in between them. "I believe that's the whole idea!"

"Think about your baby, Sullivan! Think about little Christian," pleaded Angel.

Upon hearing that, Sullivan eased her grip on Kina, her chest heaving. "You better be glad I'm pregnant. Otherwise, I would've killed you with my bare hands!"

"Sullivan, I'm so sorry," wept Kina. "I never meant for any of this to happen."

Sullivan clutched her stomach as if to reassure the baby that everything was okay. "From this point on, Kina, we're done. Don't talk to me again, don't even *look* at me. This friendship is over."

"Hold up, Sully!" butt in Lawson. "Are you seriously trying to blame Kina for this?"

"Yes, Lawson! Kina and her big mouth gave my husband a stroke. You're darn right I blame her for this!"

"No, your lies and infidelity are what gave your husband a stroke!" maintained Lawson. "This was going to come out one way or another, Sullivan. We've been telling you that all along."

"Kina had no right to say anything, especially since she did it out of malice and after a failed attempt to seduce my husband!"

"Granted, she was dead wrong for that," conceded Lawson. "But we all know that Kina hasn't been herself lately. Look at everything she's gone through these past couple of years."

Kina chimed in. "Sullivan, I never should've gone after Charles. I don't know what I was thinking."

"Is she talking to me?" Sullivan asked looking around the room, "Because I could've sworn I told all man-stealing, wannabe, jealous witches to stop talking to me!"

"Was that really called for, Sully?" asked Lawson with disdain.

Kina took another stab at explaining herself. "Sullivan—"

Sullivan flung up her right hand. "I don't want to hear it, Kina!"

"Well, you're gon' hear it!" demanded Lawson. "We're not just friends, Sully. We're sisters, all of us! Family doesn't turn its back on family."

Sullivan was dumbfounded. "You expect me to forgive her?"

"Yes, just like the Lord and Charles have forgiven you over and over again."

"My husband could have died, Lawson."

"But he didn't. Frankly, there wouldn't have been anything to tell him if you hadn't created this whole mess." Lawson turned to Angel. "Take Kina in the back and get her cleaned up so I can deal with Sullivan."

Both Angel and Kina obeyed. Neither was in a hurry to be on the losing end of Sullivan's temper.

Lawson turned her attention back to Sullivan. "You know you have to hear her out, right?"

Sullivan pouted. "I don't have to do anything."

"Kina is my cousin, and you're my best friend. I'm not about to take sides in this, neither is Angel. You and Kina are just going to have to find a way to work this out."

"I didn't see you in a hurry to work things out with Garrett or the tramp who seduced him," retorted Sullivan. "The minute you tell her that it was okay to sleep with your husband will be the minute I tell Kina it's okay to try to sleep with mine!"

In Kina's bedroom, Angel pressed an ice pack against Kina's busted lip to prevent more swelling. "Kina, I love you, and I know you've been to hell and back over the past couple of years. I think we all underestimated the toll all that took on you. Even with all that, though, I still can't understand why you'd want to do that to Sullivan. You're not a scheming, vindictive person, how could you do that to one of your best friends? We all know that Sullivan can be a drama queen, but something had to drive you to that point where you'd want to destroy her life."

"I wasn't trying to hurt her, honest, Angel. I've just been in such a dark place for so long. I thought that once E'Bell was gone, I'd have this wonderful life with my son and my new career." She shook her head. "Nothing turned out the way I thought it would. I've been so lonely and confused that most of the time I don't know whether I'm coming or going. I was just tired of feeling rejected and alone, and the pastor's been so good to me . . ."

"I'm sure he has, but that's because he's a good man, not because he's in love with you. As much as she infuriates him—and us—Charles is crazy about his wife. Maybe that makes him just plain *crazy*, but he loves her."

"I know that now. Heck, I knew it then. I just can't stand the way she treats him. He deserves better."

"That's between him and Sully. We may never understand it, but I do believe that she loves him, Kina.

I've watched her take care of him. She loves that baby too."

"She's going to hurt him again, and we all know that. I just couldn't bear to see it happen again."

"God would've revealed to Charles what He wanted him to know. He's never asked us to help Him do His job. It's when we decide to help Him out that we get into trouble."

Kina began bawling. "Sullivan is never going to forgive me, is she?"

"Never say never," cautioned Angel before being interrupted by a knock at the door. Lawson peeked inside with Sullivan in tow.

"Can we come in?" ventured Lawson. Angel nodded.

"Sullivan, I'm so sorry," blabbed Kina. "I never should've tried to interfere in your marriage. I'm sorry I betrayed your trust and went after Charles. I wasn't a friend to you and wasn't much of a Christian either. I can't tell you how awful I feel about the whole thing. I love you, and I just want you to forgive me."

Sullivan cleared her throat and crossed her arms in front of her. "You know I'm not used to being on this side of the fence. I'm usually the one who messed up and has to ask everyone else for forgiveness. I want you to know that I love you too, Kina, and I forgive you."

"Thank you, Sully! You're a good friend." In elation, Kina reached out to hug Sullivan.

Sullivan patted her on the back, stopping short of a full embrace, and gently pushed her away. "Like I said, I forgive you, but . . ."

Kina backed away a little. "But what?"

"Kina, I realize I have to take responsibility for most of this. I'm the one who cheated on Charles and set all of this in motion. If I lose him, it won't because of what you did. It'll be because of what I've done." Sullivan dropped her head. "That said, I don't think we could ever go back to being friends again, not like we were."

"Why not?" Kina asked, her voice breaking. "You said you forgave me."

"I do."

"I don't understand. Sullivan, you're one of my best friends. You know I'd never do anything to hurt you."

"See? That's the thing. I *don't* know that, Kina. Look what you tried to do to Charles and me. You told him about Vaughn and the baby for no other reason than to hurt me."

Kina shook her head. "It wasn't like that."

"In all honesty, I don't really care what it was like. Yeah, I'm sure you rationalized it in your head, but the fact is that your sole purpose for going to see Charles that night was to take my husband from me, to destroy my marriage. When seduction didn't work, you upped the ante and told him the baby I was carrying wasn't his. You didn't care how much that would hurt him; you certainly didn't care if it hurt me. Your actions could've killed him! How can things ever be the same between us after that? How could I ever trust you again?"

"Charles forgave you and gave you another chance," noted Kina, wiping a tear from her eye. Lawson draped her arm around her cousin's shoulder.

"Yes, he did, but I have an obligation not only to protect myself, but also to protect my husband and this baby. I can't risk having you so entrenched in our lives that you can hurt us again."

Kina wiggled away from Lawson. "Sullivan, that's not fair! You're talking like I'm a threat to your family, and I'm not."

"I don't intend to let you get close enough to us to be one. I want you to go to the church tomorrow and hand in your resignation. There's no way I can continue to allow you to work on Charles's behalf."

"Why are you being so mean?" bellowed Kina. "After all we've been through, after all the years we've been friends!"

"I'm not trying to be mean, Kina. It just is what it is. I'm not putting all the blame on you for what happened to Charles. I know I've gotten very good at screwing up my life, I'll be the first to admit that. One thing I haven't done, though, is try to screw up anyone else's life, especially not my friends'. Kina, I trusted you. I bared my soul to you, my deepest, darkest secrets, and you used that to try to destroy me."

"I was upset and confused," defended Kina.

"I can't risk everything I love on the possibility of you getting 'upset and confused' again. I'm sorry. I can't take that kind of chance. Now, I don't plan to make any formal announcements about the change in our friendship. When I see you, I'll still speak and be cordial. You and Kenny will always be in my prayers, and you don't have to worry about me trying to turn anyone here against you. They can still be cool with both of us. I just can't be cool with you anymore."

"What about the baby? Are you going to ban me from her too?" questioned Kina.

Sullivan nodded. "I think the best thing for all of us is to have a little distance right now. I hope you understand."

Kina appealed to Lawson. "Tell her we can work this out. That's what friends do."

"Just let it go, honey," whispered Lawson.

"I need to get out of here," mumbled Sullivan. "Lawson, call me later. Kina, *don't!*" Sullivan left Angel and Lawson alone to comfort Kina.

"I've never seen her so angry with me," Kina said quietly. "What if things can never go back to the way they were?"

"Sully just needs some time," concluded Angel. "Leave her alone and let her have it."

"She hates me, doesn't she?"

"Of course not. She loves you; she just needs the space to wrap her head around what happened."

Kina disagreed. "You didn't look in her eyes and see what I saw. She hates me. Little does she know, I hate me enough for both of us right now."

Chapter 44

"God, what has become of me?"
                              —Angel King

It had already been a stressful day, made even more stressful by the fact that Angel had to alter her plans in order to pick Morgan and Miley up at noon due to a faculty planning meeting. Feeling overwhelmed, she did the one thing that seemed to allow her to flee from the pressure these days: logging on to pornographic Web sites.

Initially, she only logged on when chatting with Channing. Now, she spent several hours out of the day perusing photos and viewing uploaded videos whether Channing was on or not. She conceded that it was a compulsion, but still wasn't convinced that it was a full-on addiction.

"Y'all stop running around in there," called Angel to the girls, who were scurrying in and out of the rooms upstairs while she hid away in the master bedroom.

"We're playing," returned Morgan, shrieking with delight.

Angel found the noise to be a distraction. "Well, go downstairs and play," she ordered them. "I can't concentrate with all that screaming."

Miley poked her head in the door. "Can we fix something to eat?"

Angel slammed her laptop shut, afraid that the tot would spy the explicit images on her monitor. "Yeah, just don't make a mess," she said before shooing them away.

"Can we make some apples and peanut butter?" asked Morgan.

"Yes," Angel responded hastily.

Miley stepped in front of her sister. "Can you come help?"

"Miley, just get the apples out of the fridge. You don't need me to help you do that."

The girls disappeared to race each other down the stairs. Angel soon became engrossed in her pornographic world again. Living vicariously through the characters on the screen was intoxicating. They were free to do the things she'd secretly thought about but would never act upon. She knew it was wrong to watch but decided that it was still better than carrying out the physical acts. After all, this was just fantasy and would end the moment she shut down her computer.

"Oww!" yelped Miley.

Angel was jarred out of her trance by Miley's scream. She rushed downstairs to the kitchen and found Miley crying and holding her bloodied hand. Morgan was mopping up the blood with a paper towel.

Angel hurried to aid Miley. "Oh my God, what happened?"

"I was trying to cut the apples," sobbed Miley.

Angel examined the cut. "What were you doing with the knife? Why didn't you come get me?"

"I did," she cried. "You told me to do it myself."

Angel couldn't believe that she'd been that careless. She gulped, riddled with guilt. "You're right . . . I did. I'm sorry, baby girl. I shouldn't have told you that."

"It hurts," Miley groaned.

"Come on, we've got to get it cleaned up. I don't think you'll need stitches—"

"Stitches!" cried Miley.

"It'll be okay. I'm a nurse, remember?"

That's when Angel remembered who she was, a nurse, a Christian, a mother to the girl, and fiancée to Duke. She'd traded in all those roles for a dirty, senseless thrill on the Internet. Now Miley was being punished for it.

Angel eventually calmed Miley down enough to bandage her hand and send both girls off to bed for a nap. When she returned to her room, the Web site was still posted on her computer screen. Disgusted with herself, Angel deleted her profile and closed her account on the site. In doing so, she had to acknowledge that she had a problem. She also knew she couldn't resolve it alone.

"God, what has become of me?" she asked aloud, plunking down on the bed. "I don't even recognize this person I've become. I need you to help me find my way back. I've not been a cheater or a pervert or a negligent mother, but I've become all three because I've allowed this sin into my life. I honestly thought I wasn't hurting anybody, but I see I was. I was hurting you, and without realizing, I was hurting myself.

"I've let this lust interfere in my relationship with the man I love, and I've let it interfere with my relationship with you. God, I'm so sorry for not watching after those precious girls you and Duke have entrusted to me. Miley could've seriously hurt herself. If anything had happened to her, I don't think I could forgive myself.

"Cleanse me, Lord. Take these thoughts and this lust out of my heart. I can't do it without your help."

Angel hugged her pillow and quietly cried into it. Even though she wasn't sure what she'd become, she knew who she was in the eyes of God. With Him, she could always go back, start over, and get it right.

Chapter 45

**"I just want a man to think, despite every-
thing I've done, that I'm still beautiful."**
                                                    —*Reginell Kerry*

The video set in Atlanta was nothing like she expected. Reginell envisioned being shuttled to and from
Savannah via a top-of-the-line limousine service. She
thought there would be a glamour squad working on
hair and makeup, whose only job was to make her
beautiful. She pictured tables overflowing with delec-
table trays of lush fresh fruit and vegetables to sink her
teeth into at will. She imagined brushing elbows with
celebrities as they were scurried on and off the set for
cameos. In short, she was expecting the star treatment.

Instead, what Reginell received was an order to
make the three-hour drive to Atlanta, a makeup artist
with an attitude who hastily slapped some powder on
her face, slung a wig on her head, and thrust her on the
set, and an overworked production assistant screaming
at her between takes while she was being herded back
and forth to the main stage with a dozen or so women
like cattle.

Mark had called her that morning before she left,
pleading with her to ditch the video and join him for
dinner. She passed up the offer, reminding him that
she had to strike while both she and the iron were hot.
That's when he told her their lives were going in two
different directions and wished her the best.

"Make it sexy . . . shake it faster . . . bend over . . . show some skin . . . take it lower," ordered the director over the blaring music on the sweltering set. "You, in the red," he motioned to Reginell, "we need you over in the hot tub with her. Lather each other up. Make it sexy."

Reginell ambled over to the tub in her red bikini. Where was a drink when she needed one? Was this really the life she wanted? Was this worth losing Mark over? More important, was it worth losing herself?

When the director yelled "Cut" for them to rearrange the set, Reginell took solace at the snack table. She struck up a conversation with the young lady she was forced to share a tub with.

"Can you believe this?" fired off Reginell to the other video vixen.

The girl's eyes lit up. "No, I mean we're actually going to be in a *real* video!" she squealed.

Reginell frowned, still outraged by the degradation of the women on the set. "No, I mean the way they're treating us. It's ridiculous!"

The girl shrugged nonchalantly and bit into a celery stalk. "I don't see nothing wrong with it."

"You don't see anything wrong with being treated like some hood rat?"

She laughed a little. "At least we're getting some camera time, right? We could be stuck in the back like those other chicks."

Reginell peered into the girl's cherub face. She didn't look a day over sixteen. Mentally, she didn't appear to be a day over six. "What's your name?"

"Peaches."

"No, what's your real name. Don't you know who you really are?"

She shrugged again. "Everybody calls me Peaches."

Another scantily clad video extra rushed over to them in excitement, almost stumbling over her six-inch stilettos. "Peaches, guess what? That road manager over there just said the band is going to be shooting a reality show and they want about four or five girls to go on tour with them and be on the show. Girl, we gon' be famous!"

Reginell shook her head in pity.

The new girl looked Reginell up and down. "What's *her* problem?"

"You honestly think you're going to be starring in some TV show?" asked Reginell. "Sweetheart, you're just going to be one of the jump-offs who get tossed around the bus whenever somebody needs to get their rocks off. They're not trying to make you a star, just a groupie."

"Yeah, whatever," she said dryly and drove a few hairpins through her hair to hold the piece in place and turned back to Peaches. "He said we've all got to audition first, though. They're only going to pick the baddest chicks to be on the show."

"I bet your audition starts right there in the back of that tour bus too," stated Reginell. "Do you think you're the first girl to come in here all wide-eyed like this? They'll tell you anything to get you to do what they want."

"I don't care," she declared. "We're about to get paid!"

"This is really going to help my acting career," Peaches added dreamily. "Once the show airs, the producers are going to really start calling."

"Is that what you think?" asked Reginell. It was scary to hear Peaches saying those words. They sounded like her own. "Intermission promised me the same thing if I did whole crew."

"Well, I guess you didn't do it right!" quipped Peaches, laughing.

"Wasn't nobody even talking to you," interjected the woman. "You ain't no different or better than the rest of us. They're calling you a ho just like they're calling us one. Come on, Peaches. They've got some drinks in the back."

Peaches started to follow her friend. Reginell stopped her. "Is this really what you want to do with your life? Being some chickenhead who gets tossed around by a bunch of egomaniacs?"

Peaches looked down. "Yeah, it's what I got to do to be famous, right?"

"What does it profit a man to gain the world and lose his soul?" quoted Reginell, remembering that Bible verse and finally coming to understand what it meant.

"What?" Peaches looked confused. "Look, I got to go." She left to join her friend.

"All right, everybody back on the set," cued the director.

Reginell dragged herself back to the center of the action, which involved yet another hot tub.

"You." The director pointed to Reginell. "Take off your top and turn your back to the camera."

It's not like you haven't done it before, she told herself. The problem was, however, that she couldn't do it anymore.

Maybe it was Mark. Maybe it was God. Maybe it was seeing girls like Peaches get caught up and lose sight of who they were as women and daughters of the King. All Reginell knew was that she'd lingered in the gutter long enough. No contract was worth her soul. Reginell climbed out of the tub and scurried across the set, covering herself with her hand.

"Hey, we're not done with you yet! Where are you going?" yelled the director.

Reginell turned around and proclaimed, "I'm going home!"

Reginell came back to Savannah with a new resolve and idea for a new ministry to help women like Peaches and herself get out of the game and start seeing themselves the way God saw them. She asked her sister to invite her friends over to share her idea and get their input.

"What is she doing here?" demanded Sullivan, walking in and seeing Kina.

"She's here because I asked her to come," replied Reginell. "I know you two have issues, but you're going to have to put them aside for a few minutes for the sake of the sisterhood."

Sullivan begrudgingly sat down, and they all listened to Reginell's spiel on the new outreach ministry she wanted to create. The conversation ultimately led to the women questioning how they ended up in their current situations and what they could do to help someone else.

"I saw myself in those girls today, y'all, and it wasn't pretty," revealed Reginell. "I finally realized that God has more planned for me than what I'm doing. I know we can't save every woman, but we can try to save some. We've got to do something to reach out to these women who are in the sex industry, who've been abused, who are lost, and who don't know how much they're worth."

"Look at my little sister," crowed Lawson with pride. "I don't think I've ever been more proud of you than I am right now."

"What you're trying to do is really inspiring," commended Sullivan. "You work out the details and present it to Charles's administrative staff. I'm sure the church will be happy to support you in this."

"Thank you, Sullivan. I just want to be able to make a difference."

"You will, Reggie. I know what it's like to feel like nobody cares and it's all you can do to get out of bed in the morning. This is wonderful thing that you're doing."

"You're amazing, you know that?" said Lawson. "I haven't told you that enough lately. In fact, I haven't told you enough of anything lately. I'm sorry."

"It's cool," she assured her. "I knew we'd get back to normal eventually."

"It's not cool, Reggie. I haven't been a very good sister to you."

"You've had a lot on your plate."

"I'm talking about before Garrett moved out. The truth is, I was jealous of you."

Reginell was taken aback. "For what?"

"It's kind of hard to explain, but seeing how much Mark cared about you made me a little crazy. I guess somewhere in the back of my mind, I wanted him to feel that way about me. I'm the one who had his baby. It felt like you were creeping in on my territory with him, and it felt like he was creeping in on mine with you. I just couldn't stomach the two of you together."

"Well, it doesn't matter now," grumbled Reginell. "Mark and me are done."

"Reggie, you know I was very happy when you found Jody last year. I want to see you happy like that again, and I've always wanted Mark to find a good woman. If the two of you can make each other happy, more power to you!"

"What about your feelings?"

"My feelings are my problem, not yours. You go on and be happy. Not that you need it, but you and Mark have my blessing."

"Thank you, Lawson." Reginell hugged her. "I just hope Mark still wants me."

"Mark loves you. Don't give up on him."

"Don't you give up on Garrett either," issued Reginell.

Sullivan joined them. "I'm praying that my husband doesn't decide to give up on me." She paused. "I've decided to tell him the truth about the baby."

"Are you sure want to do that?" asked Lawson. "Can his heart take it?"

"I have to tell him," said Sullivan. "I was crazy to think I could keep this a secret indefinitely. You all have been telling me all along that he has a right to know. I created this mess, I've got to deal with the consequences."

Angel patted her on the back. "I'm very proud of you for coming to this decision, Sullivan. It's very brave of you."

"I'm not trying to be noble. I just think he deserves to know. If he still wants to raise this baby after I tell him, I'll be eternally grateful. If he doesn't, I'll just have to accept it."

"When do you plan to tell him?" asked Lawson.

"As soon as possible. I don't want to put it off anymore."

Angel pulled Sullivan into an embrace. "Be strong, my sister. It takes a lot of strength to do what you're doing. We're praying for you."

Sullivan turned to Lawson. "If Charles can forgive me, you darn sure can forgive Garrett!" She laughed, then turned serious again. "Of course, in my case, that's a very big *if.*"

Chapter 46

"For the record, I'm perfectly capable of living without you."
—Lawson Kerry Banks

Lawson returned home from grocery shopping and found Namon sitting at the kitchen table texting. "I told you about spending all day texting those fast-tailed girls," admonished Lawson playfully.

"I wasn't texting some girl," he told her. "I was texting my dad." While Namon acknowledged Mark as his biological father, he still referred to Garrett as Dad.

Lawson's smile was replaced with the pained look of guilt, saddened by what the separation was doing to her son. "How is he?"

"He's sad just like you."

"Boy, what makes you think I'm sad?" she asked in a lighthearted tone.

"I know you, Mama. You miss him; I can tell. He misses us too and said to tell you that he still loves you."

Lawson exhaled. "You're right. I love him, and I miss him."

"Then why won't you let him come back home?"

"Sweetie, it's not that easy. You don't know everything that's happened."

"I don't care," stated Namon. "I just want you to let him come home. We used to be a family, now everything is all messed up. You and Dad aren't together.

You and Aunt Reggie are barely speaking, and now Aunt Reggie and my other dad are fighting. It's just messed up all the way around."

"Sometimes life is messy, Namon."

"Y'all act like you don't even love one another anymore."

"Of course we love one another. Reggie is my sister, and Garrett is my husband. I love the three of you more than anyone in this world. Unfortunately, I can't just snap my fingers and make everything the way it was. People's feelings have gotten hurt, and they feel betrayed."

"So if I did something bad, would you forgive me or just cut me off?" he asked her.

"I'd forgive you. You're my son."

"Then it seems like you should be able to forgive Dad too. He's a good man, Mama. Whatever he did, I know he's sorry for it."

Lawson rested a hand on his shoulder. "Namon . . . without getting into too many details, your dad really hurt me. It's not something I can just snap my fingers and—"

"And what? Forgive? That's not what you've always told me or what they preach in church."

"I know what they say in church, but this . . ." She had to stop herself from saying, *"But this is real!"* Wasn't God's commandment to love and forgive one another just as real?

Namon handed her his phone. "Just call him, Ma. At least hear what he has to say. He wants us to be a family again, and so do I. Deep down, I know that's what you want too."

It only took one call from Lawson, and Garrett was on his way back to the house he'd hoped to be able to call home again. Upon arriving, he knocked on the door, not sure if he still had key privileges.

"Hey," said Lawson and let him into house. "Come in and have a seat."

"How've you been?" asked Garrett, taking a seat on the sofa.

"As well as can be expected, I suppose. What about you?"

"I've been in my own personal hell," he admitted. "I can't sleep, I haven't been eating. It's all I can do to get up and go to work in the morning. I miss you, baby. I never even thought I could miss someone so much."

"This hasn't been a walk in the park for me either. That's why I wanted you to come over. I think it's time we made some decisions about our marriage." Garrett braced himself. "For the record, I'm perfectly capable of living without you," issued Lawson. "I'm capable of raising my son alone, of falling in love with someone else, and having a great life with another man."

"Is this what you called me over to tell me?" he asked incredulously.

"You didn't let me finish."

Garrett broke in. "Lawson, I can't speak for you, but I'm 100 percent committed to us and this life we have together. I don't want any other woman in this world except you. If I have to spend the next fifty years proving it to you, I will. Tell me what I have to do to make things right because I feel like I can't breathe without you. Just don't turn your back on our marriage."

She sat down next down to him. "I'm not giving up on us. I called you over because I wanted to tell you that I don't want to do any of those things I mentioned without you. If I love you, Garrett, that's it. That means I don't want anyone else. I know my love isn't always perfect. It's often overshadowed by my own insecuri-

ties and unrealistic expectations of you, but I'm prepared to spend the rest of my life loving you and getting it right. I want to be faithful to you, to bear your
children if need be, to leave my home, to do whatever it
takes for the honor of loving you and being your wife."

Garrett was almost moved to tears. "You mean
that?"

"You make me a better person, and I'm sorry for the
way I've treated you. I haven't been fair to you. I held
you to a standard that no human could possibly live
up to. I set you up for failure. I wanted you to accept
all of my flaws and shortcomings, but I couldn't accept
yours. I wanted you to be perfect, and that was wrong.
I'm sorry for all of the times I wasn't the wife and partner you needed me to be . . ."

Garrett folded her into his arms. "I'm sorry too,
babe, but I want to keep trying until we figure it out. I'll
do anything to make up for—"

She placed her finger on his lips. "There's nothing
you can do to take back what happened, and there's
nothing either of us can do to change it. I can't take
back lying to you or letting Reggie and Mark's relationship come between us. There comes a time when you
have to forget those things that are behind and move
toward with what's ahead," said Lawson, paraphrasing
from Philippians 3:13. "We can't move on if we keep
worrying about the past. I know we can't pretend it
didn't happen, but we don't have to let it define who we
are as a couple."

Garrett nodded. "We can do anything as long as
we're together and keep God first in our marriage and
everything else. You're my rib. As crazy, unpredictable,
and challenging as our union may be, I don't want to
be in this thing with anybody but you." He set his lips
down on hers. "I love you so much, Lawson."

Lawson sniffed. "I love you too. All I want is to have my husband back home."

He chuckled. "You ain't said nothing but a word!" He kissed her on the forehead. "Give me an hour to check out of that hotel, grab my stuff, and hightail it on back to you."

She wrapped her arms around his neck. "I'm going to give you an hour, all right," she hinted. "But it won't be for that!"

They both laughed and fell into another kiss. They both knew that there would still be challenges ahead of them and that some wounds might be slow to heal, but Lawson was with the man she loved again. For the moment, that's all that mattered.

Chapter 47

**"I've done all sorts of things that
I'm not proud of . . ."**
—Reginell Kerry

Reginell found herself at Mark's house. Using the key he'd given her, she let herself in and called out to him. "Mark!" Her heart sank when she discovered that no one was inside. "He's not here," she bemoaned. "I'm too late."

Feeling an overwhelming sense of loss, Reginell kneeled down on the plush carpeting and began to cry.

"I know I've messed up, Lord," she sobbed. "I've sinned. I've done all sorts of things that I'm not proud of, things I know aren't of you and of someone who calls herself a Christian.

"I want to change, Lord. I want to recommit myself to you and be worthy to be called a child of the King. I'm tired of living this way. I'm tired of searching. I just want to be at peace, and I want you to forgive me. Please, Jesus," pleaded Reginell.

She felt a hand on her. "Reggie?"

Reginell looked up into the face of Mark and immediately reached out for him. "Oh, Mark," she sobbed. "What have I done?"

Mark held her. "Shh, it's okay. You haven't done anything out of the range of God's forgiveness."

"The video shoot was awful! They wanted me to stand there and degrade myself, but I couldn't do it, Mark. I just couldn't."

"You listened to your heart this time," he said. He released her. "You never belonged there in the first place. A record deal isn't worth everything you had to give up. If it's God's will, it'll happen, and you won't have to do anything immoral to do it."

"I was just so sure that singing was my calling," said Reginell. "Now, I don't know what it is."

Mark helped her up. "There's no reason you can't operate in your calling for the Lord. You can still join the choir."

"You want me to trade in my stripper heels for a choir robe? I'm sure they have some sort of sin quota to join that I have, no doubt, surpassed."

"If there was a sin quota, none of us would qualify for anything. The life you've led and the things you've been through will only make your testimony that much more powerful. Not to mention that the mass choir is in talks to cut a CD. You can still have that career in music you've dreamed about."

"Mark, I haven't sung in the choir since I was little girl. I don't even feel worthy getting up there in front of all those people, knowing everything I've done."

"It's not about where you've been. It's about where you're going." He put her hand in his. "You'll get there, trust me."

"Here's hoping," quipped Reginell. "The busted shoot isn't even the worst thing that's happened."

"What's the worst thing?"

"Losing you. You told me not to go, and I didn't listen. Now it feels like we had this great thing going between us and it's over."

Mark held her face. "Who said it was over?"

"Well, I assumed that's what you meant when you told me to have a nice life."

Mark shrugged. "It was early. I can't be held accountable for anything I say before that first cup off of coffee. Besides, you know what they say about assuming, right?" joked Mark. She joined him in laughter. "It's going to take a lot more than that to get rid of me, girl." He kissed her on the lips. "I love you."

Reginell kissed him again. "I love you too."

"Now, what do you say to me taking my beautiful girlfriend out for a bite to eat, huh?"

Reginell froze. "What did you call me?"

"My girlfriend."

She wagged her finger as if rewinding the conversation. "No. Before that."

"Beautiful," replied Mark.

"That's what I thought you said." Reginell melted into a smile and felt as if her heart would burst. She channeled all of the love and appreciation she had for Mark into a long, passionate kiss.

He was taken by surprise. "What was that for?"

"That's for being who you are and loving me for who I am. For seeing me the way God sees me . . . as beautiful."

Chapter 48

"I can't build a future trying to recapture the past."

—Angel King

"It's about time you got here!" said Angel to Sullivan, letting her into the house. "I called you two hours ago."

"The baby forces me to move slower," replied Sullivan, waddling unnecessarily for a woman barely four months pregnant. She stopped when she spotted Kina. "Why do you keep inviting me when you invite her?"

"You're both my friends, and I need everyone to put their differences aside to help me. We've got a wedding to plan!"

They joined Lawson, Kina, and Reginell in the living room.

Lawson made room for Sullivan next to her. "Angel, I have to ask again, are you sure want to do this? What about Channing?"

"I've cut off all communication with him. He knows we can never be together in this world or the virtual one. That's a done deal."

"Okay, I just want you to be sure about going through with this wedding because it's not too late to change your mind," cautioned Lawson.

"I'm more than sure. I'm absolutely positive that this is what I want to do," swore Angel. "We never should've gotten divorced in the first place."

Lawson mustered up some excitement. "Well, the gang's all here, so where do you want to start?"

"Are you kidding?" Angel dragged out a box and dumped the contents in the center of the floor. "I've got to send out these invitations, I haven't picked a dress or secured a venue for the reception. We've literally done nothing to prepare for a wedding that's supposed to be happening in exactly seventy-eight days!"

"All right, calm down," coaxed Sullivan. "We've all done this before. With four weddings between us, we should be able to set this whole thing up within two boxes of cookies and one bottle of wine." She pressed her hand against her growing belly. "Better count me out on that bottle of wine, though."

Angel's house was soon transformed into wedding central. Lawson was making phone calls, Reginell was stamping envelopes, Kina made out the menu for the reception, and Sullivan helped Angel peruse catalogues for dress ideas.

"What about this one?" Sullivan held up a picture. "You could go with this sort of Grecian goddess look."

"I'm no Grecian goddess, Sully," joked Angel. "I just want something simple and elegant, like me."

"Why settle for simple and elegant when you can have fabulous and awe-inspiring like this one?" Sullivan folded the page back and passed the book to Angel.

Angel looked at the suggested retail price. "Sully, I'm not spending this kind of money on a dress I only intend to wear once."

"Here . . ." Sullivan dumped a pile of bridal magazines into Angel's lap. "I earmarked all of the good ones."

Lawson muted the television. "Angel, how many are we expecting at the reception? The reception hall needs a head count before I can book it—and a deposit!"

"Your printer is running low on ink, Angel," observed Reginell. "You got any extra?"

Kina brought her notepad over to Angel. "What were you thinking for the dinner? Buffet or a sit-down?"

"Just stop it with all the questions, okay?" cried Angel and flung the wedding catalogue across the room and buried her face in her hands. "I can't do this," she whispered.

"You're the one who wanted to go with an unknown designer and some nameless prairie gown," Sullivan pointed out.

Lawson cradled Angel. "I don't think that's what she meant, Sullivan. Angel, what's wrong?"

"Everything! I have no business planning this wedding when I know in my heart I'm making a huge mistake."

"Is this about Channing?"

"No, this is about Duke and the fact that we don't belong together."

"That's nonsense," scoffed Kina. "You two are like the perfect couple."

"We all know there's no such thing," said Lawson.

"You have such a beautiful family and a bright future ahead of you. I bet this is just cold feet, Angel. You're on happiness overload," Kina reasoned. "You're letting this thing with Channing confuse you."

"I don't think so. I haven't felt right about this engagement for a long time. Besides, if things were so great between Duke and me, Channing wouldn't have been a factor."

"Not necessarily," argued Sullivan. "I didn't cheat because I didn't love my husband. I cheated because I was bored in my marriage."

Angel touched Sullivan's hand. "No offense, Sully, but I'm not like that. I wouldn't have been to drawn to

Chan unless something was truly lacking in my relationship with Duke."

"Do you trust Duke?" asked Lawson. "Are you worried about him stepping out again?"

Angel nodded. "I can honestly say I trust Duke. I don't think he'd cheat on me again. Neither one of us is the same person we were ten years ago."

"Maybe that's the problem," inferred Sullivan. "Which Duke are you in love with—the one that he was or the man that he is today?"

"The one he is today, of course!" affirmed Angel.

"That Duke is still very much attached to Reese," noted Sullivan. "Which Angel does Duke think he's marrying? Is it the wide-eyed schoolgirl who worshipped the ground he walked on or the woman you've become, who's strong, independent, and has needs of her own?"

Angel was quiet.

Lawson eyed Angel's ring. "Angel, you don't have to go through with this if you don't want to."

Kina didn't give her a chance to answer. "Of course she wants to! Angel, you and Duke are amazing together. Don't start to second-guess yourself."

"I think you need to step back and pray on it," suggested Lawson.

"There's no need to pray," said Angel and sighed. "God has already given me the answer."

"Hey, babe, I got here as fast as I could," began Duke as he unlocked the door and walked into the house. His words trailed off as he spotted Angel's packed suitcases near the front door. "What's up with the bags? You going somewhere?"

"Yes," Angel sighed. "Sit down, honey. There's something I need to say to you."

Duke sat down on the sofa and made some room for her next to him. "What's going on here?"

"I'm moving. I'm going back to my place across town."

"Wait a minute—what? Moving? Why?"

"It's the right thing to do."

Duke nodded, understanding. "I get it. The whole shacking up thing is too much for you, and you want to wait until we're married to live together."

"Not exactly." Angel looked down at her ring one last time and slipped it off her hand. "I can't marry you, Duke."

"What?" he exclaimed. "Angel, where is this coming from?"

"It's been brewing for a while, baby. We just didn't want to see it." She presented the ring to him.

Duke refused to take it. "There's no way I'm taking that back! Angel, if I did something to upset you, I'm sorry. Tell me what it is so we can talk about it and move on."

"Yes, Duke, that's exactly what we need to do, we need to move on."

"I don't know why you're doing this. We've been planning our life together for months. This is the time we've been waiting for."

Angel stood up. "It's hard to give up on a dream sometimes, but it's even harder to accept having to settle for less than God's best. I think somewhere along the way, I was willing to forgo too much to make you happy."

"Baby, you make me happy without even trying. Just being here and being able to wake up and see your face every morning makes me happy. Don't take that away."

"That's not what I'm doing, but Duke, I have to be true to myself and to you. I've got to come to terms with the fact that this isn't what I want anymore."

Duke looked down at the ring. "We were supposed to get it right this time."

"I know," she whispered. "For years, I ached for you. I cried for that college girl whose husband walked out on her and their baby for another woman and her baby. I wanted to make things right. I never stopped loving you, and I wanted to go back to the time when we were so happy—before the divorce, before you met Theresa, before I lost our baby." She shook her head. "But you can't go back. You can forgive, but you can't really pick up like nothing's happened."

"I'm not trying to pretend like the last ten years never happened. That would be like wishing I didn't have Miley and Morgan. It would be a dishonor to my wife."

"Which wife?" Angel asked bitterly and threw up her hands. "I can't do this, Duke. I can't build a future trying to recapture the past."

"I don't think that's what we're doing."

"It's what *I've* been doing. For the longest, it felt like marrying you and loving you were such a huge waste of time, especially when I factor in all of those years of bitterness and unforgiveness I went through. Reuniting with you made it seem like maybe it wasn't such a waste after all, like maybe it was all a part of God's divine plan for my life. Believing that was a lot easier than accepting that I got married too young or that I chose the wrong mate."

Duke was hurt. "Why would you say something like that?"

"Because it's true, Duke. I'm not the love of your life. Theresa is. Just look around here—her pictures are everywhere, her stuff is still the same way she left it. You haven't even stopped referring to her as your wife. You're still in love with her, you probably always will be."

"Angel, I'm not going to deny that my wife—that *Reese*—has a very special place in my heart, but I love you. I want to marry *you!*"

Angel shook her head. "You don't want to marry me. You're lonely, and I'm good with the kids. Most important, you remarrying me and the two of us raising the girls together was Theresa's final wish. Even now, you're still trying to make her happy."

"Why can't you see how much I love you? You're my heart, Angel. I love you, the girls love you. You can't walk out of our lives this way."

"I love this family too, and I'll always be here for those girls. I'll always be your friend, Duke, but if we make the mistake of getting married, we're only going to end up back in divorce court. My heart couldn't take that again."

Duke sighed heavily. "What am I supposed to do now? I've spent the last year preparing for a life with you."

"You check in with God to see what His plans are for you. You take the time to really grieve losing Theresa. You be there for Miley and Morgan and trust God to send you the woman He wants you to have. In the meantime, you work on your relationship with Him like I'm doing."

"I'd rather work on my relationship with you."

"Duke, I know you don't like to deal with things. Your way of avoiding the problems in our marriage was getting involved with Theresa. Your way of dealing with her death was getting involved with me, but the only way you're going to get through it is to go through it. There are no shortcuts this time. God is using this as an opportunity for your development. Don't run away from it."

"You mean the way you're running away from us?"

"I'm not running away. I'm setting us both free. There's a difference." She sat down next to him again. "It would've been nice, though. I saw our wedding in my head more times than I can count. I couldn't wait for the opportunity to share with the rest of the world how much I loved you."

"You don't have to move out, Angel. Take one of the spare bedrooms or the pool house. I'll give you all the space you need, just don't leave. Don't say it's over between us. I don't think God would've brought us together again if He didn't want us to stay together."

"I know there's a reason and purpose for everything. The Bible tells us that. For the past two years, I thought the purpose of meeting Theresa was God's way of setting the groundwork for us to meet again, fall in love, and have the family and the life we wanted. I hope not—that would mean we really screwed up His plan! Maybe the point was for me to give Theresa the peace she needed, to give you and the girls the support you needed to get through this last year without her, and to give me the closure I needed to be able to move on." She touched his face. "You were my first love, my only love, Duke. How could it ever be truly over between us? But it's time to move on for both our sakes."

A few more hugs and a lot more tears, Angel found herself back home again. When she walked into the door this time, it didn't feel quite as lonely as it did before. It was full of light and peace. One day soon, it would be full of love as well.

Chapter 49

"There's something you need to know about the night you had the stroke."
—Sullivan Webb

Sullivan prayed for strength and mercy as she stood outside of her front door, preparing to go in, confirm the truth about their baby, Vaughn, and the child's true paternity. She looked down at her wedding ring. She was going into the house a married woman but could very well come out a single mother.

"Baby, I'm home," called Sullivan as she entered the foyer. Charles was sitting on the sofa reading his Bible.

Sullivan approached him with a kiss. "I hope I wasn't gone too long. Is Mavis still here?"

Charles nodded and looked toward the kitchen.

"Okay, I'm going to send her on home. There's something really important I need to talk to you about."

After dismissing the housekeeper, Sullivan returned to Charles's side. She reached for his hand, took a deep breath, and began.

"Charles, I know I've made this marriage very challenging for you, to say the least. I remember back when we first got engaged how everyone tried to warn you against marrying me. After all, what business did the daughter of a whore and a married man with three kids at home have marrying a man like you?"

Charles shook his head to indicate that he never saw her that way.

"I know you've always seen me as your princess, that's what made me fall in love with you, but I am what I am, honey. Thank God I have you and Christ in my life now, but sometimes, I am still that lost girl that you rescued. As much as I like to think I've changed, I still have some of the old me left inside. There are times when I want what I want when I want it. I don't always stop to think about who might get hurt in the process or what I stand to lose. It's in those times that I'm too caught up in me to seek God's direction. And it's during those times that I don't always do the right thing."

Sullivan rose and paced the floor as she talked. "Regardless of anything that happens next, I want you to know how very much I love you, Charles. Nothing has given me more joy or more sense of purpose than being your wife. It's my prayer that we're able to live out our lives together, but I keep screwing up. I keep hurting you and disappointing you," she confessed, her voice breaking into a sob. "You're a good man, Charles, but even you have your limits."

Charles grunted and vigorously shook his head. He reached out for her so she could know she didn't have to justify herself to him.

"No, I need to say this, Charles. Even if it costs me everything I love, you have to know the truth about the kind of woman you married."

Sullivan opened her mouth to continue when it happened. She felt something like a flutter inside of her womb. Her baby kicked for the first time.

She gasped and held her stomach. "She kicked . . . She kicked!" whispered Sullivan. She noticed Charles staring at her. She placed his hand on her stomach too.

"That's right, Charles. This is what I wanted to tell you so badly before the stroke. I'm pregnant."

Charles's eyes began to well with tears.

"I know we didn't think it would happen, but I guess God heard our prayers. We're having a baby, Charles." She took a deep breath. "But there's something you need to know about the night you had the stroke." Sullivan braided her hand into his. "Charles, do you remember what happened right before the stroke?"

Charles squinted his eyes and grunted.

"Do you remember who was with you?"

He nodded slowly. "Ka . . . Ka . . ."

"Yes, it was Kina. She brought you dinner. Do you remember what happened after that? Do you remember anything she said to you?"

Charles didn't respond.

"Honey, I think . . ." She sighed. "I think I need to tell you what she said. You have a right to know why this happened."

The truth was that Charles remembered it all quite clearly. He remembered Kina professing her love for him, he remembered rejecting her, and he remembered the bombshell report that Sullivan was carrying another man's child.

It was enough to kill him, and it almost did. It was at that point that Charles began to mediate on Hosea and God's call to him to love and accept his adulterous wife, Gomer. Like Sullivan, she'd been unfaithful and bore another man's child, but Hosea took her back under the direction of the Lord as a demonstration of God's love and faithfulness despite Israel's disobedience.

He also knew how damaged his wife was from the neglect and abuse she suffered at the hands of her parents, and he knew that God had charged him with breaking the cycle.

Charles looked at Sullivan with all sincerity and lifted his finger to quiet her before she went on. He placed his hand on her stomach and smiled.

"But I need to tell you."

Charles frowned as he shook his head, indicating that he didn't want to know and invited Sullivan into his arms.

Sullivan mouthed, "Okay" and lay her head on his chest.

In her heart, Sullivan knew that he remembered as well. The fact that he loved her and the baby enough to pretend he didn't was almost incomprehensible to her and brought her to tears.

"I don't deserve you," she replied sadly. "I don't deserve to be loved like this, to be forgiven for everything I've done to you."

"Love . . . you," sputtered Charles.

Sullivan nodded, finally understanding the sacrifice he was willing to make for her and their family. "I know you do. I just can't believe how much you love me, Charles. I've never known anything like it. What truly amazes me is as much as you love me, God loves us even more. We're the apple of His eye. It's because of His love for us that you can love me the way that you do."

She now knew what it felt like to be loved, to be protected, and understood, and finally, to be home.

Chapter 50

"Congratulations . . . I guess you're finally getting the child you wanted after all."
—*Lawson Kerry Banks*

After a harrowing nine hours of labor, Sullivan was finally able to hold her daughter in her arms, surrounded by the man she loved and her child's three surrogate aunts, Angel, Reginell, and Lawson.

"She's so beautiful," gushed Angel, allowing the baby to squeeze her finger. "Congratulations to both of you."

"Thank you, sister," said Charles, who had regained his voice after months of speech therapy. "She's our little miracle baby."

The baby yawned.

"Ohhh, look at that little mouth!" cooed Lawson. "Hi, Princess."

"You know, we can't keep calling her 'baby' and 'princess' forever," Reginell pointed out. "So what did you decide to name her? Prada? Gucci? Chanel?"

Sullivan laughed and cradled her baby's head. "Her name is Charity. Charity Faith Webb."

"That's pretty," said Angel.

"Charity means love, right?" asked Reginell for confirmation. "It sounds kind of like Charles too."

"Yes, Charity means love," answered Sullivan. "And God is love. This little girl will know the love of God and her family and be covered in love by all of you."

"Yes, she will," affirmed Charles.

"So will her mother," added Lawson.

There was a faint knock at the door. "Excuse me, Mr. Webb?"

Charles looked up and saw a nurse in the doorway. "I'll let you ladies get to know Miss Webb a little better." He kissed the top of Sullivan's head and kissed the baby. "I'll be right back, sweetheart."

"Okay, babe." She watched him leave but was too focused on the baby to wonder where he was going.

"I can't believe you're a mother, Sullivan!" exclaimed Lawson. "How does it feel?"

"You know, I spent a lot of nights crying myself to sleep and wondering if I'd ever have a moment like this." A smile shone through her pain. "But like Miss Celie said, 'Thank God I'm here!' Now, I have a testimony. I know that the blood of Jesus can cover a multitude of sins because He covered mine. I don't have to be condemned. I don't have to perpetuate this generational curse that's been on the women in my family as far back as anyone can remember. It stops with this child. My baby will know what it's like to loved and cherished. She'll know that she's precious and that she's God's little princess. She'll grow up knowing who she is in Christ and knowing that she has parents who will stop the world for her. She'll know she's beautiful and brilliant and that she's the baddest chick to walk this planet since her mother!"

They all laughed.

"Ain't that right, sugar?" Sullivan kissed the baby's nose.

Charles watched from outside of Sullivan's hospital room, clutching a sealed envelope. Inside the envelope held the results for the paternity test that he'd secretly requested for Charity. He debated whether to look at the results, having already decided to raise the child as his own regardless of what the test said. He couldn't imagine his little angel belonging to anyone other than him and Sullivan. He already loved her and would fight with everything in him to always protect her. In the end, he figured the DNA running through Charity's veins didn't really matter.

Charles folded the envelope and tucked it into his jacket. As he placed his hand on the doorknob to return to his wife and new daughter, a nagging feeling began eating away at him. He bit his lip and pulled the envelope back out. He stared at it a few seconds before saying a quick prayer and tearing open the envelope.

Back in the Sullivan's hospital room, the ladies continued to ogle and dote on baby Charity.

"I see you how you're looking at my baby, Lawson," hedged Sullivan. "If I didn't know better, I'd think you were over there getting baby fever."

Lawson giggled. "With this adorable face staring up at me, I'd have to be made of stone not to." She checked her vibrating cell phone. "I just got a text from Garrett. He wants me to meet him down in the parking lot."

"Bring him on up here," replied Sullivan. "Tell him he's got to meet his new niece."

Lawson kissed Charity's forehead. "Let's see if your Uncle Garrett wants to go home and make one of you for ourselves." She crept out of the room to find her husband.

A hip-hop ringtone came blaring from Reginell's phone. Sullivan covered her baby's ear. "Do you mind, Reggie? She's only a few hours old. I think it's a little soon for Charity to be exposed to her first cuss words."

"Okay, okay, I'll take this in the bathroom." Reginell scooted off to Sullivan's bathroom to answer the phone. It was Mark. "Hey, baby, what's up?" she asked him.

"How's the baby?"

"She's so beautiful! She's one of the few things that Sullivan has actually done right."

Mark chuckled. "Hey, don't make any plans for tonight. I want you to come over."

Reginell leaned against the sink. "Why? What's going on?"

Mark smiled and looked at the jewelry box cradled in his right hand. "You'll see. . . . I love you, Reggie."

She grinned into the phone. "I love you too. I'll see you tonight."

Lawson crisscrossed her way through the parking lot to find Garrett. "Why did you want to meet out here? Don't you want to go in and see the baby?"

"In a minute," Garrett replied brusquely. "I wanted some privacy first. There's something I need to tell you."

"What—did something happen to Namon?" she asked, panicked.

"No, he's fine." Garrett still seemed troubled. He rested his hands on her shoulders. "Lawson, there's just no easy way to say this."

Lawson gingerly touched his face. "What's going on, honey? What's wrong?"

"It's Simone," said Garrett, reaching up to squeeze her hand to comfort her as much as it was to comfort himself.

Lawson held her breath. "Who's that?"

"She's the one . . ."

Lawson rolled her eyes and finished his sentence. "She's the one you had the affair with, right?"

Garrett nodded. "Simone's been trying to get in touch with me, but I refused to return her calls after I told her it was over."

Lawson stood back with her arms folded. "Okay, so why is she calling? Does she want seconds?"

Garrett looked down, then back up at Lawson. "No . . . honey." He griped his wife's hands. "Simone is pregnant."

Lawson slowly brought her hand to her mouth. She felt herself go light-headed. "Pregnant? Did I just hear you say that she's *pregnant?*"

"That's what she's claiming," Garrett added quickly. "I haven't seen a doctor's report or gotten any kind of real confirmation."

Stunned, Lawson simply said, "A baby? Another woman is having your baby?"

Lawson eased away from him, dazed. Garrett reached out for her. "Lawson, talk to me, baby! Tell me that we'll get through this. Baby, please . . ."

Lawson's whole world came crashing down on her. For a moment she couldn't breathe. Hot tears welled in her eyes and began streaming down her cheeks. "Congratulations. . . . I guess you're finally getting the child you wanted after all."

As much as she loved Garrett, she knew it would take nothing short of a miracle for the fragile marriage to survive this time around.

Kina stood outside of Sullivan's room clutching a bouquet of pink balloons. She looked through the opened door at Reginell, Angel, and Charles doting on the newest addition to their circle. She longed to be a part of that again but knew her presence would feel more like an intrusion than a welcomed surprise.

She stopped one of the nurses passing by in the hallway. "Excuse me, ma'am? Can I trouble you for a second?"

"Yes, ma'am. Can I help you?"

Kina handed the balloons over to her. "Can you take these into room 314?"

"Are you sure you don't want to take them in yourself?"

Kina nodded. "Yeah, I'm sure . . . They look happy. I probably shouldn't interrupt."

Kina thanked the nurse and headed in the opposite direction. She reached into her purse and pulled out the one-way plane tickets she purchased for herself and Kenny, determined to find a little happiness of her own. Maybe one day she could be as happy as the rest of her friends were . . . at least as happy as they appeared to be for now.

Readers' Discussion Questions

1. Does the ladies' friendship help or hinder their walk with the Lord? How so?

2. Which character do you think showed the most growth by the end of the book? Why?

3. Do you think Kina was confused or inherently selfish?

4. Should Reginell and Mark have pursued a relationship considering that he and Lawson shared a child together? Why or why not?

5. Do you think Sullivan's troubled childhood was the real reason for her self-destructive behavior or just an excuse to do whatever she wanted?

6. Is Charles too forgiving of Sullivan, or is he an example of God's forgiveness toward us?

7. Should Sullivan have accepted Kina back into her life? Why or why not?

8. Do you think Angel and Duke's relationship would have survived if Channing had not been in the picture? Why or why not?

9. How do you think Garrett's outside child will affect his marriage to Lawson?

10. Which couple do you think has the best chance of survival? Why?

About the Author

Shana Burton is the author of *Suddenly Single, First Comes Love, Flaws and All, Catt Chasin,'* and *Flaw Less* (Urban Books, LLC) She is a bestselling author and a two-time nominee for Georgia Author of the Year (2009 Best Fiction—*First Comes Love*; 2011 Best Fiction—*Flaws and All*). She resides in Georgia with her two children. When she is not writing, she can be found gardening, dancing, or reading. She is currently working on her sixth book, *Chocolate Lovers*. Find her online on Facebook at www.facebook.com/shanajohnsonburton. Follow her on Twitter at www.twitter.com/shanajburton, or catch up with her on her blogs at www.blogspot.shanajburton.com. E-mail her at jatice@hotmail.com.

UC HIS GLORY BOOK CLUB!
www.uchisglorybookclub.net

UC His Glory Book Club is the spirit-inspired brain-child of Joylynn Jossel, Author and Acquisitions Editor of Urban Christian, and Kendra Norman-Bellamy, Author for Urban Christian. This is an online book club that hosts authors of Urban Christian. We welcome as members all men and women who have a passion for reading Christian-based fiction.

UC HIS GLORY BOOK CLUB pledges our commitment to provide support, positive feedback, encouragement, and a forum whereby members can openly discuss and review the literary works of Urban Christian authors.

There is no membership fee associated with UC His Glory Book Club; however, we do ask that you support the authors through purchasing, encouraging, providing book reviews, and of course, your prayers. We also ask that you respect our beliefs and follow the guidelines of the book club. We hope to receive your valuable input, opinions, and reviews that build up, rather than tear down our authors.

WHAT WE BELIEVE:
—We believe that Jesus is the Christ, Son of the Living God.
—We believe the Bible is the true, living Word of God.
—We believe all Urban Christian authors should

use their God-given writing abilities to honor God and share the message of the written word God has given to each of them uniquely.

—We believe in supporting Urban Christian authors in their literary endeavors by reading, purchasing, and sharing their titles with our online community.

—We believe that in everything we do in our literary arena should be done in a manner that will lead to God being glorified and honored.

We look forward to the online fellowship with you. Please visit us often at *www.uchisglorybookclub.net*.

Many Blessing to You!
Shelia E. Lipsey,
President, UC His Glory Book Club

ORDER FORM
URBAN BOOKS, LLC
78 E. Industry Ct
Deer Park, NY 11729

Name: (please print): _____

Address: _____

City/State: _____

Zip: _____

QTY	TITLES	PRICE
	3:57 A.M Timing Is Everything	$14.95
	A Man's Worth	$14.95
	A Woman's Worth	$14.95
	Abundant Rain	$14.95
	After The Feeling	$14.95
	Amaryllis	$14.95
	An Inconvenient Friend	$14.95
	Battle of Jericho	$14.95
	Be Careful What You Pray For	$14.95
	Beautiful Ugly	$14.95
	Been There Prayed That:	$14.95
	Before Redemption	$14.95

Shipping and handling-add $3.50 for 1st book, then $1.75 for each additional book.

Please send a check payable to:

Urban Books, LLC

Please allow 4-6 weeks for delivery

ORDER FORM
URBAN BOOKS, LLC
78 E. Industry Ct
Deer Park, NY 11729

Name: (please print): _____

Address: _____

City/State: _____

Zip: _____

QTY	TITLES	PRICE

Shipping and handling-add $3.50 for 1st book, then $1.75 for each additional book.

Please send a check payable to:

Urban Books, LLC

Please allow 4-6 weeks for delivery